CAPTURE THE

CW01496927

ZIYÉ TAYLOR

Contents

Content Warnings

Though Capture the Moment is more of a romantic comedy, it does tackle some strong themes...

Triggering topics may include: On page anxiety attacks and depression, mentions of drug usage, alcohol use, mentions of abusing sexual intercourse and alcohol, blackmail, vulgar language, strained maternal relationships, explicit consensual intercourse descriptions, cursing, secret keeping, and on page violence.

These scenes are graphic and may be triggering. Please only continue if you can handle it.

Remember that you are loved and seen.

Playlist

Cassandra–Taylor Swift

Delicate–Taylor Swift

Nonsense–Sabrina Carpenter

One Thing–One Direction

Pretty Little Birds–SZA (ft. Isaiah Rashad)

breathin–Ariana Grande

I Want to Write You a Song–One Direction

High–Alina Baraz

Perfect–One Direction

Let Me Love You–Ariana Grande (ft. Lil Wayne)

You & I–One Direction

C U Girl–Steve Lacy

Deeper–Summer Walker

Natural–ZAYN

I Wanna Be Yours–Arctic Monkeys

First F**k–6LACK & Jhené Aiko

Sex on the Beach–PARTYNEXTDOOR

Love Me Like You Do–Ellie Goulding

Snooze(Acoustic)–SZA (ft. Justin Bieber)

So High School–Taylor Swift

Here With ME–d4vd

Grateful–Mahalia

Honeymoon Fades–Sabrina Carpenter

Bed Chem–Sabrina Carpenter

Clit–Saurus

For all my clit-thinkers who'd love to get their smutty fantasies on or avoid it like the plague, spice can be found in the following chapters:

- Five

- Thirty-Six

- Thirty-Eight

- Thirty-Nine (Mention)

- Forty-Eight

To all the girls who think they're hard to love, you aren't. You just haven't met your Blake yet.

And to the 11 year old version of me that only wanted to read books about girls that looked like her, welcome to your first ever novel, Ziye'.

one

Blake

"Fuck, the flash is on, I just need one more..."

CLICK!

CLICK! CLICK!

CLICK!

My head feels as if I'd been punched in the back of my skull by Rocky Balboa as the sounds of a camera clicking and cursing snatches me from the shitshow of a dream I'd been having. Out of instinct, my arm reaches out toward the pink phone in the air; I groan as the girl beside me yelps.

So much for sleeping in...

I can feel the shock radiating from her as she sputters, trying, and failing, to come up with an excuse as I unlock her phone and go through the camera roll. My head pounds harder as I scroll through each of the pictures she'd taken, deleting them all.

Twenty-seven pictures in the span of...*two minutes?*

"Chelsea..." Her name falls from my lips in a rasp. She perks up and then lies on top of me. Her breasts are cold and hard as they press against my bare chest. I groan and close an eye at the sight of her.

"Twenty-seven," I croak.

"Huh?"

"You have twenty-seven seconds to put on some clothes and get the fuck out."

That sounded harsh... Maybe I should have softened the blow?

"But... But *Blakey*, I thought we were having a good time together. You wouldn't kick me out like this, right?" she stutters, and I can feel those big ass bug eyes staring at me. My headache grows pounding against my skull, and I groan again.

"You don't have to go home, but you can't stay here. My niece should be in the living room right about now, so I'll walk you through the back." My tone is stern, more than I'd thought it would be and I'm thankful because I feel like Earth has fallen off its axis drifting helplessly throughout the galaxy.

"You're such a dick, Blake Wilder," Chelsea says through gritted teeth, yanking on her underwear.

"Are you done?" I ask, shielding my eyes as she pulls back my curtains. A total dick move on her end, might I add.

I'm annoyed as she stares at me from the other side of my room, now fully clothed in her pink mini-dress from last night. As much as Chelsea likes to call me a dick, she also likes to ride it. So, I *never* take anything the hypocrite has to say seriously.

She knows that Friday mornings are reserved for my niece Delilah, I don't know why she's acting all weird this time around.

Sneaking Chelsea down the stairs without the guys noticing her is a piece of cake. I make sure to avoid all family areas such as the kitchen and living room and sneak her right out the back. We make it all the way to the back gate in complete silence before she decides to open her mouth once again, annoying the hell out of me.

"You know...you can call me sometimes, Blake. I'm always here," she purrs. *Literally.*

I don't know how one can roll the *r* in the word "here", but Chelsea manages to do so and leave my already limp dick, limper than a dog that's been hit by a car.

"Yeah...I know." And with that, I close the gate's door in her face.

As I re-enter the house, my headache seems to wash away as loud child-like giggles sound from the living room. A smile lifts on my cheeks as I make my way towards the angelic noise. I pause in the doorway of our living room and snap a photo of Braxton, Charlie, Derek, and Delilah sitting around Delilah's princess table in the center of our living room. The sight of four grown men dressed head to toe in tiny princess gowns with crowns and tiny cups in their hands brings me to my knees as I double over in laughter. I snap another photo of them and chuckle to myself as I send it to the hockey team chat.

"Shut up. You'd be in a dress too if you were on time for tea," Charlie, a senior defenseman and probably one of the most unserious people in the world, scolds me.

I stifle my laughter as he gives me the meanest mug he can muster, though it resembles an angry puppy. Charlie's long dirty blonde hair is pulled into a small bun on the top of his head, being held together by a fluffy pink scrunchie. If there was an award for the least intimidating person in the world, he'd win it.

But the reminder of me being late for teatime with Delilah does break my heart. I frown as I look down at the brown-haired princess beside her father and sigh because she's truly a gift in human form. Delilah looks up at me with a wide toothy grin, her large doe brown eyes sparkle as she sees me.

My heart melts.

I'd die for this girl.

And I'm also her favorite uncle everyone, don't listen to what that fucker Jace says.

"Deli, I'm so sorry for being late. Can you forgive me?" I stoop down to match her eye level. Delilah gives me her biggest smile to date before narrowing her eyes at me.

"Only if you get me a new plushy. Daddy says that I can't get anymore." She pouts, folding her tiny arms over herself, and *oh if that doesn't make my heart swell even larger...*

"Well, we just can't have that now, can we?" I match her pout, scooping her up in my arms. "Do you want me to beat your daddy up?" Although I already know the answer, I ask anyway and earn a slap to the back of my head from her father.

"Bad Lakey." She pouts, jutting out her bottom lip as I tickle under her chin. Delilah giggles lightly and forgets what I said about her dad as I sit her back down. She hands me my own teacup, pink with little bows on the handle.

It'd been my designated cup for the past three days. I grin cheekily and take a "sip" from the cup. Although my fingers are way too large for the handle, I still do my job as an uncle and take a sip. For all the idiots out there, this is how you keep kids happy. For example, if a toddler hands you a toy phone and says, "This is for you!" What are you going to do? *Decline it?!* No, you answer the goddamn phone and act your ass off, that's what you do.

The five of us sit and talk with Delilah; we listen to her rants about the latest sugar plum princess movie, and we laugh when she tells us the random joke she'd seen on TV. Over our almost three years as a team, and as friends, we've all grown to look at each other as family. Delilah included.

Delilah is Derek's daughter. He had her in his junior year of high school and has been taking care of her as a single dad ever since. So naturally, the guys and I have adopted her as our niece. We do everything with her from tea parties to playing with dolls to letting her do our make-up. You name it—we probably did it.

Even though I've never met Delilah's mom, I can tell that Delilah looks nothing like her. Due to the sheer fact that Delilah is the epitome of Derek from her deep brown hair to her bright brown eyes and the light freckles that twinkle across her cheeks like stars. There is no denying that Delilah is Derek Perez's daughter.

"What was that about?" Braxton whispers to me. We're on the other side of the "tea table" after Delilah decided that she wanted to sit between Derek and Charlie.

I raise an eyebrow at Brax and try to ignore him as he sighs.

"*Chelsea*, we could hear her upstairs. What was that about?" the brown-skinned man prompts again, wrinkling his nose.

"She took pictures of me sleeping." I grimace as thoughts of what she could've done with said pictures rack my mind.

"Pictures?"

"It's the price of being a celebrity," I say as a joke but can't help but feel how cringeworthy it is for the words to leave my mouth.

I'm not a celebrity, per se. But family is well known. My parents are practically every girl's teenage dream whether they're 15 or 30 with my mom being a bestselling romance author and my dad being in the NFL Hall of Fame. Then you have my older sister, Juliette. She models for a big company in New York that you've probably heard of but I can never remember the company's name. I was teased relentlessly in middle and high school for my "hot sister" or whatever that means. Those guys haven't seen Jules for the true gremlin that she is.

And then there's me, Blake Nicolas Wilder, an NHL prospect, and a pain in my mother's ass. Imagine Dad's disappointment when he found out I wanted to play *hockey* instead of football. He refused to eat breakfast with me for weeks—

"Blake, did you hear me?"

"He's daydreaming again..."

"*Uncle Lake!* Look at my tiara!" Delilah jumps in front of me, pulling me completely out of my thoughts. I smile as she shoves a glittery-pasty *thing* in my face with a smile brighter than the sun. The glitter drips onto my lap but I overlook it as I pull the "tiara" into my hands, grimacing slightly at the gooey substance.

"It's beautiful?"

"Did he just ignore us?" Braxton questions aloud, frowning at Charlie and Derek.

"I'm not ignoring you; I'm simply listening to the most important person first..."

That earns me a light punch on my shoulder from Charlie.

"Dude...we were talking about tonight's P-A-R-T-Y. Cupid and Alec should be back in a bit with all of the K-E-G-S' and we need to know if you're going to be there." Braxton stresses, folding his hands in his lap.

Ah...the infamous spelling out words bit. A wave of amusement flows through me as the big and brawny Braxton Oakley spells out simple words to hide our plans from the little angel in front of me. I nod at Brax as a response as Delilah's large eyes travel between the two of us, trying to piece the words together.

"What about you, D?" Charlie asks Derek, his gaze focused now on painting one of Delilah's fingernails as Derek takes over the other.

Derek shifts uncomfortably in his miniature pink seat, the tips of his ears reddening as he directs his attention to Delilah playing with a cup of water. "I'll be there only after I meet Deli's sitter. Mom's going back to Texas for the weekend, so I'm outsourcing tonight," he says catching Delilah's water cup with reflexes faster than light, saving it from the floor.

"What about her recital tomorrow—"

"We're home motherfuck—*Party people!*" Jace's loud voice booms from the foyer followed by a loud crashing and small expletives from Alec.

"Would it kill you to move out the doorway? People have shit to do, Heart!" he shouts.

"Well if you'd been paying attention, you'd see the God-like ass standing in front of you, Tu." Jace retorts, waltzing into the living room where the rest of us are. He runs a hand through his blonde waves, smiling wildly as his eyes land on Deli.

"CUPID!" she yells as she jumps into his arms.

Jace scoops up Delilah with a spin. "Hello little sunshine, have you caused any mayhem today?"

"Not yet..." She pouts.

"Well, let's cause some! As your favorite uncle, I declare today—"

"That's enough." Derek sighs, plucking his daughter from Jace.

"Oh, shut up." Alec waves Jace off.

"Who lied to you? I'm obviously the favorite." I scoff.

Jace simply rolls his eyes at the three of us, plopping down on our large brown couch. He lays back as if he's about to take a nap but quickly opens his eyes widely, resembling a crazed man. His light green eyes are wicked as he looks around the room. "Back to our debate from earlier, Tu Tu. I think the guys know the *true* answer." He smirks.

"Who do you think will get the most numbers, Alec or me?" Jace asks.

Alec sighs exasperatedly throwing his arms in the air clearly annoyed with this topic. "For the fortieth time, I like D-I-C-K. Not P-U-S-S-Y. But I'm more than sure that I could get a girl's number quicker than you can." Alec shrugs.

"Hush and let the others answer." Jace rolls his eyes, gesturing for one of us to continue. Unlike Braxton and Charlie who love to debate with the two idiots, Derek and I would rather not. So while those four go at it, I sidle up to the father-daughter duo.

"What time's the recital again? I got to make sure my '#1 uncle' shirt is pressed and ready," I say, sticking my tongue out at Delilah as she pokes her body up between her dad's legs.

Derek frowns. I know he's annoyed with us asking about Delilah's first ballet recital. He'd been more nervous than Deli for her to perform. "It's at 5:00, please don't be late," he says, running a hand through Deli's curls.

"When am I ever—"

"Last week, at move-in." Jace shrugs.

"Yesterday for lunch," Alec quips.

"At last year's banquet." Braxton sighs.

Charlie laughs probably the loudest I've ever heard him. "You were late to your own surprise party which *you* planned!" he guffaws I can feel my cheeks redden at the memory of being late to my own birthday two weeks ago.

I'd never had a surprise party before, and I didn't want my first ever one to be horrible, so I planned it. As for being late, my dear sister Juliette is to blame. She'd broken the internet with a photo of her and her ex-boyfriend, Carsin, in front of where we'd had our family dinner. Thus, resulting in us being surrounded by screaming fans and paparazzi. If I ever do become "famous", I hope it's never to that extent. I get hives just thinking about it.

"Well fine...but I won't ever be late for something like that. Trust me."

"I'll believe it when I see it, Wilder," Derek chuckles though his smile turns upside down with a quickness. I watch him curiously as he jumps up from Deli's small tea chair, the chair sticks to his butt as he looks around the room frantically.

"Deli go get your shoes on, we're late to meet your sitter!" Derek practically shouts, detaching himself from the chair as Delilah giggles running to the foyer with Derek in tow.

Seeing that reminds me of just how much I want to be a dad. I want to be the guy that chases his daughter around with little teacups and plastic tiaras and to have someone look at me as if I hung the sun, the moon, and all the stars in the universe. It'll be my reality someday; unfortunately, today is not that day. Someone'll love me soon just like that and I can't wait. Well... I can but—ugh. *You know what I mean.*

Anyways...

"So, what was Chelsea doing here? I *know* you didn't fuck her." Braxton chuckles, successfully stealing my peace at the reminder of Chelsea Myrtle and her god-awful *pink* phone. Who in the world needs a bright pink phone?

"And how do you know that?"

"You don't do puck bunnies... That's more Charlie's style." He shrugs as if it's the most obvious thing in the world, and I cringe.

Though, Chelsea *is* a puck bunny...I wouldn't call her one. (But she is. She's definitely one through and through.)

Chelsea has tried numerous times to hook up with most of the team. She'd been successful more times than I can count but last night I didn't go *all* the way with her.

She offered to give me a blowjob, and I'm not an idiot, so of course I let her give me one—and I'm not afraid of a little cuddle either. How she ended up completely naked, I have no idea.

I run a hand over my face, trying to stall for time, the feeling of my ears heating gives me away more than I want, and I sigh as Jace jumps from his spot on the couch.

"Oh my God! You *fucked* Moaning Myrtle!" he yells, appalled as if he were the one to do anything with Chelsea Myrtle last night.

"I didn't *fuck* her!" I try but that just causes more uproar in the room

"She sucked you off!" Charlie claps, laughing like a horse.

Can I die now? Is there a hole for me to crawl into anywhere? I try to hide behind my hands, but Jace Heart has other plans as he pulls them from my face. "Oh, this is gold." He laughs, patting my cheek, but I swat him away.

The boys had nicknamed her Moaning Myrtle after a five-hour Harry Potter binge. They coined the nickname since both Myrtle's moaned louder than life...only one of them being a little more bearable than the other.

And we both know which one I'm talking about.

"Oh, shut up, I don't need to be here for this! I'm going out, I'll be back by the time the party starts," I say waving them off as I stalk up the stairs to my room.

Fuck them and their stupid ass laughter. I'm getting donuts. Donuts never make fun of me for my sexual choices

I'd *thought* that donuts would never make fun of me.

I was wrong.

So very *wrong*.

Jace decided that he *also* needed to leave out with the excuse of us needing more beer for tonight's party, so he hopped in my passenger seat before I could tell him no. He'd spent the entire ride to The Sugar Hole, the donut shop ten minutes away from our off-campus home, making innuendos about my dick and donut holes.

Leave it to Heart to say something romantic...

Entering The Sugar Hole, we're immediately met with the sweet aroma of fried dough and happiness. I sigh, content with my new surroundings until Mr. Heart sidles up to me with the biggest shit eating grin known to man.

"Don't even think about it," I chuckle, already knowing him and whatever is traveling through his mind.

In the beginning, Jace and I hated one another. Where he was overly loud and talkative, I liked peace and was far less talkative. Though, I think he's slowly converted me into an extrovert like him, I still love my peace. There's something soothing about being content with yourself and never having to talk to a soul whenever you're on your own—

"Oh my Goodness, Cleo! Just *pick* one. We've been here for *ten minutes.*" A loud voice that I recognize as Georgia Adams, the fashion chick that was in my English class last semester, yells at her friend who's dressed in pink from head to toe. She even has a large pink bow in her hair.

What's up with girls and the color pink? I mean I love red but you don't see me wearing red twenty-four—

For a second, I lose my breath as the girl in the pink turns to face her friend with a large smile. She has the side-profile of a *goddess*. Her nose is perfectly sloped with a small stud adorning her nostril. The girl's smile is bright and welcoming...inviting, and I feel like putty as I stare at her while she laughs at her friend.

"But there's so many options! Look, they have Strawberry Glaze, Pink Truffle... Oh! Is that a Pink Kit-Kat on a donut?! I'll take two of those," she says to the woman behind the counter in a sweet tone. I'm so enraptured by her that I don't notice the blonde devil who'd been with me heading towards her.

What the fuck?

"Now, if I hadn't known any better... I'd say that you're my best friend. But that would be crazy because Cleo Jones is in New York right now, *right?*" He taunts her, twirling her ponytail between his fingers, smiling as if he *is* her best friend and *not* a stranger.

How the hell does he know *her?*

And why haven't I met her yet?

I know every girl on campus, and *she* is definitely not one of them.

The girl, Cleo, practically jumps into Jace's arms hugging him as if he wasn't the cheeky bastard that I knew. She hugged him like he was someone who she'd known for a lifetime. When they pull back from each other, they're still smiling and chatting about God knows what. I barely notice the daggers Georgia is sending Jace's way as I stride towards them, standing next to him.

"Are you two coming to our party tonight?" I ask, smiling solely at the brown-skinned girl dressed like a sugar plum princess. Maybe pink isn't *so* bad; I try to think and grimace viscerally but I have a feeling it'll grow on me.

My confidence takes a small hit as she doesn't give me the time of day. No, she turns back to Jace and gives him a small smile before focusing on the patient worker in front of her.

What the *actual* fuck?

"It'll be small," I try, my tone more hopeful than confident as I look to Jace for help. The bastard smiles at me but remains quiet.

"No pressure." I look to Georgia for help next. Though she and I hadn't talked a lot last semester, we weren't *complete* strangers.

"If Jace isn't there then yes but, if he is, you can count me out," Georgia sasses, shifting her weight with folded arms.

"Consider him gone." The joke is easy as it falls from my lips, the sugar plum princess quietly chuckles at that. I win.

One point Wilder, Universe zero.

"I don't want her there either but CJ you're more than welcome." Jace shrugs, walking to the other counter.

"Um...we'll think about it?" Cleo says more like a question than anything to Jace but it's something. She glances my way fleetingly before focusing back on her order.

I watch as the girls leave. Jace chuckles from beside me, clearly finding my small interaction amusing. "Oh, Wilder, I'd pay good money to see CJ bust your balls. But for *free?* You're giving me an early birthday gift." He grins, opening his small treat bag filled with donut holes.

"Oh, shut up and eat your fucking balls."

TWO

Cleo

"Does this dress scream 'dick me down' in a hot way or a street worker way?" Georgia asks from in front of her full-body mirror, eyeing me through the glass. She'd been dressed in an all-black mini dress with cutouts all over, it was sexy in a whore-ish way but she could make it work. She always did.

"Which one would you rather?" I look up at her for a moment then back down at my computer. Classes start in a few days, and I still haven't organized my computer or Notion. I'm so behind that it's not even funny.

My head starts to hurt just at the thought of falling behind in school. I haven't had a bad grade since eighth-grade Algebra when my teacher was a full-time substitute who only gave us busy work. I scratch the back of my neck at the thought of that time and wince as Georgia tosses a pillow at me.

"Cleo...you've got to stop stressing about school. Classes haven't even started yet!" she exclaims, moving her blonde hair over her shoulder to get a better look at her backside. Georgia purses her lips at the sight of herself and changes her dress for the *third* time.

"All the more reason to stress about school... I need to get a good head start. Besides, I have you here with me this time around." A smile dusts my cheeks as she turns to me brandishing one of her own.

"I know right, I don't know how you survived two years of college in New York without me."

I don't know either, G, I want to say, but instead, I fix her with a tight smile and return my attention to my computer. The thought of Brighton University alone gives me hives. It'd been my dream to attend my mother's alma mater to feel closer to her. That dream became a reality turned nightmare all within the span of a year. I'd been so close to accomplishing all my goals and quickly lost sight of everything all because of a crazy son of a bitch who owes me my dignity and four thousand dollars—but I digress.

The original plan for my life that I'd created at the ripe age of ten years old went as follows: Graduate high school as Valedictorian. *Check*. Get a car. *Check*. Quit Figure Skating. *Double Check*. Attend Brighton Full-Time as a Comms major. *Triple Check*. Graduate Brighton Summa Cum Laude. *Error 404*.

Because of the incident, I hightailed my ass out of New York and ended up here in Maryland two days ago, now attending my father's alma mater, Summerfield University. Dad used to play hockey in the NHL for the Washington Eagles and won three Stanley Cups before retiring. He retired while I was in high school and took up coaching for the Summerfield Men's Hockey team. I sometimes believe that Dad wanted me to be a boy so he could have another hockey player on his hands. But instead, he has a daughter who loves wearing pink, with a strong obsession for Hockey and Formula 1.

"Why aren't you getting ready? I want to get there around 11." Georgia pouts, taking a seat at the foot of the bed now dressed in a shimmery navy blue dress that stopped around her thighs. The dress highlighted her every curve and brought out the deep green hues of her eyes. She looked over my computer screen for a brief second before shutting it.

"Hey—"

"Don't *hey* me. *Ow!* Don't pinch me either! I'm trying to get you ready for your first party at SFU and you're sitting here worried about a syllabus that doesn't drop for another four days!" she whines, jutting out her plump bottom lip in a glossy pout.

"I'm not going, I have to help Dad tomorrow with training." I half shrug, opening the screen back up only for it to be shut again. Helping my father with the first training of the season had been his *first* stipulation for me to attend Summerfield, I wasn't going to disappoint him any further by not helping. Besides, what's the worst that can happen by helping a few hockey players?

"Oh, yes you are. I haven't seen my best friend for more than a week in over *two years!* I don't know what happened in New York and I won't pressure you to tell me because you will when you're ready," she starts, turning her full body towards me. Her bright green eyes are sincere as she says, "Cleo, I know whatever it is has to do with that guy and fuck him! Well—don't *actually* fuck him...you get the point." Georgia waves a hand.

"I don't think that I do..." I chuckle as she narrows her eyes at me.

"The *point* is...you're young, talented, and smart. It's okay to live life and be free and party and...I don't know where this is going but, come with me tonight, *please.* This is the first party of the semester and I have a feeling it's going to be one of the best ones," she says, smiling with a hopeful gleam in her eyes that I can't refuse.

She's right... We haven't seen each other for a while, it'd be good to let loose a little. But only a smidge, I don't think I can ever be as open as I used to be.

"Fine...but you're buying us more Strawberry Truffle donuts from that one place after," I concede.

"Oh my God! Yes! Yes! Yes!" Georgia cheers, jumping for joy as she yanks me into a bone crushing hug.

She pulls away, ecstatic and beaming with life. "Now let me dress you. You can't wear a vintage crop tweed set to a house party."

It doesn't take long for Georgia Adams to get her way and soon enough, I'm dressed in a baby pink satin dress with spaghetti straps that hug my curves in all the right places. The dress stopped around mid-thigh with light ruffles on a slant at the bottom, and on a normal day, I would never wear this. But since I can never say no to my best friend, I'll wear it—just for tonight.

"This looks perfect on you! Do a spin." She claps, green eyes gleaming as she twirls me. "I feel like there's something missing... Oh! Your bow!" Georgia pats her head as if that was the most obvious revelation before dashing into my room across the hall.

I take a moment and breathe, looking myself over in the mirror. I haven't worn anything like this in months. My fingers trail over the slanted ruffles and along the curves of my waist, tugging the skirt down a bit. When my eyes reach my hair, I realize that Georgia is in fact right. I'm missing my bow. She'd done my hair in a half up half down and left a long tendril out to frame my face. I'd done my makeup myself and matched my outfit with a pair of heels, all I need now is my bow and I'll be unstoppable.

"You have way too many pink bows... Why are there six of the same color?" Georgia asks as she reenters the room with my favorite bow in hand; I wave her off with a sigh.

"G, a girl can never have too many bows." I laugh, mimicking her mom's catchphrase from our childhood.

Georgia rolls her eyes at me and puts the bow in my hair, watching me through the mirror before shaking her head with a large smile.

"Where's Sienna?" she asked, looking around the room as if she *just* noticed that the pink haired girl was nowhere to be found.

My cousin Sienna was also our roommate. She'd originally gone to NYU but transferred to the dance program at SFU during the summer semester as there were more opportunities here.

"She said something about a babysitting gig..." I shrug, turning to face Georgia fully, she nods her head in understanding.

"Babysitting? I thought she was working at the studio for the semester..."

"You know that she changes jobs out like she does her shoes, she'll probably work at the library next week." I break into a laugh at the thought of Sienna Jones behind the counter of a library. She'd probably fall asleep as soon as she unlocks the front doors.

Growing up with Sienna, it felt like I was living with a real-life Barbie doll. Sienna, like myself, wanted pink everything. Only, unlike myself, she decided to go for pink hair. But, like Barbie, Sienna is a jack of all trades. She babysits, sings, dances. Hell, if she put her mind to it, there's no doubt that she'd run for president too.

Georgia and I do a quick once-over in the mirror to make sure we look exactly how we want before heading to the kitchen to pregame. Back in high school, we'd pregame under my kitchen table and would jump when we heard the slightest sound throughout the house. Our pregames back then always ended with one of us rubbing our heads and the other dying of laughter. I make a mental note to remind Georgia of the past when she hands me a shot of a clear liquid which I presume to be tequila.

Our go-to.

"Take it to the dome," she starts, lifting the small shot glass with a pink Las Vegas skyline printed on it, in the air.

Take it to the dome; I smile at the old saying my older cousin Zola taught us in high school. She was the very first person to slip us drinks. It was only a small miniature bottle of Patron, but I'll never forget how much older we felt drinking with the big girls. Even though we can drink on our own now, we still credit Zola whenever we take shots.

"Or take it home!" I finish the saying, throwing back the shot with a grimace.

"Ubers outside, shall we?" Georgia sidles up to me, adjusting the straps of her dress. Her smile is bright as she looks down at me.

"We shall."

Three

Cleo

THE UBER PULLS UP to a medium-sized gray craftsman-style house littered with students, blaring loud music. People are scattered everywhere–some on the porch, others on the lawn. Georgia squeezes my hand as if to reassure me that we're going to be fine as we approach the front door.

I hadn't even noticed we'd been holding hands but the small squeeze does its job and I almost instantly feel better. It's not every day that a hot guy invites me to a party...

What if everyone thinks I'm weird?

The girl dressed like a pink Teletubby with bows...

Ugh, this self-hatred has to end, but when? I haven't stopped hating myself since that night and I don't think that I ever will. Nothing could ever stop me from hating myself after what I'd done.

As we enter the house, the warm and ragged smells of alcohol and weed engulf me. There's loud rap music blasting from the speakers and we have to push our way through the crowds of people, but still, I couldn't help but notice that the house is strangely clean.

There were no weird stains from God knows what. Zero holes in the wall. Most of the drinks made their way on coasters...

What kind of college party is this?

The main wall in the living room is decorated with vinyl records and trophies in a neat array. There are small plants along shelves in the hallway and little LEGO sets placed in random spots throughout the downstairs. My eye catches on a large photograph of Sir Ruffskers, Jace's scary ass Pomeranian back at home, and I cringe at my memories of running from the animal.

Despite the current hazy state from the smokers in here, you can tell the guys are pretty neat.

"They're super neat for men!" Georgia replies to the statement I hadn't known I'd spoken aloud as we make our way to the cooler, I grab a water while she gets a can of Sam Adams.

"You'd think this place would look like a pigsty, especially with guys living here" I joke although I don't believe myself.

Jace Heart is probably the tidiest man I've ever met in my entire life. In middle school, I once colored outside the line in one of his adult coloring books (that he has because he's a dweeb) and he nearly castrated me.

I don't know if that's possible since I'm a girl and all but I will never give Jace the opportunity to find out if it is.

"Ugh do not speak of that devil in my presence, Cleo. I'm trying to have a good night without seeing him." Georgia groans as if this subject is her least favorite topic.

But I know the truth. Georgia loves Jace—platonically, of course. But she loves him nonetheless and it's obvious to me. She can never get enough of the idiot no matter how much she tries to act like she hates him.

"You love—"

Georgia's phone dinging interrupts me as her face brightens. "Hold that thought, Darius just got here... I'm going to go meet up with him. Be right back." And with that, she's gone.

In the blink of an eye, I've been ditched for a 6'2" football players dick.

She'd lasted a good...six minutes.

Looking around the empty sitting room that I found myself in, the air grows thick as realization settles in.

The one person that I knew is gone.

I haven't seen Jace or even his handsome friend yet, and fuck is it hot in here? I need something sweet, something to take my mind from this sudden heat that I'm feeling.

My feet feel as if they're being controlled by a toddler as I stumble my way into the kitchen. I'm instantly relieved to see it's empty. My vision tunnels and my feet stagger as I move toward the walk-in pantry. My mouth curves as I open the door only to drop back down.

What the fuck is this?

Chia seeds?

Whole grain granola?

Protein Penne Noodles?!

Where the fuck is the sugar? The goodies? Why is there only healthy food here? Is that... Oh my God. *Who in their right mind is eating Cookies and Cream flavored sea moss?*

I'm going to hurl.

This is preposterous on so many levels. Not only are there zero sweets, but the sweets these lunatics have are *healthy*.

"Where the fuck is the sugar?" I groan, moving over various forms of protein pasta before putting them back in their rightful spot.

"It's not kept in there," a humored voice calls back.

"Well, obviously. Help me look, I really need something sweet to bring me down." My tone is clipped, and I could honestly care less how rude I must seem. I think I'm going to go crazy if I don't get some semblance of sugar in me soon.

Who in their right minds eats Cookies and Cream sea moss when they're trying to get drunk?

"Such a princess..." The man chuckles, and with my back still to him, I chuck up the middle finger. That shot of tequila from earlier is definitely giving me more confidence than I usually have. The man sniffs a laugh as he says, "Third cabinet on the bottom left, there's a bag of powdered donuts and a few different types of cookies down there."

I sigh, turning to face my intruder more annoyed than happy he'd helped.

"I would've found them eventually," I say, taking a step closer to the tall man. Recognition slowly dawns on me as I stare at the handsome guy in front of me. I hadn't paid him any attention earlier, I'd only been able to catch a glimpse then, and could feel his stare on me. But now that he's standing in front of me, he's all that my eyes can focus on and I am not complaining.

He has the most beautiful baby blue eyes that I've ever seen. They're cloudy like a summer beach day right before a storm with hints of gray and black swirling in his irises. His face is every artist's wet dream—angular and symmetrical like a Greek God. I almost smile at the slight shift in his nose, it'd been nearly perfect but up close you can tell he'd probably broken it before. He smirks down at me, eyes glowing with something I can't quite place, and then he's stepping even closer into my space.

"Two pairs of eyes will always better than one." He shrugs mockingly whilst giving me those same weird eyes.

Are those...are those fuck me eyes?

No. Nope. Uh-uh.

Can't do this, especially not with this one, he seems like trouble. Trouble so fun it'll have you crying on your knees as he takes you from—

NO.

Stop clit-thinking, Cleo, and get a grip. I should've thanked him for finding me something to munch on, and then side-stepped him and went about my merry little way.

Instead, I say, "Does that work on all the girls?" in a voice I can barely recognize as my feet propel me closer to the large man.

His eyes, so full of expression, are brimming with humor and intrigue as he chuckles lightly.

"No, but I thought I'd give it a try with you...I'm Blake, by the way, and you are?" he asks, holding out a hand as if we hadn't seen each other earlier at The Sugar Hole.

"Not interested," I say, donning the fakest sweet smile I can muster. I didn't come to this school to fall for another athlete, and based on his build, I'd say he was either into football or boxing. Two sports that I want nothing to do with. For one, Ryan, my stepbrother, would kill me. And for two, I don't do athletes anymore. Show me an engineering major or a tech guy, and I'm your girl.

As I turn on my silver heels, goosebumps litter my arms as a warm hand clasps around my upper arm sending shockwaves down my spine. My head whips to Blake and I nearly double over in laughter at the scared puppy look he has.

"Sorry... I didn't mean to grab you like that." He scratches his neck, his cheeks reddening as he looks at his feet. The man who is probably around 6'4" looks like a dejected golden retriever as his eyes wander everywhere but me.

With a small chuckle, I brush it off. "You're fine but, don't just grab women without their permission. Now you have to get me a drink for the inconvenience," I say with a smirk.

Who is this suddenly confident woman, and what has she done with the Cleo Jones that uses her brain?

Blake's eyes widen as he stumbles and rummages the cabinets for different cocktail ingredients. I mentally capture a picture of the man as he pulls out a pink mug from the cabinet, confidently using it for his concoction.

He turns his back to me to make it before smiling coyly as he slides it to me; I look down at the dark drink and gulp before putting it up to my lips, and nearly die from whatever the fuck he put in it. It tastes like Pink Whitney and regrets. I sit the cup down as I let out a small cough.

"Never make me a drink ever again... That was one of the worst things I've ever put in my mouth."

"Well, what was the worst?" He teases, eyes glinting with mischief as he slides closer, taking up my space.

"Wouldn't you like to know..." The words slip from my mouth quicker than a cheetah capturing its prey.

"Oh, there's a lot I'd like to know, *Cleo*."

Wait... I didn't...

My shock must be written across my face because he simply chuckles.

"I heard Jace call you that earlier, so I'm assuming that's your name." He shrugs.

"Oh, so you're a sugar hoggin' creeper, is that it?" I ask teasingly and I'm surprisingly unalarmed by the fact that the stranger had known me. Instead, it felt comforting. Like there was someone that I didn't have to go through the motions of introducing myself to and slowly becoming friends with. Instead, he felt like he was already a friend.

"I'd like to think of myself as a *handsome* sugar hoggin' *observer*, Cleo. You can call me whatever you want, Princess, but make sure you add 'handsome' to the front of it" He smirks cockily as I roll my eyes.

"Princess?"

"You look like one, and from what I saw earlier, you dress like one too." He shrugs as if that's the most obvious thing in the world.

I don't even notice that the party is slowly dying down as he and I continue talking for what feels like five minutes. When I check the time my heart drops realizing it's been over an hour.

"What is it?" He asks standing over me, his voice is soft and somewhat concerned as the masculine scents of cedarwood and vanilla crowd my senses. My brain fogs as I inhale deeply.

"Huh?" My voice is breathy as I look up at him, my bark-colored eyes clashing with his ocean colored ones.

My belly heats, sending spirals through my whole body as I crane my neck to get a better look at him. His stare is so imploring as if he's searching my entire soul, picking me apart.

"You're eyes are so—"

"Come on, Wilder! It's drunk Jenga time! Bring her too."

Four

Blake

I FUCKING HATE DRUNK Jenga—and Alec Tu.

Tu Tu, not as much as Jenga, but he's a close second. Alec had looked Cleo up and down like a lion on the hunt for a gazelle, after completely dogging our moment. Cleo was finally getting comfortable around me before Tu Tu interrupted and invited the majority of our friend group, plus some random girls, to the living room for the game. I almost forgot that Alec was "strictly dickly" for a moment until he brought up how much he loved her outfit and the two of them began discussing fashion.

I sigh as I plop down on the couch between Lucki Cole, a senior left winger, and Theo Carter, our only junior D-man. Lucki gives me a curt nod, his pink curls dangling in his face as I nod back, noting his new septum ring. He and I went to the same high school and somehow ended up on the same collegiate team, it still shocks the both of us to this date. I'd been more than sure Lucki would go to the NHL straight after high school after all the prospects he'd received when he was a senior, but he declined them all to pursue graphic design here at Summerfield. He's a chill dude with only two settings, playing the fuck out of some hockey and beating ass in video games.

Theo chuckles from beside me at something the girl on his right had said and I'm not surprised to see him entertaining someone tonight. Theo almost always gets attention whenever we go out because he looks like that one actor from the 90s, with his short black curls, deep brown skin, and perfectly trimmed goatee. He stops talking as Alec calls for our attention over the EDM music playing over the speakers. Most likely from Jace. The dude is a sucker for a good beat drop.

"The rules are the same as regular Jenga, ladies and gents. Only, you have to do the dare written on the side of your piece. The lucky loser that drops the pieces must take the mystery shot. If you're allergic to cherries—*Eric*—please sit out."

My eyes wander across the table and immediately fall on Cleo. She's sitting squished between Jace and Georgia, obviously uncomfortable as she slowly sips from the second pink cup I'd given her earlier.

I chuckle as she grimaces. The first drink I'd concocted for her was out of pure fun, I honestly can't even tell you what I put in it but I know it had to be disgusting based on her reaction. The second one, however, is my go-to, something that always took the edge off.

Good ole' Cuba libre.

"Let me see these... *Ew*. Why does this one say 'kiss Jace for ten seconds'?" One of the cheerleaders, Destiny, asks with a frown looking up at the cheeky bastard.

"It's a small experiment that I'm doing. Want to test it out?" Jace asks, winking as Georgia pretends to gag beside him.

"Maybe if you were Alec, but hell no." Destiny chuckles, jokingly winking at a smug Alec. Jace frowns immediately as the guys around us groan.

"Fucking hell, Des." One of our goalies, Romeo, groans as he digs into his pocket.

"Damn it, Destiny."

"Fuck..."

The men all curse around the group as they each pull twenties from their pockets, piling them in front of Alec. Destiny frowns as she watches them and Jace sighs.

Looks like someone lost a bet.

We go over the ground rules of Jenga and within the first five minutes, Georgia has kissed Darius and "married" Cleo after drawing the kiss, marry, kill block. In-Su, our sophomore left-winger, has stripped down to his boxers, and Alec has kissed one of my LEGO figurines.

The game is getting funnier and heated by the second as we drink more enjoying our time with each other.

"Take a body shot off the person to your left."

Jace's face reddens, and for a second the statement goes over my head until I look up between him, and Cleo, who is in fact on his left. I watch as she grows shy, hiding her face behind her hands chuckling softly as Jace grabs some ingredients and a pair of shorts.

When I look at Jace and Cleo, I realize that the two are closer than I'd imagined and that he hadn't told us about her for a reason.

Cleo is one of the most gorgeous women in the world. Whenever Jace would talk about his best friend, he'd always downplay her as if she were one of the guys. He'd talk about how they played video games together and watched hockey highlights but he never mentioned that she looked like someone out of a fucking fairytale.

Jace comes back to the group with a sheepish smile, covering Cleo as she slides the shorts on under her skirt. I watch carefully, my eyes focusing on them as he lays her down on the floor, placing a pillow under her head. He's slow and a fucking tease as he lines her soft abdomen with salt, and places the shot and lime just above her cherry shaped belly ring.

It's fucking hot.

But what's *not* hot is the sensual way he licks her up and takes the shot.

It's quick and a little awkward as the two of them laugh once the shot is gone. Jace helps Cleo up with a small smile as if he didn't do a body shot off his best friend.

Leilani, a curvy dark skinned girl on the cheer team, is the next person to pull from the tower; she chuckles sneakily as she reads her card aloud.

Her plump lips curve into a sinister smirk. "Flash the group or go streaking around the house." She shows the group the card. I can practically hear the gulps from the men in the room.

Leilani is arguably the most gorgeous cheerleader in all of SFU history, but she's always hanging around the football team and Ryan Jones, so it's surprising she's here tonight with us.

Without hesitation, she lifts her shirt revealing a rack of some nicely round and perky tits, probably a D cup at max.

"Fuck me..." Theo mumbles aloud, cringing as Leilani winks at him.

Oh, she's definitely fucking him now. I wouldn't be surprised if Theo finds a whole new roster of women this season considering how much women fawn over—

"Blake, don't start that daydreaming crap now... it's your turn." Brax chuckles, from across the room.

I slightly jump at the feeling of all eyes on me and with slow movements, I steadily pull from the tower. A feeling of triumph washes over me as I successfully pull the block from the tower but all air is knocked from my lungs as I read over the block for a second time.

Is this a joke? Is God giving me a gift or is this a warning from hell?

Lucki leans over my shoulder and whistles as he reads the piece aloud. "Play 7 minutes in heaven with the person straight across from you."

His tone is teasing, but I'm not focused on him.

Instead, my eyes are trained on the wide set of brown ones in front of me. Cleo looks as if she's going to make a run for it but a shoulder squeeze from Georgia has her smiling.

Okay... She's smiling so that means she's cool with this, right?

Are you okay?' I mouth to her, but instead of responding, she jumps to her feet.

"Come on, creeper... You scared I'll bite?"

FIVE

Cleo

IF YOU TOLD ME four months ago that I would be standing in the bedroom of a handsome man that I'd met at a college party, I'd think you belonged in the psych ward.

But here I am standing in front of a man that I barely know and am expected to give him "seven minutes in heaven", or whatever the hell it is.

Blake stands a decent distance from me, shifting uncomfortably on his legs watching as I walk around his bedroom. He let me know on our walk from the living room that he didn't expect us to do anything and that I was more than welcome to snoop through his LEGO, vinyl, and film collections. So that's what I'm doing.

His room is extremely neat and tidy as if Jace did daily military cleaning checks on it. It's a little bigger than my room but has just as much personality. It's decorated to the brim with all things red and black, probably his favorite colors. His desk has a half-built LEGO set scattered across it with small figurines along a bookcase beside it, very few books were actually on the case as it's full of LEGO cars and flowers. On his dresser, there's small photographs of people who'd looked close and two 'Intro To Studio Media' textbooks placed neatly beside them with a black record player on top of it.

"So…" He rocks on his heels, unsteadily. Blake looks adorable with tomato-colored red cheeks and goofy grin. I probably look the exact same after taking five shots, back-to-back, as one of my own dares.

"I don't want to pressure you or anything, Cleo. We can just talk if you want… No rush or anything at all," he says but his eyes tell a different story. Blake's gaze on me is unwavering as he watches me stalk toward him while he rambles. "I...uh...Fuck, Cleo." He chuckles stuttering as a rush of liquid courage enables me to rub his arm.

"We could talk about the weather or...the...political state—"

"Hey, Blake..." My voice is not my own. No, this one is soft and sultry, like a siren beckoning a sailor to his doom.

I think I like it.

Blake gulps, staring down at me as he rubs his palms down the side of his pants.

"Yes?"

"Why don't you just shut up and kiss me?" I question with all the confidence in the world, but on the inside, my brain is going ballistic.

Before we'd left for the party, I listened to Georgia as she suggested that I take risks and let the night take me wherever. Right now, I'm not sure that I made the right decision.

What if I was reading his tone wrong earlier? What if he wasn't flirting at all and that was just how he talks to people? *Damnit, Cleo, why didn't you think before speaking?* He clearly doesn't want to do anything like that. If he did, he wouldn't have told me that we didn't have to—

My body being jerked into a wall by hard muscles pulls me out of the spiral I'd successfully pulled myself in. Looking up at Blake, the air from my lungs is knocked loose as he stares down at me with a look of complete and utter lust. His light blue eyes take on the color of deep ocean waves, dark and deadly—and I'm drowning in them.

He pulls me closer; sparks are sent up my spine from where his large hand decorates the small of my back with faint traces while the other holds my cheek softly as if I were a doll.

"Can I kiss you?" he asks in the softest tone I've ever heard. My heart stutters as flurries flutter in the bottom of my stomach.

"Come on, creeper... You scared or—"

Soft lips interrupt my teasing remark as Blake ravishes my mouth, haughty and hungrily.

His grip on my lower back tightens as he feverishly devours me, taking my lips into his own and never giving them back. The kiss is devastating and hungry and one of the best kisses of my life.

But that's not saying much considering I've only kissed five people—including Jace and Georgia.

He pulls away first, eyes dark as he rests his forehead on mine. "How do you want me, Princess?" His voice is hoarse and rough.

I'm startled when I look up at him but there's nothing that can prepare me for what comes out of my mouth.

"On your knees with your lips on me."

Drunk me is playing a dangerous game and I'm in the perfect mood to see where this goes.

He pauses, sharing the shock of my words with me for a second before the mischievous smirk he'd donned all night reappears. "Your wish is my command."

Seeing a man on his knees in front of me is not what I had on my Friday night BINGO card, but I am definitely not complaining as Blake makes good on his command, pushing me against his dresser and getting down on one knee.

He looks up at me for a moment, as if he's making sure that I want this. My breathing hitches and I don't think as I lean down and kiss him softly, running my fingers through his soft dark waves.

I gasp as Blake lifts up my leg and places my foot on his thigh; the silver stiletto digs into his jean clad leg but he doesn't seem to mind as he looks up at me.

His eyes drag across me slowly, as if committing this sinful image of me to memory before lightly tugging my pink laced panties to the side.

Blake groans and the sound sends shockwaves to my core as he licks his bottom lip.

"Oh, Princess, you're killing me," he mutters, rubbing a soft yet calloused hand around the swell of my ass.

I think that he won't touch me at all in the way I'd anticipated but I'm proven wrong as he begins to circle my clit with his free thumb. Blake takes his time as he works me, he watches my reactions, and smirks as my back arches off the dresser. I moan as he grows in intensity, sticking a finger in.

"Mhm..." The sounds of his fingers plunging into slippery arousal surround us in this room, drowning out the massive party outside.

"I can't wait to taste you, you sound beautiful," he says the raunchiest thing as if it were the sweetest of melodies.

I'm not usually one for dirty talk but when it's coming from him, I've become a squirming mess...and he was only two fingers deep.

"Taste me then..." I sigh as another finger slides in effortlessly.

"Trust me, Princess. I will." He chuckles huskily, thumbing my clit as he plunges faster inside of me. My back arches as my hips rock against his palm.

I didn't believe that he would actually put his mouth on my pussy until his gaze fully darkened. The intensity of my moans grow as I watch him become overtaken by a completely different aura. No longer was he the funny and shy man from the party. He is sexy and most of all intoxicating as he pulls me closer to him. Blake smiles up at me and proceeds to take me into his warm mouth, sucking and teasing me in the best way possible.

He plunges harder, faster into me with all three fingers as his mouth works me in ways I've never experienced before.

"Fuck, Blake..." I cried out clenching around him as the feeling of euphoric eroticism built larger and larger in my stomach.

"I know, Princess. I know..." His eyes held a sense of cockiness as he looked up at me, and if I hadn't been getting devoured by the man, I might've just cursed him out.

Cocky asshole.

He swirled his tongue in the most unspeakable way, sucking my clit as if it were his favorite piece of candy. The warmth in my stomach grew to an all time high as he drew me in with his mouth, unwavering and unyielding to my cries of ecstasy.

"I'm gonna'... Fuck—" Before I can finish my sentence, the sound of a lock clicking pauses me. And before I know it, the door is wide open with a tall dark-skinned man, Braxton, I think, walking in with a large smile completely unaware of the scene unfolding.

"Hey B, your time is...OH— Oh my—"

"Out," Blake commands.

Peeling myself off Blake, I shiver in embarrassment. We got caught by his *friend*.

Fuck me, and fuck this shit.

This is more embarrassing than when I fainted the first time I used a toy in the shower and my mom found me on the ground.

I run out of the room before Braxton can get a chance and make my way down the stairs thankful that the party is still going and that there is barely anyone on this floor.

Bum rushing the kitchen, I'm happy when I can instantly find Georgia, Darius, and Jace.

"Hey, doll, where ya' been?" she asks, smiling brightly with a red solo cup in hand.

"No time to chat," I rushed out turning to Darius, the only person I knew who didn't drink tonight. When Georgia had introduced us, the first thing he told me was that he wasn't drinking in case we needed a ride. So, now was the time to take him up on his offer. "Can you give us a ride?" I ask looking over my shoulder for the confused man I just left. Seeing that Blake is nowhere near, I sigh in relief.

"Yeah, of course. Let me get my keys..."

"He seems nice!" I tell Georgia as she wraps an arm around my shoulder, she smiles down at me for a second before tilting her head at me.

"I'm going to pretend you don't smell a little like sex right now because we're going to get some ice cream and then, when we get home, you're going to tell me what the fuck happened with you."

"How about now?"

"It was no five minutes ago, and it's still a no now." I roll my eyes at the pouty Georgia behind me. Since we woke up this morning and decided to clean the apartment, she's been pestering me about what did and did not happen in Blake's room last night.

"Oh come on, CJ! You've given me nothing." She groans folding another towel as *Tales of a New Girl* plays unwatched on our living room TV. I fight a laugh as she throws the towel at me, unfolding it.

"That's because nothing happened," I lie, fumbling with my middle finger's ring.

"Liar." Sienna yawns, stalking into the apartment dressed in a large t-shirt and shorts. Her pink hair wildly pulled into a bun.

"Is everyone in here fucking beside me?!" Georgia exclaims, gawking at Sienna as she plops down on the couch looking worn out.

Sienna scoffs as if what Georgia said was an insult, grabbing the discarded towel. "I'm not fucking anyone; I spent the entire night teaching an adorable four-year-old how to do a perfect Mont de Jambe and then I crashed at the studio." She sighs, running a hand over her face.

"A four-year-old?" Georgia furrows her eyebrows as she looks between Sienna and me.

"New job." We say in unison as Georgia nods in acknowledgement.

The three of us are quiet for a moment, it's calm and peaceful...and the complete opposite of Georgia Adams.

"So, did you fuck him or not, CJ? You're giving me nothing to work with here!" Georgia groans, throwing her head back, exasperated as I smile.

"No, Georgia...I did not fuck Blake last night." My smile grows as I look anywhere but my cousin and best friend, folding the towels quicker.

"But you *did* do something!" she exclaims. "So, what was it? Did you go down on him? Did *he* go down on *you*? Did you get to see—"

"Oh my God! Let the girl speak..." Sienna chuckles, throwing a towel at Georgia.

"We kissed," I reply, my cheeks burning from the unwavering smile.

"And…" Sienna prompts, now completely interested in the conversation. I don't even think she knows *who* Blake is.

"And… I may have told him I'd like to see him on his knees…" My words are out there in shy execution as my friends jump from their spots on the cream-colored couch, cheering.

"I don't know what I wanted you to say but that was the best thing you've ever said." Georgia claps as she laughs, running a hand through her blonde waves.

"You are… Oh my goodness, Cleo." Sienna guffaws.

My skin heats as they laugh louder and harder, maybe I shouldn't have told them. I don't even know him like that and I'm not the type to have random hookups at college parties… Maybe I should just forget—

"Well did you come or was he not good? Come on, you can't just leave us hanging."

"Just know that he was talented." I chuckle as the images of Blake on one knee for me, bringing me to the brink, replay throughout my mind.

"You are an icon, Cleo… Truly iconic," Georgia mocks, wiping a tear from her eye.

We continue recounting details from that night with Sienna, laughing at how Georgia describes the guys' personalities and the long game of drunk Jenga that was played. After finishing up the laundry, the three of us sit around watching TV until Georgia gasps, checking her phone.

"It's almost 8:45…." She says, looking between me and Sienna, receiving shrugs from the two of us. "And aren't you supposed to be helping your dad?! I completely forgot you told me to remind you at 8."

Oh shit…

The practice.

"Crap. Crap. Crap," I mutter jumping off the couch to find my leggings and skates.

My dad's only requirement for me to attend Summerfield University was to make sure I attended all home games and any practices he needed help with. As you can see, I'm already fucking up. The practice doesn't officially start until

9:30 a.m. but I wanted to get in at least twenty minutes of ice time, especially if I'm supposed to be helping a group of D1 athletes.

Making quick work through my closet, I find a pair of pastel pink leggings as well as my pastel pink figure skates. I already had a jacket on, so there was no need for another.

"I'll drop you off, I think there's someone I need to meet with too." Georgia smiles warmly, grabbing her keys from the coffee table.

Sienna pops up smoothly linking her arms in Georgia's with a bright smile, "I'm emotional support, of course." she grins cheekily.

I raise an eyebrow at my cousin but shrug her off. Something's up with her, I can feel it, but there's no time to dwell on it. Right now, I have 25 hockey players to deal with.

SIX

Blake

"We just had to take Betsy today... No one ever listens to me when I say that piece of shit is going to fuck us up one day and now look." Braxton throws his arms up in frustration. If I hadn't known any better, I'd say Braxton was truly upset we were late for the first practice of the season. But... knowing the bastard, I can see a glint of excitement in his eyes. He's loving this.

"Now, B. Don't blame Cap for his junk of a truck... Blame him for his refusal to get the shit fixed." I can hear the annoyance in Jace's voice before I even look at him.

Jace and I have been having the same argument about getting Betsy, my 2004 GMC Acadia, "fixed" since freshman year when we were roommates on campus. Fixed in Jace's words is "throwing that piece of shit into a compactor and having it rust out in a junkyard for all eternity."

But how can I let Betsy go?

She's been my car since I was 15 and barely knew how to drive. She's seen me at my lowest when I got dumped by Tasha Arnold in Junior year and at my highest last season when Summerfield U won our second Frozen Four in a row.

I suppress a groan as the feeling of those evil green eyes burn holes into the side of my head. Jace may be the poster child for golden retriever athletes, but the man is scary when provoked, which is why he's the perfect co-captain to my captainship this year. Never underestimate the artsy kids.

"If I knew we'd be this late, I would've told Vee she could stay over for a little longer." Charlie huffs from the back of the truck and I sigh because here we go again.

Last night, we threw a party at our house. It was where Braxton swore off women for the rest of his life, Charlie met Victoria Milani and I met *her*. The thought of Cleo sends chills down my spine, and I groan as I remember never asking for her number. Hell, I doubt she even went to SFU; I would've noticed her from a lightyear away if she'd been a student here.

Fuck, I probably would've tried to fuck her by now if she did.

Maybe it's a good thing that she doesn't go here... Women are a distraction, one that I can't afford this season. With Coach being on my ass after my shitty start last season and me being a prospect for the Washington Eagles, I can't slip up this year.

Jace is like an angry Chihuahua, and I can feel his beady-eyed stare before our eyes connect.

"Who is she?" he asks for the thirtieth time since our welcome-back party last night.

"Who is who?" Braxton turns to us, looking up from his Uber app briefly.

"The girl that's going to ruin our season if Blake doesn't get his shit together." The blonde sighs. Jace runs a hand through his golden waves and frowns as he continues studying my face.

"First off...*rude*. It's my junior year and I'm captain, J. Have some faith in me. I've already sworn off girls for the season." I shrug, lying through my teeth. Well, not *completely* lying... I have sworn off women.

Right now.

I just swore off girls, right now.

Only because in a way the golden boy is right. There can't be any distractions this year if we want another championship under our belts and I refuse to go down the same path that I did last year after my nana passed away. I plan on being the best captain the Summerfield hockey team has ever seen.

That starts with getting our asses to the ice before Coach rings our necks out.

"You? Not having sex? Has the earth stopped spinning or some shit?" Alec laughs, coming around the front of the car with the rest of us. He props himself up on the hood of my truck and frowns as the sun blinds him momentarily.

"Look... Campus is about a ten-minute walk from here. We can talk about the logistics of my non-existent sex life later but for now, I'd rather not start the season with Jones on our asses." I shrug as the guys groan before turning on my heels and starting my run to campus.

I can hear the rest of the guys behind me without looking back, their loud footsteps resemble a parade of elephants as they follow me to the rink.

"Sorry, Coach. Wilder's car broke down on our way here." Jace's voice is hurried as he runs down the stairs of the bleachers with Alec, Braxton, Charlie, and me on his tail. The four of us were already in our practice clothes, our skates already laced with the guards on as we hopped down each stair carefully yet efficiently.

"Yeah, blame Blake, his car's a piece of shit!" Braxton yells next and I want to murder him for adding extra emphasis on how crappy my truck truly is. I *know* it's a crappy piece of metal but it's *my* crappy piece of metal. However, looking at Coach from up here, I know I can't defend the truck.

"Blame me? Blame Betsy! *She* broke down on *us*. I didn't do shit!" I exclaim as I make my way onto the ice, completely bypassing everyone and gliding over to the center line.

"The three of you can cut the shit and thank Daniels for your training method today," Coach says, and though he's talking to us, he is staring somewhere else. And it isn't until I follow his gaze that I notice that we're not alone on the ice today.

She's here.

And boy does she look even better when I'm sober. Clad in a light pink outfit and figure skates, she looks like she stepped out of a Barbie wonderland. Her brown skin glows under the ugly florescent lighting of the rink and today her long black hair is pulled into a high ponytail, accentuating her soft facial structure. I'm at a loss for words as I stare at the plump pink lips from last night that tasted of strawberry and vanilla. The sight of her alone has my dick stirring.

Fuck me... I cannot get hard right now. My balls will be bluer than the sky. I want to say something...anything. However, before she or I can say anything, Coach beats us to it.

"Everyone, this is Cleo Jones. My daughter."

seven

Cleo

A LARGE FLUFF OF gold blinds me before I have a chance to speak; I can feel my skates lift from the ground. All eyes are on me and the massive golden retriever in human form. Jace's engulfs me in a hug so tight that I lose my breath and footing on the ice momentarily,.

"You should've told me you'd be here," Jace mumbles into my hair, pulling me closer to him. My heart swells as my best friend holds me in the warmest embrace I've felt all year and I can't help but feel safe.

It's only been a day since I've seen Jace Heart in person. Yet, he holds me as if it'd been an eternity. His embrace is warm and holds so much love my heart nearly bursts. He gently places me back on the ice, a large smile brightening his tanned face as he peers down at me with large sage-colored eyes.

"You get to see me train today! I can't wait to show you that move I was talking about last—"

"Ahem." Dad interrupts Jace, a cold stare darkens his already hard features as he looks between the blonde and me.

"Like I was saying to everyone. My daughter's going to be helping with today's practice..." Dad starts up again, I zone out from whatever he's saying to the boys as my skin begins to prickle.

The hair on my neck rises and it takes everything in me not to look over each of the taller men around me. You know that feeling when you know you're being watched? And it may either be a serial killer or a hot stalker... I'm hoping for the latter because I could really use a dark romance thriller kind of love right about now.

Should I be mysterious and act like I don't feel them starring?

Or should I stare back? Assert dominance, or whatever...

As a matter of fact, fuck dominance and mysteriousness.

My neck practically snaps as I turn my head to face my admirer and my breath hitches as soon as my eyes land on my hot stalker.

Only, he isn't a stalker.

He's a hookup.

And he's on my dad's hockey team.

Shit.

I immediately look away from Blake, my goosebump-riddled arms are thankfully covered by long sleeves. Coming into a new semester at a new school, I had one goal.

Stay away from the hockey team.

This goal is so simple and yet very much easier said than done. My dad coaches hockey for Christ's sake and I knew before today that Jace was on the hockey team. Though, I would *never* hook up with Jace. That ship sailed in high school when we tried to kiss, and both gagged immediately after. I still shudder at the thought of our fifteen-year-old selves playing Spin the Bottle at a party and then nearly puking on each other.

I can feel his water-colored eyes on me as I skate towards Jace when Dad finishes his spiel. His gaze burns holes into the side of my head, and it takes everything in me not to turn back to stare at the beauty of a man.

Blake Wilder.

"You're helping us today? I thought you hated ice warriors?" Jace questions me as soon as I'm in front of him.

"Ice warriors? Do we get powers or something?" a deep voice asks, sliding beside me and Jace.

He's, well, he's fucking gorgeous.

He shines a bright smile my way, his white teeth bright against his dark skin and I'm taken aback by how gorgeous this man is. He's boyishly handsome; the kind of handsome that can be a load of trouble, and oh my God, are those dimples?

I think I'm going to melt.

"I'm Braxton–" He pauses, eyes widening as ours collide. I mimic his expression as he clears his throat. "But you can call me Brax," he says, holding his hand out for mine. I stare at his outstretched hand in horror before regaining my composure and awkwardly shaking it.

"Cleo."

"Oh, I know." He smirks, sending a quick wink my way before skating back to the rest of the team.

"Ignore him." Jace chuckles, wrapping an arm around my shoulder.

"I'm trying," I say, my voice a pitch higher, and I curse myself for it when Jace rolls his eyes.

"Seriously, what're you doing here?" he asks again, gently rubbing my arms, warming me up like he did when we were kids.

I groan trying to think of a way out of this conversation and sigh as I come up with nothing. I'd known he'd want to talk about my abrupt appearance at SFU and in time, I'd hopefully tell him. But being on the ice with 24 other men was not the place to cry about my life at Brighton and the year of hell I've been through.

I help the boys with simple drills and basic techniques for the next hour and learn that not only is Blake 'Mr. Sexy Eyes and Mistakes', he's also the captain of the team and *the* Blake Wilder.

As in the Blake Wilder that my dad has been both gushing and bitching to me about for the past two years… Blake Wilder. How did I not realize who he was? I fight to push this piece of information out of my brain as I help the guys. I've talked to nearly everyone in here while also avoiding the man I'd been too close for comfort with not even two days ago.

In my small group, I have Charlie Tyson, a senior right defenseman, Braxton, who I found out is a left defenseman, and Alec Tu, one of the senior right-wingers.

The three boys keep me laughing more than teaching and I'm not mad about it as I learn all about them and the team despite my not wanting to.

They tell me about when Blake and Jace went streaking last year after winning the championship and how my dad got them a pet goldfish that lasted most of the season until Ivaan Brar, a senior right-winger, accidentally killed it. I tell them bits and pieces about myself and how it feels to have Clef Jones as my father.

I spend most of the time talking with Alec about using the puck to our team's advantage. Of the three guys, Alec is the calmest and more reserved. It took him a full ten minutes to finally say more than two words to me while Braxton and Charlie practically talked their heads off.

"*Aaannnddd* shoot!" I exclaim, nearly jumping for joy as Alec lets the puck rip from his stick back out onto the rink.

"You just saved my life." He chuckles, his nose scrunching as he watches the puck slap someone's skate.

"Sorry..."

I laugh as the player sighs, shaking his head and it isn't until the player skates off that I see him again.

Blake's blue eyes bore into my soul as we watch one another. He gives me a small smile, the crooked kind that'll make a girl's heart stop, and it takes everything in me not to smile back at him because smiling back is an invitation. When it comes to hockey players, I refuse to invite any of them back in. I didn't leave Brighton to stumble into the arms of another ice warrior.

So instead of smiling back, I look away and focus my attention back on Alec. He and I practice more one-on-one shots, while Braxton and Charlie do their own thing on the side. Getting to know Alec may be the best thing to come out of today, he speaks to me as if he's known me for years and though he's on the quieter side, he makes me feel comfortable to talk with him.

I feel like I've run four marathons back to back as I exit out of the boys' practice in the afternoon. What originally was supposed to be a two-hour session with them quickly turned into three and a half one. Dad somehow convinced me to stay and help with two more groups. So now I know way more of the team than I'd planned. Which is fine... I just don't need to learn any more names or get to know any more of the guys.

I sigh as the early September air warms my skin; it's still warm in Maryland and I am not complaining about it one bit. This warm air is exactly what I needed after spending a day in the rink with only a sweatsuit on.

Pulling out my phone I groan at the sight of two new messages.

Unknown

> you know what they say about mice

> the cats away, young Cleo but just know I'm always watching

My breath is shaky as I inhale sharply. I had to leave Brighton. It was not safe for me or anyone in the situation... I had to leave. I had to leave. I had to leave. I had to—

"Hey... You okay?"

The voice that calls out to me is warm and soft like a hand that fights to pull you out from underwater. For just this once, I let it pull me to the shore of peace and sanity.

My breathing calms as my brain tries to place where I am and what's happening. I'm still in the arena parking lot, the sun is on the verge of setting, and there is a man in front of me. My breathing shakes again and I realize I'm trembling. His eyes are cloudy as he watches me with brows dipped in concern.

"What?"

"Just breathe for a second," he says softly.

Though skeptical, I nod, taking a couple of deep breaths, and then slowly, my heartbeat steadies.

"Are you okay, Cleo?" Blake asks me.

No. I want to scream and shout at the top of my lungs that no, I am not okay. No, I am not fine. I'm scared for my life every day because of something I can't control. I'm scared of repeating history with a new man. I'm scared that everything will crumble if I ever speak about the things that I've been through. I'm just scared.

But being scared isn't going to pay the bills and crying about it won't do me any good.

That thought alone brings my breathing back.

"Yeah, of course. Why wouldn't I be?" The lie spills out of me like a tipped over glass of water.

For a second, I think Blake is going to dig deeper but he doesn't. He just throws me another crooked smile. "I'm happy I got a chance to see you again, you come here often?" he asks and cringes immediately after.

"To men's hockey practices? Or to nearly empty parking lots?" I chuckle, and then slide my phone back into my bag, steadying my shaking hand as I play with the bags cold metal strap.

"Both?" He scratches the back of his neck; the tip of his ears burns bright pink as he looks at his feet.

Cute.

Wait...no.

Not cute.

Absolutely *not* cute.

"No, I like to stay away from serial killers, you know?"

"Oh, definitely, you can never be too careful."

I can see him scratch the back of his neck again from my peripheral, a small smile tugs at my lips before I quickly drop it. The air around us is thick with awkwardness as he and I stand in front of one another not saying a word.

But what am I supposed to say? *Wow, Blake, I didn't know you played for my dad.* Or, *you have an excellent tongue...maybe the best I've ever experienced.* No, neither of those sentences will be coming from my mouth. I shift my weight onto my other leg uncomfortably.

Blake does an awkward cough before looking back up at me, his eyes lock with mine, and my stomach drops for only a moment as we stare at each other.

"About the party, I—"

"CJ! Wait up!" Jace's loud yell breaks through whatever held Blake and me in our staring contest, and I sigh as I let out the breath of air I'd been holding in.

Jace furrows his eyebrows at Blake as he approaches. Blake rolls his eyes as Jace throws an arm around my shoulders, pulling me into his side.

"Yes, sir?" I peer up at Jace as he groans.

"Oh, c'mon mama, don't call me that, you know what it does to me." Jace smirks looking down at me, I gag as he proceeds to give me "fuck me" eyes and laugh when his façade fades. "You're no good for a man's ego." He sighs looking down at me for a split second then back up at Blake.

Both Jace and Blake are about 6'4", with the same muscular build, though I'd say that Jace was slightly leaner than Blake.

"Sir, what do you want? I have to call for my ride or else I'm going to be standing out here all day."

"Uber? Baby doll, you're coming with us."

"With us? Who is *us*?" Looking around, I note that the lot is empty save for us three.

"*Us*... the guys..." He rocks on his heels, looking to Blake for help.

"Didn't your car break down?" The words spill out of me before I can stop them, and I mentally slap myself for it.

Good going, CJ.

Blake's cheeks and the tip of his ears redden as he looks everywhere but me while Jace dies of laughter.

"Then we'll all take an Uber with you. I'm not letting you out of my sight now that you're back in it *and* I have questions for you, missy." Jace's voice is stern as he looks down at me, booping my nose. I scrunch it immediately and roll my eyes; I'd rather drown on the Titanic than answer any of his questions.

"I can get to my apartment on my own." I sigh just as Jace's eyes brighten.

"Your apartment?! Do you live here? Why are you holding out on me, Cleo? You got a roommate? Is she hot?" He's practically buzzing beside me.

"*She* is Georgia." I laugh, feeling him stiffen around me.

"Gross." He grimaces.

"You go to school here? Have you always?" Blake interjects, his eyes hopeful as he looks at me.

"I just transferred," I answer with a small smile, only to be shaken by the man-child beside me.

"And you didn't tell me?!"

Shortly after Jace and I finished arguing about him asking too many questions and me not answering a single one, Braxton, Alec, and Charlie joined us in the parking lot. I like to assume that Blake ordered us an Uber but I'm not sure who truly called for the car service. So, here I am now sitting between Blake and Alec as Braxton sings in the front seat. Listening to Lovestruck by my cousin Zola, in an UberXL with singing hockey players was not how I expected my Saturday evening to go.

Zola's a big name in the music industry, she was in a popular girl group, COSMIC, but they disbanded a few years back. She and her twin sister, Zahria, played a big role in my decision to transfer to Brighton. When shit hit the fan, Zola gave me advice about handling drama with boys and keeping my "energy" protected. Zahria, on the other hand, stressed the importance of me knowing that she'd "skin any fucker alive" for me.

Her words...not mine.

"Is he always like this?" I ask no one in particular but earn snickers from both Alec and Blake.

"Yeah, we got used to him being a Zola guy *quickly*..." Blake smiles as he watches his friend sing louder with the chorus.

"Good to know." The giggle that bubbles out of me is completely foreign to my ears and I grimace as the sound rings through the car.

I've learned a few things on this short ride that I initially refused to go on: One, Blake is the second quietest of the group; Alec is the first. Two, Charlie cannot hold a pitch to save his life. And three, Braxton *can* hold one.

The car ride to the boys' house is filled with laughter and singing as Braxton and Charlie try going bar for bar in a rap battle which lasts about five minutes until Jace cuts in with a rap of his own.

I sit content as I listen to the guys joke with one another, and it isn't until we reach their house that I sort of feel sad that the ride is over. The six of us say our thanks as we hop out of the Uber and walk up to the other cars parked in the driveway. Stopping at the familiar dark green Ashton Martin SUV, I sigh as I wait for its owner to unlock it.

"Who says I'm taking you home?" Jace asks with a raised brow as he peers around the car.

"You did, or I can always call Georgia—"

"Get in the car... and stop speaking of the devil before she shows her face." He groans unlocking the door as I smile hopping in the passenger seat.

A grin plasters itself across my face as I look around the familiar car Jace's parents had gotten him for his eighteenth birthday. Jace's family is a well-off group of CEOs and entrepreneurs, who love their sons to death. This car was one of their "I love you" gifts to their youngest.

The SUV shakes as more bodies than I can count file into the backseat, my eyebrows furrow as I watch Blake, Charlie, and Braxton slide into the car. The three of them are in a quiet heated discussion as Jace gets into the driver's seat. I suppress a laugh as I hear something along the lines of *"blonde bitch"* and proceed to ignore them as we set off toward the River View complex.

The ride to my apartment is silent for the most part; I'm grateful that I don't have to deal with Jace questioning me about things I'm not ready to talk about.

Lord knows when I'll be ready to talk about last year.

"So, who's the girl, Wilder?" Jace chirps from the driver's seat, and my back stiffens as I turn my head slightly to hear his response.

Girl? Does he have a girlfriend?

This cannot be happening...

"What girl?" Blake coughs from behind me.

"The girl from last night? The one who's going to mess with our season—Oh, don't worry about Cleo, she won't tell anyone about this. Won't you, bub?" Jace asks me, briefly looking at me before focusing back on the road. For once, I want to curse the nickname we gave each other fifteen years ago because I can feel the thickness in the air as the name leaves his mouth.

My and Blake's eyes lock in the rearview mirror and I truly don't expect him to answer Jace. But when he does, my heart does a summersault.

"I don't fuck and tell, Heart."

EIGHT

Cleo

I love Mondays.

I love them because they bring a sense of newness; it's the start of a new week, a new day, and a new me. I love knowing that no matter what I did the previous week or weekend, there will always be a Monday coming up to wash away my regrets and give me a fresh start.

Today, in particular, I love the start of a new week just a little bit more.

I awoke to Georgia with a warm cup of tea and a Pink Truffle donut from The Sugar Hole with her insisting that a donut a day keeps the hangovers at bay. I hadn't been bombarded with questions from either Jace or Georgia all weekend. Hell, I haven't even seen Jace since that crazy car ride a few days ago.

But what truly tops off my Monday is that I have gone a full four hours without any interruptions from—

"*DON'T ANSWER! DON'T ANSWER! DON'T ANSWER—*" The cautionary tone of my mother's custom-made ringtone cracked the happiness spell I've been under as I pulled my vibrating phone from my purse.

Decline.

Mondays are my favorite days, even if they're the day that Lorelei Smith decides that she wants to be a parent. With a small huff, I brush off the call that I ignored and smile, stalking towards the lecture hall for Film Studies 3002.

I can't contain myself as I work my legs to move faster toward the building that is every media major's wet dream. The media building holds four lecture halls, as well as five distinct studios where students are allowed to practice and film for projects and assignments. It's also used for the school's broadcasting club to film their random videos and news segments.

This building alone played a major role in my decision to transfer.

Sucking in a deep breath, a content sigh expels from my lips as I step foot into the building. The expansive modernized atrium catches my breath as my eyes travel from the marble flooring to the high ceilings where silver light fixtures in the shape of abstract cameras brighten the naturally lit area.

"Wow—" The word gets knocked from my body as a strong force pushes me to the side, I close my eyes in anticipation of hitting a wall and sigh when the impact never comes. Instead, my body is being held by strong warm hands and I tense again as the owner of said hands apologizes.

"I'm so sorry! I thought you heard me say 'wait up' but then I realized you didn't when I practically ran you over, and then..." His words grew distant as my phone began to ring its annoying tone again, essentially blocking him out.

"DON'T ANSWER! DON'T ANSWER! DON'T ANSWER—" I ignore the call and force a smile.

Blake stands in front of me with a weary grin as he looks down at me. His beautifully blue eyes are so bright and warm, I almost get lost in them as he and I share a quick look.

"You going to get that, Princess?" he asks, warm hands letting me go, finding solitude in his pocket.

"Hm?"

"The call... You know, the *'don't answer'* one." He laughs for a moment, then looks off to the lecture hall in front of us.

"Don't worry about it... I have to go," I quip and turn on my heels, heading toward the lecture hall where I'll be for the next 16 weeks. As I enter the hall with my head down low, I can't shake the nagging feeling that I'm being followed... I almost ignore it until the creeper following me decides to bump into me for the fun of it.

"Watch it." My teeth grit, side-eyeing the tall smiling male beside me.

"Oh! Cleo Jones, look at that... We're in the same course!" Blake gasps, feigning shock as a cocky smile slowly but surely crosses his face. If I'd known that he'd follow me around like an anxiety ridden puppy, I wouldn't have let him go down on me last weekend. But oh, was he amazing at what he did... If I think hard enough, I can just feel—

No.

Absolutely not. I cannot go down that road.

"Looks like it." I sigh, pushing aside my dirty thoughts and sliding into one of the many rows in the middle of the hall.

Not too far from the front where my non-glasses wearing eyes aren't straining, and not too far from the back where there are fewer people. In the hopes of getting away from the large entity that is Blake Wilder, I sit by a girl with her head down.

From this angle, I can't see her face because her dark brown curls cover it, but she seems to be drawing something. She has an edgy vibe, wearing a leather jacket and black jeans but her aura is enchanting.

"Take a picture but make sure you get a good angle," she teases, lifting her head to reveal a dazzling red-painted smirk.

I think this might be the most beautiful human I've ever seen. Her deep brown skin glows under the ambient lighting of our lecture hall. Her cheekbones are high and soft whilst complimenting the small Marilyn Monroe mole on her upper lip. She smiles as if she's also checking me out and sticks her hand out, seeing as I'm still dumbfounded by her.

Blake snickers behind me, snapping me out of the haze.

"Denver Castillo," she says with a smile brighter than the sun.

"Cleo..." My voice is breathy as my cheeks warm. Denver's smile widens as she nods, and then it suddenly drops as her brown eyes wander behind me.

"Gross, Cleo, you brought a fly in with you." She frowns as Blake lets out the most obnoxiously loud laugh I've ever heard.

"Settle down, Seattle. You know you love having me in all the same classes as you." He responds with a mocking smile.

Am I missing something? My eyebrows furrow at his comment and Denver seems to see it as she shakes her head smiling .

"Blake's my cousin...we've been stuck in the same courses together for more than a year now." She sighs, running freshly manicured red nails through her hair.

"We're only in the same courses again because you're stalking me," he counters, humor riddling his tone.

At that, Denver rolls her eyes and unlocks her phone. The screen lights up to show an image of Noah Larkin's infamous paddock walk from last year's Bahrain Grand Prix.

"You watch Formula One?" The question is out before I have the chance to think over my words.

What if she thinks I'm a creep? What if she believes that me seeing her lock screen is an invasion of privacy? What if she—

"Damnit Cleo—" Blake groans, only to be cut off.

"Of course, I fucking love F1. You a fan?" Denver asks, eyes wide with excitement as she focuses all of her attention on me.

"Is that a question? Eren Marlowe has been my lock screen since he first debuted three years ago." I chuckle, holding up my phone to show her proof.

"Girl you're just like me! Have you seen the stats from last week's GP?" she asks, completely engaged in the conversation, and for once, my stomach flutters. This could be the new start that I needed, a new friend.

"Alejandro Sanchez should've won," Blake huffs from beside me, I'd almost forgotten he was here. My stomach clenches as I look him over completely for the first time today. He's dressed in a muscle-hugging white tee, dark jeans, and an SFU Tigers letterman jacket with a matching blue backward cap.

He's a walking wet dream; my thighs clench, but I refuse to give in.

"Don't you have anything better to do other than stalking me, creeper?" I ask.

"Why, of course not, Princess" He smirks, twirling my ponytail between his fingers.

That fucking flirt. I don't have time for this. I don't have time for him or any man so I swiftly turn back to Denver and effectively shut him out.

"Have I seen it? Baby I breathe F1, look at my Instagram. It's all I talk—"

"Wait a minute... I think I *do* know you from somewhere." She pauses, studying my face inquisitively. This action piques Blake's interest. He scoots in closer to me, his arm brushing mine ever so slightly that the close contact sends a shiver down my spine. I immediately push that feeling away.

I came here to *focus*, not *fondle* ice warriors.

"You do?" My body curls inward as if waiting for a ball to drop as Denver clasps her hands over her mouth.

Does she know me? The *real* me? Does she know the girl that I tried so hard to run away from? The one I worked so hard to leave back at Bright—

"You're fucking IcingIt on YouTube!" she gasps, and I let out a deep breath I didn't know I was holding.

"IcingIt?" Blake's question falls on deaf ears as Denver smiles widely at me, drawing closer to my face.

"Dude, I thought you went to Brighton, so I never thought I'd meet you. We're definitely friends now, I need more people that can talk F1—"

"Ladies, If you don't mind... I'd like to continue with class." A brown-skinned woman, with long locs and braces, calls from the podium at the front of the lecture hall.

We'd been talking for so long; I hadn't even noticed the professor had begun with the class. I was so into talking with Denver and gushing about last week's Grand Prix that I almost forgot that we're in a lecture in the first place.

Almost. My merry facade and happiness crumbles as a voice I know all too well speaks.

"Hello, everyone, you may know me as Olympic Figure Skater Lorelei Smith. Today, I'm here as Lorelei Smith, the director. I'll be popping in over the course of this semester to help you all with the end-of-the-term project worth 50% of your grade." My *mother* drones and my heart proceeds to plummet. Just five seconds ago, my heart was up in the clouds, and now it's practically in hell.

From the corner of my eye, I can see Blake smirking, but I brush him off and focus all of my attention on the woman who *birthed* me.

Sometimes I like to think that my parents found me on their doorstep but that fantasy crumbles every time I see my mother's face which is the exact replica of my own.

"This project will be a partnered assignment, showcasing the lives of you and your partner as well as interviewing them in various stages of their semester in a documentary style format. The best of the best will have the opportunity to work with Lorelei in her upcoming docu-series and to work as an intern at NWZ studios in the spring." My professor, Teyana Hawkins, whose name I remember from my syllabus, smiles at the various faces in the room.

An internship with NWZ has been my dream job since I was 11, more specifically as a sports analyst for On the Ice. I would kill for this chance. Hell, if Prof. Hawkins said she wanted a kidney for it...I'd give both of mine.

But *fuck* I do not want to work with my mother on this.

"I can't wait to see what you all put together this semester. Since it's the first day of classes, I will hand out everything you need for the assignment now so that you all can get a jumpstart." Professor Hawkins' voice is sweet as honey as she ruffles through a stack of manilla envelopes and cameras on a spare desk in the room.

"When I call your name, one person from each group will come up and retrieve an envelope with more details on the assignment as well as two color-coded camcorders to document everything." Professor Hawkins double checks the list on her computer before beginning the roll.

"Alana Rhodes and Ariana Smith," she starts, piquing my interest.

"Is she going by first names?" I ask no one in particular but I can feel the smugness rolling from the hockey player to my right.

"Bailey Kidd and Ben Thomas...Blake Wilder and Cleora Jones...Cora—"

Slowly, I turn my head to face the smug bastard already staring back at me with a smile.

"Hello partner, nice to make your acquaintance." He grins.

Mondays are officially the worst.

NINE

Blake

IF I HAD KNOWN that Cleo would be in my first lecture of the day, I would have dressed up like a fucking movie star. But based on the way I felt her ogling me earlier, I'd say she liked what she saw.

Catching up with Cleo after the lecture is no easy feat, even while wearing a pink dress with bows on the back of it, she walks as if she were on the Olympic track and field team.

"Wait up!" I call out to her again, a sense of deja vu tingles my brain and I feel silly as she turns on her heels.

She sighs reluctantly but stops. "What is it?" she asks, her nose scrunching as I give her my best smile.

"Is that any way to talk to your new partner, Cleopatra?"

"*That* is not my name. Just call me Cleo." She purses her lips, looking up at me.

Thank God for my birth father's genes, if I would've had my adoptive dad's height, I'd lose all my wow factor. Cleo's the perfect height for me; not too short, but not too tall either. The absolute perfect height to take into my mouth and devour.

You think she'd want to kiss me? The last time we'd seen each other was a week ago and she's been standoffish towards me. She can't say that it was because she had the worst oral experience with me, either. Her body wouldn't lie. And I for one pride myself on—

Crap. I'm getting unfocused.

"You sure? You look like a queen to me." I smirk, laying on one of the dumbest pickup lines I know, thick.

Cleo grimaces slightly and sighs, shaking her head. "We need to discuss meeting times."

"Princess, if you want to see me there's no need to plan it. I'll be where—"

"No. *Nope.* That's the *first* rule of whatever *this* is. If you and I are to work together, there will be none of *that.*" She frowns, adjusting the heavy pink tote bag on her shoulder. Instantly, I reach to grab it, ignoring her protests.

"There will be none of what? My panty-wetting charm?" Teasing her, I fix the heavy bag onto my shoulder.

"No. None of that. No flirting, no *'panty-wetting charm'.* None of it, Wilder. I need to pass my classes and I don't want any distractions, especially from an ice war—*hockey player,* like you." She is nearly seething and if I had a brain that worked when it came to this girl, I'd be a little nervous.

Good thing my brain is perfectly useless because instead of being nervous, I sling a cocky arm around her shoulder.

"I solemnly swear that there will be zero funny business. Scout's honor." I smile cheekily down at her. She couldn't be no less than 5'6" but at this angle, she looked tiny.

"You definitely weren't a Boy Scout with that mouth." She rolls her eyes but doesn't push me off as we continue down the hall. Something about the way my arm hung lazily around her felt normal as if this was the only place my arm should be. It's only been a week and I'm acting like I lost my mind.

Is it delusion? Is that what it is?

Am I becoming...*Jace?*

I cannot be him. I'm supposed to be the levelheaded, quiet friend. Not the one that randomly carries girls' bags and follows them around like a lovesick—

"Is there a reason that you're following me, Boy Scout?" Cleo's voice filters back into my ears and I realize that instead of being in the main hall, we're now in the parking lot in front of a white Audi.

Quickly, I come back to my senses.

"We have to discuss our project." I scratch the back of my neck, mentally cursing myself for the feeling of my ears heating. Why am I getting so red over one girl? She's not the first I've been with...so why do my ears feel like a hot tamale?

Cleo doesn't seem to notice my spiraling as she rocks back and forth on her heels, her dress swooshing slightly with the added air.

"Well, what days are you available? I was thinking about us going to different venues for each interview question to add something different to our video."

"I'm free Monday and Wednesdays." I shrug, trying to play it cool like my body *isn't* having the most visceral reaction to her. I'm sweating freaking bullets just looking at the woman.

Cleo rummages through the tote bag on my shoulder and pulls out a small red notebook. "Sounds good to me, I'm free every day after 4 p.m. except Saturdays because of football." She says, taking her bottom lip between her teeth.

"On Wednesdays, I'm free all day...*Oh* and I'll be at every home hockey game so if we can't meet during the week, we always have later on those nights."

"So does that mean that you're free tonight?" I question her, leaning in close. She smells fruity and sweet, almost like the Pina Colada Slurpee from 7/11. Hmm...maybe I should get one of those too. Jace will probably want one, and maybe Deli if she and Derek are over tonight. Shit... but then I'd have to ask Brax and Alec if they want some too. Charlie–

Cleo hums quietly staring up at me, her head tilting as if to question me. She's closer to me than before, and if I just take a step closer, we'd be nearly kissing.

"You okay?" She asks, amusement dancing across her features.

"I'm fine."

"Hm... to answer your question, no. I'm not free tonight, Creeper." She smiles, gently tugging the bag from my shoulder, it sags as she does so.

"Too busy thinking about me?"

"Too busy figuring out how to safely stay away from you," she mutters, but I have the hearing of a bat.

My lips curve into the biggest shit eating grin I can muster as I eye Cleo up and down, noting how she shifts her weight.

"Princess, if you want to be in my presence, all you need to do is tell me."

"Good thing that I don't... Now get up, I have to meet my cousin." She shoos me off the passenger door before stalking over to the driver's side.

She rolls down the passenger window seeing as I'm still standing in the same place staring at her like a lost puppy.

"I'll see you on Wednesday for the project, Wilder. Now please stop looking at me with those eyes" she chuckles, the sound melodic to my ears as she pushes the car into gear.

"Fine. But don't think about me too much—*Actually wait*. I didn't get your number! How are we going to talk about the project if I don't have it?" I ask, tilting my head in confusion as she smiles.

"Figure it out." She chuckles before driving off.

I'm left stunned and my heart does a weird stutter thing that I'm not going to think about right now because all that my brain can focus on is the small smile on Cleo's face before she drove off.

If it's a game that you want to play Cleo Jones, understand that I never lose.

Ten

Blake

AT HOME, I'M IMMEDIATELY bombarded with the strong scents of Derek's famous Salmon Alfredo—otherwise known as the shit we eat every Monday. I groan, kicking off my shoes at the front door remembering the way Alec scolded all of us for walking around the house with shoes on.

The sounds of yelling and hushed curse words come from the living room as I beeline it to the kitchen. Inside, Derek hovers over the stove with his all-pink *'Mother Knows Best'* apron wrapped snugly around his waist.

The apron had been a gag gift for Derek's birthday last year since he's our only culinary major on the team but the punk liked it so much he began to wear it every time he cooked at the house.

"When are you going to stop making pasta? Can we have pizza for once, or something?" I groan as he whirls around, pointing a spoon covered in sauce at me.

"Whenever *you* hockey heads decide you no longer want to be on the team. I'm trying to keep all our diets healthy." He tuts before muttering a slew of swear words in Spanish.

I chuckle as he says something with *bitch* in it as I take a seat at the dining room table adjacent to the kitchen.

"How am I a son of a bitch when you're the one that won't broaden your variety of pasta dishes?"

"Why are you in my kitchen?" He rolls his eyes, mixing the chunks of salmon with the pasta sauce.

Ignoring him, I whip out my phone and snap a picture of him before opening my messages with Denver.

Me

Hello cousin.

Seattle

Ew.

Why are you texting me? I thought I blocked you.

Me

Ouch. Not going to take all ur time.

What was Cleo's youtube again?

Seattle

Why? You crushing on her or something?

Me

No. Of course not.

I need it for...research purposes.

Seattle

Right...research...

She's IcingIt on youtube... do all your research but leave me out of it. I think her and I are going to be good friends soon.

Me

> Friends my ass…

> I highly doubt an angel like her would be friends with a gremlin like you.

Seattle

> You have five seconds to stop texting me fuckface.

Shaking my head at Denver's annoying use of her favorite nickname "fuck-face", I hop up from my seat at the kitchen table. Derek's still cooking and singing his telenovela songs when I leave him to go to my room. If there's one thing I've learned living with the guys, it's that I will not be caught dead showing interest in a girl. I refuse to have them tease me about someone who doesn't even want me.

I'll take my L in silence, *thank you very much*. Speaking of losses, I hope I'm not at a total loss with Cleo. She hasn't tried at all to talk to me between those practices and now and I can't figure out why.

Does she truly not like hockey players? Is it because her dad is my coach? Why won't she try with me, or at least flirt back? If I can't find out anything from her in person, I'll just have to find out some other way. With a light heart, I open up the YouTube app and immediately go to work, looking her up.

IcingIt Cleo and boyfriend Marcelo Rivers on the grid @
Vegas Grand Prix.

Cleo Jones and hockey star Marcelo Rivers call it quits!

Where has IcingIt been?

My hearts feels as if it's gone on a sky-fall as I read over the newest headlines all about Cleo and fucking *Marcelo Rivers*. I've played Rivers for the past two years since coming to Summerfield and he's good, I'll admit. But he's dirty. He goes for cheap shots when refs aren't looking and is just an overall asshole on the ice.

Is this the kind of man that Cleo likes? I mean, Marcelo isn't ugly, he's just... so... *ew.*

"Dude! The pasta's ready. What're you doing?!" Jace yells and before I can shut my phone off he's jumping on top of me on my bed, peeking at my screen.

My heart goes still as he remains silent for what seems like the first time in his life. Honestly, I don't think I've ever been afraid of the Hercules look-alike until now. Jace isn't a small guy he'd probably—

"You have five seconds to explain why the fuck you're looking at Cleo and *him*, or so help me God, I will rip out your throat and feed it to Charlie's kitten."

ELeven

Cleo

"So, TELL ME IF I got this right... My twin sister had 'sex' with *Blake Wilder,* the same Blake that D2 talks about every day. Now, you're trying to ignore him but you have to do a class project together? Is that right?" Ryan raises a perfectly thick brow up at me, his eyes gleaming with amusement as he stretches out on the sideline of the football field.

"Something like that..." I blow out air, rocking back and forth on my heels.

"You're fucking gross, CJ. I mean what the hell is wrong with you? I know I told you the football team is off limits but *hockey*?" Ryan curls his lips in disgust as he stands up to stretch his shoulders out. "I'm disgusted even thinking about it, why can't you just be celibate and not tell me about that shit?" he groans.

And that, everyone, is Ryan Santiago-Jones—my dumbass stepbrother. Ryan's mom, Gloria and my dad got married when the both of us were eight just three years after my mom and dad separated.

It was rough at first, not having my biological mom in the house and now having a stranger play the role of "mommy". But Ryan made the transition a lot easier—and better.

He stuck to me like glue when we first met and proclaimed us as "twins" since we were born in the same week and year, with me taking the spot as the oldest child.

Ry was always there for me, he made sure none of the guys in school would pick on me. He always watched whatever princess movie I wanted even though he was more of a superhero kid when we were younger. And he was just overall the best "twin" brother a girl could ask for.

Now, at 20 years old, Ry still calls my dad D2, and me his twin, regardless of us having completely different parents.

"You fucking asked! What was I supposed to say?!"

"Oh, I don't know. Maybe 'I'm fine, how are you?' Not tell me about your recent *sexcapades!*" He rolls his eyes before rolling out his neck.

I fold my arms over my chest and frown. "Since when have I ever *not* told you what was going on? As my brother, you're supposed to listen and give me advice! Not chastise me, you buffoon."

"Chastise?" he scoffs in disbelief.

"Yes!" I shout, my frown deepening.

"Cleo, I'm trying to look out for you, not chastise you. Blake Wilder is a whore, through and through. And I'm not trying to hear the guys talk about how my sister is being seen with the biggest manslut on campus." He shrugs as if everything he's saying is logical and sadly it is, but I'd never admit that out loud.

"Oh, and you're one to talk! Who was that cheerleader you brought home last month? Chelsea? Kelsey?"

"Her name was *Audrey*... Chelsea was the one before that." He sighs, proving my point.

For the first time in forever, I'm winning against Ry. I should gloat... Nah... Wait... Nah, I'll take the nice route.

"Exactly. You can't judge someone when you're the exact same way. Besides, I didn't have *sex* with him... I just—I'm not telling you that shit." I grimace at the thought, Ryan's always the one to give details about any and everything but I for one refuse. It's gross especially when you share the same hall with the guy.

"Good. Now, I have to go. But stay until the end of practice, some of the guys and I are heading to 88UP tonight for some 'first week' drinks," he says, giving me a lopsided grin before jogging onto the turf where the rest of the football team gathered around before practice officially began.

Unlike me, Ryan followed in Dad's footsteps and went to Summerfield immediately after high school. But like me, he went the complete opposite route in terms of sports. Growing up, Ryan and I both had a lot of time on the ice but where I excelled in figure skating and some women's hockey. Ryan was like a duckling who lost its mom when it came to anything ice related. Hence him going after the good ole' pig skin.

Originally, Dad was upset when he realized none of his kids would carry on his NHL legacy. He had a daughter who'd rather comment on hockey than be on the ice and a son who could just barely keep steady on skates. But when Dad realized that Ryan could be the next Tom Brady, there was zero hesitation in him supporting Ryan and all his football endeavors.

Dad is sweet like that; he supports hard and loves us harder. Which is also why I'm scared as fuck at the thought of him finding out why I'm really at SFU.

My body tenses just mentioning it in my *head*. I'm about to take a seat on the bench when my phone goes off like it's the end of the world. I reach into my purse and chuckle; it looks like Sienna and Georgia are up.

Bows and Ho's

Georgia Peach

> I would just like to point out to you sluts that leaving me in the house alone with zero food is a CRIME

Si Si

> At the studio, don't curse.

> I'm pretty sure the kids are reading my texts.

Georgia Peach

> Cleo why are you not in your room planning out your life????

> Don't make me get Mr.Snuffies to come find you.

You know he likes you.

ANNNDDDDD why the fuck is there only a Coke Zero and a SINGLE piece of chicken in the fridge?

Do y'all expect me to starve????????

Me

At Ry's practice.

Keep your demonic doll baby away from my shit, G.

Georgia Peach

YOU WENT TO MY MAN'S PRACTICE WITHOUT ME?!?!??

gif of man freaking out

I'll be there in 5 minutes TOPS.

With a small breathy laugh, I shake my head, then tuck my phone back into my purse, trading it for my camera to snap some pictures of the team. The boys this season look way better than last year and if they play their cards right, they're going to win this year's championship.

I'm in the zone taking pictures and small videos of the guys as some of them stop to pose for me, so much so that I don't notice the sneaky blonde preparing to attack me.

"How dare you go see my man without me? What happened to girl code?!" Georgia exclaims from behind me before plopping down to my left on the bench.

Her "man" is my brother. Georgia has had an odd crush on Ry since before any of us could remember. I believe it started when they both sprained their wrists together on the ice—I have no clue how I'm friends with the most uncoordinated people in the world, but I digress—which led to the two of them spending a month sitting on the couch watching cartoons while Jace and I played around.

But I don't think that Georgia *actually* has a crush on my brother. I think she has a crush on the idea of Ryan Jones; the nerdy kid she spent a month with, instead of Ryan Jones, the star quarterback of a major D1 football team.

"Girl code?" I tease, packing up my camera. There's no way I'm leaving that out with the clumsy girl beside me.

"Yes! You know...calling me whenever your hot brother is around." She shrugs, playing with a strand of her hair.

"'Hot brother'?" My face twists as I look out to the field where Ryan crouches, looking like a raging pit bull yelling random things to the guys. "*That* brother? You're disgusting." I grimace, repeating Ryan's earlier words.

Instead of responding to me, Georgia focuses on the field and claps for the guys as they warm up. I smile as she continues spewing nonsense to the field.

We sat on the bench for the entire practice, chatting about upcoming parties and Fall Fest, the three-day carnival styled event at the end of September. It's been so long since I've just simply talked to someone like this that I feel warm and at home.

Georgia gives me the most shit-eating grin she can muster, her eyes gleaming with mischief and I immediately regret my thoughts of her being my home.

"Damn, Jones' ass looks great." the sound of Jace's voice catches me off guard. I turn in my seat and smile at the man, only for my smile to falter as more bodies appear behind him followed by manly laughter.

"Jace..." Blake sighs, stepping from behind the blonde clad in a black compression shirt and gray gym shorts. My mouth salivates as I take in his damp brown waves and the large gym bag on his shoulder.

"His ass does look great," Alec chirps from beside Blake, shrugging.

"How does mine look?" Charlie asks with a cheeky grin, turning to poke his butt out.

"Still not my type... And relatively flat." Alec frowns as he readjusts his glasses.

"I'll take it," says the blonde, shrugging, then throwing an arm around both Alec and Braxton.

Side-eyeing Georgia, I note the overly eager look on her face as the men approach us. She's up to something... My stomach churns and I don't know if it's from fear or something else.

"What happened to girl code?" I whisper, looking back and forth between the approaching men and her.

"I like this show a lot more." She shrugs.

And as if my Wednesday couldn't get any weirder, the men's football team end their practice and trudge over to the sidelines to gather their stuff. A few of them make conversation with the five hockey players beside us but through it all, I can't shake the feeling of being watched and I am definitely *not* going to look behind myself.

No, instead I turn to Ry and give him the biggest smile I can muster.

"Ew, don't look at me like that." *My brother, ladies and gents...*

I grit my teeth at him but perk up as Tatum, the Tigers star wide receiver, and Ryan's hilarious best friend, strides over with a few bottles of water and a large smile.

"Hey, Pretty Girl," he greets me with warmth, passing a water bottle to me and Georgia.

The nickname had been an ongoing joke between us after Tatum spent the holidays with us freshman year and greeted me rather unconventionally.

"Hi, Tate." I laugh quietly as he side-hugs me, lingering just a bit before turning to the small group of large hockey players behind us giving them that weird manly greeting that guys did.

Tatum and I are good friends and there's no denying that he's handsome. He reminds me of a walking Vogue ad with his model-like features and a muscular build. However, I wouldn't say that Tatum is my type considering his closeness with Ryan. Anyone that was that close to my brother had obvious psychological issues.

Just as I think that Tatum will sit beside me, another larger figure plops down instead. The familiar scents of cedar wood and vanilla are intoxicating as the man I know all too well laughs from beside me at whatever Alec had said.

"Hey, Princess," Blake smirks, sending thrills down my spine as his eyes lock with mine.

My body tightens at his husky tone, and I fight myself to ignore him, trying to scoot away. But Georgia "girl-code" Adams has other plans as she slides in closer to me, essentially caging me between her and Blake. He grins cockily as I roll my eyes.

"Creeper." I sigh as a greeting; this only makes his smile grow wider.

He looks as if he's about to say something but immediately his features sour as both Tatum and Ryan speak at the same time.

"Are you coming tonight?" the two men ask in unison. Ryan's tone more clipped than Tatum's hopeful one as the boys look down at me on the bench.

I can feel Blake stiffen from beside me and feel his eyes on me, and though he's facing forward, feigning indifference, I know he's listening closely.

"Is the whole team going, Ry? I can't be out with you guys for a long—"

"We already have plans," Blake interrupts, now fully facing me.

I had plans? If I had plans today, I'd surely know. I keep all my plans scheduled in my little red notebook. I scrunch my eyebrows at Blake as his eyes gleam.

"Our *date*, remember?" His tone is teasing as he nudges my shoulder as the rest of the chatter from our group ultimately dies down.

At this, my brother smirks. Ryan isn't the most overprotective sibling hence him and I talking about everything. And since leaving New York and my ex-boyfriend, Ry's been pushing me to go on dates... I'm the one who's not ready.

"A date?" Ryan teases, poking my cheek and it doesn't go unnoticed the way Blake tenses beside me.

"Yup. It's Wednesday and this beauty and I have plans. So, if you'll excuse us—"

"No. I have things to—" I try to say, only for my traitorous brother and Georgia to interrupt.

"I'll do it!" She shoots up to her feet, clearly one of the few to listen to our conversation.

Ryan on the other hand is calmer as he says, "I'll schedule another hangout for us, CJ."

Well fuck me, they're basically pimping me out! I am a woman. I have rights—

"You can't get rid of me that easily, sweetheart," Blake whispers to me, his lips grazing the bottom of my ear and I shudder at the contact.

What was I saying about rights and morals again?

Right, I have...

I...uh...

Fuck me

TWELVE

Blake

WHEN IT COMES TO the female population, I'd say that I've been pretty lucky in the courting and winning hearts department. But sitting here across from Cleo inside of Doug's Diner with only an order of buffalo wings and an uncomfortable silence between us is not something that has ever happened in the history of Blake Wilder and Women.

Cleo's gaze is narrow as she watches me pick up one of the single wings on our shared plate. She eyes me suspiciously as I eat it and I almost laugh at the ridiculousness of this whole thing.

Not even two weeks ago we were practically hooking up in my bedroom—which was incredible, might I add. But now here we are on a random Wednesday in September, sitting in an off-campus diner, staring at each other like one of us has grown two heads.

I clear my throat, shifting in my soft seat as an attempt to break the silence. This had been so easy when she and I were around others but now that we're alone, I've lost all fearlessness.

"So…" she starts, looking everywhere but me as she tugs a straightened piece of her hair behind her ear. I'm thankful for her being the one to initiate whatever *this* is. So, I take the bone she threw out and run with it.

"21 questions?" I ask, cringing internally. I never said that I thought about my words before I said them.

Cleo snorts at my abruptness, covering her mouth as she chuckles at herself.

The action is adorable and heartwarming, and my ears heat up because even though it's at my expense, I'm happy to be the one to make her laugh no matter if it was accidental or not.

"How about five," she says, amusement laced in her tone.

"Fifteen." I shrug, gaining my confidence out of nowhere as I place three wings on a saucer and slide it in front of her.

Since sitting here, she hasn't eaten a single thing, other than the cherry from the Shirley Temple she'd drank.

"Ten," she counters, raising an eyebrow at the wings before taking one. "Thanks." her lips curve slightly, as if she wants to smile but refuses to do the action at the same time.

"Deal. Let's order actual food and then get started," I say happily as she takes the first bite of her wings.

For five minutes, the two of us sit in silence enjoying the rest of the wings after ordering our food. She'd ordered a fried chicken sandwich and fries that I totally would've ordered too, if we didn't have strict diets. So instead, I opt for grilled chicken and rice with broccoli. *Yum.*

As the waitress approaches with our food, setting it down in front of us, I take a second to observe Cleo.

She twirls her rings a lot when she's uncomfortable. It was something I noticed in class and last week at the party. She's doing it now as she analyzes her plate, though I can't see her hands. I have a feeling that the small ring is being fiddled with.

My gaze peruses her for longer than necessary and she shifts once again, crinkling her nose.

"Why'd you say we're going on a date?" she asked, stupefying me for a moment.

Why *did* I say that? I mean a date with Cleo would be nice but I don't do dates... I'm more of a 'meet in a bar and never see each other again' kind of guy.

It's easier that way. Less obligations, and whatnot. But staring at the girl in front of me makes me feel... *weird.* I act differently around her, and I want to know why. So instead of shying away from the conversation, I lay on a smirk and lean closer to her.

"Is that your first question?" I ask, meaning to sound teasing but my tone is huskier than I'd wanted.

I don't think the sugar plum princess will take the bait. But then a small glimmer in her eyes and slight curving of her lips draws me in.

"Was that yours?" she taunts, batting her lashes; my heart stutters but before I can lose my confidence, I pluck one of the crisp fries from her plate and smile.

"No. My first question is why did you run off that night at the party?" I ask, taking a bite of my chicken and sighing as the savory flavors melt on my tongue.

Doug deserves the world for this one piece of chicken alone. My goodness...the tanginess of the lemons mixed with the herbs—

She coughs dryly. "You sure know how to start a conversation."

Cleo smiles shyly, her arms moving fast under the table more than likely twisting her rings. She takes a bite of her sandwich before chuckling, running a hand over her face.

"Blake, I don't do hookups, or hockey players, If I'm being honest. That night was partially due to a lot of liquid courage and partially due to you being somewhat attractive." She laughs again before taking a sip of her refilled Shirley Temple.

Somewhat? I'm *somewhat* attractive? I don't know if that's a joke or she's "somewhat" blind. I've seen her squinting in the lecture hall maybe once or twice, so I probably shouldn't rule it out.

Cleo snickers as she eyes my features, my jaw agape with raised brows.

"Don't take it to heart, Boy Scout." She gives me a small smile, leaning back into the booth.

"Oh, I am. Consider my heart in mourning of my attractiveness on the impossible meter of Cleo Jones' heart."

At that, Cleo lets out the most guttural bark of laughter I've ever heard from a woman. I smile as she lets herself be free, laughing with her head thrown back without remorse.

It's liberating to be around a woman who will let herself simply be. My sister and mother are always on ten and I love them for it. But sometimes it can be exhausting knowing that they're constantly "on stage" whether metaphorically or physically.

I love the women in my life to death but this feeling of complete euphoria from another person's being is astounding.

And as for the women that I tend to take to bed, they're more worried about pleasing the name Blake Wilder than fulfilling themselves and me. I hadn't known how exhausting it truly was until the woman in front of me let out the most melodic yet chaotic laugh I'd ever heard.

I smile as Cleo reels herself back in, she looks me over with eyes filled with mirth and then frowns as they wander to my plate. Her lips curve downward as she sighs.

"Sorry he has you guys on such strict diets...I'd tried to get him to ease up when Jace first told me about it a year ago." Almost immediately my mind wanders back to Cleo and Jace and how close the two of them truly are.

He'd only given me a few details about her, even after I pestered him about her after the party. His vagueness alerted me of just how close the two of them may have been because if there was one thing Jace Heart was not, it was vague. He was more of an open book with details and pictures of wonky drawings kind of guy.

"As for your level on my scale, let's just say you're okay on there. Obviously, Eren Marlowe is at the top." She shrugs.

"He's old enough to be your dad!" I try but Cleo isn't hearing it as she waves me off.

"Eren is 26, that's nowhere near Dad. Besides, we're getting off topic. It's my turn to ask a question." Her eyes are wicked as she peers at me from the rim of her cup, they dance with mischief as she takes a sip.

"Why'd you insist that we had a date earlier today on the football field? Ry wasn't your biggest fan until—" Now she is the one trying, and I'm the one cutting her off as my stomach heats.

"How do you know Ryan and Tatum? Didn't you *just* transfer?" My tone is slightly clipped as I watch Cleo tilt her head in confusion.

My skin grows hotter as I remember how Ryan and Tatum were surrounding her and Georgia when we first entered the field. Or how cozy the three of them were. I'm a protective guy! It's only right for me to make sure girls are safe and not harass—

"How do I know my younger brother?" She guffaws, holding her shaking belly as laughter consumes her.

Younger brother? Ryan is only 20 and if he's her younger brother then does that mean that she's older than Jace—

"I can see the wheels turning in your head, so I'll just put you out of your misery. Ry and I are step-siblings, I'm a week older than him. Georgia's a year older than us, and Jace is about five months younger than me, give or take," she says, taking a bite of the large sandwich on her plate as if everything is simple. But it only leaves me with more questions, like why didn't she start at Summerfield with everyone else? Or why is she here now? And why can't I stop thinking about her and Marcelo—

"As for all other questions, and although I'd love to get to know you more, I think we should stick to more *professional* topics. I was serious when I told you a few days ago that *this* is strictly business and not the funny kind." Cleo's face is serious as she wipes at the ranch on her lip, missing it a bit. My finger itches to wipe it away but I know that the action will probably result in my castration, and I like my guy down there safe and sound.

But she wants to get to know me more. I'd say that my work here is not done but for now, I'll give her what she wants and comply.

"I already told you, you have my Scout's honor. I won't break anything if you don't. But don't be tempted by my dashing good looks while we work together for the next few weeks." I shrug, my exterior passive while my interior roars at me for being an idiot.

"Trust me… I won't." She chuckles, pushing a few fries onto my plate. I raise an eyebrow at the action as she shrugs. "They weren't crispy enough."

I fight the small smile that wants to break loose at the action and try to school my body into numbness as I watch her. If Cleo genuinely doesn't want anything romantic with me, I won't force it. But, when she's ready, I'll be here.

After my "date" with Cleo, I'm feeling giddy as I enter the house. Delilah and Jace are sitting on the couch with face masks on, watching a cartoon about a talking car. I shake my head and snap a picture at the sight before stalking off to find the mother bear of the house.

"For someone who doesn't live here, you sure are here more than I am." I chuckle as Derek jumps from his spot in front of the kitchen stove.

He gives me the nastiest look ever before turning back to the large pan filled with rolled cookie dough, more than likely chocolate chip and peanut butter.

"Deli's dance studio is closer to this house; besides, I like your kitchen." Derek shrugs, fixing the pink apron he's donning. His shoulders hunch at the mention of Deli's dance studio, and it takes everything in me not to cringe as I remembered the recital a few nights ago.

To everyone's surprise, I was in fact *on time*. I'd been there bright and early enough to see Derek and Delilah's dance teacher nearly rip each others face's off. I don't know the logistics of his argument with the fiery pink-haired teacher, all I know is that she was *not* happy with Derek.

As if sensing my curiosity, Derek shoots me a warning glare which is all I need to know that this is not a fight for any of the uncles to help with.

"So, have you figured out what you're going to do about Coach?" he asks, whirling to face me with flour dusting his nose. Derek grins wickedly as my body coils from the mention of our ironclad couch, Clef Jones. Otherwise known as Cleo Jones' scary ass dad.

"What do you mean?" I ask, finding the loose string on my hoodie suddenly interesting.

"I mean, how are you going to go about flirting with the daughter of the man who holds your balls on a tight leash? I highly doubt he'd keep you alive if he knew what happened that night at the party." Derek raises a brow at me. I sigh, throwing my head back.

Fucking Braxton can't keep a secret to save his life.

"I don't know much about her but I have seen her on social media and she seemed happy at her previous school. A girl with the lifestyle she had doesn't just leave her dream school to be up under her dad without a good reason. And I'm not saying you're not a good guy, Wilder, but you don't have a great rep with women. If Coach finds out about you clambering after his only daughter—"

"He won't. We're only classmates." I shrug, my chest tightening as Derek and I lock eyes. His eyes are soft and he looks as if he wants to continue this conversation, but instead shakes his head and sighs.

"Great. Because nothing good can come from whatever it is that the two of you did. Besides, this year is crucial for you. Scouts are watching you now more than ever."

I know Derek means well but it doesn't help the sharp feeling gracing my stomach. Sadly, he's right in a way. Flirting with Cleo Jones, no matter how fun it is, isn't something I can afford to do.

But then again... When do I ever listen to everyone else?

THIRTEEN

Cleo

Unknown

> you're dead when i catch you

> your mouth's only good for one thing

> remember that or i'll expose you for the true slut that you are

> i won't be as nice if i find you and we all know what I have against you.

> stay hidden little Cleo

MY HANDS SHAKE AND my breathing becomes unsteady as I reread the countless threats from the Unknown number. They haven't let up since I left Brighton, and I don't think they ever will. I try my hardest to even out my breathing but my attempts are futile as my throat clogs. It feels like I'm being strangled as thunderous tears prickle in my eyes and spill out like a tropical storm.

Why haven't they stopped? It's been four months since I left. Why... Why won't they stop? Why did this happen to me? I tried my hardest, I kept my mouth shut. I—

An additional ping of my phone sends my hackles raising. Are they not done? Have they come back to haunt me? I try my hardest to blink back more tears as additional texts come through from a new group chat.

Margarita Central

Georgia Peach

be ready at two babies!

#ROAAAARRRRSSS #TigressPrancing

#BIGORANGE #BIGBLUE

Denver

do I have to?

Si Si

i'll come after practice

Georgia Peach

YES denver you have to. We haven't hung out outside the apartment before and any friend of Cleo's is a friend of ours.

plus you're my new margarita bestie!!!

CJ where you at girl???

Back me up!

I chew on my bottom lip as I reread the thread, anxiety clawing at my throat. I'd introduced Denver to Georgia and Sienna three days ago after my "date" with Blake. The meeting of my new friend and older ones was eventful to say the least, ending with Georgia drunk out of her mind on our balcony with an equally drunk Denver shouting out to our neighbors about Lord knows what. Sienna and I sat back also inebriated, loudly singing along to princess musicals.

Since then, we've kind of adopted Denver. Or more like Georgia had adopted the unwilling girl and forced her to be in our group. Today's the start of football season and Georgia has deemed it as a mandatory hang out day.

I'd been happy, excited even, for today to come. But now with the orange monster of anxiety slowly sinking her claws into my throat, I'd rather stay home.

But before I can respond to the group chat, another text comes through.

Sexy Boy Scout

like the name?

I thought it suited me more than creeper

Me

Why are you texting me?

pause.

Where did you get my number from?

I never actually gave it to you...

Sexy Boy Scout

don't worry about it, see you at the game :)

Leaving Blake on read, I close my phone, lie back down on the bed, and stare at the ceiling. I thought that leaving New York would bring me a sense of peace but the demons of my past followed me into heaven. I roll over in the bed and pull the covers over my head, surrounding myself in darkness and allow myself to finally let go.

I cry my heart out, letting the world crash down over me and succumb to the dark abyss of my mind. I was never really a big crier growing up, I'd usually just laugh off my problems, but right now, I can't. I cry so much that my mouth hurts from holding in my sobs. Here, at Summerfield, I have more people around me than ever, but why do I feel so lonely? The tears soon stop and hitched shallow breathing replaces it.

I've been under the covers for so long in my own world that I don't notice when the door opens or when two other bodies surround me in the bed. I'm so stuck in the endless despair of my own darkness that I don't notice the light around me until I'm being yanked out of my own self-loathing and arms wrap around me.

I can smell her before I can hear her. Georgia's undeniable scent of coconut and vanilla soothes something deep in my soul as I feel her place a kiss on the top of the cover closer to my ear rather than my forehead.

"I know that I said you didn't have to tell us about what happened in New York, CJ," she pauses, and I can feel that she's looking over to Sienna for help with whatever *this* is.

Growing up, I was usually the one consoling others. So, I know my friends are probably scared of whatever it is that has me like this and I'm petrified at the thought of scaring them.

"But can you please talk to us? I can't stand to see you like this anymore," she finishes, slowly pulling the covers down.

"Cleo, we're always going to be here for you, but we need to know how we can help you. You always help us but we're stuck when it comes to helping you." Sienna's voice is soft and soothing, the same voice that I assume she uses with the kids at the dance studio.

Georgia coughs quietly and her voice cracking nearly breaks my heart. "You don't have to tell us everything but, please tell us something," she cries.

"The phone," I mutter, still under the covers, feeling as the two of them shuffle around for my device.

Gasps followed by quiet curses are the only thing to be heard in the near silent bedroom. Slowly, I peel back the covers and watch them read over the messages that's been plaguing me for the past year.

Sienna is the first to speak, her tone soft as her wide brown eyes look between Georgia, the phone, and me.

"Who... Who is sending you this?" she questions, scrolling through the texts.

"And why the fuck haven't we killed them for threatening you?!" Georgia shoots up from her spot near me, knocking over the small cup of water on my nightstand.

"Fuck me..." she curses, leaving to get napkins.

Sienna takes a moment before speaking up; she stares at me long and hard and then sighs before looking back at the messages, clearly shaken by them.

"You don't have to tell us everything right now, but when you do, just know that we will go to hell and back for you, Cleo. The person texting you this stuff will get what's coming to them."

"I don't know specifically who it is..." I croak, wiping my eyes of the nearly dry tears.

Georgia comes back with our mop and some napkins. "Do you have a clue on who it may be? And why are they picking on you? You're the nicest person I know." She frowns as she picks up the cup.

I gulp, looking between the women who are like my sisters and just as I'm about to spill my dirty laundry, the doorbell rings.

"Shit... Denver's here. I'll go get her and if you're up to it, we can talk about this before going to the game." Georgia gives me a soft smile before leaving.

Sienna frowns, tugging me into her arms. She cuddles me, rubbing circles on my back as I sit in her lap.

"Was this why you left New York? Is this why you're not at Brighton?"

All I can do is nod as she sighs. "Was it Marcelo? Is that who started this?" she asks, and I guess my silence is enough of an answer because Sienna pulls back from me, her gaze sharp and locked on mine.

"I'm going to skin that motherfucker and feed him to Oscar."

I can't help the chuckle that falls from my mouth at the thought of Sienna feeding my ex-boyfriend to her pet ferret. We spend a few more seconds simply embracing one another as Denver and Georgia's loud footsteps travel towards us.

"Was it my cousin? If it was my cousin, I'll call his mom on him!" Denver exclaims as she enters the room, she jumps on the bed with bright eyes, her ruby red lips curled in a large menacing smile.

Denver's like the missing piece in our friend puzzle; she fit right in perfectly when I introduced her to Sienna and Georgia and she's also been the only other person who can go "shot for shot" with the crazy blonde.

I shake my head at her antics with a small smile and stretch. "No, but, he did text me." I chuckle, showing the girls the recent messages. Denver grimaces as Sienna and Georgia each smile at the text.

"C'mon, ladies, enough moping around. We have sweaty football players to watch!"

The boys are losing so bad it's not even funny. When we'd gotten to the Tawny Reeds Stadium, it was filled to the brim with both SFU and Rhode Island University students, all excited for the first game of the season and all signs pointed to a win from Summerfield. We'd pre-gamed with a few of the frat guys from Omega Tau, and Georgia (to no one's surprise) did a keg stand with them.

Our spirits were finally high after being so low back at the apartment, only for them to droop tremendously after the very first play where SFU fumbled the ball after being tackled by the largest man I've ever seen in my life.

From there, the game went downhill and I can just feel the anger radiating from both my brother and Tatum from here.

"I thought you two said this would be fun..." Denver whispers to Georgia and me, her eyes locked on the field as she frowns.

Georgia sighs, running a hand through her straightened hair. "It usually is! I don't know what's going on with Ry but hey! It's only the first quarter...they can still make a comeback," she says skeptically.

I frown, my eyes never wavering from the field as the Rhode Island Rams score again, bringing the score to 4-12.

"Hockey is way more interesting," a deep voice whispers so close to my ear that the hair on the back of my neck raises; I jump looking over at the smiling culprit. Our faces are so close that our noses are just shy of touching as the minty smells of his breath invades my senses.

"Why are you here?" I ask, trying and failing to sound cold as Blake's smile grows wider, resembling the Cheshire Cat.

"Well, madam... If you actually read my text instead of just opening it, you would see that I told you I'd be here and that we also have to work on our project tonight." Blake shrugs leaning back, my eyes rake over him unconsciously noting his backwards cap, SFU Hockey tee, and dark light-washed jeans.

"She has plans," Georgia interjects the grinning Blake; his smile falters for a second before it returns to its usual bright state.

"No she doesn't," he retorts cheekily.

Denver groans from beside me, clearly annoyed by her cousin's presence.

"Yes she does, you idiot. Her brother invited us out for the night."

"He invited us too!" Jace speaks up from beside Blake. I jump from the sound of my best friend's voice; I'd been staring at Blake for so long that I didn't even notice the hoard of hockey players, plus a toddler, behind us.

"Oh, fuck me sideways, why are you here? *Don't you have some girl to paint or something?*" Georgia looks at the toddler and whispers before rolling her eyes and popping her gum as she looks Jace over with disdain.

He mimics the eye roll and sighs. "Did Halloween come early, or have my nightmares come true, Peach?"

He got her riled up instantly and the two of them began bickering like cats and dogs. Usually, I'd step in and cut them off before they could even start, but the roar of the crowd draws my attention back down to the field.

"Number 21, Ryan Santiago-Jones with a touchdown!"

The crowd erupts in boisterous cheers, everyone jumping out of their seats cheering for my brother, and soon enough, the game starts to turn around.

"We're all going to 88UP tonight after the game, the teams usually go there whether we win or lose to let off some steam. You guys are more than welcome to join." An invitation from Blake has my reluctant cheeks heating from his unwavering eye contact.

"We. Have. Plans," I say, getting closer to his face with every word before turning quickly back to the field.

The game goes on with the SFU Tigers leading by 15 points, we watch as Ryan and Tatum dominate the field racking up points with ease as Rhode Island's defense begins to waver. In the end, SFU takes home the win leaving us with a whopping 45-26.

Immediately after the game, we all go down to the locker rooms to wait for Ryan and Tatum.

Denver groans, shifting her weight on her heels as she leans back against the wall. She wasn't lying when she said she hated football, she was unamused the entire game and confused about what was happening on the field. It took Georgia explaining the game and its rules for Denver to somewhat understand it.

"Now listen up losers... When my man comes out those doors, don't say anything to him. Just let him come home to mama." Georgia grins before curling her lips into a snarl as she makes eye contact with Jace. The boys (though no one asked them to) decided that they would follow us down to the locker rooms. Along the way, Sienna declared that she wasn't feeling up to partying. Derek also announced that he had to take his adorable daughter, Delilah, home as well so the two of them left together since we'd driven Georgia's car here.

Jace scoffs at Georgia, his tanned skin burning red as he looks down at her. She simply sticks out her tongue at him but doesn't try arguing.

Like clockwork, the hall begins to fill with grinning football players. The boys all cheering and greeting Blake and Jace as they exit the locker room out to the main hall of the stadium. Ryan and Tatum are amongst the last to leave. My brother's grin is as bright as the sun as he approaches us but stops for a second as looks at me...wait—not me?

I follow my brother's gaze all the way to Denver?

His lips form a lopsided smile as he draws closer, walking straight past Georgia to the annoyed brunette beside me. Georgia's mouth drops as she watches Ryan lay on his "charm" to our newest friend.

"I'm Ryan," is all the man says, and I wonder if that usually works for him because he seems as confident as ever as he looks down at the unimpressed girl.

Denver looks up at Ryan, craning her neck back due to his height, and smirks. "I didn't ask."

He tilts his head at Denver as if she's a puzzle that he wants to solve and it takes everything in me not to burst out laughing as Tatum claps a hand on his shoulder.

The boys look at each other, silently conversing with their eyes before stalking towards the exit with all of us in tow. I'm walking at the back of the group and sigh as Blake falls in step beside me, smiling deviously.

"You know we never finished our game of ten questions." He chuckles, taking my tote bag from my shoulder and sliding it onto his with ease.

My belly heats at the action and I mentally fight it for being absurd. "Is this how you start a conversation, Boy Scout?" I ask peering up at him.

Blake boops my nose with a smile. I blink, confused at the action and he acts as if that didn't just happen.

"Are you saying that you agree to play the game?"

"Oh, trust me, you don't want to play any games with me."

At my words, Blake halts all movement. He rolls out his neck before looking me over.

"How about we play a game, Princess?"

"I'm listening," I say pausing just a few steps away from him.

"If you win more rounds of our games at the bar, I'll leave you alone or do your bidding for a week. But, if I win...you have to grant me three wishes." His grin is devious and enchanting as he focuses his attention on me, his eyes dancing with unspoken promises.

My stomach heats as all the possible things he could wish for swirl around in my mind.

"I'm not a genie, Creeper."

"Then you can be a fae princess... Whatever you want. But, what do you say?" he asks, stepping closer.

"Deal."

Fourteen

Blake

EVERYONE AND THEIR MOM is at 88UP tonight—literally. I think I saw Morris Brown's parents drinking beers with their kid when we walked in. I don't know what we were thinking when we decided to fit not only the entire football team but the hockey and basketball teams inside the medium sized bar but we did.

The sports themed dive bar was so filled to the brim with hormonal college kids that I'd almost mistaken Jace for the president of the Theta Nu sorority. The punch I'd earned to the shoulder from him was indeed worth it.

"I can't believe you brought your planner to the bar." Jace laughs aloud as Cleo writes away in her small red book.

The girl rolls her eyes at him, giving him a vulgar gesture before focusing back on the planner.

I watch from across the cramped table as she spends an additional five minutes doing Lord knows what before leaning across the table, snatching it from her tiny cold fingers.

I can feel the sharp looks of Jace, Georgia, and maybe even Ryan, burning in the side of my head as I plop back down in my seat but my eyes remain trained on the brown skinned girl. Her jaw drops as she furrows her brows. Oh, I love that look. She looks like an angry poodle with her little pink bows and small nose. I'd booped it earlier just to get a reaction out of her and she didn't disappoint with her small frown.

"We had a deal, Princess." I smile at her as she sighs, rolling her eyes as realization dawns on her.

"Deal?" Georgia peers between the two of us as Jace and Alec sigh.

"Oh, Cleo, please tell me you didn't make a deal with this asshole..." Alec grins, amusement dancing in his eyes as she groans, rubbing a hand over her face.

"Had I known he would be such a pest, I would've exterminated him instead..."

"Looks like you got a flea problem, CJ." Ryan chuckles and though he's speaking to Cleo, his eyes are focused steadily on the dance floor where Tatum and Denver are.

At that, Cleo groans even louder. "What do you want, Boy Scout? You get three games and that's all."

Boy Scout... I didn't think that such a stupid nickname could sound so precious coming from someone until now. I can feel everyone's eyes on me as I focus my attention on the brown-eyed woman in front of me. Her nose stud glimmering under the warm lighting of the bar.

"Darts?"

Ryan and Jace snort as soon as the word leaves my mouth, the two of them try to hide behind their drinks to mask their amusement but Georgia is the complete opposite. She bursts into laughter, leaving my mind to wonder if I was the one who'd made a deal with the devil, and not the other way around.

Cleo smirks at me, mischief and glory aligning her bright pupils as she peels herself from the brown booth the group of us occupied. I watch as she stalks towards me, my stomach dropping at her faint attempt at masking a smile.

What have I gotten myself into? This is why I don't play games without knowing my opponent first. Cleo approaches me slowly, her smile now prominent as she bends slowly to my level and I can just see the "you fucked up" look in her eyes as she smirks.

"Lead the way, Boy Scout."

And so, like the true idiot that I am, I follow her command and lead the way. The two of us reach the gaming area of the bar in no time with Georgia, Jace, Ryan, and Braxton all following behind with their phones ready to capture my inevitable defeat.

"You gonna let me win, Princess?" I try to lay on the charm, giving her my most innocent smile.

She reciprocates the action; the sight of her pearly white teeth goes straight to my cock and it takes everything in me not to adjust myself while she's looking at me like *that*.

Like I'm the guy she's about to walk like a dog. And if I'm being honest, I'd let her.

Please keep in mind that I never said that I was smart. A smart man would know when he's about to get his balls handed to him. But a *genius* would know that if it's a gorgeous girl like Cleo Jones doing the handing, then you let her.

"Not in your wildest dreams, Wilder." She chuckles getting on her tiptoes to bring our faces just a bit closer.

This girl is stunning.

I told Derek that I wouldn't flirt with her but what am I supposed to do when a woman of her magnitude smiles at me like that? Just stand there like an idiot? I mean I can...but why would I want to? Instead of backing away from her, I step a little closer, blocking out the images of our friends and her brother as I take in her sweet candy-like smell; it's so intoxicating that I could get drunk on it alone.

"What if you're my wildest dream?"

There! I said it. Sue me.

Cleo stumbles just a moment, blinking up at me before she chuckles. "Okay, okay, that's enough teasing from you. After tonight we're going back to our original deal." She laughs, shaking her head as she turns to the unused dartboard behind her.

Cleo walks up to the board with all the confidence in the world, getting darts for us before coming back to where I'm standing.

"Good luck," I say with a smile, leaning in close beside her ear.

She turns to me briefly with a smirk, mine trips at the sight of it as she says, "You're going to need it."

She remains looking at me with her shoulders rolled back and head held high as she lifts the dart up and lets it loose. My dick twitches at the unrelenting eye contact and I swear that Braxton whistles as the dart hits its target.

Bullseye.

Cleo shrugs as if she didn't just hit a bullseye without looking and sashays back to Ryan, grabbing her Blue Hawaiian from her brother.

Jace lets out a bark of laughter so loud, Russia can hear him as he claps a hand on my shoulder. "If there's one..." he tries catching his breath, "if there's one thing we never bet on with her, it's party games," he finishes, wiping a stray tear from his eyes.

I chew on my bottom lip, looking over the damage caused by the pink-loving girl behind me. I shouldn't have picked darts as my first option because I'm, one, terrible at the game, and two, can't see the board for shit without my glasses. The same glasses that I refuse to wear in public. I also decided to go contactless today because contacts fucking itch. So now, I'm stuck in front of a cool girl, our friends, and a damned dart board that holds my fate.

Fuck it.

How bad can my aim be?

I shoot the first dart and I'm immediately met with stifled laughter and snorting from the five assholes behind me. Not only did I miss the dart board, I hit the wall right beside it, lodging a small orange dart on a poster of an old singer from the eighties. I can feel her before I can see her, Cleo claps a hand on my shoulder still trying to hold back her laughter.

"Shut up..." I sigh, looking down at the near snorting girl.

"I wasn't going to say anything!" She guffaws, letting the laughter consume her fully as she bends over clutching her stomach. I can't help but to chuckle at the sight of her so tickled at my failure.

We do two more rounds of Cleo winning and me losing so bad that I may have broken a few records for being the world's worst dart thrower. After the final round of getting my ass handed to me, our friends disperse around the bar. Cleo and I make our way to the pool table a few feet away from the boards. She sets her now watered blue drink behind the pool table and chuckles, looking me over.

"For you to be a big shot, hockey player, your aim is horrible," she jokes, setting up our game.

"Says the girl who was basically bred to have good aim! I'm sorry my parents aren't in the Hall of Fame or olympians."

At this, Cleo grins and shrugs as she pulls out her phone. "True. We can't all be excellent like me."

We play four rounds of pool, the end resulting in a kick-ass tie and small videos of the two of us smack talking to each other behind our phones. Don't let anyone fool you, Cleo Jones is the most competitive woman in the world. She plays dirty and flirts her way to victory.

She winked at me, thus completely ruining my focus and resulting in me losing horrifically in one of our rounds. We're having so much fun simply being around each other letting our competitive nature take hold that I don't even notice the amount of people gathered around us until a camera flash causes her to jump.

Cleo looks around the group of students surrounding us and shyly ducks her head away from the stares of the people around her. I'm almost at her side when Georgia pulls her away from the fray of people and seemingly escorts her back to our original booth, leaving me stunned and stuck in place.

I don't stay frozen for long as I come back to my senses, and I follow them back our booth.

"What was that about?" I try, only to receive a nasty look from Cleo's blonde friend.

"Too many people and way too many cameras." Cleo sighs, and then places a hand on Georgia's as if she's telling her that she's fine and can leave. Georgia takes the hint and does just that, stalking toward the dance floor where Ryan and Denver seem to be either arguing or making googly eyes at one another.

I'll have to ask her about that later, but right now my focus is solely on the whirlwind of a woman in front of me.

One second she's confident and competitive and the next, she's hiding in her own little shell like a scared turtle.

"If we're being technical, Princess, you won our deal," I say, scooting into the booth beside her, daring to rest my arm on the top of the booth, just shy of her shoulders.

At my words, she looks up at me with a frown. "Am I supposed to tell you to leave me alone? I mean if you insist—"

"No! Absolutely not. How about I propose a trade?"

"A trade?" she echoes, skeptically.

"Mhm... Since you won, I'll give you my prize of three wishes that can be called upon at any time as long as you don't wish me away." I shrug as if my heart isn't about to burst from my chest.

What if she says no? What if she pushes me away before I even get close?

"Platonic wishes?" she asks, startling me for a second, my palms begin to sweat. Is she considering me?

Instead of showing her just how nervous I am, I feign confidence. "Whatever you want, Princess."

Cleo turns to me, she looks me over with deadly calculation before sighing, leaning her head back into my arm. My heart beat stutters at the contact but I remain painfully still. There is no way that I'm messing *this* up.

"Well," she starts, looking up at me briefly before looking back down at her lap, "my first wish is for you to take me home."

I'm shocked at her wish but not surprised, I didn't drink any alcohol since we took my car to the bar. Before leaving, we let everyone know where we're going and that I'd be back later.

I gaze at her briefly only to catch her already looking at me. Throughout the night, she'd had a fair number of drinks but she seemed to sober up a little by the time we made it to my Jeep.

Cleo grins as we make eye contact, a small dimple forms in her cheek for the briefest of moments.

"You could work in film, you know," she says, her eyes roaming over each of my facial features. My ears burn at the comment and my chest tightens as I focus back on the road.

"It's a good thing I'm a film major then." I chuckle as she gasps.

"Oh my God, Shut up! I'm like a psychic or something. Though, you do have a 'take no bullshit, I'm the boss' aura when you're not talking. I thought you were a business major, not gonna lie." She chuckles and I mimic the action as I pull up to The Sugar Hole, the only donut shop I know in the world that's open past 1 a.m.

"Business is too serious for me."

"Hmm...the more you know–" Cleo's eyes brighten at the sight of our first stop in this short journey. "I thought we were going home!" She beams, nearly opening the door before I can put the car in park.

I chuckle at her eagerness, bringing the car to a safe stop. "I thought you could use a pick-me-up, you looked a little down at the bar before we left." I shrug, hopping out of the car and nearly running to the passenger side to open it before the eager girl could.

"Thank you, sir," she babbled in a mock bow. I reciprocate the gesture, grinning like a kid in the candy store.

"My pleasure, ma'am."

Maybe bringing Cleo to a donut shop late at night was the wrong idea. As soon as we'd enter the pink-lit shop, she runs to the case where all the donuts are held and looks as if she's going to eat them all before I can make my way over. I pull out my phone and capture the moment before she realizes she's drooling in front of the sweets and straightens up.

"Asshole." She rolls her eyes as she points out the many *many* donuts that she wants to try.

"Thank you?"

"You're welcome! And since you were such a good boy taking your losses in silence, I'll buy you a donut" she beams.

"Cleo, you're not buying me a donut," I say grinning like an idiot as she whips around to look at me with a deep frown.

"And why not?" she challenged, taking a step closer. Is that sweet smell from her perfume? Or is it just her?

I'm so caught up in indulging her sweet scent that I don't notice her pulling out her wallet to pay. To her dismay, I'm still a "star hockey-player" (her words, not mine) and so I reach over her, thankful for my longer limbs and hand the cashier my card before Cleo can get her own out.

She gapes at me, shocked at how swift she'd been overtaken. I wink at her, cherishing her silent appraisal as she scoffs. We spend our time wisely as we reenter my new truck, a Red Jeep Wrangler, talking about our project and the many things we should be working on this week.

We're so caught up in each other and our conversation that no one moves to grab a donut. Cleo seems to realize at the same time as me, but when I reach for the box, she smacks my hand away.

I raise an eyebrow at the girl, snatching off my cap and throwing it into the back. "Do you have some sort of donut ritual?" I tease, reaching again only to be swatted away.

"Yes, we must sniff them first and then praise the Donut Gods and then we can eat." She deadpans.

"I—"

Before I can express any sort of confusion, she bursts into yet another fit of laughter. I think this is the most emotion I've seen from her, ever.

"No, Creeper. There's no ritual. But I do like to record little moments like this, would you be comfortable on camera?" she asks, reaching into her purse, pulling out both her phone and a small camera that I assume she vlogs with.

"Be my guest."

Cleo takes my agreement with a smile and sets up the small cameras, the only lighting to be shown in the car being the neon pink sign of The Sugar Hole.

"Blake, you are now a friend of mine, how does that make you feel?" she questions me resembling a news reporter as she looks me over.

I smile taking her in; is this what it feels like when someone comes out of their shell? Like a new world is being opened up right before your eyes?

"I feel like you should hand me a donut." I joke, giving her grabby hands. The giggle that passes her lips is the most adorable thing I've ever heard, its chaotic yet soft.

"Fine! *Only* because you're the reason we're here. How was your night tonight?" she asks and then hands me the only odd-ball-looking donut in the box. A red maple bacon donut. My eyebrows rocket at the sight of my go-to choice from the shop and I quickly shoot the grinning girl a look.

"How did you—"

"I have a gift," she shrugs as I graciously accept the sweet treat.

Cleo and I spend so much time joking around in the car, stuck in our own little world that we're both startled when our phones go off simultaneously.

Our breaths hitch in unison as we notice the time, 2:13 a.m.

Cleo answers her phone first, flinching as loud voices ring out. She stifles a small laugh as she puts the phone on speaker.

"Where the hell are you?! You said you were on the way home, CJ. I've been at the bar worried sick about you! Sienna said you never made—"

"I'm in a parking lot," Cleo cuts the shrieking girl off only for her to scream louder.

"A parking lot!? Oh, my fuck—"

"No no... not like that. Blake is with me," she tries, cringing at her tone. I wince as Georgia screams again, sounding like a dying cow.

"You're fucking my best friend in a parking lot?!" Jace is the next voice to break through the speaker, Cleo's eyes widen at his words and she stammers to come up with something.

I chuckle at her "fish out of water" look and lean across the armrest. "Cupid, if that were happening, we'd be in the house and she wouldn't be able to answer the phone. Please be serious," I joke, eyeing the blushing girl.

The line goes silent for a second before chaos ensues.

"I'm going to kill that motherfucker." Ryan curses.

"Did he say—" Jace tries only for Denver to bark out in laughter.

"Please wear protection..." Georgia sighs as Cleo gasps.

"DON'T WEAR ANYTHING!? GO HOM—"

"Toodeloo everyone!" I smile deviously hanging up in the middle of Ryan's shouting.

Cleo rolls her eyes at the action and gets comfortable in her seat.

"You're an ass." She chuckles, turning off the camera on the dashboard as I put the car in drive.

"You're too kind," I shoot back, smiling at her. And for a brief moment our eyes lock, and previous hope of staying away from her vanishes.

I realize how screwed I am when she looks at me, I can see everything from the deep swirls of the milky way dancing in her iris's to the warmth of a summer night at the beach within the depths of her pupils.

Cleo is a woman who I've only known for two weeks and yet, I find myself shy and awkward around her. I feel contrasted from my usual self in more ways than I can count.

We hold each other's gaze for so long, I'm afraid if either of us moves, then whatever trance we're in will break.

My body is compelled to hers like a moth drawn to a flame, it doesn't resonate that the closer I inch to her, the faster I'll burn.

Cleo's lips part slightly, a gleam trickling in those beautifully brown eyes that hadn't been there before. She can say that she doesn't want to do anything with me. That she doesn't want to flirt or be distracted, but her body would never lie.

We're so close our noses touch, the sweet smell of donuts escape from both our mouths as we breathe each other in. She's so close, I can practically taste her–

"THROW THAT ASS FOR A DOLLAR!!"

We jump from each other, breaths ragged as Cleo's phone blares obnoxiously.

What the fuck was that?!

Cleo fishes around for her phone, sheepishly tugging it out of her pocket.

And just like that, I know that the moment is over.

FIFTEEN

Blake

"Dude! Get your fucking head straight. There should be no reason you missed that pass!" Charlie shouts from a couple feet ahead on the ice.

I let out my fourth deep breath of the day and look up at the boiling red right defensemen. I scoff as he rolls his eyes and skates away.

Today everyone seems to be way more tense than usual and for good reason. The first game of the season is in less than three weeks and Coach has been on our ass all day. While the guys were stressed from the threats of bag skating with Clef Jones, I'm stressed from the idea of working with Clef Jones' daughter tonight.

Cleo and I haven't talked since our almost kiss two days ago. Today, I'm supposed to go over to her apartment after class and act as if everything is fine between us.

But, it isn't.

We're supposed to be doing the whole weird "friends that almost saw each other fully naked and then forgot about it" thing. But, on Saturday we almost kissed. Hell... she was going to kiss me had we not been interrupted.

She. Was. Going to. Kiss. Me.

Ugh.

Stupid phone.

I don't notice Braxton skating up to me until I feel the weight of his arm over my shoulder. "Don't worry about CT. He's in a mood because he saw Vee with one of the baseball guys yesterday."

I nod, noting that I'd have to check on Charlie before the end of the day, and begin to wrap up. Today's practice was probably the worst we've had since the start of the season and I'm shocked that I haven't been called–

"Wilder! Stay behind after practice," Coach calls out to me as the guys begin wrapping up their things, skating off the ice.

Spoke too soon.

I sigh, working fast to wrap up and get off the ice. Maybe I was wrong in thinking that I didn't fuck up eternally on the ice today. I really need to get my focus in check. I can't have the scouts from the Washington Eagles looking at me and wondering if they made a bad decision by looking to draft me. I need to show them that their decision won't be made out of stupidity.

When I approach Coach, I immediately look down at my feet. The look that he's throwing my way is searing hot, I'd get burnt if we made eye contact.

Coach frowns, looking down at his clipboard then back up at me. "Where the hell is your head at, kid? You told me last season that you were ready for this, Wilder," he says, tone full of disappointment with small traces of anger. I flinch at his words, my head hanging lower as they sink in.

Coach and I have had this talk before, mainly last season when he saw me begin to better myself near the end of the year after a major crash out with girls and alcohol in the beginning.

I will never forget the day that Clef Jones went out of his way to take me out to dinner and try to get me some help.

Last year for me was one of the best seasons and shittiest years of my life. My nana passed at the beginning of the season just when we hit a three-game winning streak. But, I never stopped playing. I played so hard to the point of exhaustion, which was probably why I turned to slight alcohol abuse and relying on sex to numb the pain from grief. Since then, I've only been with a few girls here and there and limited my alcohol intake tremendously.

I can't slip back into old habits.

Coach, Jace, and Derek stopped me way before I ever reached the point of relying on substances to numb the pain of grief; I wouldn't consider myself an alcoholic. It was just a month of bad decisions.

"I am ready." I gulp, my eyes finding the laces of my shoes before the face of the man who helped me at my lowest.

"Son, I need you more than anything right now. You entered the draft this year and I know that Washington is looking to take you on next season. You only have this year with us and then without a doubt you'll be playing in the NHL come next fall. I need you to keep your promise from last year."

The esteemed promise. How could I ever forget that?

"I won't disappoint, I just got a little distracted, but it won't happen again," I say meeting his eyes.

Coach gives me a lighthearted smile that doesn't quite reach his eyes as he claps a hand on my shoulder, and then the two of us make our way to the parking lot still side-by-side.

"Good. Now who's this girl that Jace keeps telling me is distracting you?"

I come to an abrupt stop; my heart feels as if it'll fall out of my chest as I side-eye the man.

do I tell him that the one woman distracting me is the girl that he one, told the entire team plus the football team, was off limits, and two, is *his* goddamn daughter.

"Uh..." I chuckle, scratching the hairs on the back of my neck.

"C'mon, B, I'm cool! Even my daughter tells me about her boyfriends" he chuckles, patting my back as I side eye his figure walking ahead.

Boyfriends?

As in multiple?

Now, I'm not one to hate on polyamory! Two partners can be better than one... but Cleo doesn't seem like the type to date two people at once. Well, she did date Marcelo...eh, he's not ugly. He's just... *ew.*

Ugh. Enough about him–

"Blake, you hear me?" Coaches' voices ring from his navy-blue pick-up truck in the middle of the parking lot. "If she's the one, she won't distract you during the season! She'll want to help you."

"Everyone, be sure to meet up with your assigned partners throughout the course of the semester! I know how some of y'all love to procrastinate but procrastinating this assignment will ensure failure rather than success."

The class remains silent as Professor Hawkins continues with today's lecture.

This Monday feels as if it's been dragging on for years. From my less than savory practice this morning, to the hot-n-cold attitude from Denver and Cleo's silence. Everything seems so...boring.

That's what it is.

Today is fucking boring.

Monday's in general are boring days but today? Today takes the cake on boring ass Mondays.

I scan the classroom and sigh, even my fellow classmates look boring. All except one, of course.

Today, Cleo is dressed in all pink (surprise, surprise); her choice of pink today is a light pink short-sleeved sweater set with matching trousers and sneakers. Her straightened hair is pulled into a sleek high ponytail with a tiny ribbon wrapped around it in a delicate bow.

She briefly side eyes me, obviously catching me staring but returns to her task like the good little scholar that she is. Something about her being so attentive and focused just makes me want to both bother her and watch her be in her element.

Obviously, I choose the former of the two.

With a small smile, I reach into my book bag and pull out a small sheet of paper and proceed to write her the cheesiest love note in existence.

The lecture is boring :) but staring at you for 3 hours is enough entertainment to last a lifetime.

-b.w.

I toss the note onto Cleo's lap, chuckling silently as she jumps. Cleo gives me that nastiest mug I've ever seen in my life before looking the note over and proceeding to snort so loud that Professor Hawkins has to pause in the middle of her drawn-out sentence.

Denver peers over Cleo's shoulder, snickering to herself as Professor Hawkins coughs and continues on with her lecture.

"I'm happy to be of service, Boy Scout, but please focus so I'm not the only one working on our project." She smiles sarcastically, eyes still on her computer.

"Oh, I'm focused." I drawl, resting my face on my palm.

Cleo rolls her eyes at the action and pops me with her fluffy pink pen.

I know she didn't just–

"Yup, I did that. Now, pay attention, Lover Boy."

sixteen

Cleo

"ARE YOU SURE I can come in? I don't want to ruin the whole 'no flirting just working' thing." Blake's voice is muffled as he covers his face with his hands, shielding himself from my apartment.

I roll my eyes at his antics for the fourth time in twenty minutes. We were originally going to work on our project at his place since it's bigger but Jace and Alec are home with some of the guys from the team so we figured my apartment would be the better option. With Georgia being out and about, and Sienna at the dance studio with the kids, there is no quieter place within a ten-mile radius.

"Dude, would you stop acting like you lost your mind and come in?" I ask with a small laugh as I take off my shoes and drop my bag on the kitchen island.

Blake's movements are stiff and skeptical as his eyes wander around the warm space. He visibly relaxes and a teasing smirk replaces his once frozen in place lips.

"You come here often, Princess?" He winks, leaning an elbow on the kitchen island.

"I will kick you out if you don't shut up. Now go sit in my room and wait for me." I sigh, shooing him off as he smiles down at me.

Blake stalks off towards the hall and I question if he'll know which room is mine as he stops to stare at each door. With a nod, I watch as the man reaches for the handle to the middle room before opening it, walking into my bedroom.

While he's getting situated in there, I decide to prepare some snacks with the leftover donuts from this morning and some of the fruit I'd bought yesterday when Sienna and I went grocery shopping. I'm entranced with cutting straw-berries, the act soothing my tension from today's lecture when Blake shrieks like a scared school girl. I flinch at the loud noise, almost cutting myself in the process.

"You have Princess North panties?!" Blake's deep voice shouts, my spine goes ramrod straight, the sound of footsteps are loud as they draw near. I gasp and whirl around to find him holding up the pink and purple Princess North underwear that Georgia had bought me yesterday as a joke.

I jump as Blake embarrassingly holds my fucking princess panties in the air, laughing his butt off.

"How did you find that?!" I shriek, dropping the knife as I run up to him, jumping to grab the embarrassing material from his hands.

My attitude seems to be hilarious to this psychopath because all he does is laugh harder, holding the underwear higher.

"You laid it out on your bed!"

I'm going to *kill* Georgia.

I pause in my action of reaching above him as awareness of just how close we are prickles in my mind.

Our chests are flushed together, with Blake and I both breathing so heavy, we're in sync. He looks down at me with soft eyes before coughing, taking a step back. I repeat the action and break our eye contact.

For the first time, he was the one to break contact. Not me. I don't know why my chest feels so weird at the thought of him breaking it but I hope it stops.

"Here." He smiles softly as he gently places the monstrosity of fabric in my hand. He turns on his heels to walk away smoothly but trips halfway to my door. I snicker as he throws his middle finger up at me before re-entering the bedroom.

The two of us sit in a comfortable silence for about ten minutes until the antsy man beside decides to break it. He'd been tapping his pencil on his computer for eight of those ten minutes, whilst staring at me for the full ten.

"You want pizza?" he asks, and that is not what I expected to come from his mouth. I look up at him and shrug.

"It doesn't sound bad—"

"Good. I already ordered a cheese, pepperoni, and a sausage one just in case you like a little sausage." He winks, making clicking sound as he leans back against my bed, smirking smugly.

"What if I don't like any of those flavors?" I tease lying through my teeth as I lean in close to him. I could honestly eat a cow right now; I haven't had any real food all day. I've just been snacking until now.

Blake frowns for a second, tilting his head like a lost puppy. "Then what *do* you like?"

"Well, it depends on the pizza place. If it's from Cooke's, then I get their barbecue chicken pizza. But I also love the chicken supreme without mushroom and olives from Logan's or the Cheesesteak Galore from Mika's—"

"We don't have Mika's in Maryland, Princess. That's a New York thing," he interrupts with a small, amused smile.

"And how do you know that?" I frown, folding my arms under my chest.

"Because I grew up there. Manhattan, probably born, mostly raised." He shrugs.

"Probably?" I question him, setting down my computer. Looks like work will get done later.

Blake shrugs yet again. "Yeah, probably. I was adopted a little after I was born so whenever I talk about where I was born, I always add a probably," He chuckles, ears and neck burning red. "When I was a kid, my older sister Jules would say I was born on Pluto and my parents found me because I was ugly and left on their doorstep."

"Well, were you?"

"Was I what? Ugly, or left on the step?" he questions, amusement laced in his tone.

"Both?" I respond hesitantly as he throws his head back in laughter.

"No, Princess, I was not ugly." He chuckles, pretending to flick away a tear from his eye. "But I was left on the doorstep."

My heart drops as he continues with his small chuckles that don't feel quite as humorous anymore. Blake seems like this energetic guy who doesn't care about anything other than hockey and himself, but I'm starting to learn that he's more like an onion than anything. He isn't shallow like I'd wrongfully thought, he has layers. So intricate and detailed that the average person would overlook. I want to study his layers.

I want to understand him.

So, instead of changing the subject, I dig deeper. "Does it make you—"

"Feel a type of way? Nah. If they were cowardly enough to leave me on a doorstep, then they'd be too cowardly to take good care of me, Cleo." He shrugs and for the first time, I'm stunned by the use of my own name.

Instead of calling him out on it, I try to formulate a sentence, but he interrupts yet again.

"I don't want to meet my birth parents if that's your next question. I love my parents and I thank my birth parents for leaving me on that doorstep because had they kept me, I would be living a completely different life." He gives me a small smile. A smile so soft and innocently different from his usually cocky smirks.

My chest tightens as Blake reaches into his bag, pulling out the small silver camcorder assigned to us. With a grin, Blake flicks the power button on but pauses before recording me.

"I want to know why you're scared of cameras," he says, playing with the camera's controls and I stiffen as his words process fully.

Does he know about what happened in New York? How does he know that I'm scared? I'm not scared! I just can't—I don't like… Fuck.

His eyes widen, Blake pulls the camera from his eye as the tips of his ears burn a bright red.

"I don't mean it like that! I just mean—"

I take a deep breath looking up at him before plastering on a smile, he winces at the action but I brush him off as I blink twice.

"I'm not scared of cameras. I'm scared of the monsters that are behind them."

At that, Blake tilts his head and I have a feeling that he wants to dig deeper but the doorbell chime pauses any further interrogations.

"I'll get it."

I watch as he leaves, my gaze lingering on his tight ass for a second longer than appropriate as he strides out the room. As soon as I hear him open the door, I smack a hand to my head.

I almost told a complete stranger about a past that not even my closest friends know.

Fuck me...

The brunette man enters the room with his back to me, I can tell he has a large stupid grin on his face even before he turns around. And when he does, I'm stunned to see five boxes in his arms instead of three.

Did he buy more pizzas because of me? No... I doubt that—

"I couldn't choose between barbecue and the chicken supreme so I got both since I've never tried them and I trust your opinion on food—"

My stomach growls silently, a soft moan escapes my mouth as the sweet and savory smells wafts around the air creating an intoxicating aroma. My mouth waters.

"Blake, I could seriously kiss you right now." The thought I'd been having is vocalized so loud in the now silent room.

He visibly gulps as he looks down at me on the floor. "Princess, you're making it so hard for me to do the whole just friends thing when you say things like that, looking at me like *that*." He groans.

"Looking at you? Baby, I'm looking at the five large pies in your hand." Rolling my eyes, I hop up from my seat on the floor and snatch two of the boxes from the top of the stack. Blake chuckles plopping down across from me on the spacious floor.

"Baby?" He says quietly just as I plant a slice of supreme chicken in my mouth.

This is fucking nirvana.

"Hm?" I hum at the taste of the savory slice, groaning silently as the flavor expels on my tongue.

"So, you like that nickname, too? Noted." He smirks as I flip him the bird.

"Oh, hush... you're interrupting precious C and P time." I frown my mouth full of food.

"C and P?"

"Cleo and Pizza... duh." I shrug as I continue to devour the slice.

We continue to eat the pizza in a comfortable conversation about TV when my and Blake's phones ring. We eye each other carefully before turning the screens to each other. His screen read Jace while mine read Georgia.

Uh oh...

Without further questioning, we both answer our phones.

"I fucked up!" I can hear Jace yell through the line on Blake's phone as Georgia's voice flows through mine.

"I made a horrible mistake, Cleo."

What the hell happened to them?

"Did you call fucking Cleo?!" I can hear Jace in the background of both lines.

"Yes! Because you're a fucking bleach blonde sociopath who won't leave me the hell alone! You—"

"I'm a *sociopath?!* Have you looked in the mirror, Peach? I'm pretty sure your name is plastered beside the definition in the dictionary!" Jace cuts her off as she scoffs... loudly.

"You're such a fucking cunt, asshole!" Georgia responds with a sharp edge in her tone.

"Take one to know one, dick!"

Ohh-kaay.

"Why are you two even around each other?" I ask as Blake chuckles in front of me.

The line goes dead silent and for a moment, I don't think either of them heard me until Jace screeches.

"You fuckers are together without me?!"

Blake and I look up at each other, both of us still holding the phones to our ears before smiling.

One, he mouths, holding the phone out showing me the call screen as Jace yells through the speaker.

Two, I mouth back, doing the same.

We chuckle silently as both our pointer fingers hover over the 'end call' button.

Three, we mouth together proceeding to hang up on both of our friends. They'll probably have something to say about it later but right now, I could care less.

"We've gotta do that again! Can you imagine their faces?!" he asks, doubling over in laughter. is contagious, it's so addictive and sweet that I crack up with him. He's like a kid, figuring out how to prank call for the first time. Giddy and excited for mischief. I can't say that I don't like the idea of more mischief with him–

Nope. See that's where I almost fucked up. But, you saw me catch myself, right? Right.

Anyways...

I sober up my laughter and begin pulling out the vintage 1999 camcorder we were assigned. I chuckle as the camera makes a low beeping sound, coming to life. This camera reminds me so much of the ones Gloria and Dad used to record Ryan and I with when we were younger. They'd follow us around and record everything, from us playing video games to arguing over our shared bathroom. I think they even captured Ryan and Georgia spraining their wrists on video.

"You ready?" I ask, pointing my own camera up to face him. We'd decided earlier this week that we'd intertwine our footage to make one large collage of videos. It was Blake's idea to record each other and capture the moments when we're not paying attention. The small smiles when no one's watching, and the little things we sometimes don't notice about ourselves. He told me he notices things about me but I highly doubt it.

There's not much to notice.

"I'm as ready as I'll ever be, Princess."

"What's your biggest life regret so far?" I ask him, holding the camera to my eye as I focus on the man in front of me.

Blake shifts in his seat on the ground and blows out a huff of air. "You sure know how to start a conversation, Jones." He chuckles airily, looking everywhere but at the camera.

The fairy lights around the back of my room's wall twinkle in anticipation of what he's going to say. I lean forward just a bit, in hopes of capturing his every breath on film.

"My biggest regret today is how I acted last year after my nana died." He sighs, scratching the back of his neck.

Blake's eyes wander around my room and I think he won't elaborate but he turns back to me with a small watery smile.

"She passed away before I got the chance to apologize to her. We'd been on a winning streak and she was supposed to come to one of our games but didn't make it. Hell, no one did if I'm being honest." He chuckles dryly, his eyes lock with mine and I instantly want to turn off the camera.

His voice sounds so raw and unfiltered, completely contrasting from his flirty cocky persona that I'm constantly around. For some reason, I want to protect this version of him. I want to protect the Blake who sounds so hurt and ashamed of his own actions. I want to be there for him and I have no idea why.

"My dad wanted to be there but he and my mom were in Milan for my sister's show with Asteri. She was the opening model and Nana volunteered to be the family member that showed up for me. She forgot to set her alarm and I was so mad that I iced her out." He shrugs, sniffling quietly.

"You don't have to go on if you don't feel comfortable–"

"No, I do… it's fine. I've grown up since then." He chuckles softly, interrupting me. "A few days after that, she died from a stroke. I was heartbroken, so I turned to alcohol and sex–I'm not proud of it. No. But, it was a rough time for…for me." He sighs. And the sound of his voice cracking, chips away at my heart a bit.

I don't push Blake to continue with his biggest regret, instead I watch him as he composes himself and masks his true feelings with a lopsided grin.

"I regret my actions before and after her death but I'm thankful for my friends and Coach. They helped me pick up my broken pieces."

"Would you say that they're your family as well?" I ask, holding the camera from my eye a bit as he gives me a small genuine smile.

"They're like my brothers. I'm happy they saved me when I couldn't save myself."

We finished recording our first questions with him asking me something a little more tame along the lines of "Would I rather be a rock or a worm?" After filming, we decided that since it wasn't too late and that we could watch a friendly movie.

I let Blake choose since he's the "movie connoisseur" and he ended up picking a movie about a talking cat and car duo.

"You know Svetlana is a spy, right?" he asks, pointing at the purple car on the screen.

"I'm sorry, how are you a film major again? We're watching a movie about a purple car named Svetlana and Cat called Mr. Giggles—"

"Don't hate on greatness, Jones." He tosses a small piece of popcorn my way. He'd been laying across our pink living room rug, while I took the couch. He'd said our couch was too small for all of his 'manliness' and decided to camp out on the ground.

I laugh as the popcorn hits my cheek. "I'm serious! Aren't we supposed to be watching a Psychological Thriller or something?" I ask, cracking a smile as he rolls his eyes.

"Look at you feeding into stereotypes! Not all film majors are brooding dickheads. Some of us *like* spending time watching cartoons." He smiles wide at me as I'm now the one rolling my eyes.

The apartment alarm goes off signaling the front door opening, mine and Blake's heads snap simultaneously to the front door as a grumpy pink-haired girl enters the house.

"I need a drink and some serious girl talk." Sienna frowns, stalking towards the couch. She plops down on it and lays across my lap before pulling my hand into her hair, moving it to massage her curls.

"Long day?"

"That guy will be the death of me!" she exclaims, shooting up from my lap.

"Spill, girl!" Blake quips in a mock valley girl accent, I snort at his tone but Sienna ignores him and continues.

"He won't freaking leave me alone! I'm a freaking dance teacher, not a mind reader. I love the kid, she's amazing but him? He's *so* annoying. Why should I be the one to initiate a conversation with a parent? The parent should want to know about their kid. He should want to know how his daughter is doing in dance! Hell, he's only ever picked her up from practice once, CJ!" She scoffs, running a shaky hand through her hair, clearly frustrated.

My heart hurts for Sienna as she groans. I can see her inner child hurting for the young girl in her dance class because, in a way, I think Sienna sees herself.

When we were younger, my aunt and uncle were never around for Si Si, which was why she was always at my house. They would always be on the road, whether on tour or traveling for work.

We come from a music family, with most of my aunts, uncles, and cousins being in the music industry due to my grandparents holding the torch as Jazz legends. My dad and aunt Lyric were the only two of their four siblings that hadn't gone into the music industry but Sienna's dad, Uncle Major is a super famous DJ. While her mom is a popstar.

Uncle Major and Aunt Eloisa supported Sienna in every way except emotionally. They'd send money for clothes and made sure she had the finest shoes and bags. But when it came to showing up for a recital or play, they were nowhere to be found.

"What a dick." Blake scoffs, rubbing Sienna's shoulder as she chuckles. I hadn't even noticed he'd moved to the couch.

"Do you maybe think you're projecting your feelings about auntie and uncle onto him?" I ask, bracing myself for anger as she groans.

"I don't know, honestly. But it feels shitty knowing that another little girl is out there being treated how I was." She hangs her head with a sigh.

"Then be the person you needed when you were a kid, for her." Blake shrugs as if that's the easiest thing in the world. I'm about to interject when Sienna brightens up, jumping off the couch with a large smile.

"You're so right! Thanks, Jake!" She squeals before skipping... yes, I said it, *skipping* to her bedroom.

Blake tilts his neck at the name and turns his head to me.

"Who the hell is Jake?"

seventeen

Blake

CLEO IS DYING OF laughter on the couch beside me, still repeating the name *Jake* over and over. I've been called a lot of things in my lifetime by girls but Jake, is not one of them.

I'll take *'asshole'* over some other dude's name any day.

"Something funny?" I cock my neck to the side as she wipes an absent tear, awfully tickled with the fact that her pink-haired friend called me a different guy.

"*Everything* about that was funny!" she exclaims, sighs, and then laughs even harder.

"Oh, shut up..." I chuckle as she snorts.

She's about to voice her retort when the door slams open once again, and the chime of the alarm goes off.

"Why the fuck are you here?!" an all too familiar loud voice yells over Cleo's obnoxious laughter.

The both of us freeze momentarily at the sight of the two angry blondes in the doorway. Jace stands with his hands on his hips like a hardware store dad, while Georgia rolls her eyes, stepping around him.

"Why wouldn't I be?" I cough, sobering up as I sit up on the couch, resting my elbows on my knees.

Cleo scoots in closer to me as Jace strides into the living room with an annoying smile on his face.

"Because you said you had a project! I checked your location, and *this* doesn't look like a project," he says in a matter of fact tone as if he's caught me in a dirty little secret.

I frown as he squeezes in between Cleo and I on the couch, looking me over like I'm some sort of pest before smiling sweetly at the woman beside him.

"You're interrupting, you idiot," Georgia croaks from the loveseat across the room, looking down at her tablet.

"And you're fucking annoying," he responds instantly.

"*Hey!* Be nice to each other. Why are you two arguing now?" Cleo asks, cutting the two of them with a look as sharp as a blade.

I watch Georgia for a reaction; Jace is always overreacting but I've never been around her too long to understand her. Georgia's eyes widened for a second before darting to Jace. She shakes her head subtly, but I catch it.

"Oh...you know, just Peach being annoying once again." Jace coughs.

Weird.

He's *underreacting*.

"Well, both of you cut the shit. Si Si's having a bad night and I highly doubt she wants to hear you two go back and forth about who's more annoying." Cleo's tone is stern, but I can hear the faint smile she's trying so hard to mask.

Jace doesn't say anything and neither does Georgia, the two just go silent and listen, watching the rest of the movie with Cleo and me.

We sit around, wasting away in complete silence with occasional small laughs. With Jace sitting in between us like a barrier I can't bother Cleo like I usually do. But I do manage to sneak some looks at her as she watches the movie.

Cleo laughs at the smallest things on the screen like if a character says something that no one else finds funny, she'll chuckle at it or smile. She's an expressive girl and it's hard to understand how the girl who was so vibrant and bubbly on her YouTube channel, not even a year ago, is suddenly this shy and reclusive person who's afraid of 'monsters behind cameras' or whatever that means.

From what I've noticed, Cleo is strong and doesn't want someone to save her. What she seems to want is someone who will back her up. And I'd gladly blast some monsters for her.

The girls and Jace fall asleep halfway through the third movie, and seeing him laying with his head in Cleo's lap makes my jaw tick, though I can't explain why. I haven't liked a girl since elementary and middle school.

In high school, my true love was hockey. Of course I've hooked up and had flings, I mean what D1 athlete hasn't? But I've never felt this way about a girl like how I do with Cleo. So, as I sit on the edge of her too small couch, watching my best friend sleep peacefully on the lap of the girl that I may or may not be crushing on, I can't help but kick him.

Jace jumps dramatically out of his slumber as if something *bad* happened.

"Where's the bloody rabbit?!" he startles awake speaking in a shitty British accent. He jumps from Cleo's lap causing her to stir; I shush him and point to both girls as he visibly becomes calmer.

"She looks so peaceful," he says, his tone soft and though, I'm watching Cleo, thinking the exact same thing, I startle as I track my eyes to where he's looking.

What the hell happened between Georgia and him? And why does he look less murderous than earlier?

I watch him in silence as he gets up from the couch, quietly trekking to the blonde who slept peacefully on the loveseat. He smiles softly as she mutters something under her breath before throwing her over his shoulder, like a sack of potatoes. It happens in slow motion, Georgia's eyes widening before *the kick*. I guess being friends for over ten years makes you know a person's ass because as soon as her eyes encountered Jace's butt, her foot came in contact with his dick.

I sniff a laugh as he slowly goes down wordlessly holding his crotch and take Georgia's scolding him as a sign to get Cleo to bed. My mouth curves as I look down at the sleeping woman, Cleo sleeps like an angel throughout all the chaos around her as Jace and Georgia argue quietly.

I'm gentle as I scoop her into my arms bridal style; *friends help each other get to their own beds and I'm just trying to do my good old friend a favor.*

The only time I took a girl to bed without the intention of fucking her senseless was two years ago the night of Jule's 23rd birthday. We roamed the streets of New York and ended up drunk outside of a trendy nightclub. I had to haul my sister from a cab to the penthouse level of a skyscraper. It was indeed the first, and what I assumed to be the last time, I carried a woman to a bed I wouldn't be sleeping in.

Cleo doesn't stir as I tuck her in, she just lays there motionless as if nothing has changed and for a second, I think she's dead.

I lift one of her arms and jump back as it falls wobbly. I scoot closer to her face just as someone coughs. I jump back, away from the sleeping beauty.

"Is *she* the girl?" Jace asks, leaning in the doorway with his arms folded.

I choose to ignore him and continue to tuck Cleo into bed, placing one of the large plushies I saw earlier beside her. He watches me with raised brows as I turn back around with a small faltering smile.

"Jones is going to kill you–don't tuck her in. She gets claustrophobic." He sighs, going back over to undo my work. Jace untucks her and then proceeds to lay a soft kiss on her temple. I squint at the action but don't say anything as he and I stalk towards the bedroom door.

I should kill that motherfucker for even thinking about kissing her—

Too much?

Way too much...

Anyways...

"There's nothing for him to kill me about, we're just partners."

"Partners or *partners?*" The idiot zeros in on me as if I'm a threat. Like he's her protector or something. I don't like the way he's trying to size me up either, like I'm an opponent on the ice or something. I step closer to my best friend and look him directly in the eye.

"We're partners. Now get out, she needs to sleep and I for one don't want to still be here when she or Georgia wakes up."

EIGHTEEN

Cleo

Lorelei Smith

Cleo we need to speak.

Me

There is quite literally nothing for us to talk about Lorelei.

Lorelei Smith

I am your mother.

You will meet me at Café Iteri. Friday at 12. Do not be late.

1 New message from Sexy Boy Scout

Sexy

Miss me?

Me

You have five minutes.

Sexy Boy Scout

What are your camera settings?

I can't figure out which side would make me look sexier since my face is so symmetrical and what not.

Me

Blake...

You have changed Sexy Boy Scout to Blake (Wilder)

Blake (Wilder)

I love it when you say my name.

See u after class?

Me

We have the same class...

I have to go to the mall too

Blake (Wilder)

Perfect. Can I get a fashion show?

"HOW ABOUT NOW?" BLAKE asks for the thirtieth time, interrupting yet another conversation between Denver and me.

Denver shoots her cousin a menacing glare as he smirks back at her, fully gaining my attention.

"How many times are you going to ask CJ about the mall?" Denver sighs as she carelessly rolls her camcorder in her hands. She and her partner Ethan decided to take turns weekly with the camera instead of utilizing both like Blake and me.

"Until she says yes... *duh,*" he responds in a matter-of-fact tone, Denver scoffs at him as he leans in closer to me, shutting my laptop.

"The answer is still no, Blake". I grin, opening it back up to the powerpoint of the day.

Blake has been bugging me and Denver for the past hour and a half about whether he could watch me in the changing rooms at the mall and if he and I were going to shop for one another.

I'd originally ignored him but that lasted all of five minutes until he mentioned buying donuts on the way to the mall.

Blake scoffs, resting his head on my shoulder.

"I'll let you watch me get naked." He grins cockily, looking up at me with those stunning blue eyes.

Have you ever seen a clear ocean? Not like the ones we have here in Maryland—certainly not like Ocean City. No, I'm talking tropical islands with sand so warm, you feel like you're in heaven. Blake's eyes remind me of that type of water. They're enchanting and freeing and *what the hell am I talking about?*

No. Absolutely not. No boys. *No him.*

I shrug Blake off of me and focus my attention back on Professor Hawkins. She's teaching us about atmospheres and feeling's through images and I'd be lying if I told you I was paying attention.

Those texts from my mom this morning is still weighing me down and I can't stop zoning out thinking about the one guy who should be far from my mind.

"Did you hear what I said, CJ? I can't join you guys today, I have to help this guy with something." Denver's soft voice startles me for a second. I sigh as I regroup my thoughts and focus on her.

"Huh? What guy?"

Denver rocks on her heels, avoiding eye contact with me. I stiffen as a small smile tugs on her lips. She says, "No one," before dashing out of the emptying lecture hall and I just know that it's *someone.*

"Ready for my fashion show, Princess. I will say that pink certainly looks good on you but red is my favorite so..." Blake trails off, his eyes brightening as I roll my own.

Blake is surprisingly silent the entire walk to his car and during the ride to the mall, the only sound to be heard is the soft R&B playing from his playlist.

Though it's unusual, I'm thankful for the silence, it gives me time to mussel over my thoughts.

Like, why would my mom text me out of the blue? It's been months since Lorelei Smith and I have had any sort of contact with one another. But then she shows up at the school I transferred to, claiming to be a helper in a class she couldn't care less about...

I don't buy it.

I've seen the post about my mom and that drummer guy from Australia. I'm happy for her, she's got a new boyfriend *again*.

Woopty doo.

But something about her randomly appearing in my life again after not giving a damn about me for so long doesn't sit right with me.

"Cleo?" a muffled voice calls out to me; the sound is faint to my ears as I try to swat it away.

"Oh my God, I'm going to have to do CPR—don't move!" Blake nearly shouts, my eyes shoot open at his loud tone and my breath hitches.

He's so close to my face that our noses are touching, my eyes widen, trailing down to his lips, and then back to his eyes. He smiles as if he's *not* in my personal bubble and chuckles lightly.

"How'd you sleep, Princess?" Blake muses, backing away from me. I catch my breath once again before scowling at him.

"The rules—"

"Have not been broken, that wasn't flirting... simply *observing*." he interjects before scrunching his face. I watch as Blake taps his fingers on the steering wheel and yawns.

Was I asleep?

"Now, we've got to be quick. I have a playdate at five." He's grinning from ear to ear as he hops out the car, rounding to my side. He pulls open the passenger door, bowing a little and I think my stomach does a backflip at the action. But then it falls in the middle of the flip as I recall his words.

Playdate?

"Like with a girl?" I ask, taking his offered hand as I step out of the Jeep.

"Mhm... the most beautiful girl," he adds with a little pep in his step.

Fucking gross. How does someone flirt with another person when they have a girlfriend? He went down on me not even a month ago and now he's dating someone.

I scoff, walking ahead of him into the mall. I can hear Blake trying to catch up, but I pay him no mind as I stalk towards the store that I'd came here for.

Ugh. This is why I refuse to deal with men. As soon as you start talking to someone with the intention of flirting with them, you find out that they're a two-timing weasel that wants to have his cake and eat it too.

The nerve of men.

This is why I think all men should be eradicated, not only do they do shit like that but they also mansplain everything. Like what is up with that—

"I got you a donut! I hope you like the regular pink ones with sprinkles. It was the only one they had," Blake calls out to me, jogging at my side with a large pink donut covered in rainbow sprinkles in his hand.

What was I saying about men? Right—I hate—

"I also got an Oreo one just in case." He shrugs, holding up a pink box in the other hand.

I stop in my tracks and glare at him—so maybe Blake Wilder knows that the way to my heart is through donuts, that doesn't change the fact that he's a two-timing weasel. But I do take the box from him. I can't let a perfectly good strawberry donut go to waste.

I thank him quietly as I stuff my face and ignore his light chuckles as we enter the first store. We shop around in silence for a few minutes with him showing me random clothes and me grimacing at his questionable choices in clothing.

One of the shirts said "DILFs make me horny" ...I don't even know how that ended up in a store like this.

"How about this," he starts, taking a sip of the red slushy that he ordered. I pause in my casual clothes scrolling and look up at him.

"I find four outfits for you, and you do the same, we film you trying them on for the project, and then we each answer a question from our respective lists. That way we get work done and I can style you simultaneously," he offers, shrugging nonchalantly but I can see through the act. His eyes tell me how eager he is for me to agree, so I do.

What's the worst that can happen?

I'll tell you what the worst that can happen is. I'm standing in the middle of a secluded dressing room with Blake Wilder smiling from ear to ear sitting on a beige leather couch holding a camcorder up to record me.

But that's not the bad part.

The bad part is that he has me dressed like that one guy from that one movie who wears baggy jorts and shirts that weirdly fit a niche aesthetic but make me look like a homeless bimbo with bows.

"You look adorable" he coos from the couch, recording me from head to toe.

Pouting, I look down at myself and sigh. "I look like I went shopping in my dad's closet from the 90s."

"So, fashionable?" he teases, amused at seeing me dressed completely unlike myself. The nerve of this man. I flip him off before turning back on my heels toward the fitting room.

I'll show him fashionable.

Hmph.

The shirt I picked out is a white slim-fit blouse, the kind that the super-hot secretaries in office romances wear—yeah, that type. I paired it with low-rise jeans that hug my ass in all the right ways and flare out a bit around my shins. But instead of buttoning the shirt top to bottom, I only do the three in the middle, exposing my belly ring and some light cleavage.

I'd say that this is the perfect "confidently going to tell my mother off" brunch outfit. *But wait, is this too much? Is it bland? There isn't any pink in this outfit...should I add a pink accessory? Fuck—*

"Hey, Princess, you good in there?"

"Just a second!" I call out and take a deep breath. *It's fine, this is all fine.* I psych myself up to walk out, this outfit doesn't have to be the best. It just has to look—

A whistle catches my attention as I walk down the hall of the dressing room to where Blake is seated on the couch. He's smiling so brightly that I'm taken aback momentarily, as I look at him.

"Well?" I ask, looking down at the clothing before doing a small spin.

"You are magnetic, Cleo Jones. I don't know how one woman can make both dad clothes and business chic look ethereal, but you did it."

The comment catches me so off guard that I don't know what to do with myself, so instead of responding, I turn on my heels with a stupid smile and scurry back toward the dressing room.

NINETEEN

Blake

I'M GRINNING FROM EAR TO ear, watching as Cleo scurries away. I snicker as she trips on her way to the dressing room and smile to my self at her clumsiness.

Being at the mall on a random Wednesday, watching a pretty girl play dress up, was not how I intended for my afternoon to go. Hell, I thought I'd just sit in my room and build a new LEGO set but when Cleo texted me about going to the mall, I couldn't resist the chance to hang out with her.

I'm on my phone scrolling aimlessly through the most recent trending topic on Twitter, scoffing at the outlandish things that they have to say about my sister yet again.

Who cares if she's dating that F1 guy now? Get a life people!

> *The term homie-hopper and Jules Avery go hand in hand, this supermodel is now seen with Eren Marlowe, although, we've recently spotted her smooching Twisted Vipers drummer—*

I'm getting a migraine just reading that shit.

Shutting my phone off, I sigh in frustration at the nerve of that journalist. My sister and Eren are *not* together, they've been friends since forever and besides, she'd never do that.

I put my head in my hands, tugging lightly at the strands. I'm so deep in my thoughts about my sister that I don't notice Cleo in front of me until her feet are in my line of view. When I look up at her, I'm immediately at a loss for words.

She is beautiful.

Cleo's looking down at her phone, her straightened hair no longer bound by that weird pink thing. *Hand Clip? Hair holder?* I think it's something like that. Anyways, she stands in front of me in a red dress that hugs her every curve, highlighting her chest, and extenuating her round hips. The dress is meant to look simple, *basic even,* but the words basic and Cleo Jones don't exist in the same sentence, let alone universe. And it may be because I'm taking a very *very* small liking to her that I think this.

Who am I kidding? We all know I fucking like her.

Fuck.

What do I do? I'm staring up at her like a gaping fish out of water.

C'mon, Blake... say something... anything. I'm about to open my mouth to try and speak when Cleo twirls around, her back exposed, a hint of a tattoo peaks from the bottom of the opened zipper and I groan, immediately peeling my eyes away.

Fuck me.

There's no way in *hell* I'm going to sport a hard-on with her in front of me.

"Can you zip me up?" she asks softly, pulling her hair to the side.

I gulp as I look up at the soft expand of her body, a thin red laced bra wraps around her back. The color glows off her brown skin, catching my breath. I look down at my damn near shaking hands then back up at the zipper.

Why does this feel like my first time seeing a girl naked? She's fully clothed in front of me!

Get a grip, Wilder. She's just a girl. Nothing to be scared of...

I clear my throat, slowly rising. Cleo's so close, I can smell the sweetness of her candy-like perfume. I sigh as the scent intoxicates me before lifting a shaky hand to her zipper.

We're so close that her body heat warms me and when my fingers brush against her bare skin, she shudders. I have the same effect on her that she has on me.

I take my time as I zip up the dress, smirking as she goosebumps rise along her back and neck.

"Cold?" I ask, my voice deeper than usual.

"Nope!" Cleo jumps away rushing back to the dressing room, leaving me amused and breathless.

I grin cheekily as I watch her leave and sit back down, adjusting myself on the couch. It isn't until she's fully gone that I realize her phone is still beside me, I'm about to take it back to her when it buzzes, lighting up the lock screen with several messages.

Unknown

> i'm watching you Jones

> tell anyone and it's over for you

What the fuck?

I reread the messages. Once. Twice. *Five times.* It takes me five rereads to register the cryptic messages slowly popping up on Cleo's phone. *Who is this?* Is someone playing some sick joke right now? My stomach drops as more roll in.

Unknown

> remember

> you made a deal you can't break.

A deal? At the sound of Cleo's footsteps, I quickly slide the messages over, deleting them from her lock screen, hastily throwing her phone into her purse. I pull out our camcorder to make myself seem busy as she approaches me, smiling wildly. As I stare at the smiling girl before me, I wonder how real her smiles have been since she's been here.

Has she been getting messages like this for a while now? Are they prank texts? Does Jace know?

The questions throw me for a loop, and I don't notice Cleo standing before me, pointing her camera at my face until she giggles softly, capturing my attention.

"Huh?"

"I asked if you were ready... I'm getting hungry and the only thing I had today was a blueberry-spinach smoothie." She scrunches her nose, adorably. She probably doesn't even notice the amount of cute facial expressions she makes a day.

"Blueberry-spinach?" I ask, looking down at her as she groans, frowning.

"Georgia's on a new smoothie cleanse. Yesterday was strawberry-mango. Today's blueberry-spinach. Tomorrow's something with carrots." She shrugs as if this is a regular occurrence in their apartment as we make our way to the nearest register. Cleo places down every article of clothing she'd tried on. Well, all except one.

I furrow my eyebrows, frowning as she looks up at me.

"What?"

"The dress." I tilt my head, frowning at her.

"What dress?" She asks, chuckling as if she doesn't know exactly what *dress* I'm talking about.

I groan aloud, looking from her to the cashier then back to her. If that's how she wants to play it, then fine.

I'm going to remember this.

We make our way to the food court, the both of us recording each other separately for the project. It's comfortable between us, no awkward silences and zero loss of conversation.

I know when I first met Cleo, I'd thought she'd been like me. Extroverted, yet introverted. Turns out, I was harboring a secret extrovert this *entire* time. If anyone thought I talked a lot then they certainly haven't met Cleo Jones.

I pity those of you who have yet to meet her, but if you have met Cleo and didn't introduce me to her... Fuck you. You're a bitch and I hope you step on a LEGO.

I won't apologize for that statement, either.

"*Oh!* We *have* to get that!" She squeals from beside me, latching onto my arm. I freeze, looking down at her but she's not paying me any mind as she jumps up and down pointing at the CinnaU sign.

"I thought you were a donut girl." I quip.

Cleo pauses in her momentary celebration and glares at me. "Never judge a woman and her snacks, Creeper"

"So, we're back to 'Creeper'? C'mon Princess, I thought we were making progress," I tease and there's no real reaction from her but I can see the smile in her eyes as she turns on her heel and starts towards CinnaU.

Cleo orders a cinnamon roll with extra icing, caramel drizzle, and pecans, while I get the simplest item on the menu in its simplest form. A regular cinnamon roll. Shocking, I know.

She records me as I order and I smile as I pay for our "meal", as she likes to call two large cinnamon rolls, and stalk towards an empty clean table.

"First question for Blake Wilder," she starts, holding the camcorder up to her eye just as I plop a piece of the dessert into my mouth.

"Shoot," I say as I swallow, giving her my full attention.

"Who do you admire the most and why?" She asks, beaming at me. It reminds me of how Delilah looks at Derek and my stomach flips at the thought.

"My sister," I say without hesitation.

Jules will always be the strongest woman that I know, from her struggles with anxiety and dyslexia, to becoming a supermodel and salutatorian of her graduating class. I don't believe that there's anything my older sister can't do, and I strive to be just like that.

"Juliette went from being the kid in the back of the class who kept her head down to a runway model. She inspires me in more ways than one but her perseverance makes me admire her." I shrug. Juliette can be annoying like any other sibling, don't get me wrong, but she was my first best friend. She was the first person to take me in and make me feel welcome and for that I admire her just a bit more.

"Your sister's a model? Which one?" Cleo asks, still recording as I chuckle bitterly.

"*Jules Avery.*" I sigh as her eyebrows shoot to her hairline.

Yup. An average reaction to my sisters name.

"You're Jules' brother?! Dude, she's best friends with my cousin!" Cleo's voice is high as she continues to record my face yet shuffles around in her purse for her phone.

I furrow my brow at her as she goes through her phone, excitedly scrolling. Maybe she hasn't seen the messages, yet. Cleo is grinning like a mad man when she pulls up a picture of Jules and Zahria, one of Jules' model friends in New York.

"You know the Z's?" I ask shifting my gaze between Cleo and the phone.

"Know them? I used to live with them every summer!" She exclaims.

"Our parents are siblings—same with Sienna. There's me, Aunt Lyric, Aunt Melody, Uncle Major, Dad, the twins, Zay, Ryan, Mama, and Papa," she says pointing to each of the notably famous people in her phone. I reel back as I look over the screen, shocked I hadn't put it together sooner.

"Your grandparents are Apollo and Marie Jones? *The* jazz singers?"

Cleo nods like this isn't a huge deal. Her grandparents made my childhood!

Every Sunday, my mom played Marie Jones while cleaning, and Dad would play Apollo J every night when he cooked dinner. My jaw is agape as I look further at the photo.

"Zayden Jones as in *the Quarterback*?" I gasp.

How much cooler can Cleo get?

"Yup. The one and only, he's actually super annoying once you get to know him. No sense of personal space whatsoever." She rolls her eyes.

I try to mask my fanboying, but I fail. Cleo's laughing, like *actually* laughing at me, as I continue gawking at her phone.

So let me get this straight. Not only was her dad one of the best in the NHL and her mom is an Olympic gold medalist. Her grandparents are legends in the music industry as well as her aunts, uncle, *and* cousin. Also, the number one draft pick is her cousin?

What's next? Her dog is a fucking movie star Chihuahua?

Cleo's phone dings loudly, drawing her attention away from me. She frowns as she looks at it and sighs, running a hand through her hair.

"Speaking of those devils... I forgot that Sienna and I have to talk to the twins and Zay tonight. You ready to go?" She asks, looking up briefly as I nod, collecting our bags.

"Thanks for today, Blake. I think that these clothes should be good for this weekend, right?" Cleo asks, turning in the passenger seat to look at me as we pull up to a red light.

"What's this weekend?" I question, briefly looking over at her before the light turns green.

"Fall Fest. G told me it's a big deal here so we're going for each of the days to get the full experience." She beams, bouncing in her seat excitedly.

Fuck, that *is* this weekend. I need the guys to keep it together. We can't have any distractions with our first game rolling around next week.

I have to make sure Jace and Charlie go home alone this weekend. Last Fall Fest, those two dumbasses brought back five random girls to the house. And that was just between the two of them, the fuckers nearly started a war with the basketball team because of it.

"Did you hear me?" Cleo's voice drones back in, catching me off guard as I continue driving to her apartment. "I asked if you were you going, we could get some good clips for the documentary!"

"Oh. Uh...yeah! Of course, I'll be there..."

On penis patrol.

TWENTY

Blake

WHEN I GET HOME after dropping Cleo off, I immediately see a slumped over Charlie on the couch. He looks dead from this angle, and I sigh as I approach him.

"You're never at your own house, y'know." I muse, taking the small bag of Dill Pickle flavored chips from his lap as he chuckles lightly.

"You have better WI-FI."

He's not wrong, Charlie and Braxton's internet is the worst thing I've ever used. It took five whole minutes for Siri to process the fact that I asked it a question. That was when I knew I wouldn't stay with those two dimwits ever again.

"Where were you? Date with Coach's daughter?" he asks, eyes focused on the television ahead but, I can see the glint of mischief beneath them.

"It wasn't a *date*. She needed some help with clothes, and we had to do our project." I shrug, toying with the hem of my sweatpants as I plop down next to him on the couch.

The blonde scoffs at my words, giving me a look but before he can say anything, I cut him off.

"Sorry about Vee."

Charlie tenses beside me before slowly relaxing, "It's fine. She's just a girl. My bad for snapping at practice."

I nod at the apology but still turn to look at him, "What happened with her?"

"The baseball team happened." He deadpans, jaw clenching and unclenching as he remains focused on the screen ahead.

"Oh."

"Uh-huh"

I'm about to say something else when the door swings open. Derek hurries in with Delilah sleeping peacefully in his arms, he speed walks past us to what I assume is Jace's room before coming back to the living room with three beer bottles in hand, replacing the toddler.

Charlie and I share a brief look just as he plops down in between us.

"How could she be such an asshole?" The dad frowns, taking a swig with a grimace. He hates beer. Derek once told me he'd rather drink cat pee than drink beer, yet here he is, gulping it down like a fish. "I apologize to her and then she acts like *I'm* some kind of monster!" he continues.

"Who—"

"And then she has the nerve to say she hopes I get fucked by a fish?!" he exclaims shooting to his feet, chest heaving as he looks down at our confused faces.

A fish? I mouth to Charlie; he sighs looking back up at our standing friend.

"She said and I quote *'que te folle un pez espada*[1] ' like who the hell says that to a parent?! I should give her a piece of my mind." Derek huffs, bawling his fists as he circles the living room.

Charlie is the first to stand, he pulls Derek back down to the couch as I make my way to the gaming console under the TV, turning it on.

"Would it be bad if I said it turned me on a little?" Derek asks sheepishly as I hand both him and Charlie a controller. I chuckle at the question, turning on a multiplayer game.

"Just means you're human." I smile.

"But just because you're horny doesn't mean you should go out fucking random fish. Stick to one fish and one fish only. Be a one fish man." Charlie butts in, popping some chips into his mouth.

Derek gasps, "You want me to actually *fuck a fish?*"

---

1. Que te folle un pez espada - fuck a swordfish (screw you) (Spanish

I roll my eyes at Derek and sigh, placing down the controller because there's just one fish in my sea, and I can't shake the fact that she might just be in trouble.

twenty-one

Cleo

MY MOTHER AND I have a strained relationship and it all started after she left my dad and I.

Lorelei Smith was my idol growing up. I did everything to appease the heart of my mother and looking back at all the time I wasted wanting her to love me makes me sick.

I figure skated for fourteen years to make my mother proud and we both know how that ended, but did you know that she hadn't congratulated me once in that time? I don't want to talk about it, but I also think you should know these things before I tell you about the brunch from hell that I'm currently at.

When I was seven, I won my first gold medal for figure skating. My mother was at the Vancouver Olympics that day—which was fine. I know that she's an important athlete but when I told her all about my win, her response was "mommy is busy, Ceej." It was fine the first time but after winning first place over 200 times in fourteen years, hearing the same response can be tiresome.

Gloria always congratulated me, though. She became the mother I never knew I needed, considering my own was still perfectly alive.

My mom and I have only ever agreed on one thing, me going to Brighton University just like her. And well, we all saw how that went.

"So..." Lorelei breaths out the word, looking down at the menu of Café Iteri, the industrial style café just ten minutes from campus.

The restaurant reminds me of an industrial greenhouse, with plants hanging from incandescent light fixtures in the ceiling. The walls of the restaurant are a mix of large windows, allowing in the natural light from outside, and mixture of black and gray brick in the spaces between. We're sat at a table along one of the windowed walls, seated in plush brown leathered armchairs.

I agreed to meet my mother here this morning after a nice long call from dad, begging me to just talk to her, after I'd ignored her messages.

Putting my parents against each other never ends well for any of us, especially my dad. He usually gets upset while mom gets temperamental. And me? I just become quiet during it all. Which sucks because my brain screams at me to say the most outlandish things the entire time.

"How has Summerfield been treating you?" Lorelei questions me. Her tone is bland as she continues scheming over the menu as if this isn't the first time the two of us have spoken to each other in six months.

A quiet chuckle is my only response as I follow in her footsteps and look over the extensive laminated paper.

Hmm... they have calamari. What café on a college campus serves calamari at noon?

"Why are we here, Lorelei?" I tilt my head at her, setting the menu down with a frown.

She texted last night while I was with Ryan and Tatum and told me to meet her here at noon without further explanation.

After she'd sent her last text, I tried ignoring her. I truly did. But then Blake texted me, that idiot. He'd sent me a random gif, you know... the one of the smiling Yorkie wearing a bow? Yeah, that. I can't lie and say he didn't pick up my somber mood, because he did. His text gave me a reason to laugh that night, it was like he knew how I was feeling even though we weren't near one another.

Then after Blake texted me, Dad called and in my happiest moments, I agreed to meet with my mother. And well, we all can see how that's going now.

The air between my mother and me feels like thick water. Almost like it is supposed to be fluid and easy to drink but there's just a strange thickness surrounding us that makes it hard to swallow whatever is going on between us.

"We're having this meeting because I miss my daughter—"

Bullshit.

"Do you miss me or does the press? I saw you posted up on Rodeo Drive with that drummer, Lorelei. Claiming you can't wait to expand your family. What family are you expanding? The last time I saw you was six months ago, *Mom,*" I snap, and for the first time in a long time, I feel secure to keep going. To fight back even though I don't think I'll be the one winning. I'm not usually one to disrespect authority but... I just... *Fuck.*

"Lower your tone," she hisses, looking around at the onlookers in the café. Lorelei leans in closer, her electric blue eyes are sharp and vibrant against her deep brown skin as they narrow on me.

"You will not disrespect me. Cole and I—"

"The drummer."

"My fiancé." The words are so quiet coming from her lips, I almost don't catch them.

But I do. I catch every single syllable.

My heart stutters and I'm taken aback. For just a moment, I feel like the little girl that was so excited to be in the same sport as her mom but so disappointed when she'd never see her mom in the bleachers cheering for her.

For me, skating was a way to connect with both of my parents. I didn't like playing hockey as much as I liked talking about it. But being on the ice and expressing myself through figure skating made me feel close to the woman that gave me life.

If I knew then what I did now, I would have told six-year-old CJ that no matter what you do... Mommy will always be too busy for you.

"Fiancé?" I croak, my throat dry. I reach for the peach tea I'd ordered and take a sip. Fuck, I should've ordered something stronger. *Who am I kidding?* There's not a drink strong enough in this world to keep me from feeling how my mother makes me feel.

"We got engaged in May." She shrugs with a small smile before holding out her left hand. A white gold band with a simple yet stunning teardrop diamond sits perfectly on my mothers manicured hand.

"Congratulations," I choke out, making brief eye contact with her.

She coughs, her eyes darting back to the table and just as she's about to speak up, the waiter comes over. My mother orders a club sandwich with extra tomato, her go-to, and I order a Chicken Francois, which is basically a fancy way of saying fried chicken and French toast.

We sit in silence for a few minutes before she clears her throat. "Cole has two kids, Ceej. I want you to meet them in a few weeks. We can all go to New York for Thanksgiving, and you can see Gran—"

I tune her out as she continues spewing nonsense about the future. If my mother knew me at all, she'd know that I would never step foot into New York City again. That place can go to Hell for all I care.

"I don't think—"

"And then after that you and Marcelo could probably patch things up and—"

My breath hitches in my throat.

Have you ever had the wind knocked out of you with just a single blow? I have.

When I was fourteen, I went to a concert with Jace. None of our parents knew that we went away to D.C. for the night to go to a concert, but we did. The concert was held at this tiny club downtown that literally everyone goes to, its standing room and barricade only. I'd been so close to the front, I could practically touch the singer when a behemoth of a woman got knocked into me and next thing you know, I'm practically dying from being out of breath beside a petrified Jace Heart.

That's what it feels like every time someone brings up my ex-boyfriend, Marcelo Rivers.

Marce—Marcelo and I were like a New York power couple. We did everything together. Fashion week, Hockey games, F1 races; you think it, we probably did it. Everyone in the state, probably even the country, knew about us.

He and I were inseparable for almost two years until December 4th. It was puppy love for me until the rose-colored lenses faded away and I caught him shooting up Nandrolone in his bathroom just before a game with Summerfield.

I loved him so much that I couldn't process it. Sometimes, I still can't. Marcelo is the most beloved person at Brighton University, the most favored player, and best-looking guy on campus. I couldn't fathom the idea of the person that I thought I knew the best doing something I despised the most. And it wasn't like he needed it. He was good on and off the ice.

But when I caught him, I realized that you never truly know someone. You just know the many faces that they like to put on for the world. We see the masks of their perfect selves while they hide their true vile nature under.

I hadn't meant to say that I would tell anyone, not aloud at least. But the words spilled out of me faster than I could process and before I knew it, I'd made a deal with the devil for two secrets that cost me more than I'd ever known.

I can feel myself slipping into the darkness of my past and suddenly I'm outside the girls and my apartment. I don't even remember leaving the café, but I guess that's what happens when your past gut punches you before 2 p.m.

When I enter the apartment, I spot someone on the couch and heave a breath as I stalk towards the freezer.

No ice cream. No popsicles... What kind of Hell-hole am I living in?

Frowning deeply, I turn to the pantry. Wine... Whiskey... Tequila? Yep. That's what I need.

I always feel like this whenever Marcelo is mentioned and it's not even because I miss him. No, I hope Marcelo Rivers is living his absolute best life, stepping on five LEGOs and three charger boxes a day. Instead, I feel like this because in a way, I'm mourning.

Mourning the woman, I used to be before life showed its ugliness and dealt me a bad hand.

"Cleo?" the voice is distorted behind me, kind of like it's been submerged into water.

Is it getting hot in here? I need sugar. Where are the donuts?

Soft fingers clasp around my wrist, they're cold and familiar and before I know it, I'm being squeezed into a hug. The aroma of peaches, vanilla, and warm patchouli engulf me from every angle.

I let myself fall into the pit that I've dug and let it out. I cry for the girl I was at six and the one at 18. But most of all, I cry for the 20-year-old I am right now, feeling all these things tenfold.

Before I know it, we're on the couch—Georgia, Sienna, Denver, and me. I don't know when Denver got here but I'm thankful for her presence. Her warmth is needed at times like this.

When I've calmed down a bit, Georgia sighs, placing a single cup of hot tea in front of me.

"I hate to push, CJ... I really do," She starts, sitting beside me. Her eyebrows are knitted together as if I'm a puzzle she's struggling to solve. I curl into myself a bit at her examination. "But we need to know what happened between Marcelo and you. I've been around your panic attacks about your mom, and they've never been *this* bad. So, what happened?" she asks, chewing on her bottom lip, her eyes darting behind me to Sienna and then back to me.

I sigh. How do I tell them about this? Would they hate me too if they knew? Would they call me an idiot for trusting someone so much? Fuck—

"I..."

The girls lean closer. I gulp, steadying myself trying to find the right words.

"You got this...take your time." Denver's voice is probably the softest I've ever heard it. She's looking up at me from the floor, her hand holding mine almost like if she'd let go, I'd disappear.

"Whatever I tell you, please just know that I was stupid, and I would never make that mistake ever again." My hands are suddenly much more interesting than this conversation. Have these freckles always been here?

"We'd *never* judge you. You're our sister, if you hurt, *we* hurt." Sienna encourages, giving me a reassuring smile.

"Well...um, two years ago Marce—Marcelo and I started dating and everything was fine. We were fine. You guys saw us, we were so h–happy." My voice cracks as my cheeks heat up.

Georgia squeezes my knee and nods with a small smile. The action gives me just a bit more strength, but I can't look at my friends as I lay down the most embarrassing pieces of myself out in the open.

"Then on December 4th, we had a party at his place. You know, it was typical Brighton shit. They'd throw parties before big games, and they were playing SFU and... Fuck." My throat catches, snot rolls from my nose before I hastily wipe it away.

When did I start crying? I don't cry, not really.

I sigh. "Everyone was looking for Marce...Marcelo and I went to find him. He—he was shooting up steroids and I just flipped. I was hysterical and he was angry, and it was just—"

I pause as flashes of that night speed through my brain.

"It was so... *bad*. I told him I would tell someone and that was the dumbest thing I could've ever said because then he... um. He brought up our... tape." I gulp, my body shakes as I look up, peering at my friends.

Georgia's mouth forms an 'O' as her breathing shakes, she clasps my free hand—Denver and Sienna look murderous and I feel like the biggest idiot in the world.

"I knew that he'd recorded us, and I trusted him. I *trusted* Marcelo so much that I never thought he'd throw it in my face." My lips are drying as I speak, the water from my tears drink my body arid.

"He said that if I were to tell anyone then he'd drop it—the tape, I mean. I didn't believe him. Marcelo bluffs about everything. But then, I told Karmen—my roommate...um. And well, everyone slowly began to ice me out. It was so hard to talk about *anything* when I went from being the most liked to the most hated all within the span of a week."

Sienna scoffs from behind me, I feel her as she scoots into my back and wraps her arms around my waist. She's warm, I'm thankful for her touch as she lays her head on my back whispering quiet curses.

"And then he and I came to an agreement that for four thousand dollars, this would be over—stupid, I know. But it was over for about a week until... until... the texts started. So, I left. And they've been texting me from unknown numbers ever since. I don't think it's him though, he'd never threaten me—"

"He threatened to expose your most intimate moments! Don't stand up for him." Georgia scoffs, running a shaky hand through her waves.

"Yeah...well, he wouldn't harass me."

This catches Denver's attention. "And how exactly do you know that?"

"He's not the type, when he gets what he wants he leaves you alone. Besides, he's tried to reach out to me before—"

"HE WHAT?!" Sienna jumps up from behind me, crossing over Denver and straight into my line of focus. "Give me his number," she demands.

"Huh?"

"Give me that bitch's number! He's been fucking you over for almost *a year*, Cleo. I will kill that motherfucker—"

"Calm down, Si Si... Don't go all *The Bride* on us." Georgia sighs exasperatedly as she leans back into the couch.

Denver eyes me for a long seconds before stalking towards the kitchen. Moments later, she arrives back with my phone and a bottle of Vodka.

"Is this the reason why you've been inactive?" she asks, opening the phone up. We all shared passwords in case of emergencies.

I nod.

"Well let's show those motherfuckers that they can't fuck with you. You are way too bright to let someone as sinister as them dim your light. Believe me." Denver's voice wavers as she holds the bottle up to me, I look up at her tilting my head slightly confused.

"Tonight, we show the world just how bright Cleo Jones is."

TWENTY-TWO

Cleo

Blake (Wilder)

Cinderella where art thou?

@ the ferris wheel with the feral one

Princess?

Just asked Georgia where you are, she says you're missing the first day??

I'm otw. Be prepared to smile for me.

TWENTY-THREE

Cleo

"YOU ARE THE LIGHT OF MY LIFE, MY STARLIGHT—"

"Wait, that's my line!" Georgia shouts over the loud music as Denver groans.

"Well, find a new one." The brunette shrugs, plopping down next to me on the couch. I sniff a laugh as Georgia pouts, moving down the frog face mask she'd been wearing.

After we'd all spent way too long talking about my past, Denver decided that we'd do karaoke and face masks. She said that karaoke was the best way to let out toxic energy and it was the only way to feel better, so we did exactly that.

We're now on song four of Lord knows how many; Denver and Georgia decided to sing Starlight by Astra and since Astra is our cousin, Zola, Sienna and I decided to sit this one out.

"How am I supposed to find a new line?"

Pounding on the front door halts their bickering. We all pause, eyeing one another.

"I didn't order take out." Sienna frowns as the person on the other side knocks again. I can't help but smile at her, she looks so adorable with her face mask. We're all some sort of animal as requested by Georgia. She keeps a ton of different sheet masks in her bathroom, so she's a frog while Sienna is a penguin, Denver is a duck, and I'm a piglet.

"Are those the strippers I ordered?" Denver bites her bottom lip, smiling coyly. Georgia scrunches her face and smacks Denver's arm.

"Ow! *Pinche*[1] —"

Knock!

Knock! Knock!

"Is no one going to let the strippers in?" I chuckle softly, dusting myself off as I stride towards the front door and like an idiot, I open it without checking.

But seriously, who checks the front door these days? Usually it's a delivery guy—

"Am I under arrest offi—*Blake?!*"

"Hi." His voice is deep and soft all at once, I can feel the girls' eyes on us as mine slowly meet soft blue ones.

Blake Wilder is standing at my front door, dressed in jeans, a white tee, and a backwards cap. The most basic outfit a man can wear and yet my stomach does something weird. As my eyes scan Blake, I realize he's doing the same, drinking me in like cold water on a hot summer day. I shift in my spot and clear my throat.

"Hey? What're you doing here?" I ask, standing just a little straighter.

Blake busts out the cheekiest grin I've ever seen on a guy, smiling with his whole body as his ears tint red.

"You didn't show up at Fall Fest, so..." he trails off and it's then that I notice the two boxes of LEGOs in his hands. A LEGO flower bouquet and a pink LEGO Mercedes.

Is this what it feels like to have your heart burst?

Is this what it's like to have someone think about you?

We stare at each other, our eyes intertwining in a never-ending slow dance. He knew that I wanted to go to Fall Fest and when I didn't show up for Day One, he brought his favorite activity to me to make sure I'm okay. Someone marry Blake Wilder because if you don't, I will.

Matter of fact, I take back what I said.

I'll marry him myself.

"Oh! I have these too, I asked Georgia if you were okay and when she said you weren't, I figured you could use something sweet to pick yourself up." He grins

---

1. Pinche- fucking

sheepishly, my heart spirals as he pulls out a bag with The Sugar Hole's logo on it.

Hello, ovaries? Please be ready for fertilization because I'm going to jump this man's bones—

Too much?

Yep...

Way too much.

"¿Por qué estás aquí?" [2] Denver asks suddenly close to me as she looks over my shoulder at her cousin.

Blake rolls his eyes playfully, still smiling broadly as he responds. "I know you're happy to see me, Seattle, but I'm here for Cinderella, not Drizella."

She reels back, poking her tongue in her cheek before stepping in closer to my back.

"Say it closer to my face this time." She clenches her teeth as he tilts his head back in laughter.

"If Cleo lets me in then I will." He sobers his laugh, adjusting the LEGO box sets to his hip.

When I let Blake inside, Denver mumbles something about strippers yet again before stalking off to the living room where Sienna and Georgia watch with wide eyes.

"I didn't know which set you'd want to do, so I bought two of pinkest ones I could find..." He says, scratching the back of his neck. I'm about to swoon myself to death because of this guy and I hate it.

What was rule number one again?

No boys? Or was it no more Buldak noodles after 12? Regardless, some rules are getting broken.

"She'll take both!" Georgia shouts, jumping over the couch to the foyer where Blake and I stand, staring at one another like a pair of fools.

She smiles brightly under her face mask as she confiscates the donut bag before giving me a not-so subtle wink as she makes her way to the kitchen.

---

2. Por qué estás aquí - Why are you here? (Spanish)

Some days, I'm happy to have an open floor plan apartment but today isn't the day. I shift my weight on to my right leg at the feeling of all eyes on us, watching our next move.

"Let's go to my room," I offer. Blake's eyes widened as he looks down at me almost to say, 'are you sure?', but I don't give him the time to voice his concerns as I shuffle him to the hall where my room is.

We're almost completely in my bedroom when Sienna, my lovely yet enraging cousin, shouts "Go get that dick, sis!"

We're sitting cross-legged on my floor, hovering over the pink LEGO-Mercedes with Twisted Vipers new song, Wreck U, playing softly on my Bluetooth speaker.

I steal a glance at Blake and smile at the sheer look of concentration on his face. His eyebrows are knit together as he tinkers with the four-pronged piece of plastic.

We've gotten about a quarter through the building process, neither of us bothering to speak as we help each other.

I pass him the next needed piece as he nods his thanks, humming aloud to the track. The moment is comfortable, he's working and I'm watching, soaking in every inch of his builder nature.

Blake clears his throat, smirking as he focuses on the pieces in his hands.

"Take a picture, it'll last long—"

I snap a photo immediately.

What? He told me too...

Blake shakes his head at my antics, smiling softly. I catch the small hint of red on his ears and grin as I take another picture, saving it as his contact photo.

"So, what happened earlier with your mom?" he asks, looking me directly in the eyes, ignoring my previous antics.

I gulp as I'm caught off guard. "How did you—"

"Cleo, I don't know if you've noticed this but when you talk, I actually listen." He chuckles, sucking in a sharp breath as a part of the wheel he'd been tinkering with collapses.

"Oh...um..."I laugh shakily, Blake places a soft hand on my knee, still paying close attention to the piece in his hand while also being in tune with me. It's the small push I hadn't known was needed and so I spill my guts.

I tell him about my figure skating history and how it was all for my mother's validation. I talk about how much it killed me as a kid when my parents divorced but about how safe and loved Ryan and Gloria made me feel. Then, I tell him about Marcelo and me, not all of it but I tell him that we broke up last December and since then my mother and I have barely talked. Lastly, I bring up my mother's engagement to a drummer who is a quarter of her age and the fact that I'm more than terrified to meet him and his two other kids.

Through it all, Blake listens. A few seconds into my first round of ranting, he sets down the LEGOs and gives me his undivided attention. When I get to the parts about my mother, he softly squeezes my knees as if to say, 'Don't worry, you're safe' and let me know he's here.

He's attentive and patient and so freaking kind... *I think I might like him.*

And that thought alone scares me more than all other things because liking a boy isn't simple. It's getting your hopes up in the faith that he'll reciprocate those feelings. It's choosing to give your heart to someone with zero knowledge of how they feel.

And fuck, I hate this.

No boys was the rule and it seems like I'm breaking a promise not only to my dad but to myself as well.

"Hey...look at me, you okay?" His voice is gentle as he cups my cheek in his hand. My belly flips as he circles it with his thumb, his eyes remind me of a calm breeze as he gives me all his focus.

"I'm fine." I breathe out quietly like the lovestruck chicken I am.

Blake gives me a small smile and nods. "Good, now for phase two."

"Phase two?" I tilt my head, furrowing my brows at him.

"Movie night!" he practically yells, jumping up from the floor with a triumphant smile.

I try and fail to suppress a giggle as he jogs over to my gaming center, grabbing the remote for the TV. Blake turns on the TV to a random princess movie, kicks off his shoes and turns off the light on my nightstand. He looks down at me, still on the floor expectantly as if I'm a hitch in his plan.

"You're needed in the bed, Princess." He chuckles as he plops down on my very neatly made pink flower print bed.

I cringe as he makes himself comfortable, and I guess he sees the look on my face because he freezes with his hands up.

"Zero funny business, I swear!"

I muffle my laugh at him and make my way over to the bed, climbing on top of the covers.

"Platonic cuddle? You sound like you need a hug," he offers.

With a small nod, I sigh as he wraps his arms around my waist, pulling me into him. And just like that, I'm in bed with a 6"4 hockey player 'platonically cuddling' me because I had a bad day.

Twenty-Four

Cleo

"They're so cute..."

"This is actually fucking gross."

"Rise n' shine, Lovebirds!" Someone shouts, my heart races and almost instantly, I'm jumping out of the bed. Or so, I think I am? But instead of making it out of the bed, I'm tugged back into the wall.

"Five more minutes, Mom..." a masculine voice mutters from behind me, I go rigid.

Blake?

[1] "¡Levántate estúpido!" a sharp voice breaks through his monster hold as Blake jolts awake, his eyes unfocused and bedhead shift from me in his arms to the three crazy women peering over us.

My core tightens at the lazy lopsided grin he slides my way. It's like we're in our own world, staring at one another until a cough breaks through our small universe.

"*Ew...* It's you." He sneers, obviously talking to Denver before laying back down, tugging me into him.

We both freeze at the action, seemingly noticing how easy it felt between us as well as his lack of clothing at the same time.

"Umm Blake..."

"Yeah..." he mutters, letting me go.

---

1. Levántate estúpido- Get up, Stupid! (Spanish)

That wasn't what I wanted but I guess it was what I needed.

Distance.

We need distance.

Georgia must've seen the thought making its way into my brain because she turns on her heels and proceeds to usher Sienna and Denver out of my room.

I turn back to Blake, his face is hidden in his palms, but I can make out the faint redness coloring his cheeks.

"Am I going to see you later?" he asks, his voice muffled by his hands.

"Yeah... We can meet at the concession stand and then go into the fair together if you want." I shrug as if the thought of meeting a boy at a festival doesn't have the weird moths in my stomach awakening.

The last time I'd went to a festival of any kind with a guy, it ended with him having a bloody nose at the hands of Jace Heart. The guy was a dick, and Jace, my sweetest most caring friend, handed him his ass. Respectfully. Sorry, Connor.

But that was high school.

Since then, I haven't been to any festival of any magnitude as a date—

But this isn't a date or anything.

Simply me going to the Fall Fest with my friend (who I may or may not be crushing on) to do our end of term project together. *Nothing big.*

I watch in silent admiration at the way Blake puts his clothes on; he'd found one of Jace's hoodies in my closet and frowned at it. It's then that I notice that he's doing the exact same thing that I'd done when I first entered his room, two months ago.

He's looking over my desk, softly smiling at pictures I have laid out and brushing his fingers over my donut shaped plushy.

"So, you like these little stuffed things a lot?" he asks, holding up Pickles, my stuffed Yorkie from Ryan. Ryan got it for me after we'd brought home a small Yorkie from the side of the road. We were nine and that was also the year that both of us learned that pickles taste so much better with Old Bay seasoning, so we decided to name her after it—the pickles, I mean. Not Old Bay. That would be such an odd name for a dog.

The sentiment has me smiling and without speaking, I nod at Blake.

He chews on his bottom lip as if he's deep in thought before those bright eyes of his perk up. "If I win one of these tonight, you have to make a deal with me."

I tilt my head at him, prompting him to continue.

"There's no fun in telling you about it right now, Princess. Just give me a yes or no." He shrugs, indifferently, but I can see the hint of excitement hidden behind the light flecks of his gray irises, so without thinking, I agree.

If Blake Wilder wins me a plushy tonight, I will make a deal with the Wild Card himself.

TWENTY-FIVE

Blake

"Dude, would you stop pacing? You're giving me hives." Braxton scoffs, looking up from his phone. I stop pacing for a small second to look at him before continuing.

Cleo said that she and the girls would meet us at the concessions stand at 7:30 and I've been a sweaty mess ever since. This year, SFU has pulled out all the stops for Fall Fest. Usually, it's a three-day event where you can do apple picking, hayrides around campus, and pumpkin carving.

Basic fall shit, if you ask me.

But last year the school bought more land and decided to make it into a fairground that's also open to the public. So now there's a students only side where you can do cozy fall activities with your roommates and then walk over to the fairgrounds where the carnival games and rides are.

"Daddy... Uncle Lake is sweating..." Delilah whispers rather loudly to her father, and I stop pacing to chuckle at her. She smiles as I make a silly face but I'm instantly back to my pacing when she turns to look at her dad again.

"Dude, chill out, you're scaring the kid!" Jace laughs as he approaches our group with Ricardo Ruiz and Alec. Ricardo's our backup goalie after Derek. He's usually a quiet guy who hangs out with Alec and his little brother, Rico, who's also on the team. Rico plays offense and has one of the best slapshots I've seen out of any of the sophomore guys so far.

My eyebrows shoot to my hairline as Ricardo approaches us with a smile beside Alec. I don't think I've *ever* seen him smile. Weird.

"Hey, dude!" Charlie exclaims, ever the cheerful one as he dabs up Ricardo.

Ricardo's smile is almost timid as he reciprocates the gesture with Charlie, going down the line with the rest of the guys and me.

"So, what are we waiting on—"

"That would be me! Sorry we're so late. G couldn't find her keys and then I couldn't find mine and Si Si left her room key so we all had to search for it but then I realized that I had it and well—" Cleo breathes, standing in front of me. Her chest rises fast as if to catch her breath from the rambling she'd done, "Hi."

She's dressed completely different from her usual style of pink dresses and rompers with matching bows.

Cleo's wearing baggy, low-rise jeans that complement her toned body super well, a short baggy crop top that's navy blue and white with the words COSMIC across her chest and paired it with navy blue and white *sneakers*—weird, but I like it. I look her over from head to toe and smirk as she does a little spin obviously catching me check her out, but there's still something missing.

I raise an eyebrow at her as she tilts her head in confusion. "Bow. Where's the—"

She holds her right middle finger up directly to my nose and I snort as her eyes go wide. She drops her hand immediately looking down at the ground.

"I blew out my hair earlier so I didn't want to mess it up by tying it back, so I wore my bow ring as the next best option." She shrugs and I nod because who's Cleo Jones if she doesn't wear her signature bows *somewhere*?

Sienna, Georgia, Denver and Ryan approach us. But I can't take my eyes off the bow-loving girl in front of me.

Cleo has this magnetic pull to her; no matter who you are, you're drawn to her.

Or at least I am.

We spend about five minutes discussing what rides we'd go on first and I'm about to make a suggestion when the bow-loving girl beside me tugs me away from our talkative friends.

Cleo directs me through the maze of people surrounding the game stands and pauses in front of a game where you have to shoot darts to win a prize. I groan because we all know how *good* she is at this type of stuff but I secretly love that this is the first thing she wants us to do.

In a universe surrounded by cutesy little games where the *guy* wins the girl a prize, Cleo Jones creates her own planet and dominates every single one. She wins *me* prizes and pinches my cheeks when they heat up.

For a moment, I think she might feel the same way about me as I do her. I don't let the thought leave my mind, but instead, I bask in it. I'm living vicariously through the version of me in another universe, on a *way* better planet, where Cleo "Princess" Jones is in love with me.

Is love too much? Or am I just an idiot who has the biggest, fattest crush on a girl that I can't have?

Who knows and who cares? In the wise words of Ziye' Taylor (some author that my sister won't stop talking about), "Y.O.L.O... either do or die wishing you did."

That sounds suicidal... but it's accurate for how I feel right about now.

"Okay, Boy Scout, let's see if you can redeem yourself from that horrendous game of darts you just played," Cleo chuckles to herself as we approach a "football" game.

The object of the game being you have to hurl footballs into four tiny holes to win a prize which seems easy enough. But I fucking suck at football. Why else do you think I stick with hockey?

"I'll even grant one of your *many* wishes if you succeed!" She mocks, her tone incredulous but there's a hint of amusement beneath her eyes that I won't take for granted.

I'm gonna fucking win that wish.

Cleo still has two left from our last game, and I'll be damned if I lose another chance at getting a free Cleo Jones wish.

The first two balls must have missed the memo however, because instead of going in one of the four holes, they go so far left that I almost hit the poor stall attendant.

"Sorry," I mutter sheepishly, the feeling of my ears reddening further embarrasses me.

The attendant chuckles to himself before granting me yet *another* football with a small discreet wink.

With every fiber of my being, I throw the ball and I'm so nervous I close my eyes because I'd rather not see the look of shame on such a pretty girl's face.

I don't open my eyes when the bells around us chime, or when the stall attendant lets out a low whistle. No. I open them when Cleo Jones' little body tackles me, squeezing me so tight that the air leaves my lungs for a moment too long. Had she been her brother's size, the two of us would be far, far away based on her tackling hug alone.

"Oh, my fuck! You did it, I had so much faith in you!" She beams, brown eyes dancing with excitement. Cleo's legs tighten around my torso as she squeezes her arms around my neck tighter.

I give her a look as she rolls her eyes.

"So maybe I *didn't* believe in you... but you still fucking won with your eyes closed! If I'd known you could do shit like that with your eyes closed, I would've—Never mind." She pauses and it's like she comes to her senses all at once. Cleo removes herself from me awkwardly and clears her throat.

"Got too excited?" I tease, because who am I if not a tease?

She lowers her head, and I can feel her smiling before she looks back up at me with a schooled expression. "I'm going to the bathroom... When I get back, I'll grant your wish," She mumbles before scurrying off like puppy with her tail tucked between her legs.

I'm silently laughing as I follow behind Cleo holding the four plushies she'd won plus the little otter I'd won for her, and I stand outside of the bathroom waiting for her, like the true gentleman that I am.

I'm on my phone, scrolling mindlessly through my camera roll and I can smell her before I hear her. I'm immediately annoyed as the scents of cheap perfume and burnt extensions crowd my senses.

Chelsea presses her breasts against my arm and plucks the otter plushy from my fingers before I can get a word out.

"I missed you, Blakey," She coos, toying with the *literal* toy that I'm supposed to give to my future girlfriend.

Yes, I know that I'm moving too fast and no I quite literally do not give a fuck. In my head the princess and I are married with three kids and live near a fucking beach in California. *Sue me.*

I reach for the otter and groan as Chelsea reels back causing me to fall into her; to the wondering eye, it'd look like we were embracing one another, and *yuck.* I would never—okay, that's a lie... *I have.* But I would *never* do *that* again. She gave good head, but she clearly doesn't use her brain. If she did, she'd understand that I could do without seeing her face for the next *millennium.*

Chelsea frowns as I snatch the otter from her greasy fingers and dust it off. I'm probably going to have to get Cleo a new fucking plushy because she touched it. Fuck, I don't think I can win that damn game again. That shot was beginner's luck!

"Why are you acting like this towards me, *Blakey?* I thought we had something special!" Chelsea's nasally voice whines as she latches onto my arm like a pest.

I try and fail to shake her off and I hate this because Cleo can come back any moment and I would honestly hate myself If I upset her.

"You gave me head, Chelsea, and then somehow fell asleep naked in my bed. It's not like it was the most passionate sex I've ever had," I blurt out and immediately feel like shit because Chelsea's green eyes go sad for a second and I think she'll take the hint, but no.

Fucking Moaning Myrtle smiles at me and I mean *properly* smiles. With all her teeth and shit.

"So you remember my lips on your cock?"

Fucking delusional ass—

"Is everything alright?" the voice of an angel calls out to me in a tone I can't quite register. It's not sad or mad but it's not too happy either. It's a tone that makes my skin crawl because I feel like I'm in trouble with my mom when I did nothing wrong. My eyes widen when Cleo fixates on me with a look of pure steel.

She's mad?

"Who is this bitch?"

My head reels back and I immediately stumble to Cleo's side, positioning myself in front of her.

"Watch your mouth."

"But... But Blakey!" Chelsea blubbers, eyes wide with shock.

"Watch your fucking mouth when you talk about her." My teeth are clenched and I'm so fucking livid that I don't think I can calm myself down.

I mean, who does Chelsea *Myrtle* think she is calling Cleo out of her name? How dare she? I mean seriously, Cleo, of all people?

Cold, soft fingers tug on my upper bicep from behind, the feeling sends little shockwaves up my spine and I know it's *her*.

Cleo.

She lets out a soft chuckle from behind me and I smile because I know she finds this whole situation funny even though it's pissing me so far off I can't see straight.

"Let's just go. You still have one wish to cash in," she says, looking up at me with the most beautiful brown eyes.

Most people think that blue or green eyes are the most magnificent but in reality, it's brown. Brown eyes have a vast range from being as dark as charcoal to light like warm almonds. Cleo's eyes remind me of a tawny owl. They're large and wide and full of life but also a shade of brown that is so light in the sun it's like a caramel but during the evening it's dark and rich in color.

I'm *obsessed* with her eyes.

And so instead of giving Chelsea Myrtle any more of my energy, I look down at the girl who's been invading my mind and smile. "Hungry?"

She nods, grabbing a hold of my bicep just a little tighter, shifting closer to me.

And without looking back at the gaping blonde in front of me, we turn on our heels—my bicep in her small cold hand—and make our way to the food stalls.

TWENTY-SIX

Cleo

I MADE A DEAL with a backwards-cap, dad-clothes-wearing devil. Blake looks down at me with a smile of complete and utter mischief and I know that I've sparked a deal with a man who has no limit.

My skin crawls as memories of a man from my past and how I sold him my soul in exchange for a handful of trust, filters through my mind.

I shudder and I can feel myself spiraling. Why did I come here tonight? Have I screwed myself over *again?*

Let's face it, Cleo. In the last two years, you've done that more times than you can count.

Blake steps further into my space, his warm scent crowds my senses as he looks down at me. His eyes are soft, yet mischievous and it doesn't take a genius to know that this man is dangerous.

Not in the sexy stalker or assassin way but in the heartthrob, detrimental to my ovaries and emotions kind of way.

His blue eyes sparkle as he leans in close to my ear, his warm minty breath lingers in the space between us.

"Oh, sweet, *sweet* princess, you've just made a deal with the devil." He grins mischievously before clasping his large hand around my own, dragging me around the vast fairground. I don't protest as Blake records me with our project's camcorder as I fail to hit a target in one of the fair games.

"YES! FINALLY A GAME CLEO JONES CAN'T—*Oh, come on!* How'd you make that?" he groans, licking the smile off his lips as he looks down at me.

Blake can't help the chuckle that escapes his mouth as he looks over the pin I'd just knocked down.

From the corner of my eye, I see a flash of pink rush past that catches my attention. I know who it is before I turn my head to see Sienna running away from Derek, the *hot ass* goalie on the Hockey team. He's holding a small toddler who's pointing at my running cousin. I raise a brow at the interaction before focusing back on the stunned male beside me. He gives me a small smile before wrapping his arm around my shoulder, I pause at the action, heart pounding against my chest.

Are we close enough to do things like this now? Is he my new "guy friend", or whatever Dad calls my *situationships*? Instead of dwelling on the thought of my father and the rule we'd set for me before attending SFU, I relax under Blakes touch as he guides us away from the stands to the large spinning death wheel in the middle of the festival.

The Ferris wheel.

Now, I'm no scaredy cat. But I *do* have a completely *rational* fear of metal rides that can be built overnight in the middle of a shopping mall parking lot—albeit this is a school and not a mall—the notion still stands.

Blake must sense my hesitancy because he chuckles.

"You scared, Princess?" he teases, and I roll my eyes because me, scared? *Never!* Just a little... Weary of my safety is all.

"Do I *look* scared, Wilder?"

He pauses, letting go of me and stepping back to appraise me. Blake's icy blue eyes rove over my body as he licks the corner of his lips before taking his plump bottom lip between his teeth.

"You look beautiful, Jones. But you also look scared shit—"

I smack his arm and turn on my heels to the metal wheel, my stomach and heart roaring at me to back down. My stupid head on the other hand refuses to walk away from such a challenge.

So, instead of walking the other way like a smart person, I walk *towards* the Ferris wheel with Blake in tow. I can feel his excitement from behind me as the operator lets us onto the rickety cart. My stomach drops as the cart moves sideways once Blake sits on the same side as me, clearly tilting us.

"You're too big," I say through gritted teeth and immediately wish I hadn't as I can feel the smirk he's laid on.

"That's not the first time I've been told that." He chuckles, hoisting up his phone, snatching a picture of the setting sun in the distance as we slowly climb to the top of the Ferris wheel.

"Well, let me *redact* my words... Your fat ass is making us tilt."

Blake lets out the most guttural laugh I've ever heard in my life, doubling over, letting his laughter fully consume him.

Blake Wilder has the type of laughter that halts the world, it's infectious and beautiful so much so that I don't want to make any noise because if I do, I worry that I won't be able to hear him as well as before.

He wipes a stray tear from his eyes and settles back into the seat, pulling out the camcorder from his pocket.

"What do you love about life, Cleo Jones?" He asks, still smiling from his burst of laughter and I know it's one of our interview questions but the way that he looks at me from above the camera has my stomach flipping and suddenly I'm a nervous teenager on her first date.

"I love that every day is different, and that we're never as young as we are right now. I love the idea of everyday being an adventure and the idea of one day growing old with the person I love. Maybe we'd have a kid, or three, or a fucking soccer team because who doesn't love a large family?" I ask and don't realize I'm rambling or the fact that Blake's focus is completely on me, the camera long gone in his lap as he watches me with complete fascination and adoration. "I want a large family, y'know since I have one already. I love that life gives us ample opportunities to seize the moment and savor everything it has to offer. I love that I get a restart every day and do something different, something better. I love the fact that I'm here doing shit I'd never thought I'd do last year like riding a Ferris wheel because the world didn't end when I was 19 and life goes on. I love that you're here with me and I love the fact... that I'm rambling..." I trail off, noticing the look on his face.

He's much closer now and I don't want him to move away. I want him closer to me. Blake's gaze searches my eyes softly, like a tender caress before falling to my parted lips, and then back up to my eyes.

Perfect execution of the triangle method, I will say.

His voice is soft yet hoarse all at once and I melt into a puddle as he whispers, "Can I kiss you, Princess?"

I might orgasm from his gentleness alone, and instead of responding, I pull his face to mine and melt into him as our lips crash together.

The kiss is both magnetic and exotic as our tongues dance together like the sun and the moon, star-crossed lovers that have been kept apart for far too long only to see each other during the day. But it's nearly nighttime and yet he's the sun that's still in the sky taking me whole in his mouth.

As our tongues dance, my stomach warms, and a crowd cheers. I think I'm hearing things until the cheers grow louder; we part only for a second, eyes locked on one another. Glowing orbs catch our attention at the same time and I gasp as little golden lanterns light the sky. And it's in this moment that I realize that I don't want this to end and that's what fucking terrifies me because where there's puck stars, there's drama.

I gulp as we reach the ground, I practically climb over him to escape the death wheel. I leave the bewildered man behind and want to curse myself for the action because *fuck*, I might *actually* like him, and I am *so* fucked if I do.

I send a margarita emoji (otherwise known as our SOS text) to my friends, they're quick to respond with the same. Looks like we're all in some deep shit.

They're waiting for me at the exit and bless their souls because I don't think I'd survive facing Blake right now. My stomach churns as we make our way to Sienna's car and I feel like I've made the biggest mistake of my life as I leave behind the one guy I've liked a *little* too much for the first time in a year.

TWENTY-SEVEN

Blake

AFTER CLEO KISSED ME and then became a track star before my very eyes, I found myself at 88UP, the off-campus bar where most of the SFU and Laughlin University kids hang out.

Tonight, I'm docked at the bar, nursing my fourth Manhattan, *wondering where the fuck I went wrong.*

She kissed me for fucks sake! But why does it feel all wrong? Was she uncomfortable? Was I a bad kiss—I'll stop that thought right there. I'm an *amazing* kisser.

A large figure plops down in the seat beside me, the guy already smelling like he'd had a shot—or four—as he turns to me, smiling lazily.

I recognize Ryan Jones almost immediately. He's a huge, light skin black guy with insane tattoos and a model-like face—Tu's words, not mine, but he is fucking gorgeous. Ryan gives me a sad watery smile, looking exactly how I feel. He turns back to the bar, waving down Nova, tonight's bartender. She's a student at SFU and I'm pretty sure we hooked up last year—that's beside the point... She walks over to us with a large smile, clearly happy to see the captains of both the hockey and football teams tonight.

"Jones..." She breathes, bending over on the bar as she looks him up and down quite disgustingly.

Ryan scoffs at the action and waves her off... And I mean that in the literal sense, he holds up his left hand and lazily waves her off.

Nova scoffs as she walks away, getting another bartender to service the jock. He orders four shots of vodka, I give him a lazy smile downing the one he'd offered me before turning to the man.

"Why are women so fucking confused?" I slur, resting my head on my hand.

"Tell me about it, brother." Ryan sighs, downing his second shot with ease.

"I mean first they're hot then they're cold. Yes, then fucking no," I mumble.

"In then out? Motherfucker, are we singers?" He grins lazily and I chuckle because *fuck* his sister has me in a bar, quoting some singer to him.

Ryan takes a long inhale before letting out a deep sigh. "I completely get you, dude. Why do they have to be so complicated? Like do you love me or not? Do you just want to fuck me like I'm some cum slut? Am I a boy toy or a boyfriend— Wait not that one… She doesn't do relationships." He frowns dramatically downing another shot.

Cum slut? What type of freaky—

"Why is it that every girl on this fucking campus wants me? And the one woman that I want to be with can't be fucking bothered?" He slurs, eyes hooded as he looks over at me.

"Preach, brother." I raise my glass, downing it and missing my mouth by a little but I don't care. Why should I care? Cleo obviously doesn't.

"I should text her, shouldn't I?" We say in unison and immediately hold our noses because we're immature like that.

"I'll do it if you do it!" We shout again at the same time and chuckle as we each pull out our phones.

Ryan Jones may be my new partner in crime after all, move over Jace.

"*'What are we?'* and send."

TWENTY-EIGHT

Cleo

Blake (Wilder)

Wat ER oui?

TWENTY-NINE

Cleo

GROWING UP, THE THREE of us, Georgia, Jace, and I, had sleepovers. We'd sleep in each other's beds, watch our little shows, and play all types of games together. So, when I woke up this morning with a heavy arm wrapped around my waist, a small pink and green friendship bracelet attached to its wrist, I'm not startled because I know it's Jace.

I yawn snuggling into my pillow as he nuzzles into my back, still asleep. Trying not to wake him (because he's a fucking grumpy pants when awoken) I reach over to my nightstand and grab my phone. With a deeper yawn, I scroll through last night's notifications.

Sephora's Semi-Annual Sale! Buy One, Get—*Skip.*

Message from Ryan—*Skip.*

No one out Pizzas the—*Skip.*

One new message from Blake (Wilder)... *Interesting.*

I rub my eyes as I slide open the notification from Blake and sit up as I read over the words. "Wat E...R oui? Like *baguette*? Oui? Is he trying to say we?" I mumble, sliding over to check the send time.

1:42 a.m.

What the fuck is this? Come on, Jones, wake up! Read Lover Boy's message correctly.

What...er...Are? Are! We?

"WHAT ARE WE?!" I drop the phone flat on Jace's face and cringe as he groans.

"What the fuck, CJ?"

"What the fuck is this?! Read it." I shove the brightly lit device in my best friend's face. Jace blinks once then twice too fast before shooting up in his spot, looking over at me with wide eyes.

"Let's go." His tone is stern as he looks me square in the eyes. I tilt my head at the green-eyed boy because what does he mean by *go*? Did Georgia make good on her threat last night and beat his head in?

"Go? Go where?"

"To my place, dumbass. If Wilder sent this stupid ass message, I'm gonna let him know that no one messes with my best friend but *me*."

I scoff at his ridiculousness and snatch my phone away. "He probably meant to send that to someone else..." I trail off and try to ignore the pain in my chest at the *thought* of the message being for anyone but me.

"Well, he's going to learn how to fucking read before he hits send today."

When I was 16 years old, I got my first and only car. Jace drove it around for me even though he was only 15. We'd carpool to school and pretty much anywhere until he got his own car. Georgia would usually ride with us or drive herself since she liked to be "fashionably late" to things. Sienna would sometimes ride with us too, but nothing ever compared to the rides I went on with him because of all the people in the world, he always treated me like a princess.

He treated Georgia and Sienna that way too, don't get me wrong. Mrs. Heart raised her boys the right way! But it's something about your best friend treating you how you deserve that just melts the heart.

After stopping at Dunkin' because "you can't confront hungover men on an empty stomach", (wise words from Jace Heart), we head over to the boys' townhouse. Jace stays in my car, insisting he had "things to handle" and left me to my own vices.

So now, I stand by myself dressed in a lilac donut print pajama set with a strawberry sprinkled donut in my hand, standing on the porch of the boy that I kissed last night.

Should I be here? Is confronting Blake and *potentially* getting together with him truly the best idea? I mean it's a good idea for the girl downstairs but what about the one in my heart and head?

I lift my fist, hyping myself up to knock on the black Roman-styled front door when it swings open just before my knuckles can graze it. My eyes shut off instinct because if Blake is standing in front of me, I'll be more than freaking embarrassed.

I'll be petrified.

I should've put on real pants before this...

A low whistle followed by a deep low chuckle startles me, I peel an eye open and visibly deflate at the sight of Braxton and Alec. Alec looks like a sporty deer caught in headlights as he stands in the doorway, hand still on the knob dressed in gray athletic shorts, a navy SFU Tiger's hoodie, and a black Nike sport headband. He smiles lightly at me about to speak only to be cut off by Brax. The latter is dressed almost identically, only instead of wearing shorts, he has on gray sweatpants.

"Morning run?" I ask and cringe as my voice comes out shakily.

"Something like that, Princess Cleo. Are you heading in or coming out...?" the dark-skinned male asks, a hint of a smirk tugging at his lips.

My cheeks heat up at the implication and I'm about to deny all allegations of being at the boys' place the night before when a loud voice calls out from the house.

"Are y'all going to eat breakfast or am I just wasting—Oh! Hey CJ, are you eating breakfast here too?" Derek's breathy voice is cheerful as he strides up to the front door, his face decorated with flour and a smile.

It isn't until Derek is standing next to Braxton that I realize he's wearing a pink apron with 'Mother Knows Best' written on it. I stifle my laughter as his eyes light up.

"Oh, no... I'm *uh*... is Blake here?" I cut to the chase, my nerves are jumpy and I need to get this over with.

I *have* to know what Blake meant by that text.

"Yeah, he's uh—"

I don't give Alec the time to finish his sentence as I push past the three lumberjack males and make my way to Blake's bedroom at the end of the hall.

I note to apologize to the guys later with some ice cream or something and take a deep breath as I approach Blake's bedroom door.

This is it. Behind this door, I'm going to hear some things that I may or may not like. *Fuck,* wait... maybe I should turn back around. Jace should still be outside, and I can just— *No.*

If I want to get shit done, *I have to get shit done.*

Without a second thought, I open the bedroom door. It's not unusual for Blake's room to be spotless but I am taken aback slightly at the neatness of it all, his shoes are all lined up in an even row. All his clothes are hidden from the eye and there's literally zero dust.

If I hadn't heard his small snore, I'd think the room was empty based on its stillness. Blake is under about forty blankets and his body is nearly invisible in the spotless room. I trek over to the bed and sigh as I take a seat next to the sleeping boy.

Without thinking, my hands brushes a small wavy strand of brown hair from Blakes face, it startles me momentarily. *Did I just caress Blake Wilder?*

Blake stirs in his sleep, and I immediately jump up from the bed because if there's *one thing* I won't be caught dead doing, it's caressing a sleeping hockey player.

"Mhm... Jace, I'm not helping you find the pimple dude," he grumbles, turning in the covers and it takes everything in me not to burst into a fit of laughter at him.

I stifle my laughter as I lower my lips to his ear and whisper, "I'm not Jace."

I don't think I've ever seen someone wake up from a deep sleep so fast in my life. Blake shoots up from his spot in the bed and immediately places his hands over his crotch, eyes wild and bewildered but it seems that when he notices that

I'm the one in his room, he automatically goes back into his cocky asshole-ish self.

Blake smirks, coolly moving his hands to his hips, seemingly flexing his already devastating pecs and biceps at me.

Be strong, young Cleo, do not give in. I try to tell myself, but I gulp when his smirk morphs into a lazy grin and his eyes go soft.

Be strong.

"I came to talk."

He frowns tilting his head at my cold tone. "About what?"

"What are we?" my body closes in on itself slightly as if awaiting an impact from his words. *Is it suddenly hot in here?* I twist the ring Ryan got me and chew on my bottom lip. I've never had to have the 'what are we' talk with guys. Our relationship status has always been something we both knew. But with Blake, it's different.

Everything with Blake is different because—I hate to say it—Blake isn't like other guys.

Ew.

I said it.

Don't go all "She's dickmatized" on me, *please*. I regret saying it already.

I hate that I thought it but it's true. I've never been around another guy as charming, caring or as *fucking cocky* as him and I want to see where this can go but, I know that I can't.

The saying "boys will be boys" has traumatized me all my life because they genuinely will *always* be boys. And I'm just a girl scared as fuck to find out if Blake is *the* boy or just *a* boy. Now, I know that I kissed him and not the other way around. But I also don't know how I feel about this whole thing. *Or maybe I do?*

I don't know.

Fuck, this is confusing, I'm getting a headache.

"We're—*Fuck it*."

Blake pulls me with such a strong force that I'm nearly on his lap and I don't have time to react before our lips are connected and we're back to doing that dance that I'm slowly growing to love.

My head spins as he draws me in so deeply into him, it's a fervent kiss that burns deep with passion and lust and something more that I can't place because if I do, I won't be able to say what needs to be said to him.

He runs a hand through my loose hair; I'd took down my silk press wrap when I was in the car with Jace and just completely forgot to tie it back up. As one of his hands plays in my hair and the other grips my hip, I melt into him.

Fuck—I'm falling and I *cannot* be falling for Blake Fucking Wilder.

I can't do this with *anyone*.

Fuck you heart and fuck you brain for not ringing the warning bells sooner.

He pulls away first, his cloudy blue eyes glazed over and hooded as they rove over my face.

I sigh, looking away because I *can't* see the expression on his face when I say, "We're friends. Nothing more—"

"Friend's can't kiss?"

His words are like a bucket of ice water dowsing me and bringing me back to reality. Of fucking course he'd say something like that.

This was a mistake, coming to talk to a cocky puck slapping dickhead was a mistake.

What does he mean by that? *"Friends can't kiss?"* Does he kiss all his goddamned friends like he's making love with their mouth?

What a jackass.

"And *that* is why we're *just* friends. Grow up, Blake." I stand, ignoring the sunken look on his face as I turn on my heels and walk out the door of the man that I may or may not like a little *too* much.

THIrTY

Blake

THE BOYS ALL STARE at me wide eyed with dropped jaws as I chase the most beautiful woman in the world out of my room in a pair of cartoon boxers.

"Cleo! Wait, no—" I call after her only to stop in my tracks on the lawn as she drives off faster than an F1 cart.

This was *not* how that was supposed to go.

I was supposed to tell a little joke and she'd laugh and then spend the whole day naked in my bed running our hands through each other's hair because we finally got things right between us.

Instead, I have five grown men watching me stand on the lawn practically naked with shocked expressions on their faces, probably holding up a camera to capture this moment for the team.

"You're in deep shit," is all that I hear from Jace before he pushes past me and hops into his own car presumably driving after the girl of my dreams.

Fuck.

43 times.

I texted Cleo forty-fucking-three times since last week and she has yet to even *read* a message. Neither she nor Denver have shown up to any of our lectures and I'm pretty sure Georgia and Sienna are off the radar too because whenever I try to text any of them, none of my messages go through.

This would all be easier if I could talk to either Coach or Jace but that's damn near impossible considering Jace hasn't talked to me since last week and I can't tell Coach that the girl I'm freaking out about is his own daughter.

When did life get so hard? When I was little rent was $500 and getting a girl to be my girlfriend only took me asking her out at the school dance. Now rent is $1.7k for a *studio apartment* and the girl I want is more stubborn than a hangnail.

"Leave her the fuck alone, Wilder." Jace's cold voice spits at me in the locker room.

Tonight's our first game of the season and my head is fucked, my girl hates me and my best friend has a shitty attitude too. And you know what? *I'm fed up.* I'm tired of all this shit.

"Don't tell me what to do," I snap back, shooting daggers at him with my eyes.

Is this *really* how he wants to do this? With *me* of all people?

"Or what? You think you're big shit? *You're not.* Leave her alone. I told you to fucking leave her alone before you even met her." He's seething.

I reel back at his words because what does that even mean? He's never told me that and I don't have to listen to anything this blonde motherfucker says. I'm a grown ass man. "She's an adult, who can make her own decisions, and I am too." I stand, stepping closer to my best friend as we look at each other eye to eye.

I really could go without fighting him tonight, his punches pack a bite to them.

"And she *decided* not to go with you, take a hint." His eyes narrow, jaw clenching.

"Are you jealous or something? Are you mad because she wants me and not you? Newsflash, Heart, you had 17 years to get the girl, I've nearly done it in two months."

Yeah... I knew that was going to get me punched before I even said it.

It's like a cat fight only with tall sweaty grown men in hockey padding. We each get a couple good hits in before Braxton, Derek, and Charlie haul us from each other.

Our chests heave as we stare one another down but Jace is the first to speak up. "You hurt her feelings," he says and my stomach drops.

"I didn't mean to, I honestly said it as a joke..." I sigh, grabbing the tape for my stick to keep myself busy.

"Yeah, well, she didn't take it that way and since you two are my closest friends, I need you to understand that when she hurts I *will* bring down hell for her. I've been protecting these girls since I could walk, and I'll be damned if I watch them get their hearts broken by someone that I called a friend..." He holds my gaze before sighing.

I nod in understanding and thank the hockey heavens that the rest of the team isn't here yet. We got here a few hours earlier than our call-time to do some free skating before the game.

"You're a good guy but *dude* you have to read the room... CJ is reclusive when it comes to men. She's been scorned before and it's hard for her to get back into the swing of things, especially after everything with Marcelo. I just don't need any more motherfuckers breaking my best friend's heart."

His last two sentences catch the both of us off guard, Jace's eyes widen to the size of saucers as he becomes paler at the mention of Marcelo.

My body is hot with anger at the thought of *Rivers* potentially hurting a woman like Cleo. "What did he do to her?" I ask through gritted teeth.

"Let's just say he made Hell a place on Earth for her. He was sneaky and manipulative and an overall bad guy towards her. I know you're not like him, but she doesn't. You must move at her pace and allow her to come to you first. I know I said leave her alone but that was when I was mad at you, you fucker." He chuckles, running a hand through his hair before taking a sip from his water bottle.

"Be patient and kind to her, I'm giving you my blessing so don't fuck it up or I'll have to *actually* black one of those pretty blue eyes."

I roll my eyes at the idiot to my left just as the guys poke their heads back into the locker room. I hadn't even noticed they'd left but Charlie is the first to reenter the room.

"So, what I'm hearing is that we're kicking some Brighton ass when we see them?" the long-haired man asks, smiling deviously.

"Oh, they're going to wish they'd never stepped foot in Maryland." Derek chuckles, patting my shoulder as he takes a seat in his cubby between me and Jace.

"Are we good now?" I ask the blonde on the other side of Derek as he nods with a small shrug.

"Of course, and keep your head on the ice tonight. You've got a season to open."

THIRTY-ONE

Cleo

IT'S THE FIRST GAME of the season, the rink is lit up with blue and orange lights and the boys are playing to win tonight. Since it's a home game, I'm obligated to be here by not only the pact I made with my dad but by another that I'd made with Jace last week.

Spirits are high tonight and almost everyone in a ten-mile radius of SFU is here sporting the schools' vibrant colors of navy blue and orange.

Georgia, Sienna, and I sit just a few rows behind the home box, watching the boys put on one of the best season openers I've seen in college hockey to this day.

It's been a week since Blake and I have had any contact, and to say I spent that time even more confused than I was before would be an understatement. But the girls and I took a collective mental health week where we spent most of our time doing coloring books and face masks while drowning our sorrows in pints of ice cream.

There are twenty seconds left in the last period of the game, SFU is leading by a single point but the Moran U defensemen aren't letting up on our boys. It's nasty out there as the boys fall into a heated puck battle. The crowd grows silent as we all sit on the edge of our seats, the only sound to be heard in the arena being the slapping of the puck against the sticks on the ice.

I suck in a deep breath, hoping and praying that Moran U doesn't suddenly become amazing and make the goal.

A loud slap followed by the sound of the goal horn ringing has the crowd slipping into a loud cheer and if I had blinked, I would've missed the sheer art of a goal that number 13, Blake Wilder, had scored. I jump from my seat and cheer with the rest of the crowd for the man, the myth, the legend— *Wilder.*

"I fucking hate hockey but did you see that?!" Georgia exclaims, her eyes bright as she jumps up and down pointing at the ice below.

"He scored the winning goal!" Sienna gasps looking up at the Jumbotron above with Blake's image and stats displayed on it.

For SFU to be a football university, we have one of the best hockey programs in the country. Dad says it's because he's the coach, which *may* be true. But I also believe it's because Summerfield births *legends.*

The school has produced *seventeen* Stanley Cup winners and six Olympic hockey players from both the men *and* women's teams.

It isn't until the screen displays Blake himself in current time that I realize he's not doing a cocky pose or cheering with the rest of the guys. Instead, he's looking up at something with a look of serious intensity.

My skin burns even though I'm surrounded by ice and my heart falls when my eyes lock with his steely ones.

Stay, he mouths, helmet off. His hair is curly and damp against his forehead, and my thighs rub together at the sight of him, so without thinking, I nod.

Georgia, Sienna, and I make our way to the locker-room area to wait for the boys. It's "puck bunnies" galore down here but everyone seems to be civil as we all await the group of winners.

Derek is the first to exit the locker room, he's beaming as he talks to someone on his phone, more than likely his daughter, Delilah.

Deli's a sweet kid, I met her last week at the festival and couldn't get over how adorable she was.

As Derek approaches us, his eyes lock with Sienna's. He falters in his steps, drinking her in slowly before continuing with his walk. Sienna's neck cranes as she watches him walk by, eyes softer around the edges than normal. I raise a brow at Georgia who just shrugs. We'll find out about that later, I guess.

The boys begin piling out of the locker room and we congratulate every single one until Blake and Jace exit together, laughing with one another.

Well, that's fucking new. What happened to not talking to the enemy, Jace? It's only been six hours since I last saw him, and he'd told me he wouldn't speak to Blake.

The air around us grows thick with awkwardness as the two men sidle up to us. Our friends look around as if waiting for something to happen but Blake's focus is trained solely on me. His gaze burns a hole in the side of my head, and it takes everything in me not to squirm as he lets out a low humorless laugh.

"Give your keys to Sienna," he says, and my eyes widen as I look at him up and down in disbelief.

Is he *serious?* After not talking to me for a week straight, *that's* the first thing he has to say to me?

I can sense the energy shift in our small group as Jace furrows his eyebrows at the man before clearing his throat. If this had been a few years ago and I was my old immature self, I would let Jace fight my battles and cuss Blake out for his rudeness. But I can't have him fight all my battles anymore.

"And why should I do that?" I challenge, narrowing my eyes on the annoying male.

"We have a project to do, Princess," is all he says in an indescribable tone before gently plucking my purse from my shoulder and slinging it over his.

In the car, Blake and I ride in complete silence. Though it's not terrible one, it is a bit awkward how quiet we are with one another. I don't think I've ever witnessed him be this mute since we've met. I sneak a subtle glance at him through the reflection of the car window, his figure is wonky, but I can make out the outline of his face perfectly.

"Where are we going?" I ask, trying to break the ice. I receive a small sigh in return and frown at the childishness of this all. *I'm* the one that's supposed to be mad!

I can see him smirking from the side of my eye but he doesn't respond and it isn't until we pull up at The Sugar Hole that I understand why.

He tells me to stay in the car, which is crazy because I've never just "stayed in the car" when it came to donuts, but I comply nonetheless.

It takes Blake five minutes to come back to the car with a box much smaller than the one we'd had last time and a masked bored look on his face. I peak over his shoulder as he chuckles lightly, putting the now open box full of all my favorites onto my lap. I gasp as I take a bite of a Pink Truffle donut and sigh.

"Does this mean we're good now?" Blake asks, his tone softer than before as he looks over at me with warm eyes.

"For now," is all that I can manage to get out over the mouthful of donut, as he chuckles lightly.

He's silent for a second, letting me devour two more donuts before turning to face me in his seat.

"You left that night," he says, softly. Zero hint of anger or sadness.

I scarf down the last of the strawberry donut before nodding. "I got scared and ran away. I'm sorry for leaving and then acting like a child after. Are you mad at me?" I ask, looking down at my lap, suddenly feeling smaller than before.

He lifts my chin with his thumb and pointer finger, bringing our eyes level with one another.

"I could never be mad at you, Cleo. Was I upset that I probably fucked up everything between us when I kissed you? Yes, but I wasn't mad that you ran from the Ferris wheel, I expected it. I've been watching you and I can see that you got overwhelmed with it all. And then I fucked up by joking while you were trying to be serious. Are you mad at me?" he asks, eyes soft.

You know how they say eyes are the window to the soul? Blake's eyes hold the secrets of the ocean, I want to drown in them and get to know everything there is to know about him.

"I could never be mad at you, Blake." I chuckle, repeating his earlier words as he smiles.

"Do over?"

"Do over." I nod.

Blake reaches into his backseat, shirt rolling up a bit as he pulls out the camcorder for our project, turning in my direction with a small smile, pressing record.

"Hi Cleo." He smiles, covering his right eye with the camera.

"Hi Blake." I chuckle, turning to fully face him from the passenger seat.

"Where do you feel the safest?" he asks me, his voice a mixture of softness and calming energy as I sigh.

"In what way?"

"I mean where do you feel the most secure and content that no matter what, as soon as you enter this place, it's like a weight is lifted from your shoulders."

I'm taken aback for a moment as my mind drifts over the endless places and possibilities that I can say but there are only two places that stick out the most to me.

"The beach and the bookstore." I shrug.

"Really? I think mine is my childhood bedroom, lol." He chuckles but then fully laughs, doubling over with the camera still recording.

I choke out my own laughter, belly tightening from the action.

"I know you didn't just say 'lol' in real-time." I gasp for air as Blake turns off the camera placing it in his backseat. He gives me a small look that I wouldn't have noticed if I hadn't already been looking at him. My stomach does a small flip, startling me for a second.

How am I supposed to do this whole friendship thing when *this* is how my body reacts to him?

We fall into a comfortable silence as soft R&B plays on the radio and it gives me just a second to truly think.

I know that I like Blake, but I also know that liking a guy *like* Blake as much and as quickly as I do can be dangerous to not only my grades but my mental health as well. What if he ends up just like Marcelo? What if he's just another asshole hockey—

"Again, I'm sorry about last week, Cleo." His abrupt words interrupt my train of thought. Blake gives me a small, crooked smile before running a hand through his hair. "I've never done this whole relationship thing before, and I meant for what I said to you to be a joke, but then I realized just how shitty it was as soon as you twisted your nose at me." He sighs.

Twisted my nose? I do no such—

"You twist your nose when you're annoyed, you do a little scrunch thing with it, too." He chuckles, reading my mind before continuing. "I would like to date you Cleo and show you that I'm not the guy that you think I am."

"I... I don't date," I stutter, and mentally curse myself for doing so.

I'm unsure if Blake is joking or being serious when he says he wants to date me, and it makes my head ache at the thought of him just playing games with my heart.

"We can take things slow, build a friendship before—"

"I would like to date you, Blake, but I can't. My dad and I created a plan for my first semester, and boys weren't a part of it. He doesn't want me to date anyone." I shrug playing with the hem of my shirt. How crazy is it that me, a 20-year-old woman, can't be in a relationship because "Daddy said no"? He probably thinks I'm a child now.

"We'll worry about him when the time comes but, for now, how about we go on our first official date? You can call it a hangout but for me, it'll be a date."

I think my heart just melted into a puddle, I quickly slide my mask of indifference back into place because if he knew just how much his words affected me, we'd be in the backseat of this car right now.

"I don't do relationships, Wilder," I say, feigning nonchalance.

"That's okay, Princess. I'll wait."

"What's a dealbreaker for you in a relationship?" Blake asks me, holding up our project's camcorder to his eye, smiling from behind it.

I let out a small chuckle of laughter at the man as he smiles deviously. "Was that question for the project or for you, Lover Boy?" I ask, smiling a little toying with the hem of my baby blue sweater.

Today, Blake and I are at a park to film for our project. We're sat on a Spiderman blanket, facing the small man-made lake in Summerfield Park. The mid-October air is warmer than usual but still slightly chilly hence my outfit of a sweater and jeans instead of my usual skirts.

Blake's smile is devastating and full of mischief as he gives me a playful shrug.

"A dealbreaker for me is lack of trust in any relationship. If I can't trust you, then you're not the one for me." I gulp, my heart thudding hard against my ribcage as memories of my previous relationships pound against my head.

"Then I'll be sure to have our trust be as tough as titanium, there's no breaking that," He says in a matter-of-fact tone as if it's just that simple.

I want to laugh at the naivety of his response, trust is something people build and break constantly. If he thinks that I'll freely give it to him, he has another thing coming.

"Sure, you will." I roll my eyes.

"I will! Ye of little faith, I am going to have you trusting me so hard, you won't know what hit you, Princess." Blake's face is triumphant as if he's already won as he takes a sugar cookie into his mouth.

Derek, the DILF of the team (Jace's words, not mine but I do agree) is also a culinary arts major. He made us the best lunches of chicken parmesan, fruit, and sugar cookies for today's makeshift "picnic"/project day.

"Okay! It's my turn, Lover Boy!" I exclaim as our fourth timer for our session goes off.

We usually do ten-minute intervals between questions before swapping the camera to let each person get an even amount of screen time. It was Blake's idea to do so and probably our smartest one regarding this project.

Skimming over our list of questions, I chuckle at the realization that Blake's previous one wasn't one of our regulated questions. *This boy, I swear.* I smile as my eyes land on one question in particular.

"What's something that makes you feel overwhelmed?" I frown at the question before looking up at Blake who ponders. The questions that we have to answer for the project are invasive and much worse than the ones we created, and this is an example of one. I knew that the object of the project was to document our lives and to get to know our partner and the camera on a deeper level. *But shit,* this was a *different* level.

"I get overwhelmed by a lot of things, I'm not going to lie." He chuckles, running a hand over his face before sending me the most beautiful grin I've ever seen. I covertly clench my thighs at the sight of him as he continues. "I may not seem like it because I'm such an awesome guy with an impeccable personality but I find a few things overwhelming. Crowded rooms where I know little to any people, public speaking—don't tell the guys but I hate giving out speeches in the locker room, it makes me itch." He fiddles with the baby blue bow tied across my bag's handle.

I watch Blake through the lens of the camera in a newer light as his cockiness fades and is replaced by nervousness. He continues speaking and I pray to God that I got everything on camera because the only thing that I can focus on is the softness of his features under the warm autumn sun and the way that when he carefully looks over at me, my heart beats two times too fast.

I am screwed.

So freaking screwed.

When Blake excuses himself to throw away our snacks and plastic utensils, I immediately pull out my phone and shoot an SOS text to Margarita Central.

My phone buzzes four times in my hand as I watch him come back, smiling broadly.

"Ready?" he asks, holding out a hand for me to grab, the gesture curating a pool in my panties as I grab a hold of it.

"Of course," I breathe out, grabbing his firm hand before helping him clean up our makeshift picnic area.

Blake and I ride back to my apartment listening to Twisted Vipers, singing along to their songs together. He sings the songs like we're in a rom-com, using his fist as a mic. The action makes me swoon as the music shifts to One Direction, I chuckle as Blake sings You & I to me obnoxiously loud. I pretend to ignore his singing until the opening chords of Night Changes plays.

My mouth drops as I gasp, "This is my song!"

"You got this, Princess, give it your all!" Blake shouts, holding his fist up to my mouth. I smile at the action and immediately break out into song, using the "mic".

We laugh and sing the entire ride to my place and it's only when More Life by Astra begins playing that I realize we've been driving in circles for the past fifteen minutes. My heart spins but I don't point it out to Blake as he makes yet another right turn, I never want this moment to end so I don't do anything to interrupt it.

THIRTY-TWO

Cleo

WHEN I ENTER THE house, the girls are all waiting for me in the living room, each holding looks of smugness and muddled excitement as I mosey into the shared space. I only get four steps into the living room when I'm ambushed with questions.

"What happened?!"

"Were y'all on a date?!"

"Why did you drive around the block fifteen times?" Georgia asks lastly and it's her question that has my eyebrows shooting to my hairline.

Fifteen times?!

I thought it'd been only two, maybe three...

"Uh... Hi?" I chuckle as Georgia and Sienna roll their eyes, Denver sighs already aware of just how fucked I am, considering she sat in a lecture with the two of us this morning.

"Bitch, get to the tea! I only Naired one of my pits because I saw the SOS text." Sienna groans, holding up her arms to show us the proof.

Georgia lets out a low whistle, running a finger over the bare armpit. "Damn, girl, how long was your timer?"

"Girl... get back on topic." Denver chuckles, swatting Georgia away from Sienna.

I sigh as I watch my friends begin to bicker and say the one thing that I know will break them out of it.

"I like Blake Wilder," I confess, sighing in relief at the weight lifted from my chest. I never thought admitting something as simple as having a crush could feel this relaxing, but I feel like the world is somehow brighter.

"Bitch I know that's not why I put a pause on my everything shower—" Sienna frowns, looking up at me in genuine confusion.

"Was that supposed to be the SOS?" Denver chuckles, running a hand through her waves, looking back and forth between the girls and me.

"Girl, I was watching a new episode of *Love In Cancun*! You called a meeting to deliver old news!" Georgia exclaims with a groan, laying back fully into the couch.

Well, that was *not* how I expected them to react. I frown at my friends and move from in front of the television, put off with the whole situation. Am I really *that* obvious to others?

Georgia presses resume on the current episode of *Love In Cancun* and nestles into Denver's side as Sienna trudges back to her room, presumably to finish her "everything shower", which consists of washing, deep conditioning, and putting a treatment into her pink curls while shaving and exfoliating her body in the shower with the water set to a hell-like temperature.

The last time I'd followed one of Sienna's "everything shower" guides, I nearly fainted from the humidity in the bathroom and my arms almost fell off.

We're about five minutes into the episode, and Georgia is fully invested in the nonsense that prick Cooper Turner is saying to America's sweetheart Rosetta Murano when I make the mistake of opening my mouth once again.

"I told him we couldn't date," is all that I can say before the show is promptly paused again and I am faced with two of the most confused looks I've ever seen them give me.

"And why the hell did you do that?! He's hot and funny and has the mental capacity to put up with Jace for more than five minutes!" My blonde friend shrieks as she stands, taking the spot that I'd previously held in front of the TV.

"Did he do something?" Denver's voice is laced with lethality as she looks down at me where my head lays in her lap, looking up at the ceiling.

"I'm scared." The confession burns as it comes out into the open.

Georgia lets out a choked sound trudging toward us, plopping down on the floor between us and our coffee table. "What are you scared about?" she asks warmly, running a hand through my hair.

"That she'll get hurt," Denver answers for me, her tone raw as she looks everywhere but at me and it's then that I have a feeling that I'm not the only person she's talking about.

"Is this because of Marce—he who shall not be named?" Georgia questions and when I don't answer, she lets out a groan in frustration. "Cleo Jones, you listen to me, and you listen well. Blake is *not* Marcelo, and you are not your past. I know that you're struggling with trusting him and I one hundred percent agree that you should watch your back but don't let your skepticism stop you from becoming a part of something great with someone."

That makes me sit up; I glance at Denver quickly and sure enough, she's listening as well. We only get Therapist Georgia six times a year and when that happens, it's in everyone's best interest to listen.

"Men come and go but you are forever. Why not give yourself a chance at happiness? Risks are meant to be taken in order to get what we desire. There's always risks when the heart is involved but that doesn't mean that you should just play it safe and never put your heart out there." She smiles as if she knows that she's giving us the best advice in the world... and she is. "You deserve to be loved and give it back to someone who deserves it. You both do." She finishes giving a weighty look to Denver. I furrow my eyebrows at the action as Denver nods. Whatever those two have going on must be serious based on their shared unwavering looks.

"Now go jump on that ultra hockey star dick, I heard it's amazing."

"Is video production going to be your job or mine? I mean, I'm not terrible at editing, but you *did* have a YouTube channel." Henry Ricks, my partner for my Mass Media 3004 project, chuckles as I roll my eyes at him.

Henry and I have been working together on our project since the semester began but we've only been able to meet with one another twice since he's been busy with traveling.

He's a center fielder on the baseball team and one of the coolest guys I've met since starting here.

He twists at one of his dreadlocks with a knowing smirk as I let out my own small laugh. Since it's still early in the day and a little warm out, the two of us are sitting at one of the outdoor tables by the dining hall. Henry's dark skin glows as he looks up at me holding up a picture of my YouTube channel, Icing it. My stomach dips as I remember the channel I'd practically grew up on and how I tossed it aside as soon as my life got hard.

I groan as Henry presses play on a video of me from middle school and bursts out in laughter as my younger self pounces into the frame, tugging Jace along with me.

"Man, babe, you were so adorable! All my buddies and I would watch your videos all the time." Henry smiles brightly, still watching the video and I'm about to start laughing again when a dark cloud blocks the sun. I frown at the sudden chill at my back when Henry notices it as well.

"Oh, hey man!" Henry beams at whoever is blocking out the light and my stomach twists as the smells of cedarwood and vanilla storm my senses.

Fucking Hell—

"Hey, Princess." Blake ignores Henry and plops down beside me, slinging his arm around my shoulder. I suppress a smile at Blake just as Henry begins to speak.

"Like I was saying babe, you should definitely do the editing if they'll be anywhere as good as this right here" I stiffen as Henry chuckles, completely unaware of the storm brewing in the man beside me.

"Is that so, baby? You good with your hands?" Blake asks, his voice laced with a flirty lilt as he looks down at me, his eyes dark.

I gulp, letting his words register fully before chuckling breathily. "Um..."

"Oh, she's amazing—"

"I know." Blake cuts Henry off mid-sentence, face completely devoid of emotion and it's then that Henry fully grasps that Blake isn't being friendly.

Henry, bless his heart, smiles amused. "I'll...Uh... I'll see you around, babe." He chuckles, gathering up his things and breakfast before giving me a small kiss on the cheek.

The action doesn't go unnoticed by the brooding male beside me—Blake frowns at the kiss and folds his arms over his chest.

"See you around, Hen!" I beam back and try my hardest to fight off a laugh as Blake's mouth drops in my peripheral vision. I mask my smile and bite my lip as I gather my things as well, taking a sip of the peach tea I'd ordered.

"You okay, Lover Boy?" I ask as the walking storm cloud beside me follows me silently pouting.

"Oh, me? I didn't think you cared since you were talking to *Hen*." He pouts.

"Did you have a reason for interrupting our meeting, or are you just in the mood to walk beside me while you pout?"

Blake groans from behind me before sidling next to me, wrapping his arm around my shoulder. His hold is warm and protective as we stalk toward the quad where a few students are seated with their computers.

"I originally was going to call you but after seeing you sitting with Ricks, I decided to just talk in person. Besides, I know you missed seeing my handsome face," he teases, twirling the end of my ponytail between his fingers. I pretend to be annoyed by the action, but I secretly love the attention he's giving me, so instead of pushing him off, I let him continue.

"Obviously," I muse.

"You coming to Jace's birthday?" he asks me, coming to a halt in the middle of the quad, looking down at me.

I crinkle my nose at his abruptness, I hate being the center of attention regardless of if there's only five other people around. Tugging Blake over to the large oak tree just a little bit away from the center of the quad, I turn to face him.

"Of course, I'm coming to the party that *I* planned." I can see the mental fist pumps he's doing as his eyes sparkle with his eagerness.

"It's a Halloween party baby, so you know what that means." He smirks bending down a little to match my height. I frown, I'm not *that* damn short. I am the average height of most American women, but Blake makes me seem like a garden gnome in comparison to his large frame.

"What?" I raise a brow at him.

"The freaks come out to play."

That's not... that's not the saying. "I thought the saying was the monsters come out at night?" I scrunch my nose unknowingly and mentally slap myself when I realize it.

"I can be a monster, too, but they're less sexy."

THIrTY-THree

Blake

I LET OUT A loud and obnoxious sigh as the guys recap their weekend hookups all around the Harborview University guest locker rooms. We just finished one of the shittiest games we've had since the season started two weeks ago and I'm so ready to get back to Maryland.

Although we won the game, there was a serious issue with communication on our second line and when it came down to it, they let the Harborview Lions score not once but twice, leading us to be tied until Jace scored the winning goal.

So, you can imagine why I'm a little pissed that my team is busy talking about getting laid rather than working on becoming better at the sport that we put our lives on the line for. I'm annoyed, hot, and hungry. *Bad combination.*

"Nah, that bitch is bonkers man, stay away from Moaning Myrtle. She'll bite you in the dick as soon as you try to get away," I hear Braxton mumble to one of the freshman guys, Blaise Auclair. Blaise narrows his sage green eyes on the big man before smiling. Auclair's our only French guy on the team, and a seriously weird kid at times, so it doesn't surprise me one bit when he replies.

"Maybe I want The Moaning Myrtle to bite my dick." The Frenchie shrugs with a smile.

What the fuck... I cringe at his remark and turn my attention back to my bag, rolling up my stick tape. He's a goalie, and a damn good one, but he's just so odd, is all. Derek, too...

"What about you, Wilder? You hooking up tonight?" another freshman, Jordan Smith, asks from the other side of the locker room where he and his twin brother, Jonah, lace up their sneakers.

The twins are identical but easy to tell apart since they're polar opposites. Where Jordan is loud and outgoing, Jonah would rather play video games by himself.

I tilt my head at the question and I'm about to respond when someone speaks for me.

"Of course, he has a hookup for tonight. Why do you think we call him 'Wilder', Rookie?" Kiernan Murphy, a sophomore left winger on the third line, asks with a sarcastic lilt. "It's not just because it's his last name, *I'll tell you that*," the raven-haired man adds.

"I actually—" I try yet again, only to be cut off.

"Remember when Wilder had a hookup at every school for two months?" Antonio Washington asks with a soft chuckle as if reliving one of the shittiest moments of my life with *happiness*.

I cringe at the memory of it. Not too many people know why I acted like that and for good reason because I'm not telling these fuckers *shit*. But I also don't like the way that they're talking about me and my horrible sex life last season out in the open, stuff like this can get back to Cleo and ruin any credibility that I have with her.

I'm all set to tell the truth about what I'm currently doing, and with whom, it's not like it's a secret that I'm obsessed with Cleo, but when Coach clears his throat, obviously annoyed with the subject of conversation, my skin *crawls* and I decide better of it.

"You guys know I'm focused on the game right now. No girls for me," I lie through my teeth, quietly, but of course, everyone hears it.

The guys around me let out mixtures of shock and relief. The relieved ones being my roommates—plus Alec and Derek. The guys eye me for a second before turning back to whatever they're doing.

On the bus ride back to campus, the guys are all high and mighty, cheering and talking about any and everything.

"Dude! Did you fuckwits know that condoms are only *87%* effective?!" Washington asks from a few rows behind me, rather loudly as the guys all begin to let out shocked groans.

"I just use the pull-out method!" someone, most likely Lucki Cole, shouts from the far back. His loud shout earns shouts of agreements and those of bewilderment from around the bus, and I'm about to reprimand all of the guys who are *only* using the pull-out method when Derek chimes in.

"How do you think Delilah got here?"

His question is meant to be a joking one but the twins gasp. "Which method did you use?" Jonah asks, shocking me at his forwardness.

"I pulled out." Derek frowns.

"Pull out game weak!" Someone shouts.

"You only pulled out dipshit?!" Another person exclaims as Dere hangs his head low in embarrassment.

"It was my first time!" He tried to make it better, honestly, truly. But then Jace joined in on the fun, teasing him mercilessly with Braxton and Charlie.

As the guys talk amongst themselves, I pull out my phone and check my Instagram. Cleo's been more active recently and her stories are currently to die for. *Literally.* I die of laughter every time I watch her.

In her current Insta-story, there's a video of her, Georgia, and my cousin standing in their living room obviously tipsy, wearing large sunglasses, singing the lyrics to an Astra song as Sienna laughs in the background. The girls look so happy and free and exactly like somewhere that I want to be, so without much thought I shoot a text to my favorite (and only) girl.

Me

Coming over be prepared for endless shots and karaoke

Princess

ur only allowed in if you bring snacks and margaritas babe

Me

Oh you're on!

> I'm going to go crazy in the store, the guys don't send me on snack trips for this very reason.

Princess

> Whatever you say LB

> Don't forget to bring a bag of powdered donuts too

I chuckle at the mention of the first snack we've ever had with one another and make myself comfortable for the last forty minutes of our drive back from New York. We should be getting back around 11:00 p.m. which isn't late, but damn sure isn't early so I make sure I'm the first off the bus to make it to one of the corner stores near campus.

If I'd never been to Cleo's apartment before now, I'd know that I was in the right place based solely from the loud girl group songs and shouting on the other side of the door.

"Ew, CJ! It's him!" I hear Denver from behind the door and chuckle lightly at her remark. My cousin may act like she doesn't like me, but we all know I'm secretly her favorite family member.

"Girl, he looks good as hell. He didn't come over here to just do face masks! Have you gotten a wax recently?" I can hear the soft spoken pink-haired girl loud and clear followed by loud *Shh's* and whispered arguing. I spend about five minutes standing at the front door before Cleo opens it, I pause in my tracks at her. With no makeup, her hair up in a lazy bun, and wearing pajamas with little cow plants on them, Cleo looks beautiful.

She's so beautiful that I'm taken aback for a moment and I don't fully hear what she's saying until the bag of treats and alcohol is pried away from my hands by Georgia.

"How was the game? We watched you play until *someone* got bored of it." She beams before giving a sharp look to her blonde best friend.

Georgia shrugs with a small laugh. "I couldn't sit through it, babe. I'm sure you did amazing though, Blake." She giggles.

I smile at the girls, advancing into the apartment and taking off my shoes at the door before heading into the living room where "the party" is.

"It was amazing if you think about it from a winner's perspective but shitty as hell from a captain's point of view." I sigh, silently thanking Cleo as she hands me a small glass of auburn liquid. Presumably, whiskey.

I drink up the smooth familiar liquor and smile; she had my favorite brand of whiskey stashed away in her kitchen.

"That sucks, little cousin... Anyway, did you bring the Fruit Roll-Ups?"

I roll my eyes at Denver and toss four packages to her before focusing my attention back on Cleo. She gives me a devious smile before turning on her heels toward the hallways bathroom.

The girls and I make small talk, discussing this season of *Love in Cancun* when Cleo returns holding seven colorful packets and a load of other things in her arms.

"Since you've never been here during our self-care night, I'll let you choose from any of these three," she says with a small smile before placing three different animal face masks on the coffee table.

"Huh?" I furrow my brows at her as her smile brightens.

"Today's Self-care Sunday, silly and you're just in time."

And that was how I found myself sitting in a small circle on the floor with four girls wearing a tiger face mask. The girls spend about fifteen minutes arguing about whether to watch *Love in Cancun* or a new romance movie before deciding on the reality show.

I spend that time observing their friend group dynamic and Cleo. She's sat directly beside me wearing her own pink pig face mask, stuffing white powdered donuts into her mouth as she watches that prick that everyone hates flirt with America's current sweetheart.

I don't want to be anywhere else as I sit here in my own face mask watching the woman that I have a major crush on do something she loves with the people she feels the safest with.

Cleo gives me a large powdery grin and to my surprise, she lays her tipsy little head on my shoulder. I stiffen momentarily before relaxing under her touch, bringing her close. I never want this moment to end and so I pull out my phone and do what I do best.

I capture it.

Cleo makes a goofy face at the camera before promptly telling me to delete it with fake annoyance. I'm so into talking and joking with her that when Sienna lets out a long yawn, pulling my attention to the time in the corner of the television, I'm startled.

2:15 a.m.

Fuck.

"Hey, I'll start to head out now since it's super late," I say, hastily removing myself from Cleo to stand, only to be stopped by Denver and Georgia.

"Wait, no! You can't leave this late at night," Georgia protests.

"It's too late to leave, Blake," Denver tuts, folding her arms over her chest like her word is final.

"You could just crash with CJ, I'm sure she wouldn't mind," Georgia adds sending a devious look past my shoulder to the quiet girl behind me, and my face reddens.

"I could stay on the couch!" I offer but Cleo just sighs, standing up as well.

"The couch is way too small to fit you. I promise that my bed is big enough for the both of us, just don't get too handsy, Lover Boy." She yawns, stretching her limbs.

My eyes widen at Cleo's response and I'm not one to block my own blessings, so I keep my mouth sealed as I follow Cleo to her bedroom after bidding all the nosey girls behind me a good night.

"Jace left some sweatpants here the other night, you could wear those to bed if you want." She offers me a pair of grey Nike sweatpants that... wait... *are these my sweatpants?!*

And why the fuck are they here?!

My eyebrows raise at the sight of my pants in Cleo's hands and I laugh a little at them as I head to the bathroom to change.

I'm about to leave the bathroom when I catch my reflection in the mirror. "You got this... this isn't the first girls' bed you've been in." I say to my reflection.

But *it is* the first girl that you've *liked*.

I groan, running a hand over my hair and face before reentering the room with a large smile, faking it till I make it.

Cleo's already laying in the bed, scrolling on her phone on the side closest to the bedroom window. I slip into the bed soundlessly next to her and she doesn't make any show of emotions as I get myself situated laying facing her.

"Thank you," She says with a yawn, the action causing a tendril of hair to fall into her face and without thinking I softly brush it away. Cleo shudders at the touch before relaxing into it, her eyes twinkling like all of the stars in the Milky Way as she flutters them open.

"For what?"

"Making my friends happy, Denver's been so quiet recently, and Si Si and Georgia have been a little bit upset lately, so seeing them laugh and joke around with you really made me happy tonight." She sighs contently.

"It was nothing." I smile at her as her eyes flutter shut momentarily.

"It was everything for me, Blake Wilder." She grins, rolling back her shoulders.

My heart warms and my dick twitches to life at her use of my full name. I usually hate when anyone says the full thing but coming from Cleo, it's like words of pure seduction.

"I'm a cuddler, by the way," She announces, causing me to stifle my laughter as she slides in closer to me, turning on her side. "You can be the big spoon tonight, *Blakey,*" she teases, pulling my arm around her.

I smile, tightening my grip, pulling her closer to me. I smile at the slight jump that Cleo does before bringing my lips to her ear with a smirk.

"Oh Princess, I'll be anything you want me to be." I laugh harder than intended as Cleo lets out a small groan, pinching the arm that's around her waist.

We talk quietly in the darkness of the night and when Cleo becomes eerily quiet and her breathing is heavier, I know that she's out for the count. I sigh, kissing the back of her head softly as she lets out a deep breath.

"Cleo Jones, you have my heart."

THIRTY-FOUR

Blake

"ARE YOU GOING TO just keep staring at me Lover Boy, or are you going to say something?" Cleo gives me all the sass in the world as she whirls her head to stare me down.

I sigh, content as I watch her with my head resting on the palm of my hand. Today, Cleo's hair is down in loose curls. No bows, except the one on her tote bag and she's wearing a custom pink SFU sweatsuit. The only reason that I know its custom is because no store on campus sells the color.

"You look beautiful today," I blurt out, completely ignoring the fact that this girl is turning me into a word vomiting man.

"Don't I look beautiful every day?" She asks, twisting my words. I chuckle as Cleo pulls out her phone for a small second before looking around the lecture hall as if she lost something.

"Where's Denver? She said she was coming to class today..." She trails off, taking her bottom lip between her teeth.

I inwardly groan at the sight of her and force my eyes away. I cannot get hard in a room with over 50 people. *Dead presidents*, think about dead presidents.

Clinton...

Roosevelt... Obama...

Wait—fuck. You know what I meant.

As I try and *fail* to recall all of the presidents, my mind strays back to Cleo's question and I get a small inkling that my dear old cousin may just be with Cleo's slightly younger brother. But there's no way I'm telling her that, that right there is their business. Besides I'm not fully sure if they are actually together or not.

Cleo and I work together on our project, discussing our next few location options. She wants us to do a few shots at the bookstore, one of her safe places, and I completely agree as I watch her speak on the different places to work in. Cleo's so deeply invested in her work and our shared goals that I'm fully enamored by her. And it's only when I make a stupid ass joke and Cleo snorts that my heart does the most outrageous flip its ever done.

"Go on a date with me!" I blurt out before I have a chance to think about what I'm saying. I cringe at my own stupidity, mentally slapping myself for not being rational.

"I'm sorry... What?" She asks, tilting her head like a confused puppy. Although she looks confused by my words, it's her eyes... The small shimmer of excitement in those beautiful brown eyes... That gives me the confidence to continue.

"I know you don't do relationships, and I don't either! But go on a date *with me*. Just one, that's all I'm asking for," I plead with zero regrets. We miss every shot we don't take and I'm sure as hell taking this one.

"Just one date?"

"Just one date. Saturday." I smile with all the hope in the world.

"But—"

"Please?" I beg. *God, look at what you have this girl doing to me.* "Please, Princess? If you want me to beg on my knees just know I'll be more than happy to get down on them for you," I say in a joking tone, but we all know how serious I truly am.

"Fine. One date, but I'm not promising I'll be too nice, Lover Boy"

It's been two days since Cleo agreed to go on a date with me and to say I've been on a consistent high would be an understatement. I'm ecstatic and way too eager to get tonight's game won and over with if it means I get to see her afterward.

Cleo and I knocked out another 20 percent of our project, leaving us with only six or seven more questions: it's bittersweet... I won't have an excuse to hang out with her every other day.

As Cleo dropped me off at the arena for tonight's game, she declared that she would start posting on her Youtube channel again. Which increased my mood even more. Cleo's slowly but surely breaking from that shell she'd been trapped in for Lord knows how long.

The match between SFU and Long Island U has been pretty intense with their enforcer asshole of a defenseman, Kris Moore, antagonizing everyone on the ice. Kris and I have a... history but nothing in this world can deter my good mood.

Nothing at all.

I spot Cleo in the crowd briefly as she shouts and cheers from behind the box. I send a small kiss to her then wince when my eyes drift down a bit more to find her father talking to one of the assistant coaches.

I have *got* to be more careful around him.

We're getting deeper into the game and as everything intensifies, more guys are sent to the sin bin on both sides for pettiness and small penalties. I'm watching my boys, making sure that everyone on the ice is good when a familiar voice turns my blood cold.

"I think I'll take the chick with the bows home with me tonight." Kris smugly chuckles, loud as all outdoors as he skates past me, and I don't think twice as I go after him.

Now, you're probably thinking...*No, Blake please don't do something stupid.* And I won't, especially in front of Cleo. I'm going to play it so safe you won't even know what safe is until it hits you—

"I'll fuck her so hard she'll be seeing red and yellow for the next week."

Now. *I never said I was smart and safe—just safe.* I go to swing, completely disregarding the fact that I'm on the ice and in a heated match and just as I think that I'll hit him, a blur of blue and orange stops me.

"Get your fucking head in the game!" Jace shouts, skating us away from the idiot.

I let out a huff of frustration. I almost had that sorry son of a bitch and if it wasn't for my best friend, I'd have his blood spread across the ice like jam on buttered toast.

"Nah, fuck that. Did you hear what he said?" I seethe.

"Oh, I heard. But there's nothing that she hates more than idiots on ice. Get your shit together and play to fucking win," he responds in a stern, zero-bullshit tone before skating back to his place and I'm so close to listening.

So, *so* close.

Until I hear Cleo shout, "Hey, 43, shoot that puck for me!" loud and fucking clear.

Newsflash for all the newcomers, my number is 13.

I see red.

I want to do something... Like punch that guy's head in for even *looking* at her, but then Jace's words come back to me. I need to put my all into this game because after this, Cleo Jones has a lot of explaining to do.

Forty minutes and five goals later, we won the damn thing.

I trail behind Cleo, pouting my ass off as I think about all the flirting she'd done tonight. Not only did Cleo shout out loud to Kris, but she also shouted random flirty sayings to *every single player.* Her plan was to distract them, and it worked considering we scored so many points on them. But a man can only take so much of his crush flirting with other men.

"Oh, stop being such a sour puss, you won didn't you?" She snickers from in front of me and my frown deepens at her cool tone.

I'm livid, how dare she flirt with all those guys for my benefit? Okay, when I put it like that it doesn't sound as bad but it is! My feelings are hurt.

"Here." She turns on her heels and plants a big fat kiss on my cheek.

Did I say my feelings are hurt? I meant to say that I'm the happiest man alive.

"That's for winning tonight. Congratulations, *Blakey.*"

THIrTY-FIVe

Blake

"WOULD YOU SIT THE *frick* down?" Braxton groans from my bedroom floor where he's sat with Jace and Alec building an Eiffel Tower LEGO set. Derek and Deli sit on the bed, watching cartoons on her iPad.

I chew on my thumbnail, pacing the room as I think about Cleo and I's talk from two days ago. "How can I sit when I have a *date* with our coach's daughter?!" I shriek.

The sound of my voice cracking startles me for a moment pulling me to an abrupt halt as each of the guys stare at me.

Since when the hell do I *shriek?*

"That wasn't..."

"You're p-u-s-s-y whipped." Alec chuckles, eyes focused on the miniature set in front of him.

"Am not!" I shout back but let's face it... I totally am. All I had was one taste of her. Just one taste, two months ago, and she's been all I can think about ever since.

"Are too..." Braxton sighs loudly before groaning at his phone, more than likely losing at one of the cooking games Derek got him to play.

"So, what if I am?! Have you three *seen* Cleo? She's fucking gorgeous. Sorry, Deli. As a matter of fact, don't tell me she's gorgeous, I might punch you idiots."

Jace scoffs, pausing his tinkering. He looks up at me annoyed, but I can see the amusement laced in his eyes. "Cleo has been busting your balls since you two met... It's honestly funny—"

"HELP ME!"

Jace cocks his head at my abrupt yell before a sly smile takes over his face.

"I would give you advice but my first relationship ended with a baby, so..." Derek trails off as he gathers Delilah and her things.

"Help you?" Jace asks, looking between Alec and Braxton.

Now, I know that this may be a bad idea since Jace likes to troll people for fun, but this can also be just what I need to get Cleo on my good side, for her to truly come out of her shell. So, without much thought, I slide onto the floor beside my best friend and give him my best puppy dog eyes.

"Dude..." He scrunches his face in disgust.

"Please!" I cry out reminding myself of my four-year-old cousin, Jordyn. She has the meanest puppy dog's eyes I've ever encountered.

Jace gives me a long stare before sighing, giving in to my whims, and I guess the guys take this as their sign to leave because almost immediately the four of them file out of the room.

"What do you need help with? If she agreed to go anywhere with you, nine times out of ten, it means that she likes you... I *think*. She can be a bit reclusive at times." He shrugs as if what he just told me was any news.

"Tell me something I don't know, Heart!" I groan, throwing up my arms in the air like a petulant child because that's exactly how I feel right now.

"You spent fourteen years getting to know her, I've only had sixty days. Tell me about her, who is Cleo Jones? You gotta give me something, dude."

Is this what begging is like? I've never been on the giving end of it, and I don't think I like it all too much. I'm usually the one being begged not *doing* it.

I sigh as Jace takes *forever* to find his words, he just sits in front of me staring like he's trying to crack the code on a million-dollar safe. I sink back into myself, watching him watch me.

I knew I should've just asked Georgia or Denver, those two would give me the time of day if it pertained to Cleo. I wouldn't ask the pink-haired one though, she doesn't even know my name. I mean seriously who the hell is Jake?

What if Cleo does mess with a guy named Jake and she just called me him instead? Oh my goodness, was I the misnamed side-piece?

I run a hand over my face and groan as it does nothing to calm my nerves, especially with this beady-eyed motherfucker staring at me like he's figured me out.

"You *like* her?"

Congratulations, captain fucking obvious! You've finally cracked the code.

"No... I just want to risk my spot as captain for a girl that I had a *halfway* one-night stand with two months ago *just because*". I give him a sardonic smile and immediately the small one forming on Jace's face falls.

"Okay, don't be rude, you asked me for help." Jace frowns, moving his body in a way to where he's comfortably sitting crisscrossed in front of me.

I stare blankly at him causing him to chuckle lightly. *This prick.*

"Cleo is like a breath of fresh air, whereas Georgia is like smog and the reason you need to wear masks in countries like China and shit. Cleo is like a fresh spring morning with the light morning dew, whereas Georgia is like the moment after it rains—cold, semi-pretty, *and dark.* Cleo doesn't open as easily to others but when she does it's like you're in on this wonderful secret to the joys of life. She's beautiful and clumsy and very *very* fucking nerdy about cameras—please keep her away from cameras unless you want to spend four hours looking at them in Best Buy." He pauses, looking up at the ceiling as if to think about what to say next and it is then that I see it on his face. The way his green eyes twinkle and his ears redden while talking about her has my stomach roiling.

What.

The.

Fuck?!

"You motherfucker..." I sigh, looking up at the white painted ceiling cursing the heaven's above. It would be just my luck that the girl that *I want* has a guy best friend that's fucking *in love* with her. Double points for that guy to also be *my* best friend.

FUCK ME.

FUCK.

FUCK YOU. *(WAIT...no, not fuck you? Sorry, you didn't do anything.)*

FUCK HIM, THOUGH.

FUCKING FUCKITY FUCK FUCK.

"What? You wanted me to tell you about her?" His tone is questioning as he furrows his eyebrows in confusion but what the hell is he confused about? He just practically confessed *his love* for her to *me!*

"Are you in love with her? I'm not saying I'll back off, it's every man for himself but...*are you?*" I ask, chewing on my bottom lip as I await the news that'll spin my world off its axis.

"Ew! Are you crazy? I've seen her go through puberty and her awkward stages..." He twists his face in disgust as I tilt my head at him.

"Have you *ever* loved her?" a softer, more sincere voice asks, and I don't recognize that it's my own until Jace responds with a sigh.

"Cleo and I will never be a thing like how you're thinking. We've shared baths as toddler's and beds for sleepovers, we even kissed but God no—"

"You *kissed* her?!" I shout, jumping to my feet. I think I'm going to faint. I'm seeing red and stars... but mostly fucking red.

Right now, I'm an angry bodacious bull and Jace Heart is my matador dressed in bright crimson running away from me as I charge at him.

"How the fuck did you skip over me seeing her naked?" He asks as he sprints around my bedroom, trying to get away from me but that just makes me see a brighter red as he runs out of the room.

"YOU SAW HER NAKED?!"

I take another long sip of my lemon water for the seventh time since we've been seated at Supérieure Nourriture, the latest fine dining French restaurant just twenty minutes from campus. The restaurant is the style of a candlelit dinner with basic golden candelabras at the center of each table.

My palms grow clammy as I look back up at Cleo, rubbing them against my thighs. I don't know what the hell my problem is. She and I have *shared a bed together* and now I can barely form the proper words to speak to her.

Cleo's wearing a red satin thigh length dress that clasps in a halter formation around her neck. Her long brown hair is in its signature style with half of it up and the other half down with two tendrils of hair to frame her round face.

Today, her bow of choice is on her shoes. The tiny cream bows were the first thing I'd noticed when she'd walked in front of me into the restaurant.

She shifts awkwardly as the waiter approaches us once again, asking if we're ready to order, to which Cleo asks for another five minutes to decide.

I twist the tie around my neck and frown at its tightness. Why did I even wear a tie? It's not like we're at the Met or something. I exhale deeply, a feeling of bottomless dread rumbles my stomach as realization dawns on me.

I'm completely *bombing* our first date.

"Do you feel stuffy too or is it just me?" a soft voice asks, catching my attention. Cleo's leaning across the table, her red painted lips formed in a small frown as I nod.

"You want to get out of here?"

The question causes me to wrinkle my nose but then an idea hits me, and I don't know why I hadn't thought of this before.

I give the woman in front of me a small smile before nodding, happy with my forming plan. "I think I know a place, let's get out of here." I grin, standing up from the stuffy table to hold out a hand for her.

Cleo's eyes brighten as she looks up at me from her spot before she clutches my hand and jumps out of her seat.

That's exactly how I found myself standing inside of the local Summerfield pizza shop, Pizzeria Pizza (Cliché, I know), smiling from ear to ear looking back and forth between my Jeep where Cleo sits in the front seat and to the guy making the pies I'd ordered.

I watch as Cleo films me through the windshield with her vlog camera and give it a small wave before turning back to the pizza guy.

"Hot date?" He asks, watching the exchange as I let out a low chuckle.

"The hottest."

Once I secure the pizza, I work fast to get Cleo and myself situated in the car and to our destination. She's grinning from ear to ear as she takes a bite from a slice of cheese pizza in one hand and another from her strawberry donut in the other.

During the car ride over, we laugh and talk about the semester. We even sing a few One Direction songs until we reach the final stoplight before our destination.

"Put this on your eyes for me," I say, keeping my eyes trained solely on the road as I hand her my tie.

I can hear her breath hitch as she takes the tie into her hands but Cleo, the confident girl that she is, would never let me see her off-kilter.

"You kinky bastard, I didn't know you had a thing for blindfolds." She giggles.

I smirk at her implication and place my hand on her exposed thigh.

"Oh, Princess, there's so much about me that you don't know," I tease, pulling into our destination, the smell of sea salt permeates the air as I exit the car first, leaving all of our belongings inside. I prop my phone up on a wooden plank near the car, hoping to get everything on film as I let Cleo out of the passenger side. She's definitely going to want footage of whatever happens here and I'm more than happy to do this for her.

I unbuckle her seatbelt for her, her warm fruity scent is intoxicating as I lean over her, but I suppress myself. This is about Cleo, not my horniness. Lifting her out of the car in a bridal carry, Cleo gasps from excitement as I set her down in the sand.

Her jaw drops at the sound of waves crashing in the distance and the smell of saltwater crowding our senses. I'm about to tell her to take off the blindfold but she eagerly does it before I can.

"Oh my... Blake, you didn't!" She jumps excitedly, looking back and forth between the ocean and me. Her eyes sparkle like small stars as she smiles, I can almost see her inner child smiling up at me as she throws her arms around my neck pulling me into a bone-crushing hug.

"Do you like it?" I ask as she pulls back from my neck, resting my interlocked hands on the small of her back.

"I fucking *love* it. You brought me to the beach!" She squeals, undoing us as she kicks off her heels running towards the shoreline.

As the waves come barreling back in, Cleo runs back up toward where I've wandered with the camera, smiling like a little kid in a candy store. My heart clogs in my throat, *I* did that for her.

She loosens her hair from its ponytail, ruffling it as she runs, and fuck... She looks like something out of a movie as she approaches. Her smooth brown skin glows under the natural light of the golden hour sun and is absolutely captivating.

"Well, what did you have planned? I know the cogs are spinning in that pretty little head of yours," She teases, placing her hands on her hips as she looks up at me like the little princess she is. Instead of responding to her, I held out a hand to signal for her to wait and trudge back to the Jeep, opening up the trunk where I kept a spare blanket, a cooler filled with water and Gatorade, and a small speaker.

"Welcome to our date, Princess. Follow me." I prompt her, stalking further into the beach to find a spot to set up.

She runs back to the car, grabbing our food before following me to where I set up camp. I give myself a mental pat on the back for coming up with this idea on such short notice as she plops down onto the Spiderman blanket next to me.

We sit in a comfortable silence, listening to the crashing of the ocean waves and seagulls chirping away as we eat our dinner of cheese pizza and donuts. Cleo's an iPad kid, believe it or not, so she turns on *Love in Cancun* about five minutes into our peaceful silence and insists on watching the finale with me and I'm not complaining one bit. I've grown to love the cheesy reality show since becoming friends with her and I'm *dying* to find out what happens next with America's sweetheart.

We're in the middle of a heated friendly discussion on whether or not Rosetta would pick Cooper or Judd when Cleo's phone buzzes rapidly and just as I'm about to turn away from her screen to give her privacy, I catch sight of the messages.

Unknown

don't get too comfortable little Cleo.

you know what they say about snitches, bitch.

I reel back at the last one, eyeing the woman beside me, her skin blanched of all color as she gulps.

"Who is that? Why the fuck are they talking to you like that?" I ask, blood boiling as her bottom lip wobbles slightly. If I hadn't been watching her so intently, I don't think I would have noticed it. But I am, and I did.

"It's nothing." She sighs, her voice watery as she deletes the messages from her lock screen.

"C'mon, Cleo, don't lie to me." I sigh, running a hand down my face before casting my vision back to her. "I know we're just casually dating but I want us to be friends before anything. Friends help each other and I *want* to help you. You don't deserve to be spoken to like that, regardless of whether you're in the wrong or not," I say, and mean every single word as her lower lip trembles. If I could only take it between my own and transfer all of her pain to myself, I would in a heartbeat.

Cleo seems to fight with herself for a moment, weighing the pros and cons of talking about her past life before letting out a deep and exhausted breath. And I think that's all she'll do until her porcelain mask cracks and the floodgates burst open. Cleo lets out the most heart-wrenching sob that I've ever heard and it startles me, but I instantly snap out of it when she tries and fails to calm herself.

She needs me and I want to be the one that she needs, so I reach for her, pulling her small body into my lap and hug her tight against my chest. She trembles under my touch, body heaving as she continues to cry. I massage circles into her arm with one hand and her scalp with the other, the same way I used to calm Jules down whenever she would have a panic attack.

"It's okay, baby. I got you." I soothe, rubbing small circles over her forearms as she begins to calm down.

"I... I need to... To tell you about why I left Brighton." She hiccups, snuggling deeper into my chest.

My hackles rise at the mention of her old school in New York. Is she going to tell me about Marcelo? Did he *hurt* her? *Who* are those texts from?

"I used to date this guy, Marcelo Rivers." She sniffles.

I tense at the mention of the dickhead forward for the Brighton Eagles but I have to push aside my hatred, *only* for the woman wrapped in my arms. I nod softly instead of responding. Lord knows if I use my voice, my anger will come out uncontainable.

"He and I were each other's everything, Blake, or at least I thought so then. I want to point out that I'd only ever been in one other relationship before that, so I had a really shitty idea of what love was..." She chuckles but I can tell that it takes a lot for her to say something like that about herself. "He didn't do anything to hurt me, no... He never cheated—not that I know of—and he never put his hands on me or anything like that, but he did become distant."

She chewed on her bottom lip, wiping a single tear from her cheek.

"I don't even know why I'm crying right now, it's not like I miss the asshole but *fuck* I hate that they won't leave me alone," She says with a long-frustrated sigh. "It was after a match with you guys last year, Brighton won against SFU for the first time in a *long* time, so the guys threw a major party... And I caught him doing steroids that night." Like a weight has been lifted from her shoulders, Cleo relaxes just a bit under my touch.

But my shoulders? They bunch up so hard I think that all her tension truly *did* shift to me.

Steroids? I knew Marcelo was an asshole but not a fucking idiot. I'm not too mad about the fact that he cheated in the game, I couldn't care less—we've been winning against Brighton since I started at SFU, and we'll keep winning once I retire from the NHL—but to put Cleo in the predicament of finding out like that, is what has me shaking with anger.

"He got so mad at me for barging in on him and saying that if I go to the Dean... Anyway, it was *bad*, Blake. I'd never been scared of Marcelo, he's a 6'0 hockey player, sure, but he's nothing in comparison to Ry and Jace."

She toys with the hem of my shirt before abruptly sitting up straight, looking me dead in the eyes.

"He said that if I ever told *anyone* about what I'd seen, he'd post our sex tape. I'd completely forgotten the tape existed and then he blackmailed me with it." Her face darkened as if reliving the moment he'd threatened her.

I'd never seen her look so gloomy; she radiated sunshine with her bows and pink clothing but deep-down Cleo harbored such dark things from her past. It was at that moment that I knew that whoever made Cleo feel like that, regardless of whether it was in the past, present or future, *they'd pay.*

"And then I told my roommate about what happened, stupid... I know. And then immediately after, I was outcasted by everyone—professors, students, the fucking lunch ladies. And it was only after I paid four thousand fucking dollars for my mistake that the texts started. They've been texting me since January."

January?! It's *October.*

"Cleo..." I frown, wanting so badly to ease just a fraction of her pain. She twists back around in my hold, resting her head on my chest. "What can I do to make you feel better?" I ask.

"Just hold me..." she trails off softly—and so I do.

We sit in a still position, me holding her as she and I listen to the calming tunes of our environment for all of five minutes until she jumps up from my lap with a bright smile on her face. The setting sun casts a heavenly glow behind her as she stretches, smiling from ear to ear, pulling a full 360 with her mood.

Cleo slowly lifts the bottom hem of her dress and it isn't until the soft fabric puddles on the sand by my foot that I come to the clear realization that she's stripping her clothes in front of me.

Fucking hell...

"What... What are you doing?" I cough as she turns on her heels, her matching red lace bra and underwear set does *something* to me as her ass jiggles slightly.

Have I ever told her that red was my favorite color?

She looks *amazing* in red. Fucking devilish.

"Washing the pain away... Want to join?" She cocks a raised brow at me, undoing the clasp of her bra. She turns her head to the side, eyeing me. "I mean... Why are we at the beach if not to swim?" Her voice is sultry and sweet as she rolls down her red lace panties and runs to the water, diving in.

"You coming?" she yells back to the shore, her head peeking over the water and I am enraptured by her.

I stand immediately, ripping off my shirt with eagerness. Cleo fucking Jones wants me to skinny dip with her. I hurry to take off my pants, tripping over them as I try to run before they're fully off. But who the fuck cares? That girl is going to be the death of me and I can proudly say that I will die a happy man if it means that I can spend just a little more time with her. Donning my briefs, I run to water where Cleo treads carefully and dive in.

As the sun sets behind us and the moon takes over the sun's rightful spot in the sky, I swim towards the girl of my dreams. Cleo in the light is gorgeous but in the moonlight? *She is captivating.* Her brown hair is curly from the saltwater and her skin shines a beautiful hue under the stars. I am in complete and utter awe of her, and she doesn't even know it.

"Come on, Lover Boy. I don't bite."

THIRTY-SIX

Cleo

As soon as Blake is close enough to me, I give him my evilest smirk and send a large splash of water his way. Blake has the most devious look in his eyes as he prowls towards me in the water like a starving alligator. This is the moment I realized that I fucked up.

I don't get too far in my attempt to escape his wrath and soon enough we're a laughing mess of flesh in water, splashing each other and filling the air with happiness and joy. Blake didn't have to do much to cheer me up; almost immediately after telling him about my past at Brighton, I felt an invisible weight be lifted from my shoulders. He didn't judge me for making a sex tape or interrupt me, he simply sat there and comforted me as I spilled my guts and cried to him on our *first* date.

We're splashing each other and laughing until our stomachs hurt and I don't notice the space between us receding until we're mere inches apart from one another under the setting sun.

Something in the air between us sparks to life as I beam up at the man in front of me. Blake looks like sex in human form as he wades in the water. His wavy hair sticks to his forehead and the warm tones of the pink and purple sky casts his skin in a beautiful glow as he looks down at me.

My pussy tingles from the sight of him and I can't help the yelp that escapes my lips as he pulls me into him in the water, a hand holding my lower back while the other cups my face. My heart stammers in my chest as I look up at him, the feeling of our bare chests connected sends me reeling and I can't help but smile up at him.

Blake softly pushes a curly tendril of my hair behind my ear, his raspy voice soft as he speaks.

"There you are... There's that beautiful smile," He says in a low rumble, those icy blue eyes that remind me so much of the water we're in twinkles as they flicker from my hair to my lips.

My body reacts to him as I slide closer, biting my bottom lip as his hardness presses against my belly ring. I don't have to look down to know that it's huge and when Blake adjusts his hand in my hair, pulling our face just mere centimeters apart, I know that we aren't leaving this water without consuming one another.

"I'm going to devour you, Princess," He grumbles, low and possessively but his eyes tell a much softer story as they lock with my own and I don't think twice as I connect my mouth to his.

The kiss is so much different from our previous ones, where those were like a dance, soft and sweet. This one is like a battle. Blake battles for dominance over my mouth and I put up a fight for the most part, just because I like to be a tease before I give in to him, allowing him to consume my mouth *and* me.

I moan loudly as his lips connect with the flesh of my neck and his large hand works its way from the swell of my ass to my drenched cunt.

He plays with the sensitive bud that holds all of my arousal and I arch into him as he smiles against my neck, cupping me. I groan as his tongue laps at the skin where my neck is the most sensitive and smirk at him as his strong arms grip me, pulling my body up just a bit as he takes the swell of my left breast into his mouth.

My head rolls back in pure ecstasy as he teases the pebbled skin of my breast. His teeth grazing the skin in a daring tease. I can feel his eyes on me as my breath quickens.

"Fuck, Blake..." I curse as he shifts me a little higher up, bringing my cunt to his mouth reminding me exactly why I love men in sports. They can do things that you'd never think of, and *this* is one of them.

Blake licks a long strip against my pussy, sucking and lapping up every spilled bit of my arousal into his mouth as I writhe in pleasure on his shoulders. I could care less that we're on a public beach and he's basically tongue fucking me because this right here makes it all *worth it*. My body yearns for him as he inserts his tongue further into me, pumping in and out with an intense ferocity.

My muscles tense and I'm so close to climaxing on his face that just the thought of Blake's face being decorated in my cum sends me over the edge. His low chuckle hums against my core as I ride his tongue and find the height of my pleasure comes crashing down in waves. Blake carefully settles me back in the warm water, his arms wrapped securely around me before taking my lips against his. Blake feeds me back my own pleasure and kisses me so deeply that I see stars as I taste myself on his tongue.

"Wrap your legs around me, Princess," He commands in a voice that oozes sex and I don't waste any time as I jump up in the water, wrapping myself around him.

There's only a moment of brief hesitation as we both come to the damning realization that we're missing a vital piece of our sex riddled puzzle.

We don't have a condom.

"Are you–"

"I'm on the pill. It's okay," I speak eagerly before thinking as he smirks up at me. Maybe I'm just a little bit *too ready* to have sex with him.

Blake's eyes darken as he watched me, his lips quivering in a smirk. "How do you want me, Princess?" he asks, repeating his question from just two months ago when we'd been in a similar situation and this time, I don't hesitate to answer.

"I want you so deep inside of me that the world spins, Blake Wilder, and you better not go easy on me–"

Now, because it is nearing nighttime and I hadn't seen Blake's dick before he'd jumped into the water, I had zero idea just how massive he truly was. The look in his eyes is of pure lust as he cups my bare ass in his large hands and roughly sinks me onto him.

I cry out in immense pleasure mixed with pain at his thick girth and way above average length. But Blake just eats up that sound with his mouth as he fucks me over and over again, lifting me up and down on his cock so hard I can't see straight.

"Oh my God, Blake! I'm gonna–"

"I know, baby, I know." He growls as he quickens the pace in which he connects us, pounding me senselessly.

I see stars and I'm not talking about the ones above as Blake pumps me so hard and deep, I feel him in my stomach, banging against my G-spot until I'm sent over the edge.

I'm not usually a screamer but tonight, I scream so loudly you can hear me in Nebraska as I cum all over his sweet dick. Blake lets out a groan of pleasure as his balls tighten, releasing his orgasm inside of me.

Our breaths are heavy as we stare into one another's eyes, breathing each other in deep as our heartbeats begin to align. Blake's eyes hold something I can't quite place in the darkness of the night but I can feel it as he pulls me closer than before and takes my mouth into his.

THIRTY-SEVEN

Cleo

BLAKE LEADS ME OUT of the water, his arm wrapped loosely around my waist as our naked bodies walk to where we'd set up our makeshift picnic. He pulls his button-up shirt over my head and gives my forehead a small kiss before tugging on his pants.

"I'll be right back. I'm going to get a change of clothes for us. I keep a spare of everything in the trunk," He says with a low yawn before heading back over to where his bright red Jeep is parked. I smirk at the sight of the truck and the fact that I wore red tonight knowing it was his favorite color. And after seeing the look of pure lust in Blake's eyes after he first saw me, I knew I made the right decision.

As he pops open the trunk, he does a quick look around, not thinking to look back at me, before pumping the air with his fist.

That's it, everyone. That right there is what made me fall for Blake Wilder. A fucking fist pump.

I can't see his face but I can tell that he's smiling from ear to ear as he does a small dance, gathering clothes from the trunk.

The air on the beach is chilly since we're so close to the water, so I snuggle into his button up deeper, looking out at the ocean waves.

I couldn't have asked for a more perfect first date. I got pizza, donuts, and the best goddamn sex of my life *on the beach*. I can honestly die a happy woman.

"Here." Blake's low voice startles me. I jump, whirling around to see him holding a hoodie and sweatpants for me. "Put these on. They might be a little big but you'll look good regardless."

I croak out a small thank you before pulling on each of the items and watch him as he does the same, taking a seat next to me.

"Can I?" He asks, staring me down with wide dilated eyes fixated on my large crown of curls.

Now, usually when a white man asks to touch my hair–*Hell*, when *any* man *or* woman wants to... I say no. But the look of pure awe and fascination in Blake's eyes has my heart skipping multiple beats and before I can think twice, I'm nodding my head.

Blake gasps as he softly tugs on one of my curls, twirling it with his finger and giggles–I kid you not–as the curl spirals back into its original place.

"I love your hair how you normally wear it but it's fucking gorgeous like this, baby." His voice is soft and smooth like lukewarm butter as he coo's before tugging me against him, holding me from behind.

I lean back into Blake's embrace, resting my head on his chest and watch as the ocean's waves crash against the shore.

The sun has fully set at this point and instead of being basked in darkness, the moon's light shines upon us casting a soft glow over the beach. I look up at Blake, analyzing his features and noting the small freckle he has on the bottom of his jaw.

"I had a lot of fun with you tonight," I say without thought as his body rumbles from under me with his small laugh.

"I had a lot of fun with you too, Cleo."

I scrunch my nose at the use of my name and Blake seems to notice; he throws his head back in a deep laugh as I frown.

"*Princess*. I meant Princess." He chuckles.

Good. Once you start using a nickname on someone, you can't just revoke it. That's like the universal nickname law. I don't make the rules.

We sit in a gentle silence, the only sound to be heard out of the two of us being the environment until both of our stomachs rumble at the same time. The action has us reeling with laughter but Blake recovers first.

"C'mon, there's a boardwalk just a few steps away," He says and that's how I find myself walking down a boardwalk at 10 p.m. hand-in-hand with a 6'4" hockey player.

We buy any and everything, completely bypassing Blake's strict diet for tonight only as we stuff our mouths. I'm scarfing down my second fried Oreo when Blake pauses in front of the last open game stall.

Can anyone guess what stall it is? *No?* I'll tell you. It's dart's.

Blake gives me a mischievous grin before proceeding to tug me toward the large stall. The lonely worker at the stand gives us an unenthusiastic smile as Blake hands him a fifty-dollar bill. My eyes widen at the quantity but when he gives me a quick wink, I decide that it'll be best to keep my mouth shut. He has a plan and I'm not sure if it's one that'll leave me with a dart or stuffed animal in my arms.

"I'm going to win you that flamingo," Blake announces, setting down his phone and funnel cake fries as I raise a brow at him. "I'm serious. I'm *going to* win it!" he insists, taking hold of all of the darts. He oozes confidence and I think for just a moment, he'll be like he was when we'd first played darts—shitty with terrible aim.

But as I watch him take a step back and hold the dart at eye level, I know that it'll hit its target before it ever leaves his finger tips. Within four tries of throwing darts, Blake has won not only the pink flamingo he'd set out for but also two smaller plushies of Maryland's blue crab wearing sombreros, one pink and one red.

Just like us.

As we make our way back to our spot on the beach, we're talking nonstop about any and everything. Blake tells me more about Jules and I tell him all that I know about Lorelei's wedding.

"If I was a worm, would you still want to date me?" I ask, looking over at Blake as we settle back on our blankets.

He makes a show of pondering the question before shrugging. "I'd date you in any lifetime, in any form, Cleo Jones."

Hello, heart? *Yeah... How does it feel to be snatched?*

I don't think twice as I lean in, puckering my lips. Blake meets me halfway, kissing me so soft and tenderly that my legs go numb. As we part, our eyes slowly open, solely focusing on one another. My face heats up from the searing look that he gives me as it burns into the depths of my soul. It's intoxicating and embarrassing how flustered I'm getting. I reach for a lifeline and play with the toy crabs he'd won me.

Once I make myself busy arranging Laker, his wife Leo, and their child, Phoenix the flamingo, the sound of an iPhone camera recording grabs my attention.

"What are you doing?" I ask, my tone dripping with amusement as I whirl around to the smiling man behind me.

Blake chuckles as he holds his phone up higher, more than likely to get a video of my makeshift family.

"Capturing the moment, Princess."

THIRTY-EIGHT

Cleo

As a bright light beams down on my face, I groan, trying to shut out the light with my blanket. *Fucking weighted blanket won't*—A low groan stills me in my action, I pop an eye open, looking around to gauge my surroundings. Red beady eyes and a pink sombrero meet my gaze, is that a crab in a sombrero?

Oh my God, that *wasn't* a dream.

The sound of crashing waves and seagulls calling filters into my senses as I look down at my "weighted blanket". Blake's arm is wrapped firmly around my torso, holding me securely against him. I sigh, relieved at the sight of him beside me and I don't ignore the sense of security that I feel either when I spin in his embrace, finally facing him.

Blake looks like a peaceful angel as he sleeps, his skin slightly tan from the mid-October sun beaming down on us. His dark brown hair lays messily across his forehead and just as I'm about to reach up to touch his face, his low, sleepy voice comes out to play.

"Take a picture," He grumbles, both eyes still closed and I would if I could but my phone is out of reach so I opt for the next best thing and kiss him.

He holds the back of my head in place as he deepens it and I'm just about to straddle him when my phone chimes, putting a pause on our make out.

Cupid

> Dude what the fuck are you doing at the beach?

> Okay Cleo this is getting out of control.

> Sienna and Georgia said you didn't come home last night

> Where you at chica?????

> Mama you up?

> I'll meet you at the brunch spot! Don't worry I'll get your Pina Colada too lmao

> I'm so ready to get day drunk.

> WOOT WOOOTTTTT

> BIRTHDAY BRUNCH

> BIRTHDAY BRUNCHHH

Oh my fucking goodness... I push myself out of Blake's hold, wiggling to a sitting position as I read over a few of the messages that Jace had sent.

What day is it... It can't be the 26th already. I think, but one quick glance at today's date has my heart dropping to the pits of hell. I jump up to my feet, stumbling a bit on shaky legs as I read over the messages from the group chat with the girls, all asking about my whereabouts.

"What is it?" Blake's tone is startled as he looks up at me from the ground, his hair ruffled with sleep and eyes still a bit puffy.

"The brunch! Today's Jace's birthday brunch. Fuck!" I curse.

Every year on the Saturday before October 31st, Jace, Georgia, Sienna, and I go out for brunch to celebrate our favorite Scorpio. We'd only ever missed one brunch together, and that was last year when I couldn't make it to Maryland because of midterms.

Blake seems to catch my drift as he lets out a low curse before scurrying to clean up our things. He's so quick that I don't even notice that everything is packed up until he holds a hand out to me. He makes quick work of getting us onto the road and we sit in a tense, yet comfortable silence as we ride down the highway back to campus.

The usual 45-minute trek from Summer Cove Beach to Summerfield University took 30 minutes with Blake using the back roads and smooth driving skills. It isn't until we're parked in front of his house that I begin to freak out again, only to be shut down by him.

"My house is closer than your apartment, Princess. Take a shower here. Then we can head over to your place to change and go to brunch from there. I think Jace was just trying to get you to be on time. I double checked the reservation and it's set for 1:30... It's only 10 a.m. right now. You have time." He gives my knee a reassuring squeeze. I wrap my hand around his and sigh, smiling up at him.

If Blake hadn't been with me, I'm pretty sure I would have spiraled for being a bad friend.

"Now, c'mon... I'll start a nice hot shower for you and then, we can have a little talk about last night." He says in the most soothing voice ever that I almost don't hear the end of his sentence. I tense a bit at the mention of our night on the beach, but I sigh, following him into the townhouse. I don't regret *anything*.

Hell, I'd do it again if I didn't already think that you can't recreate perfection.

"None of the guys' cars are out front so we should be fine getting up to my room without interruption," Blake says, looking back at me from the front door. His reassurance puts a part of me that I didn't know was tense, at ease, but just as I'm about to let out a deep breath, the front door swings open.

"Yeah, I'll be back! I just have to–WHAT THE FUCK?! What the *actual* fuck?! You've got to be fucking–What the fuck?!" Jace exclaims, going through the seven stages of grief.

He has his phone up to his ear, obviously talking to someone, but immediately hangs up at the sight of us. Jace's mouth drops so low that I imagine him catching flies as he flips his green eyes between Blake and I furiously.

"Happy birthday, best buddy!" I smile, ignoring his shocked and frozen state as I hug him, kissing his cheek.

Jace immediately recovers, wiping off my kiss with a look of pure disgust. "I don't want your grimy Wilder lips on me, CJ. Go brush your teeth this instant!" he yells and I roll my eyes at how extra he's being right now.

"What makes you think that we did anything? We could've just spent the night talking!" I shoot back, resting my hands on my hips to stand on my lies.

Jace gives me an unimpressed look, resembling a disappointing dad and all-knowing best friend. "Babe, you reek of sex and ocean water. Let's be so serious right now."

My mouth drops, I don't smell *that* damn bad. I'm about to stick with my lie and protest his absurdities when Blake sidles up to me and places a heavy arm over my shoulder. Jace's eyes widen a fraction larger, looking us over.

"I'm gonna fucking barf. This is grosser than when we kissed," he gags, a faint smirk hidden in his eyes as I roll my own.

"Darling, these are the best lips on the Western side of the world," I tut, folding my arms over my chest. I look up at Blake for a semblance of backup, but eyes scream internal laughter as he remains quiet in our 'bestie battle'.

"Sure they are, doll. Anyways, I've got a little minx to catch. I'll see you later, CJ. And Wilder...don't kill my best friend, they only made one of her in the bow-loving, donut-eating factory and I'd rather not lose the one that was gifted to me by said factory." Jace chuckles, patting Blake's cheek as he steps around us in the doorway, pulling down his sunshades.

I tilt my head, jaw agape at his actions as Blake and I watch Jace casually strut towards his car.

"Little minx?" I whisper as Blake scrunches his nose.

"I'm still stuck on you talking about your lips..." He sighs, gently pushing me into the house shaking his head.

"They're divine aren't they? I got them for free!" I tease, twirling on my heels.

The smile Blake gives me is full of amusement and light as he locks the door behind himself. We sit in silence for a few moments, taking one another in. It's then, in the silence of one another, that I realize two things: One, Jace was right, we reek of the ocean and sex. And two, we're the only people here.

Blake seems to realize it at the same time as me. He gently wraps his arms around my waist, but I don't miss the small glimmer in his eyes.

"Jump," He commands in a voice so deep and sultry it has my tummy boiling with heat.

Now, usually when a man tells me to do anything of the sort with any type of commanding tone, I'm quick to clap-back.

However, Blake Wilder is a walking wet dream and if he tells me to 'jump' *like that,* I'm asking *"how fucking high?"*

Immediately, I do as told, and wrap my legs around his waist with my arms around his neck. Blake's palms fall to my ass, squeezing in a teasing manner before securely holding me against him, the action has me beaming. I try to play it cool as I look down at him, but the playful smirk he sends back up to me has me giddy like a schoolgirl girl in front of her crush.

I smile so hard, I think my cheeks are broken.

He walks me up the stairs with ease, never breaking eye contact with me as he enters his bedroom, crossing straight over to his bathroom. It's only when he sets me down on his sink that I realize Blake's ears are redder than a hot tamale as he sheepishly looks around.

"Can I..." He chews on his bottom lip, looking everywhere but me. His confidence suddenly replaced with that of a nervous boy.

"Can you..." I narrow my eyebrows playfully, analyzing his jittery figure.

"Can I wash your hair?"

Have I ever mentioned that my heart has grown three sizes bigger since meeting Blake? If I haven't, then let me reiterate. My heart, like the Grinch's, has grown *exponentially*. Blake has the key to my heart and the lock that's used to hold it together.

I nod, unable to contain my excitement as Blake beams up at me. "Oh, Princess, I'm going to wash your hair so fucking good, you'll want me as your personal hairstylist." He smirks, planting a fat juicy kiss upon my lips before ducking into the cabinets under the sink to get shampoo, conditioner, and the Pineapple Pina body wash that I normally use.

"How'd you–"

"Jace left it in here, he uses it all the time. This, and a citrus one." Blake shrugs, unknowingly filling my heart even more.

That fucker Jace loves me, I know he does.

Blake pauses a beat, watching me carefully as I look up at him. "Now, if I fuck up your hair, please don't kill me!" he disclaims, turning on the shower and checking the temperature.

As he does so, it gives me the chance to look over the vast bathroom. There are black modernized appliances throughout the house that complimented the boys well but what stood out in the bathroom the most is Blake's comic-themed shower curtain.

Where his room holds all of his nerdy habits discretely, his bathroom is fully decked out in all things 'Blake'. His bathroom rug reads "Naked Babes Only", his soap dispenser is LEGO-shaped, and he has a small cluster of movie posters in front of his toilet—all framed.

I smile at the sight of the tiny LEGOs on the top of the bathroom mirror, just as Blake whirls around, grinning at me.

"Like what you see?" he asks, a teasing lilt to his tone as I roll my eyes, shifting on the cold sink counter under me.

"What's the story behind the LEGOs?" I question, my eyes flickering from the unfinished Eiffel Tower on Blake's desk, just in view of the bathroom door and the Lego soap dispenser beside me.

Blake tenses momentarily before giving me a soft smile. "When I came to my parents, the only thing that I had with me was a LEGO shaped plushy and the clothes on my back." He sighs. "My mom and dad have bought them for me ever since. We would host family building nights where we'd watch movies and just build LEGO sets for hours." Blake chuckles as his eyes glaze over with the memories of his childhood, the bittersweet memory makes my heart yearn for the older version of him and just want to hold the child version.

No one deserves the things that Blake went through as a kid. No one. I believe that if you're going to bring a child into the world the least you can do is give them your all. They didn't ask to be brought here, so it's rather selfish if you bring them into the world and treat them like trash.

Blake strides up to me slowly, and stands between my legs. He wraps his arms around my waist, squeezing it slightly before letting them rest at the swell of my ass. His eyes are an array of emotions, but the one that has my thighs tightening is one that I'm all too familiar with.

"Well, we could build something together if you want," I suggest in a tone completely at odds with my normal one. This is a tone of pure seduction and ease.

"We can do a lot more than that."

He smirks, looking down at me for a moment before bringing my lips to his own, sealing them with a kiss.

"Strip," He commands, voice husky.

What's that saying from the blue guy in the lamp? Oh... Right.

Your wish is my command.

Blake's wishing and commanding, and I'm more than willing to do what ever he wants when he looks at me like this.

As I pull his hoodie up to my waist, with the large SFU paraphernalia being the size of a mid-length dress on me, I grin as Blake helps me get it over my large array of curls.

My breasts drop from under the hoodie, Blake's gaze darkens at the sight of them in the light of his bathroom. I realize now that this is the first time we'd seen each other naked in the light and when he proceeds to strip himself bare, my eyes nearly bulge at the sight of his taught erection.

There is no way in hell that was inside of me last night. No fucking way. Blake's dick is bigger than the size of a goddamned Stanley cup... And for those that don't know what size a Stanley cup is... Go google it and come back to me.

He smirks at my obvious shock from his sizing, he's both thick in girth and large in length. I'm still in a state of shock as he picks me up from the counter, smacking my ass. The warm stinging sensation brings me back momentarily as I look up at him.

"No funny business, I swear. I just want to wash your hair." The smirk that Blake holds is anything but innocent, so I roll my eyes at him.

Yeah fucking right.

I hop in the shower, turning my back to the spray, dousing my hair in the warm water as Blake steps in facing me.

"Let me," he says, holding the shampoo bottle. I tense at the way he holds the bottle like he'll use only a quarter-sized amount of shampoo on my hair and when he notices my hesitancy, he twirls me around. "I got you, Princess. I told you zero funny business. Just think of this as me trying to save water." I can hear the smirk on his lips as he slowly massages the clarifying shampoo into my scalp.

We all know that Blake is a beast with his hands. Exhibit A: when he simultaneously fingered and ate me out when we first met. But the way that he works his fingers into my scalp, assuring that my hair is scrubbed and clean has my back arching. I moan in pleasure and he pauses, then lightly chuckles before continuing, stepping a bit closer to me.

My body reacts to him as his large length presses against the shell of my ass, and a pool of desire forms between my legs.

"Blake..."

"Yes, Princess?" His voice is strained as he twirls me around, rinsing out the shampoo in my hair.

"Please fuck me," I blurt out. His eyes widen momentarily as he smirks.

"Oh, baby, I'll do more than fuck you. I'm going to make you cum so hard you forget your own name." He grins, stepping closer to me under the spray of the shower.

Blake takes my mouth into his in a kiss filled with passion and desire. His hands grope my ass, spreading and massaging my cheeks in a way that has me grinding into him.

The small laugh he tries to conceal is dark and enticing as he rubs his hard cock against my sweetness.

"You're going to be the death of me, Cleo Jones," he says lowly, eyes clouded with a look I can't place as I look up at him.

"I'll make sure you have a lovely funeral." I smirk, pulling his mouth back to connect to mine.

The way that we mold together like a perfect set of LEGOs doesn't pass me by as we move harmoniously in the small enclosed space.

Blake spares no time as he pushes me against the wall. He looks as if he's about to get on his knees to eat me out but I shake my head at him.

I've never been one for true foreplay. Simply kissing me like you want to own me has always done the trick, so when he tilts his head in confusion, looking up at me from his knees, I smirk.

"I said I wanted you to fuck me, not tease my clit."

He doesn't say anything as he stands to his full height, towering down on me. Instead, he pulls my chin up to his face, devouring me inside out with only his lips.

"Lift your leg, baby"

I lift up my right leg slightly but that's not enough for Blake. Blake takes the leg in his hand, hauling it up against his shoulder, and rams into me without warning. I cry out in both pain and pleasure as he rocks into me with unbridled passion.

"Fuck!" I cry out as he soothes me, whispering sweet nothings into my hair as our chests rise and fall against one another.

"You're my everything, baby." His words are sweet, soft even, but the way he picks up his pace inside of me is anything but.

Blake fucks me into oblivion, the roughness of his jerky movements completely at odds with the tenderness of his words as he sucks on the soft spots of my neck, hard.

"Oh, Blake." I moan as his middle and ring finger eases between us, circling my clit as he rocks into me, building up the massive swirl of heat within me as he picks up his pace. A weird feeling of fullness blooms in my stomach.

"You want to cum, baby?" He asks and almost instantly, an uncontrollable feeling of a release flows out of me but it's not an orgasm. "Shit, that's so fucking hot," He says looking down at the sight of me, squirting on his cock.

My mouth drops as I watch the way my body reacts to him, and the sight of my pleasure mixed with his is all that I need to see before a feeling of pure ecstasy washes over me and I finally have one of the most earth-shattering orgasms on Blake's dick.

Blake finishes moments later, ruthlessly pumping into me before pulling out and finishing himself off.

In my post orgasm haze, I remain quiet as I watch Blake work. He kisses me deeply before cleaning the both of us up. Blake steps out of the shower, careful of getting the floor wet, kissing me one last time before getting a towel, and wrapping me in it.

"That's one orgasm... you up for another?" he asks, tilting his head to the side as my eyes widen.

Another one?!

"Remember, Princess, I'm going to make cum so much... You're gonna forget your name."

THIRTY-NINE

Cleo

"Can I have a bottle of hot sauce, please? Yes, that's perfect. Thank you!" Dad thanks the waitress before turning his attention back to Ryan and I across the table. "So, what's new? It's crazy to me that now that both of my kids are on the same campus, I rarely see either of y'all." Dad sighs, folding his hands over one another.

"Aw, don't lie, old man, you miss the little princess more, we just played cards last night." Ry chuckles, waving off our dad as he skims over the menu.

Of all the people on the SFU campus, my father and younger brother have been the two people whom I've seen the *least*. It makes me a little sad that I haven't spent as much time with either of them, but we've all been pretty busy with school and games.

"Well, of course, I miss my daughter! She's never around." Dad pouts as he swirls his sweet tea around in his cup. I frown at his words but choose to ignore them as Ryan finishes ordering his food and the waitress approaches me.

She's pretty in an early 2000s model kind of way with a beautiful facial structure and bold runway style makeup. As I look up at the girl named Yanai, as told by her name tag, a startled gasp erupts from Ryan as well as an angry grumble from my dad.

My eyes widen and I slowly turn to face two of the most important men in my life, each of them equally pissed off in their own ways.

"What *the fuck* is that?!" Dad whisper-yells first, pointing his knife at the badly concealed giant purple hickey coloring the skin of my neck.

Before our small brunch date, Georgia and I spent fifteen minutes trying our hardest to conceal all of the small love bites.

Looks like we missed one.

"You fucking?" Ryan sniffs, nose upturned in disgust.

Dad lets out a horrified gasp. "Your sister–*Ew*. Why the fuck would you say that shit?"

It's been a week since Blake and I spent almost a full day entangled in one another until he made me forget my own name—his words. We've seen each other since then at our shared classes and in passing, but we haven't had the opportunity to talk about *us*.

"I thought we agreed on no boys." The look that Clef Jones sends me is the same one he uses to make grown men cry on the ice. I'm used to it, having received it my whole life, so instead of cowering, I straighten my spine.

"We did," I say feigning nonchalance.

"Then who–" Ryan starts only to be cut off by the sound of whistling, the smells of cedar wood and vanilla intoxicate my senses and I know automatically who it is.

Blake.

"What happened to my sister's neck?" Ryan asks the walking man, grabbing him by the sleeve of his hoodie.

Blake startles, looking like a deer in headlights but quickly recovers, sparing me a quick glance.

"You better let go of my captain. I need him for the game this Wednesday. Besides, Cleo doesn't know Wilder from a can of paint," my father says, looking down at his phone completely unaware of the googly eyes we're shooting one another back and forth.

"Actually..." Blake starts, winking at me before facing my dad, "I know Cleo *really* well sir," He says, smirking as my dad looks up at him, tilting his head in confusion. "She and I are partners for that film project that I was telling you about right, prin–CJ?" Blake asks, eyes finally catching mine again.

I chew on my bottom lip, stifling my giggles as I nod in agreement and Ryan scoffs. I smack the back of his head and grit my teeth at him as he rolls his eyes.

"Oh, well, good. Keep an eye on one another. Wilder, if you see some dipshit around her other than Heart, whoop his ass. She has a damn hickey on her neck." My dad sneers as if the very thought of me dating disgusts him as Ryan chuckles silently from beside me, Blake lets out a choked laugh.

"Will do, Coach. Trust me, Cleo is in *good hands.*"

"Oh my fucking–OH!" I cried out as Blake inserted yet another finger into me.

After brunch with my dad earlier this morning, Blake and I went our separate ways. Him to hockey practice and classes, and me back home to spend time with the girls. I'd told them all about my brunch and my date with Blake last week. We'd all been so busy with midterms that tonight was our only time to gossip. Everything had been going fine during our girls' night until Denver got a text from the *mystery man* she's been seeing and left.

Sienna left soon after, stating that she needed to go to the studio to fine-tune choreography with her dance partner, Aidan, for the Winter Showcase.

And then there were two—just me and Georgia. We spent our time talking about who was on the grid this season until she got an important email regarding her design class and left to answer it.

Leaving me by myself even though we'd started this night as a *group.*

I'd been peacefully watching *Love on the Brain,* a new VR dating show when a knock rang through the apartment.

Blake stood at our apartment door in a pair of gray sweats and a Twisted Vipers T-shirt, holding two take-out boxes of Neo's Sushi and a box of donuts from The Sugar Hole.

Blake dropped our food on the table and opened his arms wide for me to jump into them.

Almost immediately, I jumped his bones.

Literally.

And that was how I found myself getting fingered by him yet again after two previous orgasms. Once we'd gotten ourselves cleaned up, we sat on my living room floor with both of our computers in our laps, watching *Love on the Brain* while doing homework. My legs are thrown across Blake's lap with his hand massaging small circles on them as we do our own tasks.

We feel awfully couple-y and the idea of it doesn't slip past my mind at all as we sit like this in comfortable bliss.

FOrTY

Blake

"POUR ME A SHOT MOTHERFUCKERS!" Jace shouts from the top of his lungs for the second time tonight, a bottle of champagne in his raised hand.

Tonight is Halloween and the blonde fucks 20th birthday at Breeze Nightclub. The club is filled to the brim with celebrities, socialites, and all of our friends. Breeze has four different levels shaped in a square pattern with a large dance floor on the bottom level that can be seen from each floor.

Jace closed off the top two levels for his birthday to make sure that all of his people were good before outsiders, which may sound expensive but it isn't at all...*for him*. Jace being the youngest son of the wealthiest nightclub owner in the world gives him the chance to do any and every thing he wants tonight since he *technically* owns the place.

Bottle girls dressed as different story book characters come back around with bright signs and cheers alerting all of the partygoers that tonight is in fact Jace Heart's 20th birthday.

Tonight, all of the team is out, including the freshmen—except for Derek. Delilah's at home with him this weekend instead of with her grandma so all of us went trick or treating earlier together before the party and Derek went back home to spend quality time with his daughter.

"*Idiot!* You can't get a girl's number like that... You're going to end up on one of those lists." Braxton frowns, smacking the head of one of our freshmen, Jacob McCarthy. McCarthy, who's dressed as the wolf from Red Riding Hood, groans as he looks down at his large yellow slippers and sighs as Braxton gives him a stern talking to.

I chuckle as Braxton continues grilling the guy until a girl, dressed in black lingerie with a cat headband over purple and black hair, bumps into me, spilling a small bit of her drink on my costume.

"I'm so sorry! I was *definitely* not paying attention." She sounds genuine enough until she chuckles, I raise a brow at her as she stares up at me.

"Hey! You're kinda cute, my best friend, Amalia, would eat you right up–"

"Phoenix! What're you doing here...*in that?* Hot damn, girl, do a spin!" Jace whistles, holding up the mysterious woman's hand in the air as she giggles, spinning around in a sexy move.

I quickly avert my eyes from the two, Jace can have *that*.

"A sexy sailor? Cupid, the things I would do to you if I liked dick," She teases, kissing his cheek as Jace rolls his eyes.

As the *mysterious cat* and Jace make their way back to the packed section, I follow behind, chuckling as the girl continues to bust his balls the entire way.

We're all seated in our section, some people dancing, but since it's quieter in this area, a lot of us are sitting around on the couches talking with one another.

I'm deep in an argument with Tu about whether or not he and Charlie are compatible when the guys begin howling and letting out whistles and shouts. I immediately turn to what's causing all the chaos and my mouth drops at the sight of *who* it is.

Cleo struts towards us dressed in a white corset with the tiniest white ruffled skirt I've ever seen in my life. She has on white lace gloves that end mid-bicep, with a white laced veil and frilly garter on her left leg. Her plump lips are decorated with pink gloss and she smirks as she approaches us. I don't even notice her other friends until Georgia's voice cuts off the insane thoughts that go through my mind of what I'm going to do to her tonight.

"So, are you saving Cleo tonight? Don't worry, I'll set a fire somewhere." She giggles, clearly a bit tipsy as she smiles wildly at me.

Georgia's dressed similarly to Cleo. She's clad in an all-red, off-the-shoulder corset dress that ties in the front. Her makeup is darker, accentuating her eyes and red lips. She also has a kiss print on her right cheek and a single handcuff attached to her left wrist.

"Girl please, he can barely save himself." An all too familiar voice chuckles, and it's then that I look up at my annoying cousin who just so happens to be my best friend.

Denver's in her usual color of choice, black. She has on a black lace bodysuit, *clearly* lingerie with a minuscule mesh black skirt. Denver's dark hair is in loose waves over her shoulders while her neck is decorated to look as if her throat had been sliced with blood dripping out.

My eyes widen in horror at the sight of her, "Ew! Go change, dude." I gag as she groans but before Denver can say anything else, my eyes stray back to Cleo.

Fucking hell.

Have I already mentioned that she's going to be the death of me?

"Kiss, marry, or kill us." She grins playfully as she looks up at me, though she's wearing heels, I still have a good couple inches over her.

"I'll kiss you, CJ!" one of the guys shout. I don't care who the fuck it is because she's coming home with me tonight. But I do turn to glare at every single fuck face behind me to reinstate that point.

"I'll kiss and marry you right now," I whisper in Cleo's ear. She pauses, looking me up and down as a slow smirk creeps onto her face just as she gets bumped into like how I did earlier.

"I am so sorry!" a dark skinned man with a deep voice grumbles out just as the girl behind the man slaps the back of his head.

"Watch where you're going, Jay! You almost knocked the fine girl–Cleo!?" a brown skinned girl with a blonde wig and faux scars along her face screams, hugging Cleo tight against her.

"Mali?! Oh my God! I thought you weren't coming! Girl, who is that fine ass man that you just smacked?" Cleo asks, clearly excited to see her friend.

My neck, however, snaps at her comment.

Fine?! I mean he's not ugly but...*fine?!*

"And who the hell is the sexy firefighter behind you, staring at you like a goddamn snack? Girl, he is hot! Pun intended," the friend squeals and I'm instantly smug as all outdoors.

The guy and I share an equally smug and amused look with one another over the girls' heads as they continue catching up. When we realize that they'll spend the entire night talking to one another, we converse on our own.

I soon find out that the man's name is Jayson and we talk about our equal love for our sports, his being basketball and mine obviously being hockey. It isn't until Jace calls the attention of everyone in our section to play a game of drink or dare, that I realize Jayson and I have been talking for the same amount of time as Cleo and Amalia.

"Gather around kids, the king is ready to be entertained!" Jace jeers as more and more people surround the seated area. "I'll start first." Jace perks up, resting his elbows on his knees as he looks around the group.

"Cleo! My *bestest* friend, have you ever been skinny-dipping?" Jace's eyes gleam with mischief, and my muscles tense as I stare daggers into the side of his skull.

Had Jace said any other thing to her I would've been okay with it but to basically air out our dirty laundry has me wanting to pull his intestines out through his mouth.

Cleo's eyes brim with fire as she looks down at her blonde friend; she's standing behind me talking to Amalia so I have to crane my head to watch her as she answers.

"Yeah." She shrugs as if it's nothing but I know that it's *everything* and the look that she sends my way is a clear murder sentence.

I am going to die at the hands of the bride of All Hallow's Day.

Forty-one

Cleo

BLAKE AND I SPEND the entire night practically socially distanced. Well... more like *me* socially distancing myself from him. Everywhere I go, he's there and when I figure out how to escape him, he's there *again*. It irks my nerves for the final time as I come to a halt at the bar and he slides up to me.

"Listen, baby–"

Baby?! I am not his baby.

My legs are wobbly as I turn around on him, ready to give him a piece of my mind but the six shots of vodka with Jace and Georgia are at odds with my body and I stumble a bit more than I mean to.

"How could you?" My words ring longer in my ears as Blake's eyes widen looking down at me.

The blaring music of Breeze's fourth floor overpowers my words so he bends slightly, putting his ear close to my lips. My body craves him as soon as I get a whiff of his enchanting scent.

Down girl! We're supposed to be mad.

"What's wrong?" he asks softly, rubbing the goosebumps on my arms as I throw my head back to the sky.

"You told him!" I shout but Blake doesn't seem to understand me as he tilts his head at me.

"I sold who?"

"Told!" I yell.

"*Sold?* Princess, I think you need a ride home." He frowns, gently plucking my Blue Lagoon from me, setting it back on the bar.

"I don't *need* nothing!" I pout.

"Yeah, you're done. Jump?" He asks, holding out his arms like normal and I'm so tempted to say yes but my body disagrees. That, however, does nothing to stop Blake as he nods his head and scoops me up bridal style.

"You look beautiful, by the way," He whispers in my ear, awakening the butterflies in my stomach but I want to milk this angry charade for as long as possible so instead of smiling back at him, I pout.

"Yeah. Yeah. Yeah."

When I wake up the next morning, my head is an aching mess as I squint at my surroundings. The room is still dark, I'm wrapped snugly in a red blanket.

I know immediately from the sweet smell of the covers that I'm in Blake's bed, but I don't fully notice him until I turn completely on my side to see him snuggled adorably with the covers wrapped around his head like a cocoon.

"Mornin', Princess," He rasps, opening a single eye as I smile back at him, only for it to drop as I remember that I was mad at him.

"You told Jace," is the first thing to come out of my mouth and Blake chuckles, stretching a bit before looking back at me.

"No, you told him. He'd already known by the time I told him." He sighs, opening both eyes to stare me down.

Did I really?

"I didn't–"

"You did. He told me you called him after getting piss poor drunk with the girls one night," Blake says amused by the clear frown on my face.

"I don't remember that," I groan as he wraps an arm around my waist, pulling me closer.

"I bet." He yawns, falling back asleep but I'm wide awake.

I pry myself from Blake, checking my phone for the time. I search high and low for my pink cell phone only to find it plugged in by Blake's desk and mirror.

It's then that I notice that I look completely different from the night before. My hair is covered by a pink bonnet, my face is makeup-free, and my clothes have been swapped with an oversized t-shirt.

I move swiftly around Blake's room, unaware of the now wide-awake man on the bed as I stumble over my own platform heels.

I face the bed when the faint sound of stifled laughter rings through the quiet room and narrow my eyes on Blake.

"You were mad at me last night because you thought I aired out our dirty laundry?" He asks, raising an eyebrow as I nod. Blake takes my words into consideration and nods before sliding to the edge of his bed, sitting directly in front of me. His hands find my waist, holding me in place as he speaks.

"How about this, we don't speak about our relationship to anyone until we're both ready. Our relationship is sacred to us, we shouldn't fight before we get a chance to get closer," He says and my nose scrunches at his wording.

Relationship?

This is not a relationship.

"Blake, honey...I'm going to say this once. We are not in a relationship until I have the title of girlfriend. Until I'm properly asked to be that, we aren't in a relationship. Now, I have to get back home. I forgot that I promised my brother that we'd hang out today," I say, turning on my heels to face his door, ready to get out here.

Classic, Cleo...letting past transgressions affect your current greatness.

It's not Blake's fault that I've become like this over the past couple of years, a major part of me knows that, but the less logical, smaller part of me has an inkling that if I were to pursue anything with Blake Wilder, I'd only end up hurt in the end.

"Why're you so pouty today? Did The Sugar Hole run out of Pink Truffle?" Ryan asks from the other side of our booth at Doug's Diner, his choice of location for today's lunch date.

After Dad pointed out that none of us (specifically, me) have been spending time together, Ryan and I instantly made plans to have a Brother-Sister day.

My brother runs a tattooed hand down his face, giving a passing girl a quick smile before focusing back on me.

"Nothing." I shrug, taking a sip of the Shirley Temple I'd ordered. Lemon-lime and Cherry flavors explode on my tongue, and I sigh as the cool drink is swallowed.

"You're a shit liar, sis. How's your lover boy?"

I tense a bit at the mention of my "lover boy". After I'd walked out of Blake's room, leaving him dazed and confused in bed. I turned off my phone and proceeded to ignore everyone.

My fear of commitment came about after dealing with Marcelo and his constant antics towards me. It wasn't even something I was aware of until I tried to go on a date a few weeks after our initial break up. The guy was nice, albeit, a little *too* sweet and mentioned how he was dating to marry and not for a fling.

I'd immediately left him there and proceeded to walk around Central Park until I could come to senses with the fact that my life was changing and I didn't want a man to be able to affect me anymore.

Dad wasn't the one who'd come up with the "no boys" clause of our agreement, he'd simply agreed to it and said he would hold me accountable to my word unless I genuinely wanted to give men another try.

Ryan eyes me for a long moment before tutting and nodding his head. "You have *got* to get out of your own head." He sighs.

I frown looking up at the sky as my shoulders drop in defeat, he's not wrong. I'm cock-blocking my future with Blake—and for very rational reasons. He likes playing sports, I'd rather watch. He's a red guy, I'm pink through and through. He's overly confident yet shy at times which I think is cute, but I tend to lack confidence in myself sometimes. He's like the sun, always bright and glowing, and I'm like the moon, always there, yet hidden. And as I list all of these reasons, I realize they're all completely irrational.

I'm just making excuses, so instead of bringing any of my thoughts to my brother's attention, I change the subject.

"How's that girl you're supposed to be seeing?" I ask, raising an eyebrow as he chokes on his water.

Ryan wipes his nose and mouth with a napkin before furrowing his eyebrows at me. "How do you know I'm *potentially* messing with someone?"

"Uh... because I'm not an idiot." I laugh, scrolling through my phone, checking his Instagram story. When I find what I'm looking for, I turn the phone to face him with a knowing smirk. "You've been soft-launching this same girl for a week," I say, happy that for once, I'm not in the hot seat.

Ryan smiles, looking away from me to his plate. "When I know how she feels about me then maybe I'll tell you who she is," he says.

"Yeah, sure." I roll my eyes.

We spend the next two hours with one another, talking about any and everything except for our love lives as the chilly early November day slowly fades to evening.

"I'll see you at the game next week Cleo, stay safe and text me if anything happens," he says pulling me into the most brotherly hug, making sure to tug on a few of my curls before walking towards his car parked beside mine.

"Okay! Love you, don't do anything too reckless." I tease, stalking towards my own car.

As soon as I take a seat, I lock the doors and check my phone and nearly drop it at the sight of all of the incoming messages.

Unknown

> you dumb fucking bitch. Be prepared.

> YOU WILL REGRET OPENING YOUR BIG MOUTH

> it'll be posted before you get a chance to stop me.

I'll make you wish you were never born Cleo Jones.

remember that. Bitch.

xoxo, your worst fucking nightmare.

Cupid

UH CJ?????

call me as soon as you see this

Ceej I'm serious

girl you're scaring me. don't tell me you're hurt

we're all going to your apartment.

Georgia Peach

GIRL

they did it.

I'm going to make those bastards wish they were never born.

Si Si

I'm getting our aunt to look into it all right now. Do not worry.

im so fucking sorry this happened to you CJ.

FORTY-TWO

Cleo

"WHAT THE HELL ARE we going to do?" Jace asks, pacing around the expanse of my apartment's living room. He'd brought some of the guys with him as well.

Alec, Braxton, Charlie, and Derek sit on the love seat fuming, turning their murderous gazes between one another.

"I tried to get it taken down but it's harder to do than I'd thought" Sienna sighs, pacing with Jace.

I'm sitting in the corner of the living room, on the floor by our balcony watching as my friends try their hardest to figure out how to take down the number one trending porno in America.

Cleo Jones gets railed by Marcelo Rivers.

Yep. That's the title. My body feels as if it'll cave in on itself as I try my hardest to breathe normally.

"Could we just sue? I mean, I feel like suing is our only true option–" I hear Georgia say just before everything goes black.

My breathing is rapid and I feel as if I've been dumped into the middle of a tropical storm where the current is rough and choppy enough to kill. My heart is like an angry caged bird, beating its wings against my ribcage, anxious and ready to escape.

The world around me is so dark, and I fear there's no way to find a beacon of light.

My friend's shouts grow louder but it's like static to my ears as my body shakes. I try to calm myself down but it's no use as the panic consumes me whole.

I've had panic attacks since the first and only time my mother came to one of my figure skating competitions—I bombed it immediately after noticing she was there. The panic was overwhelming then, but *nothing* compares to the increased feelings of panic and anxiety that I feel right now.

The static-like sound of my best friends voices grow louder and I try to make out their words. I truly do, but I can't and when I think that I'm going to fall off into the deep end and let a killer wave undertake me, I feel it.

Warm, large hands cuff my cheeks, and my eyes come into close contact with bright and frantic blue ones. The person, Blake, is saying something but I can't hear anything as my breathing continues to skyrocket. He's inhaling and exhaling deeply, trying to coax me into doing the same, and I do. I follow the beacon of light that is Blake Wilder out of the darkness of my mind and wrap my arms around his neck.

"It's okay sweetheart... It's okay, you're fine. I'm here and you're fine," He coos, holding me tightly as he rubs my back.

We're still seated on the floor behind the couch, near the balcony. Blake's arms are the refuge that I didn't know was needed, I allow him to pull me safely to shore.

My heart rate slows and I think that I'm fine until Blake begins soothing me again. It's then that I realize all of our friends are gone and it's just *us*.

The waterworks start back up and before I can catch myself, I'm spilling my guts.

"I'm so s-sorry, Blake. I never wanted to embarrass you, I thought I was safe. This is so bad–so fucking bad. This will affect your career so much–oh my God, did I fuck up your chance at getting drafted? Of course not...we're not dating–"

"Calm down, baby, just breathe." He chuckles, still massaging small circles into my back.

I ignore his words and start to talk only for Blake to cup my cheeks with both of his hands and turn our faces to one another, "Cleo, look at me. You having a sex tape isn't going to make me not want to be in a relationship with you. And no one other than our friends knows about us," He says softly, patting my shoulders.

And I don't know what comes over me in that moment, but maybe it's because my inner child feels understood, or maybe it's because Blake is the biggest softie I've ever met, but I spend the rest of the night going back and forth between crying and sleeping in his arms.

FORTY-THREE

Blake

I'M GOING TO KILL that motherfucker.

I was in the middle of helping River, our second-line forward, with a few shooting drills, when I received the news.

Jace was with Braxton, Alec, Charlie, and Derek when he found out about the tape being leaked. I apologized immediately to the kid, River, and hauled ass to the River View Complex.

As soon as I saw Cleo hunched into a tiny ball in the corner, I *knew* that Marcelo was a dead man walking. She looked so small and hollow, completely unlike her usually charming self.

Once Cleo fell asleep in my arms for good, I put her to bed in her room and then made my way back to the living room where everyone else sat around throwing out ideas.

"He's dead, and if one of you motherfuckers tries to stop me, consider your-selves grave buddies." I sigh, plopping down beside Jace on the couch before quickly jumping back up.

"Like what type of man would go out of their way to embarrass a woman like that? I swear to God–"

"Where is she?!" The door slams open and in walks a storm cloud of a man in the shape of none other than Ryan Santiago-Jones and usually I'd be happy as hell to see my *future* brother in law, but him walking in making even *more* noise has my blood pressure rising.

"Aye. Calm that shit down, Cleo just went to sleep and doesn't need to be woken back up because you can't enter a house without being loud as fuck," I say through gritted teeth, eyeing her brother up and down as he rolls his eyes at me, entering further into the apartment like a raging bull.

"I can come in here however the fuck I want. My sister is hurt!" He pushes me, and the action has me stumbling a bit due to his athletic nature but I could give *three* fucks about that.

"And you will be too if you don't shut the fuck up! Let her rest or so help me God, I'll–"

"Or you'll what?" He asks, stepping up to me as if ready to battle and I ain't a bitch so I take a step closer.

"I'll beat the dog shit out of–"

"ENOUGH!"

To my surprise, it's Denver breaking us up; my cousin forces herself in between us and faces Ryan. Ryan visibly calms down as his eyes wander over Denver's serious expression. He nods at her and the two seem to communicate without speaking because he pats me on the shoulder, takes Denver's hand and walks the two of them out the front door.

"What the fuck..." a person, presumably Jace, mumbles from behind me as I stalk back towards my seat on the couch.

"That was hot as fuck, now wrestle with your shirts off... *Pants optional.*" Georgia chuckles as she looks between me and the door where Ryan had just exited.

I can't help the small laugh that escapes my mouth just as Jace, the guys, and Sienna's conversation filter back into my mind.

"Once we track down the IP address and user info, I think it'll be a piece of cake to sue the poster," Sienna suggests as she gathers all of the plates and bowls the guys had.

Derek and Braxton each offer to help her with cleaning up, Sienna pauses looking them both over.

"Braxton, you can help me. Put these in the sink please?"

Derek's face is stone cold and impassive like the true goalie he is as he stands, grabbing his own keys.

"I need to get Deli from my mom's place, I can drop you three back off if you want," He offers to Alec, Jace, and Charlie. Jace waves off the offer as the other two rise to their feet.

"Tell Cleo we're all on her side. The whole team, I mean. She's a sweet girl and no one deserves to go through what she's going through." Charlie frowns, patting my shoulder as he follows the others out.

It's only when the front door closes that Denver and Ryan re-enter the house and Braxton stumbles out of the kitchen area.

"Did he just leave me?" Brax asks with a baffled chuckle as he looks around for an answer. When he realizes there won't be one, he chases after the guys leaving just the six of us in the living room.

We sit in silence for what feels like forever as the weight of our reality settles onto our shoulders. The one thing that Cleo had wanted to prevent the most is happening and all we can do is hope and pray our plan to get this fixed, works.

"We play against Brighton in two weeks," Jace grumbles, rolling around a toy fidget spinner, his usual form of stress relief, in his left hand.

I nod, my eyes trained ahead on the photo of Cleo and the girls hanging above their TV. They're all posing inside of The Sugar Hole, holding donuts, beaming with joy and it hurts to know that those smiles will never be the same because of someone else's ruthlessness.

I could just strangle him for even *thinking* of her in such an intimate way, let alone actually doing the act with her.

Fuck–

"Wilder. Dude, pay atten–"

Without thought, I speak, eyeing each person in the room, alerting them of all of my seriousness. "I'm going to make that piece of Brooklyn trash wish he was dead."

"Not if I kill him first."

Forty-Four

Cleo

IT'S BEEN THREE DAYS since my world turned upside down, 72 hours since I've had a donut, and 4,320 minutes since I've left my bed.

I haven't been to class because how could I leave when everyone has *seen* me?

How can I go anywhere after I've been exposed so *intimately*? My friends have been leaving small meals for me outside of the door and sometimes one of them would sit on the floor of my room and tell me about their day. Though it's only been three days, it feels like it's been years since I've seen the sun, or maybe it has been years.

Who knows?

I've spent the majority of the day editing my and Blake's project for film class, and smiling at the screen because who wouldn't smile at such precious memories?

"CJ, it's me, girl! Open up!" Denver shouts from outside my bedroom door, knocking on it with a special kind of force.

Denver's been coming over here more and more lately, spending time with me and making sure I'm caught up in our shared classes.

Stumbling out of the bed (literally), I groan as a bit of the light from the hallway flows into my bedroom.

"Girl, OMG, when was the last time you opened the blinds!?" Denver scrunches her nose, a bit of her Latin accent seeping through as she crosses my room to the cream curtains and blinds.

"NO–" But I'm too late; she yanks back the curtains and opens the blinds in one fell swoop, revealing the blistering sun and the complex's swimming pool.

Denver acts as if she didn't just hear my cry of terror as she spins on her heels with a large smile decorating her painted red lips.

"Blake should be here in about forty minutes which gives me just enough time to get you ready for your date—"

"Date?!" I shriek, running to my vanity mirror taking in my appearance.

Dark under eye circles, ice cream smudged hoodie, and four-day old curls... I can NOT let him see me like this.

But then again, he did watch me cry for an hour into his favorite hoodie...

STILL no.

"Yes, mami, had you checked your phone, you would've seen the fifteen messages the girls, Blake, and everyone else in the goddamn world has sent you." She sighs, rummaging through my closet.

"My phone was dead," I groan, running a hand through my curls and cringing as my nail gets caught on a tighter coil.

"Dead?! Girl—I can't. Just go take a shower and do your curl routine or something... Oh! And wear this, it's chilly outside." She pushes me into the hall bathroom, loading my arms up with goods before slamming it shut as soon as I'm inside.

It takes me twenty minutes to get my clothes on, detangle my hair, and slick it into a slick-back bun. Denver lets a low whistle as I strut into the living room, decked out in an outfit that screams Denver Castillo. I run a hand over the outfit. She chose a brown leather jacket that hung a bit loose over my body, a high neck cream crop top, and a pair of low-rise jeans and boots.

The outfit was completely at odds with my normal wear, and yet, it was exactly what I needed to have on. I twist at my bow shaped ring for good measure as Denver makes me do a twirl for her.

"He is going to eat you right up. Especially with these curls!" She gushes, gesturing to the small curly pieces that I purposely pulled out of my bun.

My cheeks heat at Denver's compliments, she's a literal goddess and gives out compliments just like one too.

Just as I'm about to offer her something to drink, Denver rises from the couch, dusts herself off, and gathers her things.

"Where are you—"

"My job here is done, that dude that I'm related to should be here any minute now! Have fun, gorgeous, and make sure you let me know when you get back safely." She winks at me, before leaving me both confused and amused in my living room.

As if on cue, the doorbell to the apartment rings as soon as she leaves.

"Were you two planning that?" I ask, opening the door wide for Blake as he smirks down at me.

"I have no idea what you're talking about, Princess." He wiggles his eyebrows before swinging his arm from behind his back, presenting me with a large bouquet of fully bloomed pink Lily's, my favorite.

But if we're being totally honest, I hadn't had a favorite flower until I'd seen these just now.

They're light and airy and perfectly me.

I love them and I love—

No.

It's way too early for that and we're not even together.

Nope.

Nu-uh.

ABSOLUTELY NOT.

"These are for you by the way... I hope you like Lily's, I asked my mom and sister to pick between Lily's and Dahlias and they chose the Dahlias but I felt like you were more of a Lily girl but then again—"

"They're amazing!" I grin up at him, carefully taking them before pulling him into the most bone crushing hug ever. Blake relaxes into the hug, pulling me closer before letting go.

I watch as his gaze darkens, taking in the full expanse of my outfit. He unconsciously licks his lips before his eyes flicker back up to my own.

"Ready?" He asks, clearing his throat as I nod, stepping out the door, locking it behind me.

On the ride to our destination, we sit in a comfortable silence, listening to a new song by Luka Espinosa, the lead singer of Twisted Vipers. The car ride is so soothing and comfortable that I drift off to sleep with a feeling of contempt and safety over me.

"Princess? Cleo...? Oh my goodness, free donuts and cameras on Highway 59!"

"Where?!" I jump up out of my sleep and immediately regret it as my head collides with something hard.

Blake groans, cursing under his breath from beside me but I can care less as I let my eyes adjust to my surroundings.

"There aren't any don—Barnes & Noble?!" My disappointment is immediately replaced with excitement as I catch sight of the four-story book store ahead.

"Oh, don't mind me, just nursing a concussion," Blake mumbles as I hop out of his Jeep.

"Don't be such a baby, Boy Scout! There's probably a book about concussions for you!"

Blake grumbles something incoherent behind me as I skip towards the store. I almost make it into the section where all of the Shapeshifter Erotica novels are when Blake pops up behind me, holding a book with a girl and guy in an ice rink on the cover.

"We should reenact one of these scenes, TikTok said that this book is—what the hell is DVP? Double vag—holy shit." He grimaces, looking down at his phone before gagging at the sight of whatever he saw.

"Put that down!" I hiss, grabbing both the book and his phone.

It's a good thing he hadn't looked up the book in my hand though, he'd probably throw up at the mention of knotting and what it *actually* is.

Spoiler alert, it has nothing to do with tying a rope or bondage.

"How about this, Princess. I buy you seven books, and a box of donuts, if you and I can reenact whatever's in... this book!" He smiles triumphantly, holding up a book about fae, that everyone and their mom, *including me*, have read and loved.

This sounds like a win-win situation to me.

I nod as Blake fist pumps the air, grabbing his phone back to presumably look up the large book.

We walk around the store, him picking up every book that I put down while I stalk through the fantasy and romance aisles. "Look at this one, babe, TikTok says he fucks her with a... with a gun? Oh my—"

I double over in laughter at the horrified expression on Blake's face as he lightly puts the dark romance book back in its rightful spot and allow him to walk us to the check-out area.

Note to self: Keep Blake far, *far* away from both TikTok and the Dark Romance section of Barnes & Noble.

Forty-Five

Cleo

"I WOULD DEFINITELY FUCK Eren Marlowe if given the chance," Denver and Georgia both sigh as they watch Eren pull off his helmet while on the grid for Sao Paulo last weekend.

Tonight, the girls decided that we needed a self-care night considering the week we've all had.

I haven't been able to talk to them all individually about what's been going on but I'm pretty sure we're all feeling annoyed with life right now.

"Eren is like seven years older than you." Sienna rolls her eyes at Georgia before ogling the man on the screen herself.

Georgia pops a black cherry into her mouth, smirking at Sienna. "And that just means he's getting closer and closer to bee-keeping age."

"Oh, gross! Eren is nowhere near that old, he's only 28."

As the girls bicker about the racer's fuck-ability, I make my way to the kitchen to gather more snacks and drinks. I'm about halfway into pouring shots for all of us when the doorbell rings.

"Did y'all order pizza or something?" I ask, making my way to the door. I receive a chorus of no's in return as I check the peephole, confused at the sight on the other side of the door, I swing it open.

"Sup, gorgeous." Jace winks, leaning against the doorframe.

"Get out the damn way." Blake's voice is strained before Jace is pushed from the doorway and is replaced by him.

Blake gives me a small smile and plants a soft kiss on my forehead before entering the apartment with his arms filled with pizza and food bags.

I'm just about to close the door when Ryan, Derek, Delilah, Braxton, and Alec enter right after Blake, bringing the full party to our apartment.

I take a step back, both in shock and awe at the sight of everyone wearing pink pajamas with my face and the words "We <3 CJ" printed across them in various ways. Even little Delilah has a nightgown with my face and the slogan on it.

They care about me.

My heart fills to the brim as the guys and Delilah smile at me and my mind can't process the fact that they care so much to the point they're wearing shirts for me.

"We told you guys to come after the race! Eren was just about to win." Denver sighs as my brother plops down next to her, sneakily stealing a few pieces of popcorn from her bowl.

"We were going to but then Deli said she wanted to be around you guys more than us." Derek frowns as his daughter makes grabby hands towards Sienna and Georgia, both girls swoon at the action, Georgia taking the toddler to sit between her and Sienna.

"It's because Deli Belly here needs girl time, Derek. I said this to you at her last practice." Sienna sighs, redoing the loose, messy pigtails in Delilah's hair.

Braxton chugs a bottle of a sports drink before belching like the true guy he is, "I told you Momma Bear, Dels needs more girls around. She's only ever around us, which is great because we love her, but she started to pick up on our tendencies."

"That's not true." Both Derek and Jace scoff just as Delilah frowns.

"Yeah, bro, that's not true! Right, Daddy?" She pouts, and Derek slaps his forehead.

I smile at the adorableness of it all before going back to the shots I'd been about to pour. Looks like we're drinking apple juice after all tonight.

"I hope it's okay that I brought the guys too... *and* that we crashed your girl's night." Blake chuckles nervously, scratching the back of his head.

"You're fine but these pajamas? I'm jealous. Why don't I have my own, personal 'We <3 CJ' merch?"

"Fuck... that's what I forgot!" Blake groans, running a hand over his face just as Delilah gasps. "I know...I know, angel" he sighs, reaching into his pocket and pulling out a $20 bill from his wallet.

Delilah jumps up from Sienna's lap and happily grabs the cash, she examines it like a shopkeeper before nodding her head in approval and turning on her heels back to Sienna and Georgia.

How freaking cute.

Since our night has been crashed by the guys and a five-year-old, we quickly turn off the most recent Grand Prix and sub it for the latest princess movie. One of which the girls and I have all been excited to watch.

I'm sitting on the couch, snuggled under Blake between him and Ryan when my phone goes off.

I jump at the sound of the ringer, my blood going cold as the guys all look back and forth between one another before it rings again.

I instantly relax at the sound of the ringer, my blackmailer has never called me. Sighing at the realization, I turn the phone over and instantly regret it.

Dad is calling...

"Answer it," Ry whispers, considerate of the movie playing.

"Absolutely not" I snap back through gritted teeth.

"Yes."

"No."

The call ends and we glare at one another just as the phone pings once again.

Dad

> since you refuse to answer my calls, we will talk about this video on Thanksgiving. Don't try to talk yourself out of this one, Cleo. I am so very disappointed in you right now.

FOrTY-SIX

Cleo

"AND THAT'S ANOTHER STELLAR slapshot from Summerfield's own Blake Wilder!" The announcer booms over the speakers of the arena's sound system as Blake does a bow and arrow pose for the jumbotron.

Today, my nerves are jumpier than ever. It's been a few weeks since my dad texted me saying that he was disappointed in me and I haven't seen him since.

I've been to almost every single home game since then but Ryan told me that dad went back home to spend time with Gloria before the holiday weekend rolled around.

His assistant coach, Vince Morgan, has been coaching the boys since and has been doing an amazing job at it.

The guys move across the ice like a well-oiled machine and are leaving it all on the ice and though I'm surrounded by all the cheers and applause of my fellow SFU students, I can't help but to feel lonely.

None of the girls were able to come to tonight's game. Hell, I haven't seen any of them since last night. And Ry is busy with a fucking *house* for his architecture lesson, granted it's made of popsicle sticks, but it's still a damn house.

My knee bounces uncontrollably as I try and fail to make myself comfortable in my seat. I'm usually fine with being by myself at games like this but with everything going on, I feel more exposed and watched than anything.

I'm just about to spring out of my seat, and rush to the bathroom as halftime starts when "Night Changes" by One Direction plays on over the loud speakers of the arena. I chuckle at the memory of the song and settle into my seat awaiting, Lola the Tiger, Summerfield U's mascot, to come skating onto the ice for her usual halftime show.

I frown as the lights go dark and Lola is nowhere to be found, pink and white light beams circle around the arena, creating a kaleidoscope affect at center ice just as a bright light blinds me momentarily.

It's then that I realize that all eyes are *truly* on me. My hackles rise as the song grows louder and I appear front and center on the large jumbotron with the words "We <3 CJ" as the label.

"Oh my—" my words are cut off by loud whistles and cheers as the boys, my boys, skate out onto the ice holding something in their hands.

Are those...*no*. Where the hell would they know how to make those? My thoughts swirl around my head as the guys slowly start to exit the ice, putting on their guards before trekking up the stairs towards *me*.

What the fuck—

"We love you, CJ!" the twins, Jordan and Jonah both hug me quickly before placing down two large and singular pink and white origami lotus flowers. The same exact ones that Jace used to make me and the girls when we were sad as kids.

As soon as the twins make their turn to leave, I'm faced with Lucki, who holds two more paper flowers. This proceeds until almost every single player has given me a flower until I'm finally faced with the creator of them all.

"I love you, Ceej," Jace whispers into my hair as he kisses the top of my forehead. I repeat the saying to my oldest friend as he tucks one of the flowers behind my ear.

I'm smiling from ear to ear as the last man, the one I hadn't known I was waiting for, stands in front of me.

"How was it, Princess?" He asks, crouching to pull me in for a hug.

"It was amazing!" I gush into his chest as he vibrates with laughter.

"Good, only the best for my girl." He grins, kissing my forehead, and God if that doesn't have my heart swelling, I don't know what will.

I wish we could stay like this forever, holding each other but Blake has a game to win.

"Win this and I'll let you do whatever you want to me tonight," I whisper into his ear; Blake stiffens for a moment before chuckling.

"Baby, I *always* win."

And that he does, the boys win in a massive shutout. The energy around the room vibrates with excitement from the Summerfield U students and everyone is talking about the crazy win.

I'm gathering my things and all of the flowers the boys had given me when two girls step into my path, each of them wearing home team paraphernalia.

"We just want to say that we stand with you." The blonde of the two pouts, pulling me into an unwarranted yet appreciated hug.

"Yeah! No one deserves to have their dirty laundry aired without them knowing, We're 100% team Cleo," The brunette that closely resembles Blake's sister Jules, minus her striking green eyes, speaks up.

"Uh... thank you?" I smile, tilting my head in confusion as both girls give me small smiles before leaving.

I would think that the whole interaction was odd had it only happened once but it hadn't. Over the ten minutes it took me to get to Blake's Jeep, I was stopped over twelve times and told the exact same thing. Apparently, both the hockey and football teams were telling the truth about the tapes to anyone who would listen and had people sign petitions to have it taken down.

Bless their hearts.

I'm beaming with happiness as Blake jogs towards me, smiling from ear to ear. He drops his duffel bag and picks me up, spinning us around.

"I won, baby!" He cheers and smiles like a kid in a candy store as he sets me down, gently, keeping his hands on my waist.

"You were amazing!" I say grinning from ear to ear as he kisses me, smiling into the quick yet hungry kiss.

"Speaking of amazing, have you seen yourself? Go on, do a quick spin, Princess." He crouches down holding his hands as if they were a camera, taking "pictures" of me.

I giggle like a kid as I spin for him, playing into his chaos.

We're so happy and peaceful joking with one another when I remember the storm cloud from a few weeks ago that's been hanging over my head.

Thanksgiving.

"Hey…um," I clear my throat, sobering up as Blake furrows his eyebrows, standing up. "Would you like to come to Thanksgiving with me?" I ask, bracing myself for his answer, hoping and praying it's anything but no.

Blake smiles down at me, his ears red as he puts a teasing hand on his hip like a Home Depot dad.

"I thought we weren't in a relationship," He teases with a smirk as I roll my own eyes.

"You're right, I'll just ask Jace—"

"Wait, I never said no!" He cuts me off, grabbing my hands up in his. "I'd love to go to Thanksgiving at your house but I do remember that I was promised something for winning tonight." He smiles deviously.

I rolled my eyes, knowing where this was going, and sure enough, Blake claimed his reward *and* then some.

"Are you sure I'm not too dressed down?" Blake asks for the tenth time as we stand on the front porch of my dad and Gloria's house in Maryland, just thirty minutes from the SFU campus. After Ryan and I moved for college, our parents moved to Maryland from New York. The only reason everyone had went to SFU was the sole fact that they'd all gotten scholarships and truly wanted to attend the school first. Whereas I attended Brighton for the sole fact that I wanted my mother's validation. But that's neither here nor there.

"You look perfectly fine, Boy Scout, but if you keep running your hands through your hair, you're going to look like we took the backseat of your Jeep for a test drive." I chuckle, smoothening down his hair.

Blake frowns at the innuendo just as the front door to the house swings open.

"Absolutely not." My father's deep voice startles me momentarily as he stands in the doorway, looking down his nose at both Blake and me. The action should be impossible considering my father's shorter stature of just 5'10" but he manages to do so.

"Hi, Coach..." Blake grimaces as my dad rolls his eyes.

Gloria appears right behind my father with the most welcoming smile imaginable as she pushes Dad to the side, opening the door wider.

"Cleo, my baby! Is this the boy you spoke to me about?" She asks loudly as she pulls me into a tight hug before doing the same to Blake. Her familiar scent of lavender and citrus lingers against my skin and I instantly feel at ease as we step into the house, ignoring my dad's mugging glare.

I'm immediately greeted with the smell of fresh pastelitos, chicken, and Gloria's famous black beans and rice. Also known as my favorite meal curated at the hands of Gloria Jones. Having a Black father and Dominican stepmom means that dinner is always excellent in our house, and I've been saving my appetite since this morning for whatever my parents cooked tonight.

"Yeah, Glori, this is Blake." I smile down at her as she gasps.

"Wait... Blake? Like Blake Wilder? Oh, the girls in my book club are going to have a field day with this! Can I take a picture with you, honey?" she asks practically gushing over him as my dad's frown deepens.

Blake on the other hand, instantly perks up, stepping up to my stepmom to take a photo.

"You better step back, son," Dad warns, still trying to do his macho man routine.

Blake visibly gulps at his commanding tone but looks back and forth between Gloria and my dad. Gloria waves off the scary man at her shoulder as she pulls out her phone snapping a photo of her and Blake.

"Don't mind him, honey. Clef, you aren't fooling anyone with that act, now come help me with the pastelitos. I just got a new manicure and can't have the grease touch my polish." Gloria tsks, walking off towards the kitchen.

"Coming, honey." My dad frowns following behind.

They are the true embodiment of 'walk him like a dog'. Whatever Gloria says, goes, and it's been like that forever.

"I like her." Blake chuckles, much more relaxed as he follows me into the dining room area where Ryan's already seated in his usual spot. I opt for the seat across from him just so Blake can sit beside me, and then I place my phone down before going to wash my hands. Blake does the same before taking a seat beside me.

We're deep into eating without a peep from anyone until Dad decides to open his mouth in the most rude, yet funniest, way.

"Why is Blake in my house, Cleo?" He asks, not missing a beat as he plops a spoonful of rice and beans into his mouth.

I nearly choke on my food at his forwardness and Blake stills momentarily beside me. "Gloria said I can bring a *friend*," I say through a mouthful of pastelitos.

"You and Blake aren't just friends though, sis." Ryan eggs on adding to the mix, I drop my half-eaten fried meat and dough on my plate as I look up at the smug bastard.

"And you and Denver aren't just friends, either, right?" I ask, tilting my head as Gloria gasps and Blake chokes on his rice.

"Denver!? Who is this Denver and why haven't I heard of her yet, Julio?" Gloria asks, her jaw dropped as she eyes her son suspiciously.

Ryan mouths an obscenity at me as I discreetly flip him off. Serves him right to air out my business.

"She's my cousin!"

"She's my *friend*."

Both Blake and Ryan speak at the same time, the both of them eyeing one another down. The two men share an unspoken agreement with one another, each of their eyes widening momentarily before falling onto Gloria in a relaxed manner.

Gloria glares at her son but turns on a sweet smile for Blake as she looks over at him. After that, dinner runs smoothly for the most part with Gloria making conversation with Blake and me, Dad glaring holes into the side of Blake's head, and Ryan laughing at it all.

"C'mon, Clef help me wash the dishes." Gloria smiles warmly at my father as she begins gathering all the plates from the table.

"I can help! It's only fair—" Blake tries but Gloria just waves him off.

"Nonsense, you're a guest and Clef's been glaring at you this entire time. Besides, I'm sure Cleo and Ry would like nothing more than to get out of doing the dishes." She chuckles, hauling Dad into the kitchen.

Blake nods as the older couple enters the kitchen and almost instantly visibly relaxes.

"I didn't think you'd last more than five minutes with them." Ryan cackles from in front of us as Blake sighs, agreeing.

"It wasn't that bad." I frown at my brother, throwing an ice cube at him from my empty cup.

He grimaces as it hits him square in the cheek and cringes as he wipes away the water it left behind.

"Clef was about to stare the poor kid into a coma." Ry chuckles.

"I'm going to have to bag skate for the next three weeks because of this," Blake groans, jokingly. I rub his shoulder, hiding my laughter at the sad truth. If there was one thing my dad loved to give out as punishment, it was bag skating.

Forty-seven

Blake

"So... What are your intentions with my daughter?" Coach asks, completely out of nowhere. He'd been sitting on the back porch, watching Cleo and Ryan run around the backyard, tackling one another until now. Though the question was out of nowhere, it wasn't unexpected so, without hesitation, I turn to face him.

"I intend to treat your daughter like the princess that she is, and love her unconditionally. I want to be the safety net that Cleo looks to when her anxiety gets the better of her and the person that makes her laugh whenever she's gone on one of her spells of boredom. I intend on being the guy who wakes up at 5 a.m. to buy her Pink Truffle donuts from The Sugar Hole because she likes them fresh and the guy who's there whenever she wants to go shopping because let's face it, the girl's a shopaholic," I say, stunned with my honesty and how fluid everything I said came out. I had never admitted these feelings out loud or to myself before, but I'm glad that I did because the more that I think of my words, the more I agree with them.

I want to be all those things and more for Cleo and I intend on doing it all sooner rather than later.

"Do you know who posted that tape of her?" He asks, still focused on his kids in front of us as he speaks in a lower tone.

"Jace, Sienna, and I are still looking into it but we're getting down to the bottom of it," I assure him with a light pat on his shoulder.

"Oh, Thank God. How has she been doing?"

"She had a bad panic attack when she first found out about it being leaked but I think her being home has been good for her so far, this is the most I've seen her smile in weeks." I sigh, following Coaches line of sight to the "twins".

"I talked to her about it yesterday when you boys were watching that princess movie on the couch and she wasn't as open about it with me. I'm happy she has someone like you, Blake. I know that I get on you at times and like to play the role of the macho man, but you're a good kid."

"Aw! Thanks, Coach. Look at you, going all soft on me." I cheese at him, harder than ever, wrapping an arm around his shoulder as he groans.

"I take it all back, you're the most annoying kid I've ever met." He chuckles, and I shake my head laughing with him. "But seriously kid, you break my daughter's heart, I won't hesitate to kill you and spread the remains all over the Potomac."

I gulp, taking a step back from the shorter guy because as much as I love my Coach, I know that he doesn't make light threats.

Later that evening, Thanksgiving at the Jones' is in full swing. A-list celebrities and athletes walk around the house carelessly for the simple fact that they're all a part of the Jones family.

I'm at a loss for words as some of my favorite singers and athletes sit around the living room and dining room, all eating the delicious food that Gloria, Coach, and Ryan made this morning and last night.

Cleo emphasizes that she's not allowed in the kitchen after The Great Popcorn Fire of '17 where she left popcorn in the microwave for too long and in turn almost burnt down the house.

Sienna and Cleo sit around on the living room floor; Cleo eats while the two of them talk and laugh until the door rings.

"Blake, can you get that?" Cleo asks, completely zoned in on her conversation with the pink haired ballerina in front of her.

Nodding, my stomach fills with butterflies at the thought of me opening the door at her parent's place. *Cleo trusts me to the point that she has me opening the door.* I'm smiling from ear to ear as I open the door, only for my smile to drop and the butterflies to wither away at the sight of the person in front of me.

"Ew. She *actually* invited you." Denver rolls her eyes as I open the door. I immediately walked her back down the stairs. What the fuck is she doing here? My cousin isn't dressed in her usual choice of clothing this time; instead of her signature leather jacket, she wore a cardigan and replaced her normal red lip with a pink gloss.

What the hell?

"Why are you here?" I ask, stepping out into the cold November air with her, I instantly tug off my jacket passing it to her. Denver's a cold person both literally and figuratively and my aunt would kill me if her anemic daughter died from being frozen to death.

"Why wouldn't I be? Now move out of my way, this apple pie is going to get cold from being out here." She sighs trying to walk around me but I'm in front of her almost immediately.

"Who invited you? This was supposed to be *my* weekend to impress the in-laws. I can't have your snarky ass messing up my first impression," I groan as my cousin stomps on my foot.

"And this is also my chance to impress Ry—Cleo's parents. So do me a favor and get the fuck out—"

"You said Ryan!" I beam, mouth dropped as Denver throws me a searing glare.

"What's taking you two so long?" Cleo's amused tone filters into our conversation as she stands at the top of the stairs with her hands on her hips with both Ryan and Sienna on either side of her.

"Oh, this is too good." Sienna chuckles, clapping her hands slowly as Ryan tries and fails to pick his jaw up from the floor.

Ryan doesn't waste any time talking to anyone and simply walks down the stairs, grabs the pan of apple pie from Denver's arms, and walks her back into the house. I chuckle as he shuts the door behind the both of them, locking it.

Cleo doubles over in a fit of laughter as the lock firmly clicks. The house had one of those fancy doors where all you had to do was enter a pin to get into the house, so she wastes zero time unlocking it again.

"Why'd you invite Denver?" I ask as Cleo sobers up, following her back into the house with Sienna.

"Because that'll teach my dear old brother a thing or two about laughing at me."

Cleo's family dinner goes off without a hitch, her family welcomes Denver and me as if we were their own, with her older cousins teasing us about dating and her grandma fawning over my *impeccable* bone structure.

I have to tell my mom that freaking Marie Jones just pinched my cheek and called me *her* 'handsome boy'.

I fucking love it here.

"Having fun?" Cleo's teasing tone is like music to my ears as she saunters over to where I'm seated on the couch. She leans her body over the top of the couch, wrapping her arms around my neck, forcing me to look up at her but I'm not complaining.

I love looking up at her, especially when my tongue is deep inside of her as she grinds on it. That's my favorite view of all.

Wait, no... second favorite.

Her little annoyed nose scrunch takes the cake.

"I'm having a blast. I'm pretty sure your grandma loves me!" I try my hardest to tamper down my excitement but it's hard especially when her grandmother is a musical icon.

"I can tell..." She chuckles. "Would you like to go out tomorrow, just us? I know we haven't had time to go out with one another since we've been on this side of town and—"

"I'd love to." I cut her off, kissing her cheek.

I'd love nothing more than to kiss her pouty lips but I settle for the cheek especially since I can still feel her dads glare on me.

"Great, we can leave at two!" She smiles brightly before yawning quietly.

I grin up at her, watching as she stretches before agreeing.

"It's a date."

"Wait, no! Mine is *way* better than yours!" Cleo groans as I switch over our gourmet hot chocolate.

I chuckle at her failed attempt at grabbing the hot cocoa from my hands yet again before finally swapping it with her *again*. When we'd first ordered at the hot cocoa stand in the middle of the park, she'd ordered a signature hot cocoa which is basic hot chocolate with nothing in it while I went with the hot chocolate deluxe, the added bells and whistles being just what was needed for today's brisk walk in the park.

"We've traded twice already," I chuckle as she trips a little in her step trying to keep up with my long strides. I slow down seeing as she's having trouble and shorten my steps.

"Yes, well, I think we must trade again. You know that they say...third times a charm," She chimes back in the worst English accent imaginable, and to anyone else in the world, it might be corny and fucking *awful* but to me, it's fucking hilarious.

I feel like that one girl from that one movie franchise that's always overly laughing at her male co-star's horrible jokes.

That's how Cleo makes me feel and it's exactly how I want to feel forever so without thinking, I open my big ass mouth and ask her a bizarre question.

"Will you be my girlfriend?" I ask and in my head, I think I sound normal but in reality it comes out more like: "Uh...W-Will you b-be my girlf-friend?"

An idiot, I tell ya'.

There's no response to my question and my hands grow clammy because of it. What if I fucked up our little arrangement? I remember she said she didn't date but then she also said that she wasn't mine until I made it official...

Fuck.

Why are women so complicated? Why can't she just wear a shirt with her thoughts on it so I can know exactly what she has going on in her head?

And fuck why didn't I think this through?

I was supposed to take her to a fancy dinner, set the tone and mood for the night. Ask the waiter to write the words on a plate with a donut on it and propose my question to her that way.

Instead, I blurted it out in the middle of a random park in Maryland while the two of us are going back and forth over which of us has the better hot chocolate flavor.

Cleo's like a statue behind me as she stares with wide eyes, and I stare back at her, gaining a bit more confidence the more that I look at her. I walk back to where she is and stand in front of her. I plaster on my most confident smile as I pluck her hot cocoa from her hands and replace it with my own.

"Cleo Jones, will you be my girlfriend?"

FORTY-EIGHT

Cleo

I'VE NEVER JUMPED INTO someone's arms so fast in my life, hot chocolate be damned.

Blake must've sensed the jump before it'd happened because he quickly grabbed both of our drinks and sat them down before I barreled into his arms.

"So, is that a yes?" the smartass asks, his voice muffled by my hair as I giggle

I freaking giggled! *That's* how excited I am to be his girlfriend. I feel like I'm at freaking WonderWorld watching their signature fireworks show in front of the pink WonderWorld castle.

"Of course it's a yes!" I beam, kissing him with all the joy in the world.

The idea of Blake and I being together has crossed my mind more than I can count over the course of the past month, especially after all that he's been doing to get my sex tape taken down. Hell, he'd done such a good job at keeping me distracted from it that I'd nearly forgotten about it all until I got back home.

Dad and I had a very short conversation about it and he'd explained that he wasn't disappointed in the fact that it was posted, but more so the fact that I allowed myself to be recorded in such an intimate way—which is understandable.

I felt the exact same way.

Blake sets me back on the ground with the largest grin I've ever seen as he wraps an arm around my shoulder.

"So *girlfriend*, what is it that you want to do for the rest of the day?"

"I have quite a few ideas, *boyfriend*."

And just like that, we find ourselves in the driveway of my dad's house, making out with each other like that one Wonder cartoon from the early 2000s.

I climb across the center console onto Blake's lap for easier access, and since he owns a Jeep, the center is practically nonexistent. Blake smirks at me, pushing my hips down onto his hard erection, and I whimper as my sensitive heat comes in contact with his hardening dick.

"Fucking hell, Wilder," I mumble as he rocks my hips against him, pushing me harder into him.

"Say that shit again," He growls, tightening his already tight grip on my hips.

"Say what?" I kiss the shell of his ear softly, working my way down his neck.

Blake groans as my touch lingers along the most sensitive part of his neck and I lick it just to toy with him a little longer.

"Fuck, Princess." He curses, lifting my hips off his waist, pulling down his pants and boxers. Blake's dick jumps in all its glory as soon as it's released from his underwear.

My eyes gleam at the sight of him as he gives himself a few strokes before reaching into his glove compartment, and pulling out a condom.

I don't waste any time as I pull my panties to the side, my skirt giving me quick access to the flimsy material.

"We have to be quick..." my voice is breathy as Blake pulls me in for a searing kiss, he's smiling as he pulls away, looking me square in the eyes.

"Baby, I can cum just from the sight of you, my job is to make sure you finish."

He's quick like a cheetah, adjusting me directly over him and I clench around his length almost immediately as he slowly sinks me down on him.

We breathe each other in, allowing me to adjust to his thick length. Blake eyes me for a moment and once he sees that I'm okay, he goes to work, thrusting up into me.

He fucks me like he never wants to lose me, he grips me tightly, holding my body into his as he works himself into me.

"Fuck! Fuck! Fuck!" I cry out as he pulls my hair back, leaving me to stare up at the ceiling as he drills into my aching pussy.

I'm thanking every deity in the world that my parents aren't home because there's no saving us from this one.

And let's face it.

I don't want to be saved.

"That's it, Princess. Say it," he growls as his thrusts grow rapid, and I'm a screaming mess as he pounds without pause.

"Fuck me!" I scream.

Blake's muscles tense and I'm meeting the same fate as him soon enough as he pumps deeper and deeper. He's so deep, I can feel him in my stomach as he hits the one spot that's been begging to be fucked.

Blake fucks my g-spot until I see stars and soon enough, I'm a quivering mess as I fall into my own release. My head falls into the crook of his now sweaty neck and I sigh, trying to regain my breathing.

"You okay?" He asks, concern mixed with smugness as he rubs circles on my back.

"Fucking amazing. Want to go again?" I pop my head up to look at him.

Blake rests his head back, laughing at my eager expression just as a knock on the foggy tinted window startles the both of us.

"Is that—"

"I know damn well y'all aint fucking in my parents' driveway."

FOrTY-NIne

Blake

IT'S BEEN A WEEK since Cleo jumped in my arms and basically professed her undying love to me then I fucked her in her parents driveway only to be caught by her brother.

That's not how you remember it?

Well... you need your memory checked because that's *exactly* how I remember it.

My and Cleo's time has been epic with one another since then, and when I say epic, I mean *epic.*

Epic sex, epic conversation, and an epic fucking woman. I mean, what more can a man ask for?

We've just finished the last few questions for our project in Film Studies. Though, ending the one thing that has kept us close is sad, I find the whole situation to be bittersweet.

We no longer have the barrier of our camcorders and premade conversation starters which now that I think about it wasn't something that was needed. Cleo and I are *magnetic* together with or without a camera capturing every single moment between us. She understands me in a way that no one else seems to, she gets that sometimes I just need a moment to myself to regroup and think, and I understand just how she feels when she thinks no one cares to pay attention to her.

I would say she's like the Bonnie to my Clyde but, I'd rather not compare us to a couple of idiots in love that robbed banks only to end up killing themselves in a car crash. No, we're better than that because we're simply Blake and Cleo.

Cleo and Blake.

The Princess and her Lover Boy.

We're sitting on my living room couch back at the guys and I's townhouse, putting the finishing touches on the project and studying for finals when the front door swings open followed by loud chatter and cheers.

Cleo perks her nosy little head up, trying to see whoever's causing all the chaos but I'm selfish and would rather her attention stay on me, so I steal a kiss and all of her attention again.

"Ew. That's disgusting." Jace gags just as we pull away from one other, and Cleo giggles at the sight of our friend standing in front of us looking like he wishes he was anywhere else but here. I'm about to flip him off and send him back to where he came from when a ball of sunshine squeals and barrels into my arms.

"Uncle Lake!" Delilah shouts to the top of her lungs like most kids do instead of speaking in normal tones.

I wince at her loud octave but put on my biggest smile for the little angel in my arms. "Hi, Del—"

"Is Cleo my new auntie?! Daddy said—" She cuts me off just as Derek pries her from my arms, putting a hand over her mouth.

"I said that was a secret between us, Dels." Derek nervously laughs as Deli tries to speak from under his hand as he sits them down on the loveseat across the living room.

Jace smiles at the action, his eyes resembling hearts as he watches the father and daughter interact. It's like he's in a daze standing in front of us, watching them.

"Sorry! I forgot why I came home for a second. I have news..." He pauses, looking each and every one of us in the eye for dramatic affect.

"Well get on with it." Cleo sighs, sitting up on the couch, wiggling out my grip.

I frown at the loss of her warmth and tug her back into me. There's no way I'm letting that slide again, whatever he has to say he's going to have to say it while she's cuddled up into me.

Cleo doesn't acknowledge my clinginess for a second as she gives Jace her full attention.

He pauses for an extra second, a slow smirk pulling across his face.

"We got the video down!" Jace cheers.

Our eyes widen at the news, and Cleo's mouth drops as she looks around the room. Derek gives her a subtle nod, smiling like the true dad that he is as she gasps.

"Wait, you're serious?! Oh, my goodness... How?! I've been searching for ways to get it down for the longest."

"Don't worry about it, sweetheart. Just know that you have the *best* best friend in the world. Now, where's my hug?" he asks with a smug smirk, opening his arms for her.

Cleo seems like she'll get up to hug him but looks up at me and settles back into her spot beside me.

"His cousin Caroline hacked the site and got the video taken down and removed from all search engines... Sienna's been working with your aunt to get all the legal stuff situated. We're still waiting on Caroline to send the IP address over so you can sue the blackmailer," says Derek, clearly over Jace's over the top persona.

Jace, on the other hand, is still standing with his arms out waiting for Cleo's hug and the prick has the nerve to wink at me.

"Sit your stupid a-s-s down before I have to smack you for propositioning my girlfriend." I deadpan.

Jace frowns, sitting down beside Cleo.

"How dare you let that peasant talk to me like that CJ, I was here first!" he exclaims, folding his arms over his chest.

Cleo pays the dork zero mind, turning her attention to Derek.

"You guys play Brighton on Friday, right?" She asks, clearly ignoring both Jace and me as the blonde sighs dramatically.

"Yep, it's supposed to be a full house too." Derek sighs, placing Delilah on the empty cushion next to him. He's been more out of it than usual when it comes to hockey. I think it's because of his hips but he won't ever admit that something's wrong unless it's a critical injury.

"Hey, B?" Cleo leans back into my chest; her sweet scent coats my senses as her curly hair rubs against my chin.

Since our time earlier last month, she's been wearing it curly more often and I am not complaining one bit. I love her hair no matter the style.

"Kick their asses." She sighs, twisting to snuggle into my arms.

Could a woman be any more perfect? The answer is no... No one tops Cleo Jones.

"Sure thing, baby. Just say the word, and I'll burn their entire world down."

FIFTY

Cleo

"THOSE BOYS BETTER TAKE Brighton by the balls and crush them to smithereens then dance on their fucking graves! I didn't wear this stupid jersey for nothing."

Denver and I pause in our strides towards the concession stand, sharing an equally horrified and confused look before looking back at Georgia.

"Tone it down, blondie." Denver chuckles, wrapping an arm over Georgia's shoulder as Georgia laughs.

"I'm serious! It's bad enough that Si Si had to practice for the winter showcase, but if they add losing to Brighton on top of that? I think I might die." She pretends to faint in Denver's arms, and Denver chuckles at the antics, holding a hand out to me.

"I'm pretty sure they'll win, the guys were pumped when I FaceTimed them earlier," I say, hooking arms with Denver as we make our way to the front of the line.

"Good. I made a bet on SFU and would cry myself to sleep if I lost $500 tonight."

I roll my eyes at Denver, moving forward.

Tonight's the big night, SFU vs Brighton, and everyone within a 50-mile radius is in the arena tonight. I think I even saw my Film and Communications professors here together! Georgia orders our snacks for us as Denver and I small-talk about tonight's winner when I suddenly have to pee, yet again. We'd taken a few shots along with some wine coolers before coming and being the idiot that I am, I broke the seal before leaving the apartment so now my bladder is constantly full.

"Hold on girl, I have to pee again" I sigh, handing her my pink tote bag.

Denver chuckles as I scurry away to the ladies room, practically clutching myself and I'm so focused on trying to get to the restroom that I don't pay attention to my surroundings and walk straight into a red-haired girl.

"Fuck girl, I'm so sorry! I wasn't paying attention," I apologize like any normal person with a sense of decency would when the girl sighs.

Fuck... Did I make her spill something?

I begin to question myself but come to an abrupt stop when the scent of her perfume invades my nostrils.

Lemon and *ginger.*

The scent is so disturbingly familiar that I know it anywhere, I don't even have to see her face to know it's her. I don't know if I should be happy or scared shitless as she dusts herself off.

"It's fine..." Karmen, my ex-roommate, sighs, and I don't think she knows it's me that she's talking to.

"Karms? Girl! Oh my God! How've you been?!" I'm ecstatic to see her familiar face, so much so that I pull her in for a hug, completely unaware of her clear "fuck off" energy.

She's stiff under my touch and is almost repulsed as she pushes me off.

"Cleora," She scoffs, using my full first name, and I'm taken aback by the action, I furrow my brows ready to speak but just as I'm about to try to talk to her, she turns on her heels and sashays away.

But that's when I see it.

Across her back in big bold and black letters is the number 65 with the word Rivers spread across the top.

I think I'm going to be sick.

I completely forget about the fact that I had to pee more than anything just five seconds ago and trudge back to my friends.

Denver tilts her head in obvious confusion as she hands me my drink but doesn't press the issue as we walk into the arena and take a seat a little bit away from the box but close enough that we can touch the acrylic.

"Am I late?" Ryan's voice startles me momentarily as he takes a seat behind us, wearing a sweater with Jace's number on it. It'd been Jace's gift to all of us after his birthday and seems to be the perfect outfit for tonight's big match.

"Just on time. Wilder's been dogging them this entire period! I hate to say it, but I love hockey now!" Georgia exclaims before letting out a loud cheer for the guys, standing up to show off the sweater Jace had given her. Being the true fashion major that she was, Georgia took the dull blue and orange sweater and made it her own by cropping it and adding creative flare and gems to it.

I smile up at her and do the same, pulling off my coat, standing up to show off the large number 13 on my back. Blake skates toward us almost instantly; he bumps his back into the tempered glass. We cheer as he continues with the game clearly focused.

Ryan's scoffing catches my attention as Marcelo makes a near-perfect goal, I raise a brow at my brother as he curls his lip.

"I should fuck him up for even being here."

"And if you do that, who am I going to bother all day long?" I ask, nudging his shoulder.

Ryan's jaw clenches momentarily before he gives me a halfhearted smile. "Then I'll have *you* beat his ass and I'll post your bail."

"I wouldn't last five minutes in jail." I frown, grimacing as Jace takes a nasty yet legal hit from one of the defensemen on the Brighton team.

"You wouldn't make it past the squad car, babe," Georgia teases, taking a swig of her Stella Artois. Suddenly my best friend is a beer girl that likes hockey?

"OH COME ON! THAT WAS A FOUL PLAY AND YOU KNOW IT REF!"

We all turn a stunned look to Denver who stands with her hands in the air with red painted lips ajar. She looks shocked by herself as we all stare at one another before bursting into a fit of laughter.

Maybe hockey is becoming all of our favorite sport after—

A loud whistle followed by dead silence and a loud cry of something both dreadful and filled with pain ricochets through the air and everyone in the arena goes still.

"Was that Blake? Are the boys okay?" are my first thoughts as my eyes frantically scan the array of blue, orange, black, and purple.

I find the puck first, just mere centimeters from making a goal, and then move onto the man clutching his wrist just a few paces away kneeling on the ice.

Blonde hair, tan skin, and the number 26.

No.

No.

No.

NO.

Jace's cries are the sounds of a man who's career in both professional hockey and fine arts has just been crushed.

Blake, Braxton, and Charlie are immediately by his side. They're all saying things that can't be heard over the chatter of the arena.

"Is he okay?!" Georgia's voice is panicked and shaky as she tries to get a better look at our friend but it's no use seeing as more and more players are surrounding him.

"Fuck!" My dad yells from the bench where all the other boys on the 2nd and 3rd lines sit on the edge of their seats, ready to jump in and help their teammate.

Everything had been going nearly perfect, the boys were 2-1 and we were slowly moving into the second period only to have something fatal happen to one of the star players.

I curse myself for not paying full attention to the ice and feel my heart drop as two medics carefully walk onto the ice and help Jace skate off. His hand limp in the other.

His wrist is an array of blue and red but there was no mistaking one fact.

It's broken.

"What happened? Wait—"

"He pushed him. Marcelo fucking body checked him. I don't know what Jace said or did but now the idiot's wrist looks like a run over dog... I'm going to go make sure he's okay and call his mom." Georgia sighs gathering her things, and I'm stunned that she even knew what happened considering we were in a full-blown conversation when everything occurred.

"I can go and help—"

"No, you stay here. This is your day, CJ. Let's just pray the guys win this thing." And with that she's gone, stalking towards where Jace and the medics disappeared off to.

The game continues on with nastier hits and jabs and more boys spending time in the sin bin on both teams than necessary. We're well into the third period when the line changes again and Blake skates to where the benches are. I can't speak to him, but I can see the clear anger radiating from him.

He's pissed and that's exactly how he needs to be to win this game.

One of the freshmen, Jacob McCarthy, from the third line got traded to take over Jace's spot and he's been working nonstop to keep up with the men on the first line. Lucki Cole and Jack Tyler are on the move working with their center, River Ruiz, to score before the next shift change.

The boys are so in sync that I'm taken aback as they move like a well-oiled machine up and down the ice. It's only when River tries and fails to score a goal that my dad gears up for another line change and Blake is back on the ice.

Blake moves with the precision of a trained assassin, he's stealthy and quick on his feet as he maneuvers the puck with ease. I can see why Washington is so interested in him as a player, he's fucking awesome. When I become a commentator, I hope that he plays one of my first games because being able to talk about someone as skilled as him would be an honor.

I'm not just saying that because he's my boyfriend, either. Blake is simply *that* good.

He signals for his wingers to spread out, Alec takes the hint and rockets into motion, getting ready for whatever the brunette has up his sleeve, but Marcelo and his boys see it at the same time and are immediately on it.

The boys fight for the puck and it's so close that I think I might need Blake's glasses to see what's going on down on the ice but a loud buzzer goes off signaling a goal has been scored and that the game is over.

The crowd is silent for a still moment before loud cheers and cries of joy burst through the arena. Waves of blue and orange soar into the air as everyone from SFU cheers for their home team.

And on the big jumbotron above, Blake cheers with his boys, holding up Jacob's stick.

Jacob, the freshman, scored the game winning shot.

Just as I'm about to stand and cheer with the rest of the arena, my phone buzzes. I tense at the reminder of tonight not being truly over and sigh as I read over the text.

Cupid

> IP address of the blackmailer. Do you by chance know a Karmen Tate?

All the blood in my body chills.

I can feel her steel gray eyes watching me from a few rows behind.

My eyes lock with Karmen and it all comes back to me.

The way her face changed after I told her about everything that night. The long lingering gazes she would send Marcelo when we'd be out together and the way she would almost always find a way to interrupt our dates.

She was the one blackmailing me, not *him* and I know exactly how she did it.

Karmen's tech savvy. She's always been good with computers and it was one of my favorite things about her. Having a roommate that was a computer science major was the best thing in the world for me because not only was she good at fixing our Netflix when it glitched, she could also hack into private internet servers when we were out and needed to use wifi. I'd never thought to think about her leaking the tape because she'd never been that big in my mind.

She *was* my friend.

But why would she do this to me? I was nothing but nice to her. My blood boils to a level so hot I think the earth's core and I are battling for the hottest thing in the world.

I don't waste any time in approaching her and I don't know what's come over me as I do, but I do know that I am done with all of this. I'm done with the threats, the constant looking over my shoulder, and I'm done with this coward.

"It was you, you did this to me?! What the fuck is your problem?!" I yell, stopping in front of her.

Karmen's face is shocked as she looks down at me, she folds her arm over her chest and scoffs then looks at her friend. It's then that I notice she's befriended all of the people that I thought were my friends all those months ago and I see red.

"I said what the fuck is your—"

"You want to know my problem?" She stands, her eyes cold and daring as she snarls at me. "I fucking *hate* you. He was *mine* first. *I* was the one that introduced you two and then little Ms. Pink Bows and Donuts, Cleora fucking Jones just had to waltz in and steal my man—*my fucking life.*" She spits.

"Your life? Karmen I didn't even know you—"

"But didn't you?! It was obvious that I loved Marcelo, he was my best friend and then you had the nerve to date him. The nerve to flaunt him and then fuck in the room three doors down. So, yeah, I took the tape from his computer and yeah I fucking texted you but so what!? What you did was so much worse, Cleora. I had everything taken away by you." Karmen's chest heaves, her red hair is like fire as she spouts nonsense at me.

"But what made you post it?! I was quiet. I walked around for *months*, looking over my shoulder like a pathetic bitch because you were too much of a coward to talk to me! You exposed me!" I shout, not caring who can hear.

My skin feels as if there's claws gnawing at my throat but I don't back down. I need to hear this and I need to talk to this bitch face to face.

"I wasn't going to at first but then *you left*. And you just wouldn't leave him alone. It didn't matter if you moved to butt fuck Summerfield, Maryland. It didn't matter that you got new friends or became whatever you are because you were *always* there. He'd fucking talk about you nonstop as if *you* didn't leave. But it was the day that idiot Blake or Jake or whatever his name is posted you two on the beach looking happier than anything that I snapped. You were never supposed to be happy. Do you know that Marcelo saw that picture and texted you *thirty* times? Did you know that I had to be the one to tell him not to worry about *you?!* So, yeah. I got fucking livid and I posted it. But you've done so much worse," She seethes.

Is this bitch crazy?

"Woah you posted the tape? Marce was worried shitless about it—" Katy, one of my ex-friends and roommate looks horrified as she stands up with Maria, the other girl we'd shared a dorm with.

"He'll be fine, it's not like his face was in it—"

"You sick bitch." I chuckle humorlessly and before I can say a word, a fist is sent soaring past me and straight into Karmen's eye.

"Ow! Fuck! Fuck. Fuck!?" Denver screeches, reeling her hand back and clutching it to her chest.

"I told you not to punch her if you didn't know how to! You could've broken your hand on that weird bitch's face!" Ryan groans as he examines her knuckles.

"You're going to pay for that—" is all I hear before I'm pushed by the psychotic redhead.

"Lay another finger on my niece and I'll have you sued for not only defamation of character, extortion, and libel, I'll have you in court by Monday for assault and battery. I suggest you mosey along and I'll be in touch with you soon." The familiar lethal lilt of Aunt Melody's icy voice is like music to my ears as her eyes sneer down at Karmen.

"You're—"

"Add in the fact that Marcelo was a *minor* during the time of that video and you'll have a really sticky situation on your hands, Ms.Tate. I suggest you leave."

The color drains from Karmen's face as she looks around the group of us, clearly outnumbered. When she notices that Katy and Maria aren't following behind her, she scoffs and snatches up her things and leaves.

I almost forget that we're in a crowded arena filled with college kids until chatter and confused whispers fill the air; my breathing picks up and I feel the panic attack starting but my aunt moves quickly to calm me.

"We're sorry, Cleo. We'll sort everything out and get everyone to apologize to you. You didn't deserve any of that." Katy frowns.

"Yeah, we had no idea she was like that. She made it seem like you were crazy..." Maria gives me a sad smile as she and Katy leave with the rest of the crowd.

"C'mon, let's get out of here." Ryan smiles shortly, hauling us all out.

FIFTY-ONE

Cleo

Unread Messages from Marcelo R.

Marcelo R.

I fucked up

Please CJ

Text me back please

Are you happy?

It's been 7 months baby please

Are you fucking kidding me??

Fucking blake?

How dare you??

The beach????????

What the fuck cleo?

Please just txt me back

Tell me you two aren't together

Tell me this isn't true

How could you move on so fast?????

I thought you loved me!!!!

Cleo i swear to God

CLEO

WHY ARE YOU WITH HIM

ANSWER ME

BABY PLEASE

DON'T LET US END LIKE THIS

I STILL FUCKING LOVE YOU

CLEO STOP THIS ANSWER ME

Im sorry

I shouldn't have gotten angry

Forgive me?

Cleo i hope you're happy

You know where home is

I love you baby

Forever us, never them

FIFTY-TWO

Blake

"You're an amazing kid, Wilder. That was some excellent team work that I saw out there. The way you aided Heart after his injury and how you helped the other members adjust on the ice was exactly what we want to see of you in Washington. We'll be in touch." Travis Liberdade, the head coach for the Washington Eagles, shakes my hand. I think I'm going to faint from all of this excitement as he claps a hand on my shoulder before leaving.

I'm so pumped! I have to tell Cleo and the guys—

"I'm calling our fucking lawyer on that psychotic bitch, Dad. Cleora Emory Jones will rue the day she let her crazy guard dog touch me!" a red-haired girl shouts expletives into her phone as she stomps past me towards the front door of the arena.

Cleora? What the hell was that? I tilt my head in confusion as I walk towards where Cleo and a few others stand only to stop in my tracks at the tall dark-skinned man looming around my girlfriend.

I don't think as I walk up to him, grabbing his shirt.

"You got a lot of balls talking to my girl, Rivers. I should kick your ass to next Friday after everything you did," I say through gritted teeth as Marcelo frowns, looking clear past me to Cleo.

"Put him down, Lover Boy. He's apologizing." She sighs, defeated, as I drop him.

The fuck did I miss? The question must be evident on my face because Ryan claps a hand on my shoulder with a knowing look, promptly walking me away from the two just far enough to hear their conversation.

"But where does that leave us?" Marcelo asks, Cleo pears up at him with obvious disgust.

"What do you mean?"

"I mean," He steps forward, and Cleo shoots me a look as she takes a giant step back, frowning at him, "Where does this whole situation leave you and—"

"I'll stop you right there. I've heard enough. Lover Boy, take me to The Sugar Hole?" Cleo raises a brow at me, challenging me to say anything but I keep quiet, smirking as I wrap an arm around her.

"Already on it."

FIFTY-THREE

Cleo

"Throughout this semester, we've had ups and downs." Blake projects his voice to the crowded room of students and faculty.

"We've seen each others highs and lows and even grown close in the process of it all." I smile up at our professor who I definitely should've spent more time with over the course of the semester.

My mother sits directly beside her, scowling throughout the entirety of our presentation. I think she's a statue for a moment, considering her lack of movement and frown when she begins to smile and nod at the presentation.

The video cuts to scenes of Blake and I running on the beach to some of me simply dancing in his passenger seat. There are videos of me and him talking about life, completely straying from our presentation before focusing back on the topic. The way that Blake looks at me in the videos awakens the moths in my stomach, giving them a new light as the videos go on.

"Woah, woah, woah! What're you doing?" My voice on the screen is loud as Blake chuckles, shaking the camcorder.

"I'm capturing the moment, duh."

And then it ends, there are a few claps, and some snaps around the class and though it's not the standing ovation I'd dreamt of, it's better than nothing.

Professor Hawkins' smile is bright as she thanks us for presenting and begins to speak to the next group. As I'm walking past the judges table, a hand grabs me, startling my movement. I grimace as I look down at my mothers red nails, curled around my wrist.

"You didn't answer my text. I told you—"

"Let me go. I will not be a part of any weddings and to be frank, if our project is picked, I'd rather jump off a bridge than work with you. We are done, Lorelei. And I'd rather you not text me or use your resources to show up at my classes and become a guest for the semester again," I whisper, cutting her off.

The look she sends me is one of simmering rage but I could care less. After everything with Karmen this past weekend, I've been on a rampage of telling people exactly how I felt and my mom is now one of them.

"You okay?" Blake asks as I take my rightful spot beside him, and I nod resting my cheek on his shoulder.

"I am now."

A few days later, just before winter break, Blake and I find ourselves sitting on the couch of his townhouse watching a documentary on the creation of LEGOs.

We've decided that since we're still a newer couple that we'll spend our time separately during Christmas and meet back up on the 29th to prepare for the new year with all of our friends here at the townhouse.

"So, when I get drafted next year, are you going to wear a shirt that says 'I love my boyfriend' or do I wear an 'I love Cleo' shirt? How does this work?"

Blake chuckles as I smack his shoulder playfully.

There is no way in hell I'll be wearing a shirt that says 'I love my boyfriend' on it.

"I love you." I chuckle, seemingly unaware of the big three words that I just dropped on him.

Blake's stunned gasp is what snaps me back to reality and we both freeze. Him, a shocked happy expression and me, completely mortified that I let it slip like that. It was supposed to be cute and romantic! I'd at least hoped I said it when I wasn't dressed like the cookie monster.

"Princess, you don't know how long I've waited for you to say that. There aren't any words in this universe that can describe how much I need you in my life. I need you like the moon needs the sun baby, I love—" Blake is cut off by the front door slamming open, he groans and then seemingly pauses as loud smacking noises and rumbling flows through the room.

Two *extremely* familiar figures stumble through the living room in a heated make out session, they grind against each other, trying to rip one another's clothes off.

I'm about to scream. My mouth is hung so low, I'll catch flies and just as I'm about to say something, Blake does it for me.

"OH MY FUCKING GOD—"

The End

Epilogue

One Year Later...

"AND WE'RE LIVE! I'M your host Cleo Jones and welcome to *On the Ice!* where I give you the latest and greatest on all things hockey. Today's special guest is Clef Jones!" I announce to the cameras in front of me, and then gesture to my father sat beside me.

My dad gives the camera a small head nod; I roll my eyes, smiling at him.

He's been gushing about his feature on *On the Ice!* since he was asked to be a special guest on my show. Tonight, the Washington Eagles are playing the New Jersey Angels and it's also Blake's debut game.

Initially, I was upset that I would possibly miss Blake's debut with the Washington Eagles since I'm still an intern, I had zero hope of being able to see the game in person. But then the host of *On the Ice!* got pneumonia and the producers claimed they'd seen my commentary videos and YouTube channel, next thing you know, I'm sitting behind the Eagles' bench watching the game with my dad.

On the Ice! is a newer segment on VSN where the commentators are speaking on the game in real time and capturing their genuine emotions on the game when everything first happens.

Since Dad is a big a name in the NHL, he'd been asked to participate in today's segment before I was ever thought of.

"C'mon, kid! I didn't make that bet for nothing!" Dad shouts as Blake skates onto the ice for the beginning of the game.

I scream at the top of my lungs, completely ignoring the stunned look from my camera man, Reggie, as Blake skates circles around the rink, raising his stick to get the crowd hype.

My heart swells at the look of pure joy on my boyfriends face, his light blue eyes sparkle under the spotlights on the ice.

I can't wait until he shows the world what he's made of.

Blake is like a fucking rocket on the ice tonight to the point it's hard to keep up with his speed and agility. He skates circles around the other team and though I can barely see his face, I know he's smirking at his opponents.

He makes a single shot, a stellar slap shot that is so beautifully executed it has my thighs clenching and my heart rocketing against my chest.

What can I say? I'm a sucker for a man in a uniform.

"I taught him that!" Dad jeers to the camera, smiling like a proud father.

I roll my eyes, "Sure you did, Dad. Just like how you taught me how to braid my hair."

If there's one thing Clef Jones is going to do, it's act like he taught someone something. Dad chuckles at me, slinging an arm over my shoulder as the game continues on. We're on the edge of our seats as Blake and one of his teammates, Moritz, a cool guy with an epic wrist shot, send the puck soaring between one another, avoiding their opponents with ease.

I chew on my bottom lip, ignoring my dad as Blake gains the puck only to be checked immediately after and had I not been a fan of the sport, I would've marched down onto the ice myself, but it's because I am an avid fan of hockey that I see it.

Just before Blake gets knocked over, he sends the puck spiraling through the air and had it been anyone else in the world, the puck would've gone the opposite direction of the goal.

But since it's Blake Wilder at the other end of the stick, the puck soars into the goal, alerting the loud buzzer.

My mouth drops in pure shock as Dad and I stare at one another, the camera, and then back to the ice where the teams cheers are loud as they barrel towards my boyfriend.

He fucking did it.

As I pack up equipment with Reggie, I feel an overwhelming sense of giddiness and happiness.

Blake scored the winning freaking shot. Did he bust his ass immediately after? Yes. But did the puck go in? Also, yes.

"Slow down, soldier, your man isn't going anywhere." Reggie chuckles as we make our way to the locker rooms. Reggie's cousin, Fitz, is a defenseman on the team so he's equally as excited as I am.

"Oh, shut up, Reg. Did you see how perfect that shot was?!" I practically yell because of all my excitement. Reggie chuckles, rolling his eyes at me as the players file out. I completely ignore them all. I know exactly who I'm looking for and they're not him.

It takes no effort for me to spot my boyfriend within the crowd of tall men, the smile on his face sends a swarm of butterflies up my body as he rushes towards me pulling me into a hug.

"Did you see me, baby?!" His excitement fuels my own as he lifts me up before gently placing me down.

"I was like a fucking bullet, Princess. It was so much fun!" Blake grins looking down at me, his eyes hood over as he stares into my brown eyes and I grin cheekily as he leans down to my ear.

"Winner gets whatever he wants, Princess," He tells me more than asks, taking a quick look at me.

My body shudders for an all-new reason, other than the chill of the arena.

"Whatever he wants." I nod.

The look Blake sends me is of pure hunger, one of his teammates doesn't seem to notice as he clasps his shoulder.

"You coming to dinner, Wild Card?"

"Nah... I'm looking at mine right now. Catch you guys later, though." Blake's eyes never waver from my own as he steps toward me. I choke on my own laugh, looking up at him but I know without saying that his words were *not* an empty promise.

And he proves it to me again and again until I can barely stand the next day.

Gotta love hockey.

Or let me say... *Gotta love Blake Wilder.*

Acknowledgements

Thank you so much for reading Capture the Moment. It takes an army to write a book and this book could not have been written without the help of some of my very close friends, family, and lots of hours of wondering what the hell I'm doing writing a romance novel.

First, I'd like to say thank you to my friends Chase, Briana, Brianna, Sofia, Essance, Genesis, Riya, and Miah. Without these people, Capture the Moment would not be the book that it is today. Chase, thank you so much for pushing me to write this book on that cool winter day in December. If you'd have never pushed me to write out of my comfort zone, this book would have never happened. Briana, thank you for listening to me read and rant about this romance novel and helping me figure out where everything should go. You've truly helped me so much this year, and I just want you to know that I am thankful for you. Brianna, girl I love you. You've been here since the beginning and quite literally helped me get through the biggest plot of this book. If I'd never asked you to help me plot my book, there wouldn't be the iconic beach scene and Cleo would never knew who blackmailed her.

As for Sofia, Essance, Genesis, and Riya, I would like to thank you four for being as eager about this book as me. You have helped me in more ways than I can ever describe by being there for me when I needed help plotting and pointing out mini mistakes throughout the book.

Miah, girl I love you! Thank you so much for being so encouraging and supportive of me from the very beginning. You were my first ever "author friend" and have truly inspired me and helped me to get to where I am today!

To my Mom and Dad's, I would like to say thank you to the three of you. Without your tremendous amount of support and pushing me to reach my goals as an author, I don't think that Capture the Moment would've ever been written. Had you all not gifted me a Chromebook at 11 years old, I never would've began storytelling. You three have been the best parents ever and I love you all so much for all of your support.

To my boyfriend, thank you for being my real life Blake Wilder. From staying up until Lord knows when, playing with LEGOS and watching movies to helping me through my panic attacks, you have truly been there for me through every step.

And lastly, to my readers and loyal besties on Instagram, thank you so much for all of your support! There have been many days in 2024 where I wanted to give up and stop writing and then I'd get an encouraging message from one of you telling me you couldn't wait to read CTM. You all don't know how much that meant to me. There wouldn't be a Capture the Moment without you, so I say thank you.

XOXO,

Author Z

About the author

Ziyé (ZYE-yay) Taylor is an American author born and raised in the DC, Maryland, and Virginia area. She currently lives in Texas and writes romance novels while attending college part-time at LSU.

When Ziyé was 11, she began to write her own shortstories on the app, Wattpad. She began to publish her stories at age 13. Ziyé has surpassed 300k reads on the app and has accumulated a small loyal fanbase of readers. She became an author because of her love of reading and whilst being on Wattpad, she noticed that there weren't a lot of books that represented herself. This prompted her to begin writing stories of her own. She wants to write books that everyone can relate to, no matter their shape, gender, or race. Her sources of inspiration are music and her environment. Often times, ideas come to her randomly and she jots them down in the notes app of her phone.

Ziyé's favorite shows are The Vampire Diaries, New Girl, Teen Wolf, and The Originals. She spends a lot of her time rewatching these shows with her dog, Koko and her little sister. If she isn't watching these shows she can be found watching the movies White Chicks, Harry Potter, or The Princess Diaries 2. Her favorite music genres are Pop and R&B with SZA and Sabrina Carpenter being her current favorite artists.

For more information on Ziyés upcoming works please check out her website at https://authorziyetaylor.com